FINAL CUTS

FINAL CUTS

> > > > > > > > > > >

New Tales of Hollywood Horror and Other Spectacles

Edited by ELLEN DATLOW

BLUMHOUSE BOOKS | ANCHOR BOOKS

A Division of Penguin Random House LLC

New York

A BLUMHOUSE BOOKS/ANCHOR BOOKS ORIGINAL, JUNE 2020

Cataloging-in-Publication Data is available at the
Library of Congress.

Anchor Books Trade Paperback ISBN: 978-0-525-56575-8
eBook ISBN: 978-0-525-56576-5

Book design by Anna B. Knighton

www.anchorbooks.com

Printed in the United States of America
10 9 8 7 6 5 4 3 2 1

CONTENTS

INTRODUCTION

From the first moving picture publicly shown in 1895—the Lumière brothers' fifty-second film *L'arrivée d'un train en gare de La Ciotat* (translated into English as *The Arrival of a Train at La Ciotat Station*)—the medium has maintained its hold on society's imagination. There's a power to movies—watching them in the privacy of one's home or in the weird intimacy of a darkened theater with hundreds of strangers all looking at the same thing on the screen.

The first real horror movie, only about three minutes long, is *The Haunted Castle*, also translated as *The House of the Devil*, made by French director Georges Méliès in 1896. However, an argument could be made that the one-minute-long *Le squelette joyeux*, *The Dancing Skeleton*, made by Auguste and Louis Lumière in 1895—meant to be more amusing than scary—is the very first. Another of Georges Méliès's early horror films, *Une nuit terrible*, translated as *A Terrible Night*, also came out in 1896. It's about an insomniac, played by Méliès, who discovers a giant spider on his bed and fights it off. *The X-ray Fiend*, made by George Albert Smith in 1897, is little more than a scene of a man and woman flirting and a professor turning on an X-ray machine (a brand-new invention) so that the audience sees them as skeletons, something that today seems comic but at the time would likely have frightened the audience. Both Méliès and Smith made other little horror films in the next couple of years. In 1898 two horror films were released by a Japanese film company: *Shinin no sosei*, which translates to *Resurrection of a Corpse*, and *Bake Jizo*, which translates to *Jizo the Spook*, both written by Eijiro Hatta.

And horror movies have continued to be made ever since.

Writers have a complicated relationship with movies and movie-making. Some write directly for the screen; others have had their work adapted for it, with mixed results. There have been lots of memoirs by screenwriters and other movie creators about their experiences in the industry, some positive, many negative. This might be primarily because while writing prose is generally a solo enterprise, writing for and working on movies is always a collaborative process, one during which compromises are made over and over again, often to the extent that the original piece of text that inspired the movie is unrecognizable to its author.

Surprisingly, there have been only a few anthologies featuring movie horror and dark fantasy: the most prominent are David J. Schow's *Silver Scream*; *Midnight Premiere*, edited by Tom Piccirilli; *It Came from the Drive-In!*, edited by Norman Partridge and Martin H. Greenberg; *The Hollywood Nightmare*, edited by Peter Haining; and my own, *The Cutting Room*, a reprint anthology.

So an anthology of all new dark and strange fiction inspired by cinema and television seems like a natural in our worldwide movie-obsessed culture. Stories about inexplicable happenings on the screen and behind it, *Final Cuts* contains accident-prone rehearsals, spectral performances, shadows that appear only on film, home movies made for one person to view, snuff films, the worldwide phenomenon of livestreaming *everything*, and even movies made to open our world to terrifying, otherworldly creatures. Some of these stories examine the rich arcana and artifacts of movie lore; some create new ones.

A seemingly innocent domestic drama made in Hong Kong has a startling effect on its viewers; a serial killer in Pakistan wants his execution televised all over the world; a film set in Kuala Lumpur is host to dark and hungry ghosts; a moviegoer obsessed with a lost documentary made by Werner Herzog discovers more than he bargained for. These are only a few of the stories featured herein.

I invite you to this journey into the surreal, the uncanny, the dark hidden behind, in front of, and even within the silver screen.

With thanks to ReelRundown.com for the historical information.

FINAL CUTS

DAS GESICHT

Dale Bailey

A FLY ALIGHTS ON THE TABLE, grooms itself, is gone.

Even now, after all these years, it is all the old man can do not to recoil. Even now, he remembers the flies. Even now, he dreams of them.

He looks at the woman across from him. She is young, impossibly so. His experience of aging—and he is now irrefutably old, born at the rag end of a long-dead century—is that he lives on unchanged while everything around him grows progressively younger.

His infirmities give this notion the lie. He looks at the world through a film of cataracts. Constipation binds his guts. But inwardly, he feels the same as he'd felt five decades ago.

Inwardly, he is terrified.

Udo Heldt's words have lodged inside his head like fishhooks. *Peel back the surface of the world and it's all butchery, isn't it? Everything. Butchery and filth and corruption.*

What will this young woman—this Eleanor Farrell—make of

the sentiment, he wonders. For it's Udo Heldt who brought her here.

She's come to ask about *Das Gesicht.*

She's come to ask about *The Face.*

> > >

He'd nearly turned her away.

He'd spent more than fifty years trying to unlive it, disremember it, undream it from his dreams, and if he had not been entirely successful, neither had he wholly failed. He was eighty-eight years old. He'd spent the first third of his life chasing down his aspirations. He'd spent the rest of it running away from them. He'd renounced the calling that had summoned him across an ocean, to the broken shelf of a continent not his own. He'd forsaken the lush boulevards of Los Angeles for the grimy streets of Brooklyn. He'd abandoned the woman he'd loved.

No.

He did not want to think of Udo Heldt.

He did not want to think of *Das Gesicht.*

"The film is lost," he'd told her when she called. "It was never released. Why should it interest you?"

"It may not have been released, but it was screened. I've tracked down nearly a dozen oblique allusions to it," she said. "Three or four diaries, a handful of letters in private collections. No one wanted to talk about what actually happened at the screening—but no one seemed to be able to forget it, either."

"Please, Miss—"

"Farrell," she said. "Look, Mr. King. It's of historical interest, if nothing else. Lon Chaney was said to be there. James Whale. A handful of others. Pola Negri. Tod Browning. They were universally revolted by it. Chaney called it vile, Tod Browning blasphemous."

"It was a long time ago. No one wants to hear those old stories."

"I promise you. I'm not doing some *Hollywood Babylon* hack job," she'd told him.

"You are chasing ghosts," he'd said.

"Even ghosts should have their say." And then, to his undoing: "You should give her a voice. After all, you loved her, didn't you?"

She didn't say her name. She didn't have to.

There had not been a day in nearly sixty years that the old man had not thought of her. Not one. Not since the day in 1919 (had it really been so long ago?) when he'd strolled into a Berlin cinema on a whim. Not since he'd seen her in *Küss Mich*, a movie of little distinction, in a role of even less. The next day, he'd returned to the theater with Heldt. And when the lights went down, the director, too, through the camera's eye, saw not the woman on the screen—not Catrin Ammermann, as she was then billed— but the woman she was striving to become.

By the time she took the role of the young wife in *Der Ver- dammte Schlüssel* almost a year later, Heldt had dubbed her Catrin Amour. But it was the man operating the camera—it was Hein- rich König, it was the old man—who'd made her a star.

Now, in his dim, second-floor walk-up, with traffic whisper- ing outside the curtained windows and dust sifting down on the tables and the antimacassars and the framed black-and-white photos that throng every surface—now that Eleanòr Farrell has flown across the country to speak with him—now that her little cassette recorder is unwinding its reel, patient as the hours— now that Catrin Amour is dead and beyond hurt—now, he can say it. And why shouldn't he? All her life she had been no one and she had wanted desperately to be someone. All the great ones are alike in that way, he tells Miss Farrell: they are forever chrysalids on the verge of a magnificent transformation. That is the secret of his profession. You do not shoot the woman in front of the camera. You shoot the woman she wishes to become.

"Alchemy, Udo called it," he says.

"What was he like?"

How is he to answer that, the old man wonders. He remembers Heldt as a small, sinewy man, with a shock of dark hair and fervid, black eyes. He remembers his near-crippling limp, the legacy of an Allied round at Passchendaele. "I'm lucky to have a leg at all," Heldt had once told him. "The fucking surgeon was a butcher. He should have cut the fucking thing off and handed me a crutch."

The cinema was his crutch.

Only on the set did Udo Heldt know anything akin to joy—and even there, his fury infused every frame the old man had shot on his behalf. *Der Verdammte Schlüssel*, his first film, ends with the gory decapitation of Bluebeard's young wife, betrayed by the bloody key.

"Did you serve in the war?" Miss Farrell asks.

The old man nods. He'd been wounded in the first days of fighting, at Liège. Unlike Heldt, he'd been spared the endless horror that followed: the gas, the artillery, the grenades, and, most of all, the vast wasteland of barbed wire and landmines between the rat-infested trenches, where Lewis guns spat out death at five hundred rounds a minute, and flyblown corpses bloomed like roses.

Dulce et decorum est pro patria mori.

Heinrich König had survived intact.

The war had scooped out Udo Heldt's soul.

> > >

The old man falls into silent rumination.

Miss Farrell gets up to look at the photos. They stand by the dozen on bookshelves and end tables: flappers and vamps and innocents alike, icons of the silent era: Mary Pickford, Norma Talmadge, Theda Bara. So many others. The old man wonders if Miss Farrell sees herself among them. She is not a beautiful woman; she is pale and freckled, with a sharp nose and green, inquisitive eyes. But in the right hands—in *his* hands—the camera could be coaxed to love her.

Such is the alchemy of the aperture, the paradox of the eye.

Heldt was already musing aloud about these issues when he wrote *Die Wölfe*. They had storyboarded the film together. The old man can remember it almost shot by shot even now, though little footage survives beyond the scene that juxtaposes the hunter's death against his wife's garden party, crosscutting his face, twisted in horror as he is torn apart by wolves, with those of the revelers, garish with laughter, and effectively dissolving the line between agony and exhilaration.

No one but Heldt could have conceived that sequence.

No one but the old man could have shot it.

Miss Farrell runs her finger across the top of one picture frame. Lifts another one to her face.

"Clara Bow," the old man says.

He can lay his hand upon any one of the photos, even in the dark.

"This is you beside her?"

"Yes."

He studies her studying him, measuring him against the amiable rogue in the photo, with his unhandsome, equine face. He is no longer so tall. His jacket hangs upon him. His age-yellowed collar sags at the neck. His tie is too narrow.

It has been years since he's entertained a caller.

"You came to Hollywood in '21," Miss Farrell says, placing the picture back on the shelf, angling it into something proximate its original position. He will have to adjust it when she is gone.

"Yes," he told her as she takes her seat across from him. "Sol Wurtzel at Fox had seen *Die Wölfe*. We came together, the three of us. Udo would have it no other way."

They'd crossed on the *Hansa*, an unhappy time. The old man, Heinrich, had been in love with Catrin Amour, of course. He'd been in love with her from the moment he walked into that Berlin cinema. But she had eyes only for Heldt. Somewhere along the way he'd become *ihr Liebhaber*, her lover, her Svengali. Catrin believed that he'd made her a star, little understanding that he could not have done it on his own. He needed the camera eye. The camera needed the man behind it.

They were alone upon the deep when everything went wrong.

Catrin Amour came pounding at Heinrich's stateroom door well after midnight, in some cold, dead hour when the ship rolling gently through the swells lulled the soul into a sleep like death. Waking, he'd thought there'd been a disaster—a boiler that had blown out the hull, an iceberg collision, the *Titanic* torn asunder as the frigid deep engulfed her. It *had* been a disaster, of course, but a purely personal one that would cleave not the ship, but their little trio, along fault lines none of them had before acknowledged.

Catrin was incoherent, sobbing. There had been an altercation. She could tell him nothing—she *would* tell him nothing—beyond that solitary admission, and he could have read that much in the bruise blossoming upon her cheek. He found her some ice, put her to bed, and spent the rest of the night pacing the tiny stateroom, torn between fury and fear.

Catrin awoke toward dawn. Ignoring his protests, she let herself out into the corridor. She had to see Heldt. She had to apologize. She had to make things right.

Heinrich thought it had ended there.

But late that afternoon, Heldt found him alone on the fore-deck, leaning against the railing and staring out over the heaving, black water. The sky smoldered. The wind coming in across the waves whipped their hair. The air smelled of brine.

They stood there for a long time, the old man at a loss for words.

Finally, Heldt said, "Something happened to me in the war. I never told you about it. This was in the summer of '17, when the advance had ground to a halt. We spent most of our time hunkered down in the trenches, smoking and playing cards, while the boys behind us lobbed shells at the enemy lines. It was a gloomy day, and the night that followed was black as sin, moonless, with lowering clouds and gusts of icy rain. You couldn't see much beyond three or four feet.

"It was after midnight when we went over the top. It was chaos, Heinrich. You could hear the intermittent boom of the sixty-pounders and the chunk of the Lewis guns chopping rounds into the mud. Tracers slashed green streaks through the darkness. When a shell dropped, the sky would light up a smoky crimson, revealing the hellish doomscape around you: men screaming and dying, their bodies dancing grotesquely in the blizzard of .303s. And everywhere the stench of gas and gunpowder and the miasma of rotting corpses that had not yet been recovered—that might never be recovered.

"And then I heard the whistle of a descending shell. The night exploded around me. I squeezed shut my eyes, I took a breath—

"—and I was staring up into the flawless blue vault of a bright morning sky. I hurt—everything hurt, Heinrich—but I was whole. I'd survived. The explosion had driven me back into a deep pit in the wasteland. The stench of the place was unbearable. I haven't the words to describe it.

"A constant, low hum filled the air. It was the buzz of flies, Heinrich. Thousands of them. Dense, whirling clouds of them, their bodies glistening black and green when they came to rest upon me. I still hear that loathsome insect drone. I will see the sheen of their eyes until the day I die. I'd fallen into a pit of corpses, and the flies had come to feed."

The old man cannot bring himself to share the details that followed. Eleanor Farrell is already looking at him in dismay. Yet he can't help recalling Heldt's description of the flies gathering around his eyes, of the flies clogging his nostrils and worming their way between his lips.

The rest, though—

"I lurched up," Heldt had told him. "Waving my arms to keep them away, I staggered toward the rim of the pit. I began to climb, clawing my way through mud and snarls of barbed wire and decomposing bodies."

He'd been almost to the top when the hand had closed around his ankle. Slipping to his knees, Heldt found himself staring down into the countenance of a wounded Tommy. Half his face had been shot away, revealing a complex ligature of muscle and tendon, with here and there a white grin of bone. His eyeball lay exposed within its shattered orbit. Flies massed everywhere upon this broken visage. They sipped at the wells of his nostrils and devoured the raw flesh that strung his jaw. They squirmed into the crevice beneath his eyeball to glut themselves upon his brain.

"Kill me," the Tommy whispered. Heldt reached for the blade sheathed at his belt. It was the only thing to do. It would be a mercy. And then he had a nightmare vision of his companions in the trenches—men who'd eaten and gambled and battled alongside him—*Dreckfressers* like himself, mud gluttons conscripted into a war they'd never chosen to fight, gunned down by British machine guns. He turned away.

"*Lassen sie schlemmen,*" he said. Let them feast.

He kicked loose the Tommy's hand and clambered up out of the pit. He'd made it safely back to the German line by nightfall.

The *Hansa* plowed on through the murky water.

"Why did you tell me this?" Heinrich had asked at last.

Heldt stared out at the sea. "That is when I learned the true nature of all things. Peel back the surface of the world, and it's all butchery, isn't it? Everything. Butchery and filth and corruption." And then Heldt met his gaze. "There is nothing I will not do, Heinrich. Nothing."

> > >

Miss Farrell's little recorder winds the tape tight, and snaps off. She digs a fresh cassette out of her bag and gets the machine running again.

"What happened in Hollywood?" she asks.

The old man snorts.

"Hollywood was Udo Heldt's undoing," he says. "In the end, Hollywood undid us all. *Der Verdammte Schlüssel* and *Die Wölfe* were widely admired. But they were not the kind of films Sol Wurtzel could make at Fox. He'd thought Heldt could be tamed, that his enormous talents could be channeled into more conventional pictures. But Heldt could not be tamed. He was a great filmmaker, but what made him great was that he had an unflinching vision. Strip him of that vision, and put him to work making romantic comedies—"

The old man laughs.

Not that Heldt would make romantic comedies—or any other movie Wurtzel sent him.

They reached a stalemate: Heldt made no films at all.

Catrin and Heinrich, meanwhile, both found work quickly

enough. Catrin's star never reached the heights it had risen to in Germany, but she was well-known and well-paid; in the day of silent film, language and accent were no barrier to stardom. Soon she and Heldt were living in the Hollywood Hills—unmarried, igniting the kind of small scandal that kept her safely in the public eye.

And Heinrich's skills were much in demand. His work was never less than professional, often excellent. He worked with most of the stars of the era—

—here Eleanor Farrell glances around at the photos once again—

—and the ones he didn't work with he met. But *Der Verdammte Schlüssel* and *Die Wölfe* nagged him. With Heldt, he had been great. He wanted to be great again.

By this time, the wounds inflicted on the *Hansa* had healed—imperfectly, true, but well enough that Catrin, Heldt, and Heinrich spent many long evenings together, hashing over the latest Hollywood gossip. Catrin contrived not to mention the occasional bruises that shadowed her face, and Heinrich contrived not to notice them. Udo drank, and late at night, when Catrin had retreated upstairs to bed, he talked film.

He had seen everything. He saw every picture that came out of Europe. He screened all of *der Blödsinn*, the drivel—his word—produced in Hollywood. A withering critic, he scorned even the best films, reserving the occasional kind word for Heinrich's work on otherwise worthless pictures, and for Murnau and Wiene and some few other Germans in their darker modes. "But even they flinch when they come hard up against the truth," Heldt would say. Heinrich did not ask what he meant by truth. He remembered all too well their conversation aboard the *Hansa*. He would not forget the horror of the Tommy's fate. He knew that he'd been obscurely threatened. *Butchery, filth,* and *corruption*—these words lingered in his mind.

But Heldt had still more to say on film in the abstract. Commercial pictures, with their neat plots and their happy endings, were a perversion of the cinema, he argued. The image may tell a story. It may coax and manipulate. It may deceive. But it must not lie. It may be a fiction, but inside the fiction there must be truth. "The biggest lie cinema tells," he said, "is embedded in the very medium itself, is it not—the paradox of the moving image, which is still, and the still image, which moves."

So it went, Heldt's talk of pictures and paradoxes—so it might have gone on forever, the old man supposes, but for what happened on Monday, October 13, 1924. The date is scored into the old man's memory. It was the night Udo Heldt destroyed Catrin Amour's film career; it was the night *Das Gesicht* was born.

Catrin would never speak of what had happened. All the old man knew was that a hammering at his door once again woke him deep in the blackest hour of the morning. Swimming up out of the depths was very much like waking that night on the *Hansa*—a sense of confusion resolving into the certainty of disaster: icebergs, torpedoes, exploded boilers, something beautiful shattered and devoured by the deep, a world consumed by a war that would not end.

It was Catrin, of course. Heinrich's forebodings as he pulled on his dressing gown proved correct. Heldt had carved open her cheek. A doctor was summoned. The police were not—Catrin wouldn't permit it. It was clear to all of them that her career in pictures was over.

For a few weeks, they all waited for something to happen. Nothing happened. Heldt showed up neither in anger nor remorse. The picture Catrin was about to start shooting was quietly recast. The few rumors in the press were swiftly extinguished. The studios kept the gossip columns on a pretty short leash in those days. Catrin Amour, it became known, had tired of acting. She had chosen a life of seclusion. She might well go back to Germany.

In the meantime, her slashed cheek healed into a puckered scar. The doctor had done his work as well as he could. So had Heldt. Catrin stayed on with Heinrich. He and Catrin were companions, nothing more. They never shared a bedroom. This was Catrin's decision, not Heinrich's.

"I loved her very much," the old man tells Miss Farrell.

Miss Farrell says nothing. What is there to say?

The reels of her tape recorder continue to turn, eating time.

The old man clears his throat. "Then I ran into Heldt again. I was eating lunch at the counter of the Musso & Frank Grill, when he slid onto the stool next to me—"

> > >

"Why don't you move on down the counter?" Heinrich had said.

Heldt didn't bother responding. "I want you to shoot a picture for me, Heinrich," he said—though by this time the old man had started calling himself Henry King.

"I asked you to move on down the counter."

"Just think about it," Heldt said, and then he moved on down the counter, and out the door onto the street.

The hell he would think about it, Heinrich told himself.

Yet he thought about little else. He thought about *Der Verdammte Schlüssel* and he thought about *Die Wölfe* and he thought about the trivial picture he was working on now, and the featherweight of a director, who barely knew which end of the camera to point at his actors. Heinrich might as well have been directing the picture himself. He supposed he was.

He mentioned the encounter at the Musso & Frank Grill to

Catrin, who took little interest in the business these days—or anything else, for that matter. They rarely talked, and when they did talk, they said nothing of consequence. Heinrich had once told her he didn't even see the scar when he looked at her. She replied that she saw nothing else. But when he said that he'd run into Heldt, a light came into her eyes that he hadn't seen for months. He realized that she was still in love with him.

Which is how, a few nights later, they wound up at Heldt's house—though, of course, it was really Catrin's house, too. That night Heinrich learned that she didn't seem to resent anything Heldt did or wanted from her. It was her money that had paid for it, just as it was her money that Heldt had been subsisting on during their time apart. But Catrin didn't resent it. It turned out that she'd even consent to go back in front of the camera for him. And it turned out that Heinrich would consent to stand behind it.

But what was the project Heldt had in mind?

He wanted to work inside the paradox, he said, where the still picture and the moving one meet. And then he went on to describe the film he had in mind. *Das Gesicht*, Heldt called it. *The Face*. It sounded like the most static—and least interesting— picture Heinrich could imagine. It would, nonetheless, be the most difficult challenge Catrin would ever confront as an actress. She would need to do the impossible. She would need to remain utterly still—utterly—for an hour and more.

And Catrin was not alone.

"Technically, it was the most difficult challenge I ever faced, as well," the old man tells Eleanor Farrell. "Together, the three of us would make a great film—or we would fail. We made a great film, Miss Farrell. Thank God, it does not survive."

> > >

"You will want to know how it was done, of course. Does it matter? Would you understand if I explained it? Alchemy, Heldt called it. But *Das Gesicht*—there is alchemy, and there is alchemy."

The old man shakes his head.

"Did something happen on the set of *Das Gesicht*?" the young woman asks.

"Nothing unexpected, Miss Farrell. I was present for the entire shoot—a single day, but a trying one. The finished film looked like a single take, but such a long take was, of course, impossible. It is impossible even now. Like all films, *Das Gesicht* was an illusion. Like all films, it was constructed in the editing room."

"What happened at the screening, Mr. King?"

The old man sighs. He doesn't answer for a long time.

> > >

"I wondered even then who would be interested in such a film," he says when he finally resumes. "Technicians like myself, perhaps, who would want to know how we had pulled off the illusion of the long take. And there would be interest among Hollywood's aristocracy, who would wonder if Heldt's new film—privately financed and shot in a rented studio—could possibly live up to the achievements of *Der Verdammte Schlüssel* and *Die Wölfe*. But as for a real audience? The film had none. There would be no release. It was art for art's sake, I suppose: an expression of a single man's private obsession. He insisted that it would be his finest film."

"And Catrin Amour?"

"She never spoke to me of it. She loved him, of course, as I loved her, perhaps to a greater and in a different degree. She loved him enough to surrender up her ruination for his art. As far as I could tell, she did so without ill will or regret. I never asked her why. Any such inquiry seemed to me somehow obscene. So we shot the film and retreated to the editing room, painstakingly matching up and splicing shots. The details"—the old man shrugs—"they will have little interest to you. You wish to know of the screening. You wish to know of the film itself. You wish to hear about *Das Gesicht*."

Eleanor Farrell does not respond.

She lets the silence spin out, trusting, he supposes, that he will come to it in his time. And he will. Having come this far, what can he do but unburden himself? And so, slowly—haltingly—he begins to speak.

Between the three of them—Heinrich, Catrin Amour, and Udo Heldt—they put together a select guest list: James Whale and Tod Browning and Lon Chaney were there, as Miss Farrell had said. But there were others, Barbara La Marr, Sol Wurtzel, Louise Brooks, and Nita Naldi. The great cinematographers of the day, G. W. Bitzer and John Arnold. Others. Perhaps twenty-five people, no more. The old man cannot recall them all, not after all these years. Heldt's greatest regret was that the German directors he respected—Murnau, Wiene, Lang—would not be present—though he told Heinrich that he hoped to take the film to Germany, as well.

And so they gathered in a small screening room on the Fox lot. Heinrich was there, of course. And Catrin Amour came, too. Udo Heldt escorted her in just as the lights were going down, her face artfully veiled to reveal the unmarked arc of one high cheekbone—and to hide the scar that Udo had slashed into her face on the other side. The men murmured, standing to greet her. She merely nodded and let Udo lead her to her seat in the gathering dark.

The room fell silent but for the whir of the projector as it cast out its light upon the screen. The title came up, white on black—

—Das Gesicht—

—and dissolved into darkness. Then the screen brightened to reveal an image of a woman's face—Catrin Amour's unmarred face—in medium-close profile and to the right of center, so that it commanded the screen without overwhelming it. She was beautiful, the old man says. Not even the tiniest imperfection was visible, not even a pore. There was an audible intake of breath at this vision: Catrin Amour, her lips relaxed into an enigmatic half smile, her hair falling in dark waves around her shoulders. Everything about the image was utterly still. If you saw it as the audience saw it, if you saw it here before you, the old man says, nodding at the pictures that surround them—if you saw it before you now, you would mistake it for a still photo—until the woman blinked. And when the woman on-screen *did* blink—when Catrin Amour blinked at last—someone laughed in the darkness, mirthlessly, a release of tension, nothing more.

And still the image held.

What at first was confusing—was this a moving picture at all?—became gradually mesmerizing, because the image both fulfilled and defied every expectation. It lived entirely in the paradox of the moving image.

If you have ever spent a long time living with a child, the old man says to Eleanor Farrell, you may have had the experience of looking at a photo from many months in the past and feeling a moment of shock, an instant of cognitive dissonance, for the child before you is palpably different from the child in the photo—yet the change has happened so gradually, right before your eyes, day by day, that you barely notice it until confronted with her image from another era.

This was the experience of watching *Das Gesicht*. The image appeared never to move. You only occasionally awakened to realize that the angle of vision had changed: you were no longer looking at Catrin Amour in pure profile but from a subtly different perspective, as though the camera was tracking slowly, impossibly slowly, in an arc around her. It was a still picture. And then you realized that the still picture had been a moving one all along—and thus the paradox was exposed. Catrin Amour blinked, and you awoke from your trance to realize that she was no longer as she had been.

The film ran an hour. That's how long it took to describe that arc around Catrin Amour's face, how long it took the viewer to progress from perfection into imperfection, from the unscarred face to the horrifically mutilated one: Udo Heldt's not very subtle metaphor for his vision of the world as he had shared it on the *Hansa*: *Peel back the surface of the world, Heinrich, and it's all butchery, isn't it?*

In the moment the scar was fully revealed, you could feel the mood of the audience shift: This was the masterpiece of the man who had made *Der Verdammte Schlüssel* and *Die Wölfe*?

The old man pauses again. He is a long time gathering his thoughts.

This time Miss Farrell risks a question. "That was it?"

The old man recognizes the implication in her voice. She too has been duped. She has traveled all the way across the country for this revelation? This was *Das Gesicht*? The old man is briefly tempted to answer her in the affirmative.

But he has come too far to stop now.

"No, Miss Farrell," he says. "There is more." He doesn't wait to hear the follow-up question. He plunges on. "Chaney was right. It was a vile picture. It was a blasphemous one." He takes a long breath. "What you must understand, Miss Farrell, is that I was there—I was there on the set of the film. I was there in the editing room for weeks. With my hands I shaped the illusion of the unbroken take. With my hands I created the trickery. I had seen every frame of that footage, including the many, many feet we left on the cutting-room floor, a hundred times or more. And what I saw next, I did not see on the set. What I saw next, I never filmed."

What the old man had seen next—what they had all seen next—was nothing more, and nothing less, than a fly emerge from Catrin Amour's left nostril. An optical illusion, a speck of dust on the print, a flaw in the film, Heinrich thought. And then the camera, a camera he had been operating, moved in for a tight shot—a shot he had never taken. And in this new shot, a second fly emerged from Catrin's nostril. It took flight and landed on the scar Udo Heldt had carved into her cheek. A third fly followed. Another. And then another.

She might have been a mannequin, the woman on the screen was so still. Then her mouth bulged grotesquely, as though she were going to vomit, and flies boiled forth from within her. She spewed them out in handfuls, in clots, in seething mouthfuls; she spewed them out by the hundreds. They massed on her neck and chin, launching themselves intermittently into the cloud that swirled around her. And still they came, streaming out of her mouth and nostrils in swarms. And Catrin Amour—the Catrin Amour on the screen—remained utterly unmoved.

Flies began one by one to land on the camera lens, blurring the image of *das Gesicht*—of the face—into a spume of bodies, engorged with putrescence. They probed the air for the carrion stench of food. Heinrich flinched from the scrutiny of the enormous compound eyes—from the filth and corruption that lay exposed before him, the sordid truth inside the lie. At last, the loathsome creatures obscured the image of *das Gesicht*'s defiled beauty altogether. Catrin Amour was gone. The screen writhed with insectile turmoil an instant longer—

—and then it went abruptly black.

For a heartbeat, silence reigned.

Catrin Amour began to scream. Someone fumbled on the lights, plunging the room into chaos. Some few of the audience—Lon Chaney among them—sat in stunned horror. Most reeled blindly toward the doors. In the back row, someone retched. Heinrich stumbled in Catrin's direction, shoving people aside.

Udo Heldt was already there, tearing away Catrin's veil.

Heinrich lurched to a halt, snatching at the back of a seat to support himself.

He could no longer see Catrin's face.

He could no longer see anything but scar.

> > >

Eleanor Farrell says nothing.

The daylight behind the curtains has faded, draping shadows over the photographs surrounding them: still images that move now only in the old man's imagination, that speak only in his memory.

The old man wonders if she believes him. He wonders if he cares.

"Saying it was true," the young woman says at last. "How could it have happened?"

"I don't know," Heinrich König says. "I know only the things I have seen, Miss Farrell. Whether they are true things—" He shrugs. "The camera also lies."

She pauses, clearly unsatisfied with this response, but what is he to say?

There is mystery in the world.

"What happened next?"

"You know the rest. I destroyed the print. I destroyed the negative. I destroyed everything. I did it that night. And when I was finished, I drove east. I was done with pictures."

"And Catrin?"

"I left her to him, to my shame. I did not return to Los Angeles for her funeral after the suicide."

"Yet you loved her."

"I loved Catrin Ammermann. I loved the woman she was striving to become. I loved the dream of Catrin Amour. But after *Das Gesicht*, I could not see her any longer. I could see only the scar she made in the world."

"And Udo Heldt?"

"He died in a car accident three years later, Miss Farrell. You know this. The fact is readily available."

"I don't know how you feel about it."

"Do my feelings matter?" he asks, and when she does not answer, he says, "I did not grieve Udo Heldt. I am glad his movies—our movies—are gone from the world. I repent the finest work I ever did. I repudiate it. I disavow *Der Verdammte Schlüssel* and I disavow *Die Wölfe*. If I had been able to destroy them, too, I would have. I take comfort that only fragments survive."

"But—"

The old man reaches out and touches a button on her recorder. The reels grind to a halt. Into the silence that follows, he says, "You are still young, Miss Farrell. Forget *Das Gesicht*. Find a happier illusion and hope that it is true."

And then, slowly, the old man stands—a difficult process, but, he reflects, not one that he would willingly surrender. He supposes that he will soon have no choice in the matter.

He straightens his tie and glances at Miss Farrell. He wants to give her the foolish advice that old men call wisdom, but he has already indulged himself sufficiently in that respect: perhaps she will forget *Das Gesicht* and perhaps she will not. He hopes so— for in unburdening himself, he understands, he has burdened her. And he has given Udo Heldt's picture new life. He would give her something else, if he could. Perhaps he will not have to adjust the angle of Clara Bow's photograph, after all.

She hesitates for a moment when he extends it to her.

"Mr. King, I couldn't—"

"Please, Miss Farrell. Let me grant you a brighter memory for your visit than the one I have already given you."

She gazes at the photo. "It's inscribed."

"Yes. I was new to America when that picture was made. She was kind to me."

"Okay, then." The young woman tucks the photo into her bag. She smiles—she is more beautiful than he had thought—and thanks him. And that is enough. He sees her out and then he is alone in the dark apartment.

He sits quietly, listening to the traffic outside, and looking at the photos that surround him—mementos of a life he'd surrendered more than five decades ago. He'd led several other lives in the interim, but it is that first one—the life he'd shared with Udo Heldt and Catrin Amour—that matters.

After a time, he eats sparingly—a can of soup, nothing more—and then he sees himself to bed.

Sleep is a long time coming. He keeps thinking of the films he made with Udo Heldt. He keeps thinking of *Das Gesicht*.

He disavows it. He disavows them all.

He lays very still.

In the darkness above him, a fly cuts circles in the air.

DRUNK PHYSICS

Kelley Armstrong

DRUNK PHYSICS STARTED IN A BAR, naturally. A bunch of physics postgrads hanging out, blowing off thesis stress, getting wasted and getting loud, and pissing off the group of math postgrads quietly working through theorems at the next table.

Six of us crammed into the booth. Trinity and I were the only girls—I do remember that. We weren't exactly friends, but if Trinity wanted a drink with the guys, she always asked me to come along. I was her wingman, a warning to the guys that none of them would be escorting Trinity home, however noble their intentions.

I'm a good drinker. Well, not "good" in the sense I can hold my liquor. I absolutely cannot. I just become someone different, someone fun and funny and vastly more entertaining than sober Hannah. Being drunk doesn't just lower my inhibitions—it atomically annihilates them while never destroying my common sense. All the clever and cool retorts I'd normally think but never say? They actually come out of my mouth. Plenty of silly nonsense, too, but never anything cruel.

So, I'm in the college pub with the guys, downing a fizzy pink something—that's how I order drinks: just give me a fizzy pink something or a blue sour whatever. Bartenders either love me or hate me. This one thinks I'm adorable, and I suspect there are more than two shots in my drink. One minute I'm expounding on this show *Drunk History* and the next I'm riffing on a *Drunk Physics* version of it, and the guys are laughing so hard they're snorting beer. Even Trinity chuckles as she sips her wine cocktail.

Then Rory says, "You should totally do that. Put it on YouTube."

"Be my guest," I say.

"No, *you*, Hannah." Liu waves an unsteady finger in my face. "You and Trin. Together. You'd rack up the views. You're hilarious, and Trin's . . . Well, Trin's Trin."

Trinity is gorgeous. That's what he means. She looks like Hollywood's idea of a physics doctoral student, the sort who makes actual physics majors roll their eyes because, come on, we don't look like that. Except Trinity does. Long curly black hair, huge amber eyes, a slender but curvy body. I'm embarrassed to admit that the first time I saw her in class, I almost offered to help her find her room because she was clearly in the wrong place.

"So, *Drunk Physics*, huh?" Trinity says. "How would that work?"

"You guys drink," Liu says. "A lot. You get wasted, and then you try to explain a physics concept and post the result on a YouTube channel."

"It *would* be hilarious," Rory says. "You should do it, Hannah."

The other guys take up a chant of "Do it! Do it!" banging the scarred table. I roll my eyes. Trinity shrugs and says, "Sure, why not."

I look at her. "Seriously?"

A soft smile. "Seriously. It'd be fun."

And so *Drunk Physics* was born.

> > >

Six months later

I wake on the couch, groaning and reaching for my water bottle, which I've learned to put on the table before we start filming.

As I chug lukewarm water, Trinity's figure sways in front of me. She's seated at the desk, and she isn't actually swaying—that's just me.

Trinity's gaze is fixed on a massive computer screen where my drunken image gestures wildly. Thankfully, the sound is off. It's last night's *Drunk Girl Physics* episode. Yes, we had a name change. Apparently, *Drunk Physics* wasn't as original as I thought. We decided to play on the element that made our show unique. *Drunk Girl Physics*. DGP to its fans, and to my everlasting shock, we actually have those. A lot.

Six months ago, Trinity and I started with a laptop and a cheap microphone. Now we have this ginormous computer monitor, connected to a top-of-the-line laptop, professional-grade cameras and microphones, all courtesy of Webizode.com, a startup channel for web series. We began on YouTube, but that was an exercise in humility. Oh, we got traffic—thanks to incredibly kind shout-outs from a few stars in the science-web-series biz—but we also got the kind of attention no one wants. For Trinity, that was endless chatter asking her to show some body part or another. For me, it was the opposite.

Don't undress, please, Hannah.

Well, it's a good thing she's funny, 'cause no one would be watching her otherwise.

Despite a rocketing viewership—and actual income—we'd been ready to quit, deciding no amount of money was worth the humiliation. Then Webizode came along, offering us a home with awesome comment moderation. They gave us the equipment, too, plus promotion, exposure, and enough income for Trinity and me to leave grad-school housing. We found this gorgeous old house to rent, and yes, Trinity swears she gets spooky vibes from it, but honestly, I think she'd say that about any house more than twenty years old.

While we loved having our own house, it was Webizode's moderation we appreciated most. Still, the morning after our latest upload, Trinity is scrolling through comments, ready to hit our personal report button if anything slipped through.

"All good?" I croak as I rise from the couch, the floor tilting underfoot.

She doesn't turn. "That was a really shitty thing to do, Hannah."

"Wh-what?" I blink and stagger to the desk as my head and stomach spin . . . in opposite directions, of course.

God, I need to drink less for these videos. Except that's the point, as Webizode pointed out when I tried subbing water for half my vodka shots. Our fans noticed and were not impressed, and neither was Webizode.

In six months, I've exhausted every hangover remedy on the planet. The only thing that helps is having a full stomach pretaping and then drinking enough water afterward that I might as well sleep in the bathroom. I may have actually done that once or twice.

I look down at Trinity, my lurching brain struggling to remember why I'm here.

Oh, right.

"What'd I do?" I say.

She turns on the volume and hits Play on the frozen video.

I'm saying, "The prevailing theory of time is that it moves in a straight line, like this." I demonstrate with an empty shot glass, which does not move in any actual semblance of "straight."

"Which means that to travel through time, you'd need to . . ." I did something on-screen with the two empty glasses.

I groan. "Time travel? Really?"

On-screen, I continue drunkenly explaining concepts that I don't even understand sober.

"But that presumes that time is orderly, when it could actually be," my drunken self says, and then launches into a *Doctor Who* quote about time being like a ball of *"wibbly-wobbly, timey-wimey stuff."*

"What?" on-screen Trinity says.

I continue to quote the show with, *"Things don't always happen in the right order."*

Trinity hits Stop and glares at me. I sink into a chair and blink at the screen. Then I blink at her.

"I made a fool of myself," I say. "Situation normal. But I'm not seeing what . . ."

She jabs a finger at a section of the comments.

trekgal98: Twenty points to Hannah for the Doctor Who refs!

larrybarry: And they both zoomed right over Trinity's head.

trekgal98: Are you surprised?

larrybarry: LOL

It seems like an innocuous exchange. It *is* innocuous—all comments pass through Webizode's moderation. Profanity is removed. Insults and innuendo are blocked. Trinity, though, cannot help scraping away those layers of idle comments to find the insult hidden within, and she's found it here as she always does when I make a geek-culture reference that she doesn't get.

"You promised to stop doing that," she says.

I throw up my hands. "I'm drunk, and I'm blathering nonsense."

"You do it on purpose. You know our audience, and you play to them, and you make me look like an idiot."

"Not watching a TV show hardly makes you an idiot, Trin. In fact, it makes you smart. Unlike me, you don't waste your study hours watching Netflix."

"Because I need to study. You don't. You're a freaking genius."

And that's what it comes down to. What it always comes down to. Trinity has decided that I'm smarter than her and that our Webizode audience prefers me. She's . . . not wrong.

Damn it. I hate saying that. I've gotten to know Trinity much better in the last six months, and I consider her a friend. Yet the more I get to know her, the less I envy her. Yes, she's gorgeous. Smart, too, or she wouldn't be in our doctoral program. But she has an insecure core that desperately needs to be more than a pretty face. She is accustomed to being the center of attention, and when the spotlight slides my way, she deflates, her anxieties twisting into anger that homes in on me, as if I've stolen that spotlight from her.

"I didn't mean it, Trin," I say evenly. "You know that. I'm making a fool of myself." I wave at the screen. "Time travel? I don't even know what I'm saying there. Lunatic fringe."

"They love it," she says. "Check the stats."

I peer at the counter and frown. The episode has been up for fewer than eight hours, and it's already gotten more views than last week's.

"That can't be about me babbling incoherent sci-fi references," I say. "There must be something else."

I zoom through the comments. I don't get far before I find

what I'm looking for, and I groan anew. Then I fast-forward the video. About halfway through our segment, a dim light appears over Trinity's shoulder. It gradually becomes brighter until there is very clearly a translucent amorphous blob hovering there.

"Ghost," I say.

"What?"

I point at the shape. "This is a ghostly orb. At least, it is according to our viewers."

Trinity reads the comments and then squints at the screen. "That thing?"

"Hey, you're the one who said this place was haunted. There's your proof."

She gives me a hard look. "I said this house gave me a weird feeling, and you're never going to let me forget that, are you?"

I tap the screen. "Looks like a ghost to me."

She rolls her eyes. "It's light glare. Even I know that."

"Well, more clicks will make Webizode happy." I shut off the monitor. "I'll make you a deal. I won't bug you about ghosts again, and you won't bug me about time travel."

"Fair enough. You want the shower first?"

"I want coffee first. And after." I purse my lips. "Think I can rig the brewer up to the nozzle and shower in it?"

She rolls her eyes and heads for the bathroom.

> > >

The orb is back. It's right where it was in the last segment, hovering over Trinity's shoulder.

I'd set my alarm to get up before Trinity could check our latest episode. I wasn't looking for the orb. I'd forgotten all about it. I just wanted to comment-skim, make sure I hadn't said anything else to upset her.

After the last episode, I emailed our contact at Webizode and asked whether they could delete any future comments on my geek-culture references. They refused. It'd be a game of Whack-A-Mole, really. Delete one, and another commenter would gleefully jump in, thinking they were the first to recognize it, claiming whatever cosmic cookies the universe awarded for that.

I knew Webizode would refuse. That was just my opening gambit, so they'd be more likely to agree when I asked them to instead delete comments about Trinity failing to recognize my references. While they said yes, I was still checking.

I only get through the first page before someone mentions the orb. I check, and sure enough, there it is.

It seems . . . brighter? No, clearer. It looks like a reflection of the moon, a pale sphere with cratered shadows. There's only one window in this room, though, and it's behind the camera with a permanently closed blackout blind to avoid light cast by passing cars.

I read the comments.

schrodingers_cow: I see a face in the orb. Don't you?

jazzhands1999: Uh, no. I see the reflection of a light bulb.

kalebsmom: That's not a light bulb. It's an orb. And I see a face, too. Zoom in. Eyes. Mouth. Nose. It's all there.

I blow the video up to full screen. Yes, there are dark blotches approximately where you'd find eyes and a mouth, but it's like spotting dragon-shaped clouds. People see what they want, and apparently, they want ghosts.

I keep scrolling through comments. Some are about our episode, but more and more are about the orb, people new to our channel tuning in just for that.

I won't argue with a little publicity, though I'd rather it were for the actual show. As our marketing team at Webizode says, it doesn't matter why people come—just get them there, present a good product, and some will stay. Which is probably why Webizode hasn't argued about the high heating bills that keep Trinity in tank tops year-round.

I'm popping two aspirin when Trinity comes downstairs as fresh and bright-eyed as ever.

"Your ghost has returned," I say as I swivel the keyboard her way. "Sorry, *our* ghost. According to the comments, it now has a face."

"What?" She seems genuinely startled, and I chastise myself for joking around. She believes in this stuff. I hurry on to tell her that I do not see a face in what is obviously a lighting glitch.

As she skims the comments, I say, "So the question is whether we investigate the anomaly or not."

She pales. "Investigate a ghost? I hope you're kidding, Hannah. You don't mess with that sort of thing."

"I mean investigate the *real* cause of the light. What's causing the reflection. Do we embrace our scientist credo and conduct a ghost-busting investigation . . . or do we let people keep thinking it's a ghost if that bumps our stats."

She doesn't answer. She's stopped on a section of comments. When I turn to head into the kitchen, she says, "I thought you went through these."

"I did."

"And you weren't going to mention this?" Her nail stabs the screen, making the image shudder.

I read the comments.

gonegirl5: You see me, don't you? I know you do.

gonegirl5: Did you really think you'd get away with it?

"Yeah," I say. "I read that. Random bullshit. I don't know how it got through moderation. Sometimes I wonder whether there's a real person monitoring it or just a bot looking for key words."

"Webizode said it's a real person. They guaranteed that in our contract."

"Then it's an intern looking for key words, and since those comments don't have any, they ignored them. I'll mention it to them."

> > >

After the next episode, I wake to Trinity shaking me hard enough that I jolt upright with an uncharacteristic snarl.

"Could you not do that?" I mutter as I sit up, rubbing my eyes.

"You weren't waking," she says. "You're still drunk."

"Yeah, that's what six shots of tequila will do to a girl. We need to stop accepting those damn challenges."

I'm grumbling, but the truth is that I watered my shots, and as a result, I'm barely hungover. Trinity has been on edge. Yesterday, I made the mistake of glancing sidelong at the new clubbing dress she planned to wear on camera. I was eyeing the tiny sheath of shimmering fabric, thinking, "Damn, I wish I could wear that," but she took my look as criticism, and we had to delay the taping while she changed. I watered down my tequila while she was gone, knowing it wouldn't take much to set her off again.

I glance at our stats. Fifty percent more views. Double the comments. Triple the link shares.

"Ugh," I say. "Casper must be back."

"I'm glad you find this amusing. How about *this*?" She points at two comments.

gonegirl5: You thought I was gone, didn't you? You thought you got away with it.

gonegirl5: I'm dead, and it's your fault, and I'm going to make sure everyone knows.

I snicker.

Trinity slowly turns on me. "You think *everything's* funny, don't you, Hannah?"

"No. I do, however, think *this* is funny." I intone the comments in an ominous voice. "It's B-movie dialogue. *I know what you did last summer.* I'm actually surprised it doesn't say that. Maybe it'd be too on the nose."

"Someone is accusing me of being responsible for their death, Hannah. That is not, in any way, amusing."

"You?" I read the comments again. "I don't see anything saying these are about you, Trin."

She points at the orb. Is it clearer now? It *seems* clearer. I definitely see what looks like eyes and a—

I shake that off. The power of suggestion.

"Still not seeing why this is about you," I say.

"It's over *my* shoulder. The ghost is always right there, next to me."

"Trinity," I say, as carefully as I can. "That is not a ghost. It's a lighting anomaly. One person decides it's an orb, and suddenly everyone sees spooks, and then someone's gotta take it to the next level and accuse us of murder."

"It doesn't say 'murder.' It just says we're responsible."

"Maybe that's why the comment moderation didn't pick it up. It lacks whatever words are on the intern's watch list. I'll report it." I hit a few keys. "And now we'll prove this is not a ghostly orb. It isn't worth a bump in stats if it upsets you."

"You think I'm overreacting."

"No, I think it's understandably unsettling," I say evenly as I pull up the original video. "I'll find out what's going on, and our next show will be spook-free."

> > >

"It's not there," Trinity whispers.

In front of us, the screen is divided into two panels. One shows the online show from two weeks ago, paused where the orb is clearest. The other window is a direct feed from the camera, stopped at the same spot.

There is no orb on the original video.

I'd started with last night's show. When I didn't find the orb there, I went back to the previous show. Same thing. Now I'm at the first one. There is undeniably an orb in the online version and not even a hint of stray light in the original.

At a noise, I look over to see Trinity gripping the mouse, her hand trembling so much it chitters against the desktop.

"Hey," I say, squeezing her arm. "This is good news. It means the orb didn't originate at our end. There's definitely no ghost. Someone tampered with the online version."

She glances at me, her eyes blank.

"Someone tampered with the episodes," I say again, slower. "It's happening on the back end. At Webizode. They're screwing with our uploaded video."

"Why would they do that?"

"For the views," I say, stopping myself before I add "obviously." "It's someone's idea of a marketing ploy. They're probably also responsible for the original comments, identifying the orb as a ghost. Interns, right? Some sixteen-year-old marketing exec wannabe who's trying to wow the boss with a creative scheme."

Trinity nods dully. "Okay."

"We have to—" My phone rings. Webizode's number fills the screen. "Perfect timing. Let me handle this. An intern is about to be sacked."

> > >

I'm not nearly as badass on the phone call. I'm polite and calm. Our contact—Oscar—is touching base about the comment I flagged, but I want to talk about the video first. I explain that I've examined the original video, and there's no sign of an orb. Then I pause to let that sink in.

He's quiet long enough that I'm about to prod, when he speaks in that way of his that I'm sure he thinks is gentle but is patronizing as hell. Is that what Trinity hears when I address her concerns? Shit. I'll need to be more careful. There's a fine line between "gentle" and "patronizing," and I might be straying as far over it as Oscar is.

"I know you girls are very invested in the success of your show, Hannah," he says. "We all are. But I might suggest that if you have marketing ideas, you run them past our team first. That's what we're here for."

"Marketing ideas?"

"Your brand is science," he says in that same slow, patronizing way. "You are both brilliant girls, and even while inebriated, you explain complex concepts in a way that's both enlightening and entertaining. You have a great package, and you don't need to muddy it with . . ." He pauses, as if struggling for words. "Off-brand theatrics."

"You think *we're* doing this? I just said it's not on our uploaded—"

"I know you've seen a jump in stats, but you're attracting the wrong kind of viewers, ones who will dilute your brand."

"We aren't—"

"We've noticed you girls haven't discussed the orb on camera, and we weren't sure you realized it was there. We were debating whether to tell you to adjust your lighting. If it's a marketing ploy, though? That would be a violation of your contract."

"We didn't put it there. We don't *want* it there. The fact that it's not on the original means it's coming from the other end of the process."

A long pause. "You think *we're* doing this?"

"I don't actually care. Just make it stop. It's upsetting—" I glance at Trinity, who's listening in. "Upsetting *us*. Now, what I originally messaged about is something else that's upsetting us. Those comments. I'm presuming the fact that they don't actually say 'murder' gets them past comment moderation. Your moderator needs to be more careful."

"That's why I was calling, Hannah. To discuss the comments. They're bypassing moderation."

"Exactly. Whoever is moderating is letting them—"

"No, I mean they're *bypassing* moderation. And the only account that can do that is the one you two share."

"Sure, our account isn't moderated but . . . Wait. Are you suggesting—?"

Trinity hits the Speaker button. "Oscar? Trinity here. Are you saying someone posted those comments from *our* computer?"

"Yes," he says.

"The call is coming from inside the house," I intone.

She glares at me.

"That means someone's hacked our account," I say.

Oscar doesn't reply.

"Track the IP address," I say. "Find out where exactly those comments came from."

More silence.

"You already have, haven't you?" I say carefully.

"Yes."

And I don't need to ask what he found.

The call really did come from inside the house.

> > >

After I end the call with Oscar, I text Rory. Thirty minutes later, he's at our place, dissecting the videos and the comments for signs of tampering. Rory might be a physics postgrad, but his area of expertise is quantum computing . . . and he did his share of hacking in his misspent youth.

If Trinity doesn't match anyone's idea of a physics doctoral student, Rory is a walking stereotype, effortlessly managing to convey both computer geek and science nerd wound in a double helix. He's not much taller than me, slight and reedy. His saving grace is his hair, which is an adorable boy-band mop of dark curls. Today he's wearing a "Super Jew" T-shirt and blue jeans that I'm pretty sure he irons—he might even starch them. That sounds less than complimentary, but to me, guys like Rory really *are* superheroes in disguise—sweet, funny, smart as hell, packaged in a way that lets them pass under the radar of girls like Trinity. I do not fail to notice how fast Rory replied to my SOS, even on a Sunday morning, and I won't pretend I'm not pleased by that.

After an hour of work, Rory leans back in the swivel chair and adjusts his glasses. "I don't know what to tell you, Hannah."

"The truth?"

"That I can't find any sign of outside tampering. I don't know how those orbs are getting on the video, but it seems to be the same one you've uploaded. No one is taking it down, tweaking it and putting it up again. As for the comments, everything indicates that they really did come from this computer."

I swear under my breath. Then I say, "It's not me."

"You'd hardly call me in to investigate if it was. The real culprit must be . . ." His eyes cut toward the back of the house.

"I don't think it's Trin, either. She's really freaked out by all this."

"Hmm." He eyes the closed door again and lowers his voice. "Trin likes attention, and since you guys switched to Webizode, you're the one getting it. You're the cool, quirky science geek. Trin is the window dressing. The straight man to your comedian." He lowers his voice even more. "Does she know you've been fielding offers for solo projects?"

"I delete those as soon as they come in. Trin and I were having trouble even before this. She thinks I'm mocking her with my geek-culture references and . . ." I sigh. "Managing her moods is harder than I expected."

"Mm-hmm."

I turn back to the computer. "She's going to think I'm doing this. How do I convince her I'm not?"

"By ending the show."

When I stiffen, he says, "It started as a lark. But between Trinity's bullshit and the weekly hangovers, you're not having fun anymore. You already have job offers—*real* job offers in your field just waiting for you to graduate. You don't need this show, Hannah."

"Trinity does. It means a lot to her. Both the exposure and the money."

"Which is not a good reason for *you* to continue, when she's the reason you're miserable."

"We're fine," I say, taking the keyboard and busying myself checking comments.

"You said Trinity is really freaked out by those comments," he says. "Does that seem like an overreaction?" He leans in, his dark eyes twinkling with amusement. "Maybe our Trin is a secret killer, tormented by her guilty conscience."

I groan.

"You did say she believes in ghosts," he says. "Maybe she's convinced her past has literally come back to haunt her."

He starts making ghost noises, and I laugh, telling him to cut it out. That's when Trinity walks in. She looks from me to Rory.

"Did I just hear you two talking about ghosts?" she says.

"Uh, no, we—" I begin.

"You were making fun of me, weren't you, Hannah."

Rory rolls his chair between us. "No, I was joking about ghosts, and Hannah was telling me to stop." He gets to his feet. "I have a lab this morning, and I need to run. First, though . . ." He reaches into his backpack and hands me a wrapped mug. "Almost forgot this."

I unroll the paper to find a Doctor Who mug with the "timey-wimey stuff" quote I'd paraphrased on the show. As I laugh, I catch Trinity's expression.

I quickly rewrap the mug. "I'll put this in my room."

She snatches the mug and sticks it on the desk, facing the camera, with "There" and a defiant look my way. Rory counters with a narrowed-eyes glare, but Trinity doesn't notice, just plunks herself into the chair with, "So, did you find any evidence of tampering?"

> > >

So these comments came from our account. From our *computer*. And they're being posted after Trinity goes upstairs to bed and I am alone, sleeping it off on the couch.

I'm the logical culprit. Trinity isn't buying my protests and excuses. She's convinced I'm responsible, and I need to fix that.

I keep thinking of what Rory said about Trinity seeming suspiciously freaked out. His comment about her having murdered someone was a joke. And yet . . .

The more paranoid Trinity becomes, the more I wonder whether there is something in her past to warrant it. Not that she's actually killed anyone. But whenever I slip and say we're being accused of murder, she's always quick to clarify that the comments never say that. Only that one of us is *responsible* for a death.

I'd joked about *I Know What You Did Last Summer*, in which a group of teens accidentally hit and kill a pedestrian. What if there's something like that in Trinity's past?

It doesn't even need to be that dramatic. I'd been at summer camp with a girl who drowned, and I still feel guilty for not noticing her go under the water . . . even if a dozen other kids and three counselors didn't notice, either. Survivor guilt, my mom calls it.

Someone could know that Trinity feels guilty over an accidental death and be trolling her. Tormenting her. If there's something in Trinity's past—connected to those comments or not—it'd help me understand her paranoia.

I conduct my search in the library. If the public computers weren't crammed with undergrads, I'd have used those to better hide my search history. Is *that* paranoid? Maybe, but I need only to imagine Trinity discovering what I've searched, and my back tenses, triggering an ache that suggests I've been more stressed lately than I like to admit.

I think of what Rory said, about quitting the show. I'd be fine with that. I might even be relieved. My parents are both corporate researchers, and while we're hardly rich, I don't need the show income—I've been stashing it in a savings account. Also, I'm really tired of the drinking. The occasional pub night with friends used to be fun. Now I nurse a Coke . . . or blow off the invitations altogether.

The problem is Trinity. I can't be the bitch who takes away a critical source of income. And maybe I won't need to be, because I find the answer to my question a lot faster than I imagined.

In high school, Trinity was blamed for the suicide of a bullied classmate.

My gut clenches reading that. I won't pretend that I don't know what it's like to be bullied. I mostly flew too far under the radar to attract attention, but there was one girl in high school who decided I was a vastly underappreciated and overlooked target. Even today, I'll tense seeing her first name online.

Trinity isn't named in the actual articles about her classmate's suicide. They only refer to bullying by "an unnamed sixteen-year-old classmate who has not been charged at this time." It's social media that fingers Trinity as the perpetrator, and even there, while no one disputes she's the one accused, they hotly debate her guilt.

The short version is this: When Trinity was sixteen, a classmate—Vanessa Lyons—committed suicide. In her note, she alleged ongoing and systematic harassment by Trinity, who had been her best friend in middle school. Vanessa claimed Trinity had dumped her as a friend after becoming a cheerleader and joining the popular clique. When Vanessa tried to maintain a civil relationship, Trinity turned on her, bullying and berating her until depression claimed Vanessa's life.

It's a common story that carries the mournful ring of truth. Girls are BFFs, but then one grows into a gorgeous cheerleader and the other . . . does not. Popular girl ditches uncool friend, who flounders, trying to make sense of it, and when she reaches out, popular girl drives her away with insults that lacerate the friend's already paper-thin self-confidence, driving her to a place where suicide seems the only option. In death, she can finally accuse her true killer.

Reading that article, I cannot help but picture the orb behind Trinity. Cannot help but see those messages again.

In death, she can finally accuse her true killer.

I shiver even as I berate myself for it. Vanessa Lyons's ghost has not returned to wreak beyond-the-grave vengeance. Someone else has, though. Someone who blames Trinity.

The problem is that few people *did* seem to blame Trinity. On social media, her friends defended her, insisting Trinity had never said anything unkind about Vanessa in their hearing. Of course they would say that, being her friends. But only a couple of other classmates claimed to have witnessed the bullying, and no one put much stock in their credibility. Most of those blaming Trinity never saw or heard anything—they simply condemned her with variations on "Of course she did it. Girls like her are total bitches."

Reading this and knowing Trinity, I'm not persuaded she's guilty. I do know why she's freaking out, though.

She's convinced Vanessa Lyons has come back to haunt her.

> > >

I try to cancel the next episode of *Drunk Girl Physics*. Trinity won't hear of it. The show must go on, apparently. I do convince her to let us switch seats. That way, if the orb appears over me, I'll know it's just a random asshole hacker, nothing to do with the death of Vanessa Lyons.

I set my alarm for seven the next morning to beat Trinity to the comment section. When I wake, I find a text from Rory. He asks me to call him as soon as I wake. The fact he's asking for a call rather than a text means it's urgent.

He picks up on the first ring.

"First, I need to apologize," he says. "I overstepped my bounds and did something that, in retrospect, is going to seem really skeevy. It was for a good reason, though."

"Okay . . ."

"I set up a spy camera on the desk in your office."

"Uh . . ."

He hurries on. "I only activated it after last night's episode went live, and it's focused on the computer. I can't see the rest of the room. I just wanted to monitor the keyboard after you uploaded the show."

"To see which of us was tampering with the film and posting the comments."

"Yes." He exhales, as if in relief that I understand. "Not that I thought it was you. Honestly, I expected to catch Trin."

The hairs on my neck prickle. "But it was me? Drunk sleepwalking?"

"No, no. Nobody tampered with it, Hannah. That's what I wanted to tell you. I have the entire night of tape, and no one came near the desk."

"Okay, is the orb gone, then?"

His hesitation tells me otherwise, and I hurry to the computer.

"Two minutes, ten seconds," he says.

I find the spot. As I watch, the orb manifests over Trinity's seated form.

"Shit," I say.

"You switched spots," he says. "That was a good idea."

"No," I say. "It was actually really stupid. Now she's going to see that and—"

"See what?" says a voice behind me. I wheel as Trinity walks in. She stops. "Who are you talking to, Hannah?"

"J-just Rory." Did I stammer? Why the hell did I stammer?

Her gaze slides to the screen, and she blanches. I mumble something to Rory and hang up.

"Someone's hacking the system," I say quickly. "That's what Rory was calling about. He put a camera in here and—"

"He put a spy camera in our *house*?"

"He apologized. He could only see this desk, and he only turned it on after we posted the show. He was watching in case I was posting the comments in my sleep or something."

"Or *something*?" Her voice hardens. "He was trying to catch me. Except he didn't. He caught you. That's why he called. He installed a secret camera and caught you doing it, and he called to warn you. He thought he was going to catch me, and instead, he caught the girl he likes. That puts him in a really nasty position."

"I didn't do anything, Trinity," I say. "Ask Rory."

"He'll lie for you."

"Then ask him to show you the tape."

"He'll have erased it by now."

"What the hell?" I stop myself and take a deep breath. "Explain why I'd do this to you. Why I'd undermine our show like this."

"You're not undermining it. Our show is more popular than ever, and you don't want to ruin it—you want it all for yourself. You want me to quit."

"*No.* I'd quit myself before I—"

"Do you think I haven't seen those solo offers? They send them to our damn show address. I find them in the trash folder."

"I delete them because I'm not interested. If I wanted you off the show, Trinity, I sure as hell wouldn't do something as silly as this."

"It's not silly. It's clever, and you're always clever, Hannah. You know I believe in ghosts. You know I've said this house has a weird vibe. You found out about my past, didn't you? What I was accused of. You used that to fake a very public haunting. An on-screen haunting, complete with accusatory comments. You're hoping I'll quit. If that doesn't work, then eventually someone will dig up my past and humiliate me, forcing me off your show."

I take a deep breath. "Yes, I know about Vanessa. I found out yesterday. You were freaking out, and it worried me, and I had to investigate. Whether or not you bullied her—"

"I didn't." She spits the words and steps up to my face. "She bullied me."

I open my mouth.

Trinity continues. "You don't believe that, do you? No one did. Obviously, the pretty, popular girl was the bully. That's why you don't even bother to name me in those comments. Everyone will presume it's me. Geeky little Hannah wouldn't bully anyone. But Trinity? Oh, yes, she's just the type."

"I know you and Vanessa stopped being friends—"

"Because she was a nasty, vicious *bitch*, always putting me down to pull herself up. I made new friends, and Vanessa couldn't handle that. She came at me all the harder, posting from anonymous accounts, telling people I was a slut, a two-faced bitch, anorexic, all the things that kids are quick to believe about someone who looks like me."

"And then she . . . killed herself?"

Trinity laughs. It's an ugly, raw laugh. "Oh, she didn't mean to. That's the irony. Vanessa was like you—a clever girl who always had a plan. She wrote a suicide note blaming me, and then she took just enough pills to be rushed to the hospital for a good stomach pumping. Except she passed out from the sleeping pills and choked to death on her own vomit. Joke's on her. Only it wasn't, because the school believed her suicide note. Zero tolerance for bullying. It didn't matter that they had absolutely no proof. I had to go live with my aunt so I could attend a new school. I spent the rest of high school on depression meds and suicide watch. The fact I'm here—getting my PhD, no less—is a freaking miracle."

"No," I say. "It's a sign of hard work and resilience. What happened to you was shitty, Trin, but—"

"Oh, spare me your patronizing bullshit, Hannah. You're gingerly patting me on the head like a rabid rottweiler who has you cornered. I'm not going to hurt you. But I am going to make sure you don't get away with this. I'll prove you're behind the orbs and the comments."

"Sure. Go for it. You may find your efforts hampered by the small fact that I didn't actually do anything but—"

She wheels on me. "You aren't going to give up, are you? You're determined to make me look like a fool."

"Nope, actually, right now, I'm just determined to end this conversation, go out and enjoy my Sunday while you dig for evidence you're never going to find. I've tried to be reasonable, Trin, to pussyfoot around your paranoia. If anyone is behind this, it's you." I start to step past her. "If this is a cry for attention, I'm not listening anymore."

She grabs my arm. "Don't you dare—"

I wheel to throw her off, and she flings me. My stockinged feet slide on the hardwood. When I stumble, she shoves me with all her might. I fly backward, feet sailing out from under me, head striking the desk edge.

The last thing I see is Trinity, staring in wide-eyed horror as I crumple to the floor.

> > >

I wake on the office floor, my head throbbing. I grab the chair, which of course wheels away, and I sprawl face-first onto the hardwood.

"Trin?" I manage to croak.

There's no answer. I lift my head and peer around an empty office. There's blood on the floor, and when I touch the back of my head, I feel sticky, wet hair. I wince as my fingers brush a gash in my scalp.

Blinking hard, I grab the desk edge and pull myself up. I'm standing in front of the computer monitor. On the screen is Trinity with that orb behind her. Except what was an orb is now changing into a very clear figure.

A ghostly figure standing behind Trinity.

Standing right where I am.

Below it, there's a new comment.

gonegirl5: You killed me, as surely as if you'd bashed my head into that desk.

No.

That's not . . .

It can't be. It makes no sense.

And yet . . .

I swallow hard. When I look at the figure again, I can make out long dark hair and what looks like a pale T-shirt. In the reflection of that screen, I see myself . . . with long dark hair and a gray tee.

I am the ghost behind Trinity.

I am the ghost accusing her.

Not Vanessa Lyons.

Me.

But that isn't possible. We saw the orb three weeks ago. The comments started three weeks ago. How could I be the one . . . ?

My gaze shifts to the mug prominently displayed on the screen. The *Doctor Who* mug from Rory, with the time travel quote I'd said on the show.

Things don't always happen in the right order . . .

Footsteps thunder down the hallway.

"Hannah? Hannah!"

It's Rory.

Oh God, *Rory*. He's about to race in and find my body. I spin, as if I can stop him, but he's already frozen in the doorway, his gaze on the floor. Then it lifts to me.

"Sit," he says, rolling the chair toward me. "You hit your head, and there's blood . . . Damn it! Where the hell is Trinity? Did she just shove you down and take off?"

"You can see me?"

His brow furrows. "Of course I can . . ." He sputters a ragged laugh. "How badly did you hit your head, Hannah? No, you're not a ghost. Sit down for a minute, and then we're getting you to the hospital."

As he puts me in the chair, he explains that he saw part of the fight on the hidden camera. Without any sound, he only caught a glimpse of Trinity pushing me, in the screen reflection. Then he saw me crumple to the floor. He caught an Uber and spent twenty minutes banging on the door before breaking in through a back window.

"Fucking Trinity," he mutters. "I hope this is the hint you need, Hannah. She's no friend of yours, and you have to get out before . . ."

He trails off, his gaze fixed on something behind me. I turn to see he's looking at blood on the floor, a pool of it creeping from behind the desk.

I'm about to say that's just mine. Then I realize it's in the wrong spot—I fell on the other side of the desk, and this is a *pool* of blood, trickling along a crack between the floorboards.

That's when I see Trinity's sneaker.

I bolt up from the chair so fast my head lurches. Rory grabs my arm to steady me. Then we make our way to the desk. There, on the other side, sits Trinity, holding her slashed wrists on her lap. Dead eyes stare at us.

There's a note by her leg. I pick it up as Rory hurries to check for a pulse that I know he won't find.

I skim the note. It's barely legible, a crazed rant about my trick with the orb and the comments, how I tried to drive her off, and we argued, and I fell, and Trinity knew everyone would blame her, just as they did with Vanessa.

"She thought she killed me," I whisper.

"What?" Rory takes the note and skims it. "Wow. I knew she was unstable, but she lost it. She totally lost it."

He's still talking. I don't hear him. I'm staring at the screen as that figure behind Trinity slowly comes into focus. It's a slender young woman with long dark hair. I see the ghost's shirt—a pale blue V-neck. My gaze goes to Trinity's body . . . wearing a pale blue V-neck.

That's when the comments begin to scroll.

gonegirl5: You're alive, and I'm not, and that's your fault, Hannah.

gonegirl5: Everyone's going to know what you did to me.

gonegirl5: I'll make sure of it.

EXHALATION #10

A. C. Wise

IT'S NOT A SNUFF FILM, at least not the traditional kind. The single MiniDV cassette was recovered from the glove box of a crashed beige Ford Taurus. The car had passed through a metal guardrail and flipped at least once on its way down the incline on the other side. No body was found. The license plate had been removed, the VIN sanded away, no identifying information left behind.

The handwritten label on the cassette reads *Exhalation #10*. The film it contains is fifty-eight minutes long; fifty-six minutes of a woman's last breaths, and her death finally at the 56:19 mark.

Henry watches the whole thing.

The padded envelope the tape arrived in bears Paul's handwriting, as does the tape's label—a copy of the original, safely tucked away in an evidence locker. It's no more than a half-hour drive between them; Paul could have delivered the tape in person, but Henry understands why he would not. Even knowing this tape is not the original, even touching it only to slip it into a machine for playback, Henry feels his fingers coated with an invisible residue of filth.

Expensive equipment surrounds him—sound-mixing boards, multiple screens and devices for playback, machines for converting from one format to another. Paul warned him about the tape over the phone, and still Henry wasn't prepared.

During the entire fifty-eight minutes of play time, the woman's body slumps against a concrete wall, barely conscious. She's starved, one arm chained above her head to a thick pipe. The light is dim, the shadows thick. The angle of her head, lolled against her shoulder, hides her face. The camera watches for fifty-eight minutes, capturing faint, involuntary movements—her body too weak for anything else—until her breathing stops.

Henry looks it up: on average, it takes a person ten days to die without food or water. The number ten on the label implies there are nine other tapes, an hour recorded every day. Or are there other tapes capturing every possible moment to ensure her death ended up on film?

"Just listen," Paul had told him. "Maybe you'll hear something we missed."

Henry's ears are golden. That's what his Sound Design professor at NYU said back in Henry's college days. As a kid, Henry's older brother, Lionel, had called it a superpower. By whatever name, what it means is that as Henry watches the tape, he can't help hearing every hitch, every rasp. Every time the woman's breath wants to stop, and every time her autonomic system forces one more gasp of air into her lungs.

He never would have agreed to watch the tape if he hadn't been a little bit drunk and a little bit in love, which he's been more or less since the day he met Paul in film school. Paul, whose eye for framing, for details, for the perfect shot is the equivalent of Henry's golden ear. Paul, whose cop father was shot in the line of duty three months short of graduation, causing him to abandon his own moviemaking dreams and follow in his footsteps by becoming a cop as well.

Henry has always known better than to chase after straight boys, but what he knows intellectually and logically has never been a defense against Paul. So when Paul called at his wit's end and asked him to just listen to the tape, please, Henry agreed.

After fifty-six minutes and nineteen seconds, the woman dies. After another two minutes and forty-one seconds, the tape ends. Henry shuts down the screen and stops just short of pulling the plug from the wall.

> > >

"Jesus Christ, Paul, what did I just watch?"

A half-empty bottle sits at Henry's elbow in his bedroom, his phone pressed to his ear. He locked the door of the editing suite behind him, but the movie continues, crawling beneath his skin.

"I know. I'm sorry. I wouldn't ask if . . . I didn't know what else to do."

Henry catches the faint sound of Paul running his fingers through his hair, static hushing down the line. Or, at least, he imagines he hears the sound. Even after all this time he's not always sure if what he thinks he hears is just in his head, or whether he really does have a "superpower."

After watching the video of the dying woman, he's even less sure. He watched the whole thing and didn't hear anything to help Paul. But he can't shake the feeling there *is* something there—a sound trapped on the edge of hearing, one he hasn't heard yet. A sound that's just waiting for Henry to watch the video again, which is the last thing in the world he wants to do.

"I'm sorry," Paul says again. "It's just . . . It's like I hit a brick wall. I have no goddamn idea where this woman died, who she is, or who killed her. I couldn't see anything on the tape, and you can hear things no one else can hear. You can tell which goddamn road a car is on just by the sound of the tires."

In Paul's voice—just barely ragged—is his fear, his frustration. His anger. Not at Henry, but at the world for allowing a woman to die that way. The ghost of the woman's breath lingers in the whorls of Henry's ears. Do the shadows, carving the woman up into distinct segments, stain Paul's eyelids like bruises every time he blinks?

"I'll try," Henry says, because what else is there to say? Because it's Paul. He will listen to the tape a hundred times if he has to. He'll listen for the sounds that aren't there—something in the cadence of the woman's breathing, the whirr of an air duct he didn't notice the first time, something that will give her location away.

"Thank you." Paul's words are weary, frayed, and Henry knows it won't be a stray bullet for him, like the one that took his father. It'll be a broken heart.

The drug overdoses, the traffic accidents, the little boy running into the street after his ball, the old man freezing to death in an alleyway with nowhere else to go. They will erode Paul, like water wearing down stone, until there's nothing left.

Closer than Paul's sorrow is the clink of glass on glass as Henry pours another drink. The bottle's rim skips against the glass. Ice shifts with a sigh. He pictures Paul sitting on the edge of his bed, and it occurs to him too late that he didn't bother to look at the clock before he called. He listens for Maddy in the background pretending to be asleep, rolling away and grinding her teeth in frustration at yet another of duty's late-night calls.

Henry likes Maddy. He loves her, even. If Paul had to marry a woman, he's glad Maddy was the one. From the first time Paul introduced them, Henry could see the places Paul and Maddy fit, the way their bodies gravitated to one another—hips bumping as they moved through the kitchen preparing dinner, fingers touching as they passed plates. They made sense in all the ways Paul and Henry did not, even though their own friendship had been instant, cemented when Paul came across Henry drunkenly trying to break into an ex-boyfriend's apartment to get his camera back, and offered to boost him through the window.

At the end of that first dinner with Maddy, Henry had sat on the deck with her, finishing the last of the wine while Paul washed dishes.

"Does he know?" Maddy had asked.

Her gaze went to the kitchen window, a square of yellow light framing Paul at the sink. There was no jealousy in her voice, only sympathetic understanding.

"I don't know."

"I won't tell if you don't." Maddy reached over and squeezed Henry's hand, and from that moment, their relationship had been set, loving the same man, lamenting his choice of career.

Henry wants to tell Paul to wrap himself around Maddy, take comfort in the shape of her, and forget about the woman, but he knows Paul too well.

"I'll call you if I hear anything," Henry says.

"Henry?" Paul says as Henry moves to hang up.

"Yeah?"

"Are you still working on the—"

"The movie? Yeah. Still."

His movie. Their movie. The one they started together at NYU, back when they had dreams, back before Paul's father died. The one Henry is now making, failing to make, alone.

"Good. That's good," Paul says. "You'll have to show it to me someday."

"Yeah. Sure." Henry rubs his forehead. "Get some sleep, okay?"

Henry hangs up. In the space behind his eyes, a woman breathes and breathes and breathes until she doesn't breathe anymore.

> > >

Sweat soaks thirteen-year-old Henry's sheets, sticking the T-shirt and boxer shorts he sleeps in against his skin. His mother left the windows open, but there's no breeze, only the oppressive heat they drove through to get to the rental cabin. His brother snores in the bunk above him, one hand dangling over the side.

The noise comes out of nowhere, starting as a hum, building to a scream, slamming into Henry full force. Henry claps his hands to his ears. Animal instinct sends him rabbiting from the bed. His legs tangle in the sheets, and he crashes to the floor. The sound is still there, tied to the heat, the weight and thickness of the air birthed in horrible sound.

"Henry?" Lionel's voice is sleep muffled above him.

Henry barely hears it over the other sound, rising in pitch, inserting itself between his bones and his skin. There's another sound tucked inside it, too, worse still. A broken sound full of distress and pain.

Footsteps. His mother's and father's voices join his brother's. Hands pry his hands from his ears.

"Can't you hear it?" Henry's voice comes in a panicked whine, his breath in hitching gulps.

"Henry." His mother shakes him, and his eyes snap into focus.

"It's just cicadas. See?" His father points to the window.

A single insect body clings to the screen. Lionel trots over and flicks the insect away before pulling the window closed.

"What's wrong with him?" Lionel asks.

Even with the window shut, the noise remains, filling every corner of the room.

"Can't you hear?" Henry's hands creep toward his ears again.

His mother gets him a glass of water. His father and brother watch him with wary eyes. They don't hear it. They hear the cicadas' song, but not the broken, stuttering sound that digs and scrapes at Henry's bones. No one hears it except for him.

Later, Henry learns that the sound is the cicadas' distress call, the noise they make when they're threatened or in pain. And over the course of the two weeks at the lake, Henry learns his hearing is different from the rest of his family's, possibly from almost everyone else he knows. There are tones, nuances, threads of sound that are lost to others. It's as though he's developed an extra sense, and he hates it.

Lionel, however, turns it into a game, dragging Henry around to various parts of the lake, asking him what he hears, getting Henry to challenge him to see if he can hear it, too. Henry's big brother grins, amazed at every sound Henry describes—birds murmuring in distant trees, small animals in the burrows, dropped fishing lines, an aluminum rowboat tapping against a dock all the way across the lake.

Henry almost allows himself to relax, to have fun, until on one of their excursions he hears the crying girl.

Henry and Lionel are deep enough in the woods surrounding the lake that the dense, midsummer foliage screens them from the road, the water, and the other cottages. Henry scans the tree trunks, looking for shed cicada shells. The sound comes, like it did the first night, out of nowhere—a ticking, struggling sound like hitching breath. Except this time it's not hidden in cicada song but stark and alone, somewhere between mechanical and organic, full of pain.

Henry freezes, cold despite the sweat-slick summer air. Lionel is almost out of sight between the trees before he notices Henry is no longer with him.

"What's wrong?" Lionel trots back, touching Henry's arm.

Henry flinches. He's sharply aware of his own breath. His chest is too tight. Underneath the insect sound there is something else—distinctly human, horribly afraid. He tries to speak, and the only sound that emerges is an extended exhalation, a "hhhhhhhh" that goes on and on.

Lionel's repeated questions fade. Henry stumbles away from his brother, half-blinded by stinging eyes, catching tree trunks for support. He follows the sound, its insistence a knife-sharp tug at his core. He needs to find the source of the sound. He needs . . .

Henry crashes to his knees, nearly falling into a hole opened up in the ground. The edges are ragged and soft, the forest floor swallowing itself in greedy mouthfuls. There's a caught breath of alarm from below him, wet with tears, weak with exhaustion, fading.

"There's someone down there," Henry pants, the words coming out between clenched teeth, his whole body shuddering. He's doubled over now, arms wrapped around his middle, where the sound burrows inside him.

"What—" Lionel starts, but then he looks, seeing what Henry sees.

The girl is barely visible. The tree canopy blocks direct sunlight, and the hole is deep enough that the child is a mere smudge at the bottom.

"Get . . ." Henry's voice breaks. Tears stream on his cheeks. "Mom. Dad. Get help."

Lionel sprints away, and despite the pain, Henry stretches out flat on his stomach. Leaves crackle, branches poke at him. Things crawl through the earth underneath him, worms and beetles and blind moles further undermining its integrity, impossible things he shouldn't be able to hear. He stretches his arm as far as he can, pressing his cheek against the ground. He doesn't expect the girl to be able to reach him, but he hopes his presence might comfort her.

"It's okay." His shoulder feels like it will pop out of its socket. "I'm not going to leave you."

From the dark of the earth, the girl sniffles. Henry stretches further still, imagining small fingers reaching back for him.

"It's okay," he says again, terrified the girl will die before rescue comes. Terrified it will be his fault, his failure, if she does. "Just hold on, okay? Hold on."

> > >

The second time, Henry listens to the tape with his eyes closed. It scarcely matters. He still sees the woman, slumped and taking her last shallow breaths, but inside the theater of his mind she is so much worse. She's carved up by shadow, her skin blotched as though already rotting from within. At any moment she will raise her head and glare at Henry, his powerlessness, his voyeurism.

He stretches after any glimmer of identifying sound, wondering if his unwanted superpower has finally chosen this moment to abandon him. Then, all at once, the sound is there, sharp as a physical blow.

A faint burr, rising from nothing to a scream. The cicada song he can't help but hear as a herald of doom. It knocks the breath from his lungs, bringing in its place the heat of summer days, air heavy and close and pressed against the window screens. He shoves his chair back from the desk so hard he almost topples, and stares, wide-eyed. The image on the screen doesn't change. After a moment, he forces himself to hit rewind. Play.

Ragged breath, stuttering and catching. There's no hint of

insect song. Even though Henry knows exactly when the rise and fall of the woman's chest will cease, he holds his own breath. Every time her breath falters, he finds himself wishing the painful sound would just stop. It's a horrible thought, but he can't help it, his own lungs screaming as he waits, waits, waits to hear whether she will breathe again.

Then, a sound so faint yet so distinct Henry both can't believe he missed it and isn't certain it's really there. He reverses the tape again, afraid the sound will vanish. Sweat prickles, sour and hot in his armpits. He barely hears the woman breathing this time, his strange powers of hearing focused on the almost-imperceptible sound of a train.

A primal response of exaltation—Henry wants to shout and punch the air in triumph. And at the same time, the woman on the screen is still dying, has been dead for days, weeks, months, even, and there's nothing he can do. Henry forces himself to listen one last time, just to be sure. The train is more distinct this time, the lonely howl of approaching a crossing. Goose bumps break out across Henry's skin. His body wants to tremble, and he clenches his teeth as though he's freezing cold.

He must have imagined the cicadas, even though the noise felt so real, a visceral sensation crawling beneath his skin. The train, though, the train is real. He can isolate the sound, play it for Paul. It's an actual clue.

He thinks of the summer at the lake when he was thirteen years old, Lionel snoring in the bunk above him. That first terrible night where it seemed as though all the cicadas in the trees around the lake had found their way into the room. Then, later, how their song had led him to the almost-buried girl.

Henry reaches for the phone.

"I'm going to send a sound file your way," he says when Paul answers. "It's something. I don't know if it's enough."

"What is it?" Water runs in the background, accompanied by the clatter of Paul doing dishes. Henry imagines the phone balanced precariously between Paul's ear and shoulder, the lines of concern bracketing his mouth and crowded between his eyes.

"A train. It sounds like it's coming up to a crossing."

"That's brilliant." For a moment there's genuine elation in Paul's voice, the same sense of victory Henry felt moments ago. And just as quickly, the weight settles back in. "It might give us a radius to search, based on where the car was found, and assuming the killer was somewhat local to that area."

There's a grimness to Paul's voice, a hint of distraction as though he's already half forgotten Henry is on the other end of the phone, his thoughts churning.

"Thank you," Paul says after a moment, coming back to himself.

The water stops, but Henry pictures Paul still standing at the sink, hands dripping, looking lost.

"I should—" Paul starts, and Henry says, "Wait."

He takes a breath. He knows what he's about to ask is unreasonable, but he needs to see. Without the safety and filter of a camera and a video screen in the way.

"When you go looking, I want to go with you."

"Henry, I—"

"I know," Henry interrupts. His left hand clenches and unclenches until he consciously forces himself to relax. "I know, but you probably weren't supposed to send me the tape, either."

Henry waits. He doesn't say please. Paul takes a breath, wants to say no. But Henry is already in this, Paul invited him in, and he's determined to see it through.

"Fine. I'll call you, okay?"

They hang up, and Henry returns to his computer to isolate the clip and send it to Paul. Once that's done, Henry opens up another file, the one containing the jumble of clips he shot with Paul at NYU. Back when they had big dreams. Back before Paul's father died. Back before fifty-eight minutes of a woman breathing out her last in an unknown room.

Henry chooses a clip at random and lets it play. A young man sits in the back seat of a car, leaning his head against the window. He's traveling across the country, from a small town to a big city. The same journey Henry himself had taken, though he'd only crossed a state. There are other clips following a boy who grew up in the city, in his father's too-big shadow, but both boys' heads are full of dreams. Two halves of the same story, trying to find a way to fit together into a whole. Except now the film will always be unfinished, missing its other half.

Even though he knows he will never finish the movie without Paul, Henry still thinks about the sounds that should accompany the clip. It's an exercise he engages in from time to time, torturing himself, unwilling to let the movie go. Here, he would put the hum of tires, but heard through the bones of the young man's skull, an echo chamber created where his forehead meets the glass.

The perfect soundscape would also evoke fields cropped to stubble, the smell of dust and baking tar and asphalt. It would convey nerves as the boy leaves behind everything he's ever known for bright lights and subway systems. Most importantly, it would also put the audience in the boy's shoes as he dreams of kissing another boy without worrying about being seen by someone he knows, without his parents' disappointment and the judgment of neighbors' faces around him in church every Sunday.

Henry watches the reflections slide by on-screen—telephone poles and clouds seen at a strange angle. His own drive was full of wind-and-road hum broken by his parents' attempts at conversation, trying to patch things already torn between them. Henry had gotten good at filtering by then, shutting out things he didn't want to hear. Maybe he should have given his parents a chance, but love offered on the condition of pretending to be someone else didn't interest him then, and it doesn't interest him now.

Between one frame and the next, the image on the screen jumps, and Henry jumps with it. Trees, jagged things like cracks in the sky, replace the cloud and telephone pole reflections. The car window itself is gone, and the camera looks up at the whip-thin branches from a low angle.

Then the image snaps back into place just as Henry slaps the pause button. He knows what he and Paul shot. He has watched the clips countless times, and everything about the trees cracking their way across the sky is wrong, wrong, wrong.

When the phone rings, Henry almost jumps out of his skin. He knocks the phone off the desk reaching for it, leaving him sounding weirdly out of breath when he finally brings it to his ear.

"I'll pick you up tomorrow around ten," Paul says. "I have an idea."

"Okay." Henry lets out a shaky breath.

His pulse judders, refusing to calm. He needs a drink and a shower. Then maybe a whole pot of coffee, because the last thing he wants to do is sleep. When he blinks, he sees thin black branches crisscrossing the sky, and he hears the rising whine of cicada song.

> > >

There is a legend that says cicadas were humans once. They sang so beautifully that the Muses enchanted them to sing long past the point when they would normally grow tired, so they could provide entertainment throughout the night while the gods feasted.

But the enchantment worked too well. The singers stopped eating. They stopped sleeping. They forgot how to do anything except sing.

They starved to death, and even then the enchantment held. They kept singing, unaware they'd died. Their bodies rotted, and their song went on, until one of the Muses took pity on them and fashioned them new bodies with chitinous shells and wings. Bodies with the illusion of immortality that could live for years underground, buried as if dead but waiting to wake again.

Cicadas are intimately acquainted with pain, because they know what it is to die a slow death as a spectacle for someone else's pleasure. But they do not die when they are buried. They merely dream, and listen to other buried things, things that perhaps should not have been buried at all. They remember what they hear. When they wake, they are ready to tell the secrets they know. When they wake, they sing.

> > >

Paul drives, Henry in the passenger seat beside him, a bag of powdered donuts between them, and two steaming cups of coffee in the cup holders.

"Isn't that playing a bit to stereotype?" Henry points. Paul grins, brushing powdered sugar from his jeans.

"So sue me. They're delicious." He helps himself to another. Henry's stomach is too tight for food, but he keeps sipping his coffee, even though his nerves are already singing.

Paul mapped out a widening radius from where the car with the MiniDV in the glove box was found, circling the nearby railroad crossings. It isn't much, but it's something. They're out here hoping that whoever killed the woman crashed his car on the way back to his home, which might be the place he killed the woman. Maybe they'll find her body there, or maybe he was on the way back from burying her somewhere else. Maybe they'll find him. Henry is both prepared and unprepared for this scenario.

Right now, he's not letting himself think that far ahead. He's focusing on the plan, tenuous as it is, driving around to likely locations where he will *listen*. Henry feels like a television psychic, which is to say a total fraud. He wants to enjoy the relative silence of the car, the tick of the turn signal, the engine revving up and down. He wants to enjoy spending time with Paul, catching up, just old friends. He doesn't want to be thinking of snuff films and ghosts, and on top of that there's a nervous ache in his chest that keeps him conscious of every time he glances at Paul, wondering if his gaze lingers too long.

Trees border the road. It's early fall, and most are denuded of their leaves. Henry peers between the trunks, looking for deer. The sound, when it comes, is every bit as unexpected and violent as the last time. A reverberating hum, rising to a scream—cicada song, but with another noise tucked inside it this time, one he remembers from when he was a child.

That hitching, broken sound. Like gears in a machine struggling to catch. Like a baby's cry. A wounded animal. Henry jerks, his body instinctively trying to flee. His head strikes the window and pain blooms in his forehead above his right eye.

"Are you—"

Concern tinges Paul's voice, but Henry barely hears it. The sound has hooks beneath his skin, wanting to drag him in among the trees.

"Turn here." Henry bites the words out through the pain, the song filling him up until there's no space left for breath.

Paul looks at him askance but flicks the turn signal, putting them on a road that quickly gives way to gravel and dust. The trees grow closer here, their branches whip-thin, the same ones he saw in the corrupted clip of their film.

"Pull over."

Henry's breath comes easier now, the pain fading to a dull ache like a bruise. The cicada song forms an undercurrent, less urgent but not completely gone. Paul kills the engine. His expression is full of concern. Henry wants to thank him for his trust, but whatever waits for them in the woods is no cause for either of them to be thankful.

He climbs out of the car, buries his hands in his pockets, and walks. Leaves crunch as Paul trots behind him. Nervous energy suffuses the air between. Henry hears the questions Paul wants to ask, held trapped behind his teeth. It's nothing Henry can explain, so he keeps walking, head down.

When Henry stops, it's so sudden Paul almost trips. Tree branches cross the sky in the exact configuration Henry saw in the film, only the angle is wrong. Henry should be seeing them from lower down. From the height of a child.

The burr of cicadas grows louder, the steady drone rising to an ecstatic yell. Henry forces himself to keep his eyes on the trees, turning to walk backward. He pictures a girl being led through the trees, a man's hand clamped on her upper arm. Her death waits for her among the trees, and so does a camera on a tripod.

Henry is thirteen years old again, listening to the crying girl, lost and frightened and in pain. The hours after her discovery blur in his mind, though certain moments stand out sharp as splinters beneath his skin. The scent of leaf rot and dirt, his cheek pressed to the forest floor. His parents lifting him bodily out of the way as the rescue crew arrived, and Henry scrabbling at the earth, refusing to let go, terrified of leaving the girl alone.

He remembers seeing the girl's face for the first time but not what she looked like. In his mind, her features are as blurred and indistinct as they were at the bottom of the hole—eyes and mouth dark wounds opened in her pale skin.

There were endless questions from his parents, from the rescue crew—how had he found the girl, did he see her fall, was it an accident, did someone hurt her? They called Henry a hero, and he wanted none of it. He remembers burying himself under the blankets on the bottom bunk in the cabin, wishing he could stay there for years like a cicada, only emerging with everyone long gone.

Now, as then, the insect song times itself to the blood pounding like a headache in Henry's skull. He's sharply aware of Paul watching him, eyes wide, as Henry stops and turns around.

The shack is half-hidden in the trees, scarcely bigger than a garden shed. There's a catch in Paul's breath, and Henry glances over to see Paul's hand go to his service revolver.

The door isn't locked, but it sticks, warped with weather and clogged with leaves. Henry holds his breath, expecting a stench, expecting a horror movie jump scare, but there's nothing inside but more dead leaves and a pile of filthy rags. A small wooden mallet rests up against one wall.

Paul uses a flashlight to sweep the room, even though they can see every corner from the door. A seam in the floor catches the light, and once Paul points it out, Henry can't unsee it. Paul kneels, prying up boards with a kind of frantic energy, using the edge of a penknife.

"It's another tape." Paul straightens. There's dirt under his nails.

"He killed more than one person." Henry swallows against a sour taste at the back of his throat. He knew, the moment he saw the corrupted bit of film, the moment he heard the cicadas scream, but he'd wanted desperately to be wrong.

Paul holds the tape in a handkerchief, turning it so Henry can see the handwritten label—*Exsanguination*.

"I brought my camcorder. It's in the car." Henry feels the beginning of tremors, starting in the soles of his feet and working their way up his spine. Adrenaline. Animal fear. Some intuition made him pack film equipment before leaving the house, and Henry loathes that part of himself now.

Back in the car, Paul runs the heater, even though there's barely a chill in the air. Sweat builds inside Henry's sweatshirt as he fumbles with the tape, wearing the cotton gloves Paul gave him to preserve fingerprints. He flips the camcorder's small screen so they can both see, but hesitates a moment before hitting play, as if that could change the outcome. Henry knows all movies are ghost stories, frozen slices of time, endlessly replayed. Whatever will happen has already happened. The only thing he and Paul can do is witness it.

Static shoots across the screen, then the image steadies. The girl can't be more than ten years old. Her hair is very long and hangs over her shoulder in a braid. She stands in the center of the shack, dressed in shorts and a T-shirt. Dim light comes through a single grimy window. She shivers.

A man in a bulky jacket and ski mask steps into frame. He picks up the mallet leaned against the wall in the shed, now in a plastic evidence bag in the back of Paul's car, and he methodically breaks every one of the girl's fingers.

The image cuts, then the man and girl are outside. The camera sits on a tripod, watching as the man leads the girl to the spot framed by two stubby trees. The girl is barefoot. She sobs, a sound of pure exhaustion that reminds Henry of the little girl in the hole. This girl's ankles are tied. Her hands free, but useless, her fingers all wrong angles, pulped and shattered.

The man unbraids the girl's hair. He employs the same care

he used breaking her fingers. Once it's unbound, it hangs well past the middle of her back. The man lifts and winds strands of it into the spindly branches of the trees growing behind her, creating a wild halo of knots and snarls and twigs.

The girl cannot flee when the man pulls out a knife. She thrashes, a panicked, trapped animal, but the knots of her hair hold her fast. He cuts. Long slashes cover her exposed thighs, her knees, her calves, her arms.

How long does it take a person to bleed to death? Henry and Paul are about to find out.

After what seems like an eternity, long after the girl has stopped struggling, the man steps out of frame. The camera watches as the trees bow, the girl slumps. Branches crack, freeing strands of her hair, but far too late.

Henry gets the door open just as bile and black coffee hits the back of his throat. He heaves and spits until his stomach is empty. Paul places a hand on his back, the only point of warmth in a world gone freezing cold. Henry leans back into the car, and Paul puts his arms around Henry, holding him until the shaking stops.

"I'm sorry," Paul says. "I shouldn't have dragged you into this."

The expression on Paul's face when he says it is a blow to Henry's freshly emptied gut. The pain in Paul's eyes is real, yes, but what accompanies it isn't quite regret. Instead, guilt underlies the pain, and Paul's gaze shifts away.

In that moment, Henry knows that Paul wouldn't change a thing if he could. He would still ask Henry to watch the tape, no matter how many times the scenario replayed. This death, among every other he's witnessed, is too big to hold alone. He needs to share the burden with someone, and that someone couldn't be Maddy. Because that kind of death spreads like rot, corrupting everything it touches, like it corrupted Henry and Paul's film, their past, their shared dream. Henry understands.

If Paul shared that pain with Maddy, it would become the only thing he would see anytime he looked at her, and the only thing he could do to save himself would be to let her go. And Maddy isn't someone Paul is willing to let go.

"I'm sorry," Paul says again.

"Me too." Henry reaches for the passenger-side door and pulls it closed. He can't look at Paul. His face aches, like a headache in every part of his skull at once. Paul shifts the car into drive.

"Are you . . ." Paul's words fall into the silence after they've been driving for a few moments, but he stops, as if realizing the inappropriateness of what he was about to say.

Henry hears the words anyway. *"Are you seeing anyone now?"* Bitterness rises to the back of his throat, even though his stomach is empty. Paul could have asked the question any time during the drive, if he really wanted to know, if the question was genuine curiosity and not born of guilt. Paul asked Henry to share his burden, and now it hurts him to think that Henry might have to carry it alone in turn. Henry hears the words even when Paul doesn't say them, his golden ear catching sounds no one else ever would.

"I hope you find someone," Paul says finally as he pulls back onto the road. "You shouldn't be alone. No one should."

Henry knows what Paul is saying; he should find someone to share his burden, too. Henry can't imagine someone loving him enough to take on that kind of pain; he can't imagine ever wanting someone to. He knows what that kind of love feels like from the other side.

The heater makes a struggling, wheezing sound, and Paul switches it off, rolling his window down. Air roars through the cabin, and cold sweat dries on Henry's skin. If it weren't for Henry's golden ear, the wind would swallow Paul's next words whole.

"I'm sorry it couldn't be me."

> > >

It's a good two days before Henry brings himself to check the other clips he shot with Paul. The rot has spread to every single one of them. There's an open barn door looking out onto a barren field, rising up to block the buildings of Manhattan, a water stain on a ceiling spreading to cover the boy's face as he gets his first glimpse of the city, a crack of light under a closet door instead of the flickering gap between subway trains. Each new image is a hole punched in an already fragile structure, unwinding it even more.

Henry understands what the scenes are now, after watching *Exsanguination.* They are films made by ghosts, the last image each of the killer's victims saw before they died. What he doesn't understand is why he is seeing them. Is it because he had the misfortune to hear what shouldn't have been there for him to hear? The cicadas, linking him to the woman whose last sight was of trees through a grimy window. Her death linking him to the deaths of the other ghosts.

Henry shakes himself, thinking of his and Paul's drive home from their aborted attempt to find answers. Awkward silence reigned until Henry stood outside the car, looking in through the driver's window at Paul. Then their fragmentary sentences had jumbled on top of each other.

"You don't have to—" from Paul.

And, "Next time you go—" from Henry.

Standing there, trying not to shiver, Henry had extracted a promise.

"Call me before you go looking. I mean it. I'm coming with you." He almost said, *whether you like it or not,* but Henry knows it isn't a matter of like; it's a matter of need. He saw the gratitude in Paul's eyes and his self-loathing underneath it, hating the fact that he should need to ask Henry to do this thing, that he should be too cowardly to refuse and demand Henry stay home. One way or another, they will both see this through to the end.

Henry doesn't tell Paul about the images corrupting their film. But he watches them again, obsessively, alone, until each is imprinted on his eyelids. His dreams are full of doorways and trees and slivers of light. At the end of the week, Paul finally calls, his voice weary and strained.

"Tomorrow afternoon," Paul says.

Henry barely lets him get the words out before saying, "I'll be ready."

> > >

They drive away from the city. Henry's stomach is heavy with dread and the sense of déjà vu. He clenches his jaw, already braced for the sound of cicadas, and speaks without looking Paul's way.

"We're looking for a house with a barn."

From the corner of his eye, Henry sees Paul half turn to him, a question and confusion giving a troubled look to his eyes. But he doesn't ask out loud, and Henry doesn't explain. They drive in relative silence until they reach the first railroad crossing on Paul's map, intending to circle outward from there.

It takes Henry some time to realize that the sound he's been bracing for has been there all along, a susurrus underlying the tire hum and road noise, a constant ache at the base of his skull. How long has he been listening to the cicadas? How long have they been driving?

Fragments of conversation reach him. He realizes Paul has been asking questions, and he's been answering them, but he has no sense of the words coming from his mouth, or even any idea what they're talking about. Suddenly the noise in his head spikes and with it, the pain. Henry grinds his teeth so hard he swears his molars will crack.

"Here." The word has the same ticking, struggling quality as the cicada's distress call.

Henry is thirteen years old again, wanting to clap his hands over his ears, wanting to crawl away from the sound.

"What—"

"Turn here." Henry barks the words, harsh, and Paul obeys, the car fishtailing as Paul slews them onto a long, narrow drive. The drive rises, and when they crest the hill, Henry catches sight of a farmhouse. Paul stops the car. From this vantage point, Henry can just make out the roof of a barn where the land dips down again.

Henry is first out of the car, placing one hand against the hood to steady himself. He closes his eyes, and listens. He's queasy, breathing shallowly, but there, as if simply waiting for him to arrive, the mournful, unspooling call of a train sounds in the distance.

"You hear it, too, right?" Henry opens his eyes, finally turning to Paul.

Paul inclines his head, the barest of motions. He looks shaken in a way Henry has never seen before.

"This is the place," Henry says, moving toward the front door.

A sagging porch wraps around the house on two sides. To the right, straggly trees stretch toward the sky. Without having to look, Henry knows there is a basement window looking up at those trees.

Paul draws his service revolver. The sound of him knocking is the loudest thing Henry has ever heard. When there's no answer, Paul tries the knob. It isn't locked. Paul leads and Henry follows, stepping into the gloom of an unlit hallway. The stench hits Henry immediately, and he pulls his shirt up over his nose.

Stairs lead up to the left. Rooms open from the entryway on either side, filled with sheet-covered furniture and windows sealed over with plywood boards. Paul climbs the stairs, and again, Henry follows. Up here, the scent is worse. There are brownish smears on the wall, as if someone reached out a bloody hand to steady themselves and left the blood to dry.

At the top of the stairs and to the left is a door bearing a full bloody handprint. It hangs partially open, and Paul nudges it open the rest of the way. Henry's view is over Paul's shoulder, not even fully stepped into the room, and even that is too much.

The corpse on the bed is partially decomposed, lying on rumpled sheets nearly black with filth. There are no flies, the body is too far gone for that, but Henry hears them anyway, the ghostly echo of their buzz. But just because the flies are gone doesn't mean there aren't other scavengers. A beetle crawls over the man's foot.

Henry bolts down the stairs before he realizes it, back in the kitchen where unwashed dishes pile on the countertops, with more in the sink. Garbage fills the bin by the door. The air here smells sour, but after the room upstairs, it's almost a relief.

Henry thinks of the wrecked car, and imagines the killer somehow pulling himself from the wreck, somehow managing to make it back home, only to die here, bleeding out the way the girl in the woods did. He wants to feel satisfaction for the strange twist of justice, but there's only sickness, and beneath that, a hollow still needing to be filled.

Henry turns toward the basement door. It seems to glare back at him until he makes himself cross the room and open it. Wooden steps, the kind built with boards that leave gaps of darkness between, lead down.

He finds a light switch, but he doesn't bother. Light filters in from the high basement window. It matches the light on the tape where the woman breathed and died and so it is enough.

Beneath the window, a pipe rises from the unfinished floor. There's a tripod aimed at the pipe, a camera sitting on the tripod, the compartment where the tape was ejected standing open. At the base of the pipe, there are marks on the floor. When Henry bends close to see, they resolve into words. *Find me.*

Henry's breath emerges in a whine. For once, his ears fail him. He doesn't hear Paul descending the stairs until Paul is beside him, touching his shoulder. Henry can't bring himself to look up. He can't even bring himself to stand. He stays crouched where he is, swaying slightly. When he does finally look up, it isn't at Paul, it's at the window. On the other side of the dirty glass, stark, black branches crisscross the gray sky. Henry looks at them for a very long time. And he breathes.

> > >

There are twelve more tapes. They arrive in a padded envelope, each one labeled like the originals, copies written in Paul's hand—*Exhalation 1–9, Contusion, Asphyxiation,* and *Delirium.* Henry didn't ask, but Paul knew he would need to see them. Even so, it's several weeks before Henry can bring himself to watch.

In *Asphyxiation,* a man hangs from the rafters of the barn, slowly strangling to death under his own weight. In *Contusion,* a little boy is beaten within in an inch of his life and locked in a dark closet, only the faintest sliver of light showing underneath the door. In *Delirium,* an old man is strapped to a bed, injected with a syringe, and left to scream out his life with only the water spot on the ceiling for company.

Paul informs Henry by email that four bodies were unearthed

on the property—the old man, the young boy, the hanged man, and the girl. But not the woman. Paul informs Henry that the search is ongoing, her body may have been dumped in the woods somewhere, buried or unburied. It may even have been on the way back that the killer crashed and crawled free of the wreck, leaving the tape behind.

What made her special? Or is she special at all? Perhaps the killer was afraid of burying yet another body so close to his home. Maybe he was planning to dig up the others and move them, too, but he never got the chance. Or maybe, just maybe, he woke in the middle of the night to an insistent cicada's scream and tried to get the woman's corpse as far away as he could. As if that would ever make them stop.

Henry watches the clips one last time, the ones he and Paul shot, the ones corrupted with ghosts. The frames are back to normal, only the footage he and Paul shot of city streets and subway rides—no stark trees, no water-stained ceiling. Henry sees those things nonetheless. He will see them every time he looks at the film. The only thing he can do to save himself is let them go.

After he watches the clips for the last time, he deletes every last one.

> > >

When Henry finally makes his movie, his great masterpiece, it's no longer about a boy leaving the country for the city and finding his true home and meeting a boy from the city who grew up in his father's shadow. The city no longer belongs to the boy Henry used to be, and the boy who grew up in his father's shadow never belonged to him at all.

Before he begins work on the movie, Henry moves to a city on the other coast, one smelling of the sea. The trees rising up against the sky there are straight and singular; their branches do not fracture and crack across the sky. That fact goes a little way toward easing his sleep, though he still dreams.

While working on the movie that is no longer about a boy, Henry meets a very sweet assistant director of photography who smiles in a way Henry can't help but return. Soon, Henry finds himself smiling constantly.

Even though the movie Henry makes isn't the one he thought he would make when he first dreamed of neon and subways and fame, it earns him an Oscar nomination. He is in love with the assistant director of photography, and he is loved in turn. He is happy in the city smelling of the sea, as happy as he can be. The love he has with the assistant director of photography—whose eye is good, but not quite golden—isn't the kind of love that would willingly take the burden of death and pain from Henry's shoulders. For that, Henry is grateful. He would crack under the weight of that kind of love, and besides, half his burden already belongs to the man he willingly took it from years ago.

At first, Maddy sends a card every Christmas, and Henry and Paul exchange emails on their respective birthdays. But Henry knew, even on the day he packed up the last of his belongings to drive to the other coast, when he said *see you later* to Paul, he was really saying *goodbye*. Paul chose, and Henry consented to his choice. Maybe Paul's relationship with Maddy could have survived the weight of his pain, but sharing his burden with Maddy wasn't a risk Paul was willing to take.

Henry is the one to drop their email chain, "forgetting" to reply to Paul's wishes of happy birthday. When Paul's birthday rolls around, Henry "forgets" again. It's a mercy—not for him, but for their friendship. Henry can't bear to watch something else die slowly, rotting from within, struggling for one last breath to stay alive. Perhaps it isn't fair, but Henry imagines he hears

Paul's sigh of relief across the miles, imagines the lines of tension in his shoulders finally slackening as he lets the last bit of the burden of the woman's death go.

For his part, Henry holds on tighter than before. The movie that earns him his Oscar nomination is about a woman, one who is a stranger, yet one he knows intimately. He saw her at her weakest. He watched her die. The words scratched in the floor where the woman breathed her last, *find me*, are also written on Henry's heart.

He cannot find the woman physically, so he transforms the words into a plea to find *her*, who she was in life or who she might have been. Henry imagines the best life he can for her, and he puts it on film. It is the only gift he can give her; it isn't enough.

When Henry wins his Oscar, his husband, the assistant director of photography, is beside him, bursting with pride. They both climb the stage, along with the rest of the crew. The score from their film plays as they arrange themselves around the microphone. Henry tries not to clench his jaw. A thread winds through the music, so faint no one else would ever hear—the faint burr of rising insect song.

Paradoxically, it is making the movie he never expected to make that finally allows Henry to understand the movie he tried to make years ago. Even though he destroyed the clips, that first movie still exists in his mind. He dreams it, asleep and waking. In the theater of his mind, it is constantly interrupted by windows seen at the wrong angle, water stains, and slivers of light, and scored entirely by insect screams.

The movie that doesn't exist isn't a coming-of-age story. It isn't a story about friendship. It's a love story, just not the traditional kind.

Because what else could watching so many hours of death be?

How else to explain letting those frames of death corrupt his film, reach its roots back to the place where their friendship began and swallow it whole? What other name is there for Henry's lost hours of sleep, and the knowledge that he wouldn't say no, even if Paul asked for his help again. Even now. When Henry would still, always, say yes every time.

Every time Henry looks back on the film in his mind, all he sees is pain, the burden he willingly took from Paul so he wouldn't have to carry it alone. Even so, Henry will never let it go. The movie doesn't exist, he destroyed every last frame, but it will always own a piece of Henry's heart. And so will the man he made it for.

SCREAM QUEEN

Nathan Ballingrud

"CAN YOU SHIFT your chair a little bit . . . no. Here. Let me—"

She stood while Alan adjusted the angle of her chair an inch. When she sat down again, he saw immediately that the lighting was better. He was hoping to get at least part of the interview using the natural light coming in through the picture window in her living room. It highlighted the contours of her face brilliantly. She was old—beautifully, regally old—and he wanted to play it up.

She let him angle her shoulders the way he liked; a natural pro, he thought. God bless her for that. Standing back a few feet, he gave her a quick critical appraisal.

She was seventy-two years old, she wore her hair long, and she was dressed in jeans and a red flannel shirt with the sleeves fastidiously buttoned at her wrists—too hot for Texas, Alan would have thought, but then he wasn't on the far side of seventy. Her face resembled a weathered rock. She looked goddamn beautiful, and it was hard for him not to smile like a stricken fool. "How's it look, Mark?"

Mark was standing behind the camera. When he didn't answer, Alan turned to look at him. Mark was staring at the screen, giving him a thumbs-up.

"I can't see you when my back is turned," Alan said. "You have to speak out loud."

"Sorry."

Jennifer Drummond smiled, careful not to alter her position. "Are you a student, Mark?" she asked. Her voice sounded strong, and she articulated well. This was going to be so good.

"Yup. I'm in my last semester at USC."

Alan waited for Mark to brag about the fancy new job waiting for him after graduation, but surprisingly he managed to restrain himself.

"How nice! That's where Lionel went," she said.

"Yes, ma'am, I know. John Carpenter, Lionel Teller, Dan O'Bannon—a lot of the old-school horror guys went there. I feel like I'm part of a tradition."

Her smile faded a little, turning private. "Well. I didn't know those other gentlemen. I only knew Lionel."

Alan didn't want this conversation to happen yet. Better to wait until they started filming. He wanted her answers spontaneous and fresh. She might look robust, but he didn't want her telling the story once off camera and then deciding it was time for a nap. "We'll get to all that," he said. "I'm going to get in close for a sec, okay? I don't want you to think I'm getting fresh."

He loomed over her, fixing the microphone to the collar of her shirt. He half expected her to make some joke about not having been this close to a man since the Nixon Administration—she was a famous recluse—but she remained still and quiet. He caught the scent of perfume as he leaned in, and wondered if he should feel flattered.

Stupid to feel this giddy about a woman nearly twenty years

his senior, but he couldn't help it. He'd been in love with her since he first watched her movie on a VHS tape when was a kid.

Alan's dream was making his own movies, but he was in his midfifties now, and his middle-of-the-night thoughts told him he'd missed his chance. He hadn't given up, though. Not yet. And in the meantime he made his living hustling work like this—producing featurettes and press-kit material for feature films, both new and old, for release on disc. It was a precarious life, made more so as the advent of streaming services eroded the audience for physical copies of films, but it kept him in the business he loved. He picked up ad hoc work as a waiter or a barista to fill in the gaps. Somehow it all worked out. So far, anyway.

This one was going to strain the wallet. He and Mark had driven from Los Angeles to north Texas for this interview, hauling their equipment with them in Alan's 2005 Camry, and the cost in time and gas was going to be more than the small sum they'd make for the finished product. They were staying in a hotel in nearby Templeton, making the fifteen-mile drive to her isolated ranch house this morning. If the interview was with anyone else, they wouldn't have been able to justify it.

But this was Jennifer Drummond. He'd take the goddamn hit. Mark, to his credit, felt the same.

Drummond had only one film to her credit. Written and directed by Lionel Teller, and released in 1970, *Blood Savage* crackled across the grindhouse circuit like chain lightning, where it was received with great enthusiasm by gore hounds and lovers of sleazy exploitation, before being ushered off-screen by the next tide of cheap thrills. It should have faded into obscurity, like most films of its kind—there was no arguing its low quality made it tough to watch—but people kept talking about this one. *Blood Savage* had a vitality that overcame its tiny budget, its bad script, and its terrible actors. Most people credited Lionel Teller for this:

somehow he tapped into the ugly zeitgeist, as the optimism and the righteousness of the flower power generation wilted under all the assassinations, the Vietnam War, the Manson cult—Teller channeled all that infected energy and poured it into this nasty little film, which spat directly into the eye of an audience that had learned to crave abuse.

Some, though, credited the extraordinary performance of Jennifer Drummond, the lanky Southern girl with the long blond hair and the cornflower eyes. She'd come from nowhere, like every other actor in the movie, but unlike the others, she seemed to possess a natural talent for the job. Where the others moved woodenly, conscious of the camera, she was indifferent to its presence; while others looked as though they were waiting tensely for their cues before lurching into awkward speech, she seemed in easy conversation with the world. As the movie accrued its cult following over the years, she was sometimes compared to Mia Farrow in *Rosemary's Baby*, or Isabelle Adjani in *Possession*. She was the kind of person you fell in love with on sight.

Her defining moment was the midnight scene in the barn. The lights were placed outside so she was lit only by hard white beams sliding in through the wood slats. The horses huffed and whinnied in their stalls. As the scene progressed they reared and panicked, slamming their back hooves into the wood. Drummond's jittery depiction of a woman inhabited by the devil mesmerized, even terrified. Naked, she shuddered and spat, undulated like something underwater. And then that godawful, howling, throat-ripping scream. Alan felt a happy thrill thinking about it. The scene displayed none of the obvious special effects enhancing Linda Blair's more famous performance a few years later; but there was a sense of taboo about it, leaving the audience feeling as though it had witnessed something it shouldn't have. Something genuinely evil. The scene wasn't the climax of the movie—just a throwaway scare, the second-act demise of a supporting character—but the rest of the movie dragged on in a predictable series of ridiculous plot points. Drummond's performance in the barn became the foundation for the movie's cult status. You could find echoes of it in the bigger, better films that followed, and it was still referenced by horror movie junkies as the possession scene yet to be topped. Naturally, rumors circulated that the possession was genuine. A fun bit of urban legend, which only heightened the movie's appeal.

Despite its flaws, *Blood Savage* could have made Jennifer Drummond into a star—a bona fide scream queen—if she'd been at all interested.

"How's that, Miss Drummond? Are you comfortable?"

"I'm just fine, thank you."

Alan went back to the camera and checked the positioning. He came around once more and tugged gently on the bottom of her shirt, straightening a wrinkle near her shoulder. He didn't know why he was fussing with this part so much. Inevitably, she would move and shift as she spoke; but the process was a kind of ritual, and it helped him settle into his role.

He positioned himself in the stiff-backed chair, which had been arranged opposite her, taken from its place in front of the hearth. He hunched forward. It didn't matter what he looked like; he wouldn't be in the shot. They'd try to edit her answers so they wouldn't even need his questions in the finished cut, but he'd be careful to articulate anyway, just in case.

He fixed his own mic to his collar. "I figure we can get a good twenty-five or thirty minutes to start, and then we'll break for lunch. Does that sound okay?"

"It sounds fine." She didn't seem nervous or impatient.

"Mark, how's the sound?"

"You're both coming through loud and clear," Mark said.

"Well, Miss Drummond? Shall we begin?"

She smiled and sat up a little straighter in her chair. "I'm ready," she said.

"So, I'm going to start kind of generally, hit the basics, and then as we go we'll focus on particular topics. There are some points I definitely want to touch on—Lionel Teller, the barn scene, your life afterward—but really I just want to see where the conversation takes us. I think these things always turn out better when there's an organic quality to them. Okay?"

"Sure."

"Okay. So. What were you doing before you were cast in *Blood Savage*? Did you have any acting experience at all?"

"Christ, no." She laughed. "Have you *seen* the movie? None of us did!"

Alan smiled encouragement.

"I wanted to be a painter. I'd dropped out of college years before and was just kind of drifting. I was apolitical, which sounds terrible, but it's true. No protests for me. I had this idea I was going to have a show in Dallas and get discovered by some fancy New York art dealer. Me and some friends were renting out this big house, sharing all the costs. None of us ever had a real job, we were always late on rent. It was a miracle we didn't get evicted."

"So, how did you get involved with *Blood Savage*?"

"Lionel was over at the house one night. He was dating one of my roommates. It was the usual stupid thing. We were all stoned, he and I hit it off. We spent the whole night talking about art. I wanted to talk about Warhol and Picasso. He was into the surrealists and Grand Guignol theater."

"Did he talk about Satanism?"

"Not right away. That came later."

"Okay. I interrupted you. Please continue."

"Well, there isn't much more. He started in about the movie

he was going to shoot, and all his high talk about art went right out the window. It was just a cheap horror flick. A chance to show naked girls and a lot of blood."

"What did you think about that?"

"Well, I thought it was all very silly and childish, but I was hoping he'd ask me to be in it."

"Really? Even though you thought it was childish?"

Drummond smiled. "I was silly and childish myself. Why wouldn't I be interested? Besides, it was a movie. Everybody wanted to be in the movies."

"Did he ask you that night?"

"Yes he did. And I said yes right away. I thought I was going to be a movie star."

"What about your dreams of being a painter?"

"Why couldn't I be both?" She didn't seem wistful or sad. She spoke about those old feelings as if they belonged to someone else, someone she'd been assigned to observe, and she was making a field report.

"A lot of people think you could have *been* a movie star, if you'd wanted to be. Me, for example. I mean . . . I'm sure you get this all the time, but a lot of us think you gave one of the all-time great performances in horror cinema. You could have been up there with icons like Barbara Crampton and Jamie Lee Curtis." He realized he'd phrased that tactlessly, and he felt himself blush. "I mean, I think you already are, but . . ."

"I don't know who those women are," she said. "I don't keep up with the movies. But I'm sure it's a flattering comparison."

"It is!"

"Well, thank you. But I think you're full of shit." She smiled when she said it, but it was clear she meant it. "I didn't invite you here to blow smoke up my ass."

Despite the rebuke, Alan was thrilled. She was no washed-up

relic. She had a sharp tongue and she wasn't afraid to flash a little steel. The classic Texas no-bullshit personality. He began to wonder if there might be more to this interview than simply press-kit material. Maybe he could turn this into a book, or a documentary even. Maybe this was the beginning of something.

"You're not talking about my acting," she said. "My acting was terrible. We were all terrible. None of us had a future in the movies, including Lionel. You're talking about the barn scene."

He cast a glance at Mark, who looked up from his place at the sound board. This was what they'd come for.

"Yes," Alan said. "I guess I'm talking about the barn scene."

She looked out the window. The day had just crossed noon. The rolling hills and the brush were bathed in light. There was nothing around them but open land for as far as he could see. Nevertheless, the black energy of that scene intruded into the room. Goose bumps rippled over his skin.

When she didn't speak, Alan pressed her. "The rest of the movie has plenty of charm, but that scene seems like something spliced in from another project altogether. There's a rawness to it, a realness, the rest of the movie doesn't have. And I've tried to figure out what it is. It's not like there's anything inexplicable happening on-screen. No rotating heads or impossible contortions. It's just, I guess you'd say an *eeriness*. A sense of transgression."

She watched him while he fumbled through his thoughts. It made him nervous, which surprised him; he'd done a million of these things, sometimes with big stars. What should he be nervous about?

"And like, it's iconic for so many people of my generation." He said *like*. He was talking like a fucking teenager.

"So many men, you mean," she said.

He paused. He cast another glance at Mark, but Mark was now

focused solely on the sound board. "That's true. It's a very sexual scene."

"Why do you think so?"

Nothing in her inflection had changed; her expression was neutral, not hostile. And yet Alan felt as though the balance had shifted, and his footing was unsteady. He tried to get it back. "Were you uncomfortable performing the scene naked?"

"Of course. Who wouldn't be? But there was nothing squalid about it. Everyone was very respectful. What I think is interesting is how uncomfortable *you* seem."

She watched him for another moment and then reached over to an end table and fished a pack of cigarettes from a drawer. She leaned back in her seat and lit one up. All his careful compositional arrangements came undone, but there was no stopping that, and he didn't care. He was on the verge of getting something good.

Fuck it, he thought. *Be candid*. He could always edit this later. "You were a sexual fantasy for a lot of boys my age," he said. "Maybe that's why I'm uncomfortable talking about it." Heat crawled up the back of his neck. He feared he'd crossed a line. Some people like to ambush their interview subjects with sensitive or intrusive questions, making them uncomfortable in hopes of getting at some emotional payoff. They didn't care if it upset the person or embarrassed them. If it was for an in-depth feature, that was one thing; but for press-kit material like this, he'd always considered it a cheap move. Alan did not consider himself one of those guys. And he *liked* Jennifer Drummond; he respected her. The thought of putting her in a bad position appalled him.

And yet.

"Of course," she said. "A lot of teenage boys like to look at naked girls. There's nothing wrong with adolescent libido. Girls have libidos, too, it might surprise you to know."

He accepted the chastisement with a smile and a shrug. "I know, but—"

"Fantasies are normal, and as long as they're kept in context, they're usually healthy, too. You can let them go too far, though." She paused and took a pull from her cigarette. He noticed nicotine stains on her fingers. "It never occurred to me to think people might find the barn scene charged in that way, but it wouldn't have bothered me very much. We filmed it in 1969. It was a wild time."

"It never occurred to you? Forgive me, but that seems a little hard to believe."

"You can believe what you like."

He paused to regroup. "Let's talk about Lionel Teller and his obsession with Satanism. Obviously, at this point, he'd already started talking about it openly. Can you tell me about that?"

She looked down at her hands, fidgeting in her lap. The cigarette burned between her fingers, untouched. "What you have to know about Lionel is that he was an egomaniac. He had to have the first and last word on everything. He was obsessed with black magic—reading everything he could get his hands on about Anton LaVey, Aleister Crowley, who knows what else. We all thought it was a bunch of nonsense, but God forbid he heard you say such a thing. He'd fly into one of his tantrums, and it could last a long time. He could hold a grudge like you wouldn't believe. He'd host rituals and séances at his house, and he'd expect the cast and crew to come. He'd feel personally slighted if someone didn't attend. I made that mistake once—he didn't talk to me for a week."

"What were those sessions like? Does anything stand out?" He glanced over at Mark, who was watching her intently. Seeing Alan's glance, he flashed him a thumbs-up.

"They were boring, mostly. Lionel was impossible. We got

stoned, we drank. But there wasn't much fun to be had. A few of the others took it seriously, I suppose. Jake McDonell, the leading man, was so scared one night he drove away in the middle of it. Lionel had to meet him the next day and convince him not to quit. But most of us just did it to go along."

"I've never heard that story," Alan said. "Have you, Mark?"

"Nope. New to me."

"McDonell was going to quit the movie?"

"He did quit it. For a night, anyway. Lionel was very persuasive, though. That man could talk anyone into anything he wanted." She paused, thinking. "Jake was convinced something had come to the house. Even after Lionel talked him into coming back, he asked us all, at one time or another, if we'd heard it."

"Heard it doing what?"

"Walking. Breathing."

"Did you believe it?"

"No. Not then."

"But . . . later?" Alan felt his excitement ramping up. Was she going to cop to believing in black magic? On *his* featurette?

"When it came time to shoot the scene, Lionel believed filming a real ceremony would give it—and the whole production, really—a sense of legitimacy. Something genuine the audience would respond to, even if it was just—you know, subconsciously."

"Did anybody object? Jake?"

"By that time, no. We knew what he was like. And Jake, well. Despite his tough guy attitude, he was meek in his heart. He always did what he was told." She seemed to remember she had the cigarette in her hand and brought it up for a deep draw.

"Do you know the rumors circulating around the movie?"

Silence stretched between them. She took another pull before she said, "No."

Alan had the strong sense she was lying. But if she'd been as reclusive as she claimed, he guessed it was possible. "An urban legend has grown up around the movie, specifically around the barn scene. You were so good, and the scene is so creepy, some people say you were actually possessed."

"Oh. Well, yes. I was."

Alan and Mark exchanged a glance. "You're saying Lionel used actual summoning rites to film the scene?"

The question irritated her. "Lionel didn't *do* anything, except give us the script and stand behind the camera. *We* did it. We said the words and made the motions. And I opened my heart to it. Please don't give him credit he doesn't deserve."

"I'm sorry." He took a breath, watching the sunlight move across her face as she turned her head. "But I want to be clear. You're saying you actually summoned a real demon onto the set."

"I'm saying more than that. I'm saying I was physically possessed by a demonic entity, and that same entity has not left my body in almost fifty years."

Alan was stunned. How to respond? His new ambitions for a book about her shifted; she was either a crank after all, or she was exhibiting some late-life William Castle–style showmanship. Either would be a compelling subject.

"Are you, um—are you possessed right now?"

"We can talk more about it after lunch," Miss Drummond said. "I'm feeling a little tired. I could use a break." Her enthusiasm seemed reduced from its former high; she looked distracted, almost sad.

Alarmed, Alan said, "Maybe we can push a little further? We're just getting into the good stuff." If they stopped now, she might never come back to this subject. Or she might be more circumspect about it.

"I don't know . . ."

"Another few minutes. I don't want to lose momentum—"

Mark spoke up. "Alan. Let's get some lunch. I'm starving anyway."

Alan kept his mouth clamped shut; it was everything he could do not to tell his partner to shut his goddamn mouth. This was *his* interview. Mark was just the fucking tech support.

Jennifer Drummond smiled at him, arching one eyebrow. "You wouldn't push an old lady when she's tired, would you, Alan?"

He flushed. "Of course not, Miss Drummond. I'm sorry. I didn't mean to be rude." Recognizing the interview was at an intermission whether he liked it or not, he removed the microphone from his collar.

She patted his hand. "Call me Jennifer," she said. "I don't stand on ceremony. Now look, you boys go into town and get yourselves something to eat. I recommend Paco's. I would have prepared something for you myself, but frankly I wasn't up to it. I'm sorry to be such a poor host. I'm out of practice, you know."

He leaned over, unclipping her mic, too. "Please don't say that. You've been more than gracious. I wish you'd join us. My treat."

"Heavens, no. I'm going to have myself a little siesta. I don't believe I've talked this much in one sitting in ten years. If I'm asleep when you get back, just knock on the door. I'm a light sleeper."

"If you're sure."

"Don't ever ask an old Texas lady if she's sure. If she said it, then that's how it is."

Alan smiled. "Yes, ma'am."

"Good. Well, that's it, then. Go fill your bellies and come on back in a couple hours. Say three or four?" When they agreed, she headed back to her bedroom, leaving them by themselves. Alan and Mark stepped out into the heat. The sun burned in a thin blue sky. Wind billowed over the land, smelling of sagebrush. They regarded one another quietly for a moment. Then, despite his irritation with him, Alan broke out into a smile. "Holy shit, dude."

Mark headed to the car. "Come on, man. We need to talk."

> > >

They skipped Paco's and headed straight for the bar, a dingy little hole called the Canteen. The place was dark, cool, and empty, the bartender a threadbare soul who seemed stunned by the way they manifested into his world from the glare of daylight. They ordered a couple burgers and some beers. He served them and retreated into a shadowy recess.

They hadn't talked much in the car. Alan was fit to burst, but Mark was clearly troubled by something and put him off with a brusque "I need to think." Now that they were settled in and had a few sips of beer in them, he loosened up. "I think she needs help, man."

"What do you mean?"

"I mean she's not well."

The irritation Alan had felt back at the house bubbled back up. "Come on. You have nothing to base that on."

"Are you kidding me?"

"You don't know her story. She's been living in this godforsaken town for half a century, she's probably grateful for the attention. She's feeding the legend."

Mark shook his head. "I don't know, man. I think that's wishful thinking."

Alan took a pull from his beer. "You shouldn't make judgments about the person you're interviewing until you've let them speak their mind, and even then you should probably try to refrain. We need to remain objective."

"Oh, here we go."

"What the fuck is that supposed to mean?"

"You talk to me like I'm a child. You do it all the time. I don't need a lecture on what to think. And don't talk to me about being objective."

"You *are* a child!" He tried to say it like he was kidding, but he didn't sell it very well.

"Look, this woman was taken advantage of," Mark said. "She was forced to attend these stupid rituals by some alpha-male douchebag, made to perform this fucked-up scene in the nude, which she admitted made her uncomfortable—surrounded by God knows how many of them lighting their fucking candles and doing their stupid devil chants!—and she ended up becoming the wet dream of half the maladjusted teenage boys across America. And she was probably mentally ill already. Undiagnosed and untreated. And now here she is, thinking she has some actual demon roosting in her head. And we're putting her on camera. Exploiting her all over again. No wonder she ran away."

Alan stared at his plate, reeling from this little speech. "I'm surprised to hear you say that," he said. "If that's what you think, what are you even doing here? You seemed thrilled about it on the way out."

Mark pushed his empty mug away and called for another one. "I'm doing this because I love horror movies. Just like you. And because it's going to be great material, and that's what we're here to get. You know, Alan: *professionalism*. That doesn't mean I have to pretend I don't know what we're really doing."

The bartender put another beer in front of Mark.

"That's the last one," Alan said. "We're not done today."

"You're a piece of work," Mark said, turning to face him. "You just have to make your little power plays. Christ, I'll be glad to move on from this."

There it was. Alan knew Mark wouldn't be able to resist throwing his new gig in his face. A few more months and he'd be on set with a big studio production, making some real money. Not hustling anymore. Making the leap Alan never could manage. A young man with a future.

They'd been working on and off as a team for two years. They'd developed a good rapport. Mark had listened to Alan talk about the movie he was going to make someday, how he was going to get the funding, the strings he would pull to get some surprise stunt casting. "I've been in this business for a while," Alan had said, often. "I'm owed a lot of favors." He'd promised Mark he'd give him a job, too; they'd climb up the ladder together. Mark had always been encouraging.

And then Mark got the call. A USC buddy had done all right for herself, landed a good job at Lucasfilm, and when a position opened up in her department, she called in her old friend.

He knew he shouldn't take out his frustrations on Mark. It wasn't the kid's fault Alan had somehow managed to waste the best working years of his own life. Alan should be happy for the guy.

But he felt like a goddamned idiot. He felt ashamed of his whole life.

"Well," he said. "You'll be out of here soon enough. Then you can go suck Hollywood's big dick."

"Okay, I'm done." Mark stood, leaving his beer unfinished. He threw down a few bills. "Hey, bartender, you got cabs in this town?"

The bartender nodded.

"Call me one, please." To Alan, he said, "I'll meet you back at her place."

"Fine."

Mark walked out the door, and Alan finished his lunch, taking his time about it. She'd asked for a few hours, and he was enjoying the cool and the quiet. He only hoped the dumb kid didn't wake her when he got back to the house.

Finished, he pushed his plate away and ordered another beer. He went over the argument in his mind, searching for justifications and weaknesses. He already regretted shitting on Mark's opportunity—the kid was good at his job, and he deserved it—but then he considered that little speech about taking advantage of Jennifer and got angry all over again. Who was Mark to decide she was crazy? Why not clever and playful? The self-righteous prick.

Glancing up, he was surprised to find the bartender standing right there, staring at him. "Um . . . you need me to pay my tab or something? Are you closing already?"

"No, no." The guy seemed nervous. Alan couldn't get a read on his age. Late forties? Early sixties? He seemed gray and indistinct; his whole presence was like an apology. "I was wondering if you fellas were here for Miss Drummond."

Hang on now. "What makes you say that?"

"Well, it ain't hard to figure out. You were talking kind of loud."

"I guess that's fair. Okay, yeah, we're here to interview her. You know she was in the movies, right?"

The knowledge seemed to surprise the bartender. "No, I did not."

"Yeah, man. She's a big deal." He smiled, feeling a little buzzed. He picked up his mug and offered an imaginary toast to him. "At least, to the discerning cinephile, she is."

"Well, isn't that something. I was hoping you all were here 'cause she was starting up her service again, but I guess that's not it."

Alan, about to drain his beer and fashion his exit, paused. He kept smiling, but it was a curious smile now. "What's your name, man?"

"Tom."

"Tom, how about another one of these? I want to hear about this service."

"I guess I probably better not talk about it."

"Why not?"

He seemed to take the question seriously and mulled it over for a minute. "Miss Drummond is a private person. That's probably pretty clear to you, since you had to come all this way to find her. It's not my place to tell her story. Not anyone's, really." He put a little emphasis on the last, making it clear what he thought of Alan's purpose here.

"Look. Tom. I don't know Miss Drummond very well personally, but I've been an admirer my whole life. I would not do anything to put her in a bad light. Just the reverse, actually. You heard my colleague. He thinks she's mentally unsound. Do you think so?"

"No I do not."

"Neither do I. I want the world to fall back in love with her. If she was holding church services or something along those lines, it could go a long way to helping me make that happen."

Tom ruminated. It was clear to Alan that he didn't do much of anything before giving it considerable thought. He supposed that was a virtue, but it made him impatient.

"She deserves that," the bartender said. "She deserves to be loved."

"We're on the same page, Tom. How about that beer?"

Pouring another draft, Tom said, "She used to hold it up at her house. This was a whole lot of years ago. I was just a kid myself." He produced an old ghost of a grin. "Not too young to fall in love, though."

"But this *was* like a church service, right?"

"I guess you could call it that." He became cautious again, as though he'd startled himself with his little flare of enthusiasm. "I don't really remember the specifics."

"What *do* you remember?"

"This was way back in the seventies. Like I say, I was young. She was in the same house she's at now. I don't remember how she came to be there, but I know she was a fairly recent addition to the scenery. My dad kept on calling them 'the city slickers,' even when they'd been here for years."

"Wait. 'Them'?"

"Her and her boyfriend."

Alan sat up, tried to clear his head. "She had a boyfriend? What was his name?"

"Can't remember his last name, but his first name was Lionel. I remember 'cause it was the same name as the model trains. You remember those?"

"Lionel Teller?"

"Maybe."

"Holy shit." He rubbed his eyes. "So he was here with her. And he was what, hosting these services with her? What were they like?"

Tom's memory turned out to be ill-defined. He had a round-about way of speaking, once he got going, so it took longer than it should have for Alan to get an impressionistic notion of these "services." It seemed everyone in town attended them, and there was little rhyme or reason dictating when they were held. From time to time an urge would come into their heads, and they'd go. Little Tom's parents would take his hands into theirs, and together they'd walk with others from Templeton in a loose procession to the Drummond house. People congregated outside until she and Teller came out.

"I remember she had a silver light, real powerful but not really shining beyond her own skin. Almost too bright to look at. But

I couldn't not look. None of us could bear to look at anything else. Sometimes it was Miss Drummond in the middle of the light, sometimes it was something else."

"Something else?"

"Something holy. Something with a lot of limbs and a lot of faces. Its head spun like a carousel, showing them all to us. Or showing us to them."

He couldn't remember what would occur next. He believed it was possible that nothing happened at all, that the observance was the whole point; each side watching the other, the very act of looking fulfilling some unarticulated need.

After each service, Tom said, there were one or two fewer people making the walk home. No one wondered too much what happened to the missing people, not even later, when the services stopped. It was sort of understood that they were gone, and it was natural that they should be.

"You weren't scared?"

Tom thought about it. "'Scared' seems like too easy a word for what it was. We loved her, and as anyone who's lived a while knows, love and fear aren't strangers to each other. We felt like she was ours. She belonged to us, whatever that meant."

It meant quite a lot, it turned out. Lionel Teller became the object of some jealousy from people in town. Each time they were sent home—"or maybe 'released' is a better word," Tom said—Teller retreated into the house with her. His exposure to that magnificent light, and to the presence inside it, was ongoing. Why did he deserve it, and not they?

Well, that all stopped, eventually.

"What do you mean? What happened?"

"Somebody killed him."

"Killed Lionel Teller? How?"

"Hard, that's how. A mob of folks tore him to pieces."

". . . What year was this?"

"Seventy-five, seventy-six? Difficult to say for sure."

"Jesus Christ. How is it possible this has never gotten out? Doesn't anybody from this town ever gossip? Ever go online, even?"

Tom shrugged. He slid him another beer; Alan realized with some surprise that he'd downed three or four. There was no window in the bar to measure the sunlight. He checked his phone: he was late.

"It's just not something we think about, I guess."

"Do you know how crazy that sounds?"

Tom wasn't pleased by the question. "You weren't here for it. You don't understand. Hell, I wouldn't have thought of it at all if you two hadn't come into town and started shouting at each other."

Alan had to go. He stood, felt his head swim. He didn't want to leave this guy on a bad note, though. Fuck the featurette; he was definitely going to come back here and make a documentary. Lionel Teller murdered! This was what was going to save him. What a godsend. But what would it do to *her*? Was he really prepared to throw her to the wolves? He paid his bill and left a generous tip. His brain scrambled to process what he'd heard, to figure out how he was going to proceed. Maybe Mark was right: maybe she was crazy, and it was contagious. Maybe everybody in this town was batshit.

His scalp prickled. He'd seen enough horror movies to know what was supposed to come next. He imagined the people of Templeton arrayed outside the bar, staring at the door with dead eyes, waiting for him to come out. "I'm curious," he said. "If no one's said anything all these years, why now? Why are you telling me? Makes me kind of nervous."

Tom didn't smile. He said, "Nobody's set foot in that house

since that Lionel son of a bitch got hisself killed. And she's been quiet as the grave since then. If she's invited you fellas in, I figure she's getting ready to start back up again. I miss it. I miss her. I still dream about her, and that silver light." He paused. "Tell you the truth? I'm not worried about you telling anybody. Nobody who sees that light ever chooses to leave this place."

Alan had nothing to say to that. He nodded noncommittally and headed out the door, where the late afternoon was still warm and the parking lot was empty of angry townsfolk, where his car waited right where he'd left it and started easily when he turned his key. He turned onto the road and drove the fifteen miles toward Jennifer Drummond's house, the sky a gorgeous rose hue above him.

It was the magic hour.

> > >

He drove slowly. He was closer to drunk than he liked, and he was already very late; he didn't want to compound his problems by getting pulled over by a Texas cop. By the time he pulled up to the ranch house, daylight had receded to a ghostly echo in the sky. Night with all its distant stars loomed behind it. Getting out of his car, he paused to stare up into it. He rarely left LA anymore, and when he did, it was usually for another metropolis like New York or Toronto, so it had been a long time since he'd been intimidated by the sky. Like any student of the genre, he knew the decreed reaction to this kind of display: a feeling of smallness, of inconsequence. But as he progressed further into middle age, he no longer needed an empty sky to feel cosmic horror; the deep, formless awareness of a wasted life engulfed him every night. It was the impetus for many two a.m. breakdowns. He always felt afraid.

Light shone from the living room window, warm and welcoming. He crunched a few Altoids to mask the smell of beer and climbed the steps, bracing himself for Mark's withering look. He rapped once on the door and then walked in. "Sorry I'm late. I was interviewing some of the local wildlife."

He was struck by a sudden gust of rot stench, a rolling wave of it, which made his eyes water. Involuntarily he brought his hand over his mouth. It passed in seconds, replaced by the scent of sandalwood incense. He noticed a stick of it smoking in a corner.

Jennifer Drummond was sitting in the same chair she'd used for the interview. Mark sat across from her, in the chair Alan had used. Alan paused. The room was gravid with moment, as though he'd intruded upon some delicate transaction. Jennifer looked at him and smiled in a way that seemed wounded and hesitant. Mark lowered his head and wiped a hand over his eyes.

"Uh, is everything okay?"

"Who were you talking to?" Jennifer asked.

"The bartender at the Canteen. Tom. I lost track of time."

"Alan," Mark said. "I think we need to go."

Jennifer looked startled. "Nonsense."

"Yeah, really. It's late. We can come back and finish in the morning." Saying this, he looked up at Alan. His eyes were red and swollen. He'd been crying.

"Mark? What the hell happened?"

Jennifer put a hand on Mark's wrist. He flinched. "Mark thinks I'm crazy," she said.

"Goddamn it."

"That's not how I put it," Mark said.

"He was trying to protect me." She looked away from Alan and back at Mark. "But you were being presumptuous. Weren't you, Mark."

He nodded, his face lowered. Alan could see the backs of his ears turn red. Mark was trying to hold back tears. He felt deeply unsettled. Something was badly wrong. "Miss Drummond—Jennifer—I think Mark is right. It *is* late, and he looks like he might be feeling sick. It's probably best to come back and finish in the morning."

She ignored him. "Go sit on the couch, Mark."

Mark did what he was told, avoiding Alan's eyes as he brushed past him. Jennifer gestured to the vacated chair. Alan remained standing. "What's going on here?"

"I had to show him," she said. "I didn't like his insinuations."

Alan sought for something to say, some way of defending Mark without risking her trust. There wasn't any. Instead he just stared at Mark, who sat on the couch like some chastened little boy, struggling to keep his composure.

"What did you show him?"

For a moment she seemed to be on the verge of tears herself. "I didn't want to." Her hands were clutched tightly in her lap, knuckles white with tension. Then she closed her eyes and he could see a resolve settle over her like a garment. When she spoke again, all trace of weakness was gone: "I won't be told who I am anymore."

"Then tell me yourself. Who *are* you, Jennifer?"

She smiled politely and settled back into her chair. "Sit down, and I'll tell you. Turn the camera on. Let's finish."

Alan did as she asked. The light had all but gone from the world outside, and he drew shut the curtains. He gestured for Mark to return to his place at the sound board. In a couple of minutes they were ready to record. He resumed his seat and took a deep breath.

"Tell me what you want to tell me," he said.

"Lionel was a monster. He was charming and funny when he needed to be, but once you got right down to it, he only cared about what he wanted. Power. Over the people in his life, over his actors, and over me. Especially over me." As she continued to speak—describing Lionel's exacting direction, his rages, the way he eroded her will over a period of several days before the barn scene, insulting her abilities and criticizing her appearance when she disrobed for the night's shoot, leaving her vulnerable and defenseless—that rancid odor intruded into the room once more: first an unpleasant tickle in the nose, swelling quickly into the brute stink of decay.

Alan ignored it for as long as he could bear to; then he pulled his shirt up over his mouth, squeezing shut his watering eyes. Jennifer continued talking for a few seconds, then trailed to a stop. She made no effort to cover her nose, nor did she seem offended by the smell. She only seemed sad.

"Jesus," Alan said. "What *is* that?"

She continued as if he hadn't said anything. "When I realized what had happened—what had moved into me—I came out here. I wanted to be far away from people so it couldn't hurt anyone. I wanted to isolate it. Lionel didn't care. He followed me, and I was too weak to refuse him. He wanted to feed it and see what happened. He wanted to make a documentary—the film that would make him a star. The two of them together overwhelmed me for a while. But Lionel didn't last long. The people loved me." She stopped. "Well. It was really the demon they loved. But they thought it was me. Maybe that's the same thing. They did what I wanted them to do."

Somebody killed him . . . a mob of folks tore him to pieces.

"So Lionel was filming when he was here? Where are the reels?"

"Under the house."

"Buried? They might be ruined."

"Not buried. In the nest."

"What are you talking about, Jennifer?"

"After Lionel was gone, it was just the two of us. It was strong, but I was stronger. I locked myself in this house, cut myself off from everyone. I killed it, finally. I starved it. It took years. So many years." She put her hands on her chest, her belly. "It's rotting inside me now."

Alan fought back a wave of nausea. His head swam. "What do you mean? What do you mean it's rotting inside you?" He stood up, for what purpose he wasn't sure. He was confused. He needed fresh air. The stink had grown even worse. It was like something physical in his throat. "What did you show Mark?" he said. "What was it?"

From the corner, Mark started weeping. He didn't try to stifle it; he sounded like a child who had lost something, or was lost himself.

"I didn't mean to." Jennifer's voice trembled, her resolve crumbling. "When he told me I was crazy, I just—I got so angry. I lost control for a minute. I didn't mean to hurt him."

"Jennifer. Please let me see."

"Not here," she said. She rose from her chair and headed down the hallway to her bedroom. The stink of decay followed her. She left a tarry sediment on the floor with each footstep. Alan put the camera onto his shoulder and followed.

Her bedroom was unlit, the bed itself upturned and leaning against the wall, its underside covered in a heavy layer of dust. A great hole had been excavated in the floor, rough steps descending in a steep gradient. Darkness pulsed from inside it.

Jennifer began to change. Her clothes fell from her body in rotten tatters, like the wrappings of a mummy. The skin shifted on her body, turning a pallid gray, covered with black patches of mold. It glistened with some kind of interior light—a luminous rot. She seemed taller, stronger, more beautiful. She was naked, but her body was androgynous: gorgeous, magnetic, dead.

Through her failing flesh he saw an equine skull bearing too many pale, sightless eyes. She was at once regal and putrid, her body wavering between her own elderly form and the holy beauty of the Corpse, as though seen beneath rippling water.

The light on his camera surged and went out.

Alan fell to his knees, his cognition crumbling beneath the weight of this like rotten wood. Something primordial in his brain shrieked and danced. His clasped his hands together under his chin, his lips seeking a prayer he'd never learned.

"Don't you pray to it," Jennifer said, her voice leaking from that cracked skull like a gas. "Don't you dare."

Alan couldn't fathom the strength of resolution it would have taken to do what she had done. To endure a contest of wills that spanned decades, to tame a hunger that had crossed the gulf between this world and whatever aching hole it had crawled from—it beggared the mind. It cast into harsh relief the meandering path of his own life: the passive hoping, the cowardly wait.

Even in death the Corpse exerted its influence. Alan felt the snapped-bone shock of a fundamental reordering in his brain. He peered through its eyes. He saw that Mark was dead, despite the heart beating the blood through his body. Like Tom and the people of Templeton, he had borne witness to a beauty so terrible that it would ruin everything that followed it. Mark felt his body rotting around him and would long for an escape from it for whatever years remained to him. Alan saw a small handful of people making their way along the empty road from Templeton, the bartender and a few others, not pulled by the mysterious impulse of decades ago but by a doomed hope that she remembered them, that she called them back to her. They would wait outside her house as they had before, shivering in the dark, though this time no light would come. And he saw Jennifer Drummond, her whole life thwarted by the desperate war she'd fought for her own body and her own mind, lonely now in her victory.

She descended into the hole, and he trailed behind her. The stuttering, decayed light from her body illuminated the walls in brief flashes. It was a nest, walled in human faces, scores of them peering out from battlements of melded flesh, their mouths blackly gaping, their eyes cataractous and blind. It was like walking through an abandoned wasps' nest. Once, it rang with screams and hosannas.

Their silence now was obscene. The demon was dead, but this woman still lived. She was still sweetly beautiful, she still yearned to fill her heart's need. "Is it too late?" she asked.

She started to dance, a gorgeous rotted thing, undulating in the way she had done so long ago. Tears spilled down Alan's face. He fixed the camera on her, recording it all using her own spoiled light. He was making terrible sounds. They echoed in the nest and soon it seemed the faces joined his effort, like a choir in a cathedral.

FAMILY

Lisa Morton

"DO YOU WANT to go see a horror movie?"

Dave looked up from the script notes he was jotting on his iPad. Fiona lounged in the conference room doorway, arms crossed, eyebrows raised.

His hand paused, stylus in midair. "I wanted to finish getting these comments down for the next draft . . ."

"So get them down and let's go."

Dave frowned, slightly perplexed; Fiona had been in the same script conference he had a few moments ago. In fact, Fiona was the one who'd gotten him, an unproduced American screenwriter with a legendary spec action script as his entire résumé, this job.

"There's a lot here . . ." Glancing at what he'd already written down, Dave couldn't see how they possibly expected him to deliver a revised draft of *Hard Chase* in time. They'd flown him to Hong Kong and agreed to put him up in a hotel for a month, and that had been three weeks ago. These executives liked working closely with their writers; would they cut him loose once he returned to the States?

Fiona looked over her shoulder before stepping into the room and sitting next to him. When she spoke, her voice was soft, but she couldn't have been *too* worried about anyone overhearing because she hadn't bothered to close the door. "Trust me, the script is going well. I work with these guys, I do a lot of these meetings, I can tell."

"Really?"

She smiled. "Really. They're glad they brought you over for the job." Dave didn't know the junior development executive well, but he had no reason to disbelieve her—she'd worked with the writers on Dragon Galaxy's last hit, an action comedy called *Run to Chill*, so at just twenty-eight Fiona Shu was respected within the still mostly male upper echelon of the company. He knew they were also impressed by the film degree she'd acquired from an American university, to say nothing of the fact that she was equally fluent in English, Cantonese, and Mandarin, but he wondered just how much power they'd really let her wield. A vice president of production named Li Ka-fai had exclaimed angrily in Cantonese halfway through the meeting; even though Fiona had calmed the man down, Dave was still sure he'd lost the job.

"I'll let you in on a little secret." She lowered her voice and leaned in. "We're talking to Chow Lok-hang about directing."

Dave looked up. "Chow Lok-hang? As in, *the* Chow Lok-hang? I didn't even realize he was still alive."

"He's retired, not dead, but he's considering making this his big comeback movie."

"You know Chow's *Greener Fields* is the whole reason I got interested in Hong Kong cinema. Well, that and *The Killer*."

"I know. I read your blog on it."

Dave smiled, shook his head. "Of course you did." He paused for a second before asking, "Wasn't Chow part of that whole Hong Kong way of making movies where they didn't use scripts?"

Fiona shrugged. "Times have changed. If Hong Kong wants to compete against South Korea and the mainland in the global market, we need great scripts. Chow knows that." She stood, and spoke loudly. "Now finish up those notes, and let's go get scared."

> > >

Fiona dragged him down to the subway station. As they stood on the platform waiting for the next train, she checked her phone. "There's a three-thirty showing in Tsim Sha Tsui. We'll just make it."

The train pulled in and they boarded. At this time of the afternoon, it was only half-full. Dave took a seat near an elderly woman whose face was so creased it was hard to make out her features. He imagined asking her what she'd lived through, what she'd seen, if she'd spent her life in Hong Kong or had (as so many others) come here from somewhere else. He wished he was more fluent in Cantonese, the vanishing tongue still spoken throughout Hong Kong.

As the subway carried them beneath the harbor and toward the Kowloon Peninsula, Dave asked, "So what's this movie called?"

"*Family.*"

"And why are you so interested in it?"

"You haven't heard of it?"

He shook his head. "I've barely had time to eat over the last three weeks, let alone follow the new movies."

"It's a first-time female director named Fan Chiu-yi, who we're thinking about working with."

"Ah. So that's why we're abandoning work in the middle of the day to go to a movie."

Fiona shrugged. "Well, that's part of it, but I'm also really curious about this one. It's about a dysfunctional family in Guangzhou. The grandfather's an old-school patriarch who won't give up traditional ways, and he's always clashing with the rest of the family, especially his granddaughter, who's in the tech industry."

"So how is it a horror movie? I mean, aside from the idea of anyone working in the tech industry."

Fiona gave his arm a friendly punch and then went on. "The grandfather dies and comes back to haunt the rest of the family."

Dave thought back to what he knew of NRTA, or the National Radio and Television Administration; they reviewed all films released in China and were notorious for banning anything with even a whiff of the supernatural, which didn't jibe with the state's Communist philosophy. "So it's a horror movie like the one that was so big last year . . . what was it, *The Door* or something?"

Grinning, Fiona said, "You mean the one that turned out to be all in the protagonist's head?"

"I thought that was the only way to get a ghost movie past NRTA."

"I thought so, too, but somehow *Family* did it. It just finished its first week on the mainland and was a big surprise hit."

Dave thought back to the glorious Hong Kong horror films of the '80s, movies like *A Chinese Ghost Story* or *Zu: Warriors from the Magic Mountain* that had gleefully embraced fantastic happenings—giant tongues pursuing victims through nighttime forests, monks fighting demonic energy balls with their endlessly long eyebrows, seductive fox spirits seducing naive young warriors—and rued the passing of that enchanted era. "It's probably too much to hope for even one hopping vampire."

Fiona laughed, mainly because she'd recently admitted to Dave that she'd never seen a single entry in the *Mr. Vampire* series ("I was too young"). "I think this one is more serious than that."

"Too bad," Dave muttered.

The train pulled into the Tsim Sha Tsui station and they disembarked. Fiona led the way past herb shops, souvenir stalls, a McDonald's fast-food joint, and a 7-Eleven convenience store as they spoke idly of people they worked with, which executives Dave should be most cautious around, and the vanished Kowloon Walled City, a massive city-within-the-city that had been torn down when Fiona was five. She didn't remember that, but she'd been nine when Hong Kong had been given up by the British and set up as a special administrative region under China, and she remembered enough to know the city had changed since then as it had wrestled with its new identity. In the past, there'd been less tension, fewer soldiers and protestors, more money and opportunity.

Dave talked about his family, about how he was still close to his father, a retired engineer, and his mom, a teacher. His only sibling, Matt, lived in Boston; Dave hadn't spoken to him in a year. He confessed to Fiona that he'd always felt like a failure in his father's eyes, that his father didn't consider screenwriting a "real job." She did her best to assure him that his father must be very proud of him.

When they reached the theater, Fiona chose their seats, paid for two tickets, and led the way as they filed in.

Around twenty patrons were seated for the matinee, a mix of older retired people and a few younger students. As they waited, Dave scrolled through his phone, checking a couple of sites for #familymovie.

The comments included "scariest movie EVER," "I was so scared I couldn't sleep for a week," and "how did the government let this out?"

"Wow," Dave muttered, causing Fiona to look up from her own phone. "The comments on this movie are *intense*."

"I know," she said.

The lights went down and after a few commercials, the movie

started. Dave was relieved to find it bore English captions. He was also startled to see the name Fan Lung show up in the credits. "Fan Lung?" he whispered to Fiona. "The Fan Lung who was a Shaw Brothers star?"

"Yes. It's his first movie in nearly forty years. The director is his granddaughter."

The opening half hour of the movie sketched in the Hui family's history: their home in Guangzhou, where the grandfather, played by Fan Lung, had once worked as a tax collector for the government and still remembered when the Yangtze River had been filled with British vessels and pirates. His son was a mix of old and new, a man who'd worked hard for the government but had never held to his father's severe and inflexible ideas of traditional values. The grandson had moved to Canada, leaving both father and grandfather angry, but the daughter had stayed; she worked as a programmer for a major tech firm and was a true capitalist. The mother was a quiet woman who'd spent her life obeying the men around her. Mother (a classic character actress Dave recognized from dozens of Hong Kong movies) secretly burned with resentment toward the men around her, evidenced by glares they never saw, the way she scrubbed dishes with angry energy, the small confidences she shared with her daughter.

Family certainly didn't have the setup of a typical horror film; in its first thirty minutes, no one died, no spirits were glimpsed, and the audience watched quietly. It was shot in dark, shadowed hues, with corners of the frame fading off into darkness, but that look served it well as a drama about a family ruled by a strict patriarch who appreciated only the values of the past.

Then, at the thirty-five-minute mark, the grandfather died.

Five minutes after that, a young woman to Dave's right cried out, "*Gui!*"

He blinked, jerking upright in his seat—what had she said?

Had he missed something? He peered at the screen, confused; the scene was mother and daughter in the kitchen, sharing memories of the grandfather.

An older man two rows below Dave gasped. He abruptly rose and fled the theater.

Leaning over to Fiona, Dave asked, "What happened?"

"I don't know," she whispered back.

In the movie, the mother erupted in anger, revealing how she'd secretly hated the old man her whole life, a life full of petty dismissals and major cruelties perpetrated on her.

A woman on the other side of the theater choked back a terrified sob and staggered out, doing whatever she could to avoid looking at the screen.

The film continued with the old man's funeral, for which the youngest son returned from Canada. He argued with his father about his choice. As they shouted at each other, the daughter stood by, silent and disregarded. When the funeral ended, the brother left Guangzhou and the father finally turned to the daughter, accepting her as the real heir of the family. The ending was sweet without being maudlin as the family reconciled around the daughter.

The lights went up. The audience had been reduced by a full third. Dave glanced from those filing out to Fiona. She looked back at him before rising and exiting. Dave followed.

Outside, as they headed back to the subway, Dave asked, "What the fuck just happened?"

Fiona frowned. "I have no idea."

"Is there something I missed because . . . well, because I'm . . . not . . ." He didn't know how to say it: *Because I'm not Chinese.*

But a glance at Fiona told him that wasn't the case. "No. Maybe it's the way the movie is shot . . . ? It does look like a horror film."

Shrugging, Dave said, "Maybe, but . . . that one woman

screamed. That's a pretty intense reaction to something that just *looks* like a horror movie. And what was that word that one woman used . . . ?"

"*Gui*—'ghost.' "

That night, back in his hotel room, Dave took a break from working on the script to google comments on *Family*. Major reviews all covered it as a family drama. An article in the *South China Morning Post* noted that NRTA was reconsidering the film, "which some have described as a frightening ghost story." Another article mentioned that Fan Lung had come out of retirement to play the patriarch because his granddaughter had begged him to, but had died when he had one day of shooting left (they'd restructured the script to accommodate the loss). Dave remembered Fan Lung as a handsome young martial arts master in the Shaw Brothers kung fu epics of the '70s; he'd starred in the comedic-action film *My Cousin the Boxer*, a performance that was said to have been hugely influential on Jackie Chan. Just when Fan had been set to become an international star, he'd been in a terrible car accident that he'd never fully recovered from, making it impossible for him to continue as a physically active actor.

Family was the only film he'd made since 1979. It was his granddaughter Fan Chiu-yi's first film, and had earned her high critical marks . . . and more than a little controversy. In interviews she avoided any discussion of the film as a ghost story, preferring to talk instead about what it had been like directing her grandfather.

That night, Dave dreamed of finding himself in a towering, shadowy place he recognized from photos as the Kowloon Walled City. He wandered its gloomy corridors, lit by flickering fluorescents, the sky nothing but a gray sliver thirteen stories overhead. The floors were slick with noxious moisture, unidentifiable trash piled in dim corners. He thought he was alone, but then he glimpsed a face, just a flash of a grimace, in the doorway of an unlit apartment. He grew increasingly uneasy, unable to find a way out, anxious. When he heard the thunderous crashes of walls crumbling, the booms of demolition explosions, his dread forced him to run, and run—

He awoke to find rain pattering against his hotel window, and a text from Fiona on his phone: *Guess what? Fan Chiu-yi coming 2 offices 2day for meeting, 11 am.*

Twenty minutes later Dave was heading for the subway entrance. He'd made a habit of stopping at a local bakery every morning for a custard tart and a *yuenyeung*, the popular regional mix of coffee and tea that Fiona called "Chinese coffee." He liked the young girl who worked at the bakery; she was trying to learn English, and Dave enjoyed helping her out in exchange for picking up a few choice Cantonese phrases. She told Dave she wanted to be called Anita, and that someday she hoped to travel to his hometown of Los Angeles.

When he saw her this morning, though, she looked ill and was shaking so badly that she slopped much of his drink before getting it into his paper cup. He knew she'd lost her grandmother several weeks ago, but she'd said she'd barely known the old lady, who lived on a farm outside Shenzhen.

"*Nei ho ma?*" he asked, trying to get the inflections right.

Anita shook her head. "*Mo ah.* Last night I see this movie. I am so scare I do not sleep."

Dave asked, "Was the movie *Family?*"

Anita looked at him. "*Hai ah.* You see it?"

He nodded.

She asked, "You are not scare?"

Somehow feeling guilty, Dave said, "No. Why did it scare you so much?"

Busying herself with getting his tart, the girl answered, "The *gui*—the ghost. It is very scary. Green, and big head." She placed the tart in a cardboard box and gestured with her hands around her head.

Without further comment, Dave paid for his tart and *yuen-yeung*, wished Anita well, and walked away, thinking: *There are two cuts of the film out there. It's the only possible answer.*

> > >

At eleven thirty, Dave looked up from the desk Fiona had loaned him to see her approaching with another young woman. Where Fiona was tall and chic, the other woman was smaller, with spiky blue hair, a leather jacket, and torn jeans. "Dave, this is Fan Chiu-yi." Fiona turned and spoke to the other woman in Cantonese; the woman listened, smiled, extended a hand to Dave. She had a confident grip and eyes that assessed him quickly.

Dave said, "I'm so pleased to meet you. Congratulations on the success of *Family*."

As Fiona translated, Dave was slightly disappointed to realize that Fan Chiu-yi spoke no English, although his deeper disappointment was in his own inability to grasp Cantonese. After a brief exchange, Fiona turned to Dave. "She says we can call her Chiu-yi. She's going to join us for lunch."

"Oh, fantastic."

Fiona led the way to a huge restaurant on the second floor of the skyscraper that housed Dragon Galaxy's production offices; the restaurant was still serving dim sum, the carts loaded with small plates of food moving between tables, and Fiona selected various items for the three of them. As they sampled steamed buns filled with barbecued pork, *siu mai* with quail's egg, and spareribs with black bean sauce, Fiona served as interpreter. Fiona spoke to Chiu-yi, gesturing and nodding at Dave, who wondered what she was saying. When Chiu-yi smiled broadly at Dave, Fiona said, "I just told her that you know all of her grandfather's movies."

"Yes, I'm a big fan. I especially love the work he did with Chor Yuen. *The Cursed Blade* is an underrated classic."

Fiona translated, and the look on Chiu-yi's face told Dave that she genuinely approved. When she was done speaking, Fiona said, "That was her grandfather's favorite of his movies. She wishes you could have met him. He loved to talk about his film work."

Dave asked, "Why did he stop acting for so long?"

Fiona gave the question to Chiu-yi, and then turned back to Dave with her answer. "He didn't believe he was a real actor. He always thought of himself as more of a stuntman."

"That's a pity. He's really good in *Family*."

Chiu-yi glowed, responded. Fiona said, "She's glad you think that. She told him the same thing, but he didn't believe her. He loved movies; if he hadn't had that heart attack at the end of shooting, he might have had a whole second career."

The conversation wandered through Fan Lung's career, what he'd done after leaving the film industry (real estate, which he'd been good at), and how he'd provided most of the financing for *Family*. When the talk turned to that film's script, Chiu-yi stopped eating and looked down at her food, melancholy. She spoke for a while; Fiona listened intently, waiting for the other woman to finish before turning to Dave. "She says that while much of *Family* is based on her life, the part that isn't is what happened after her grandfather died. In the movie, the son returns from Canada for the old man's funeral, but in real life she has brothers in both Canada and Beijing who didn't come for Grandfather's funeral. It was very upsetting."

Dave decided it was now or never. He pushed his plates aside and leaned forward. "Chiu-yi, why did you make two cuts of the movie?"

Fiona's eyes widened; Dave realized the possibility had somehow not occurred to her before. After a second, she turned to Chiu-yi and asked the question.

The young director's response was a bitter laugh, followed by a short answer that Fiona translated as "I didn't."

"Then who did?"

"No one. There's only one cut."

Fiona and Dave exchanged a look before Fiona leaned in to ask something of her own. Dave was surprised to see that Chiu-yi was on the verge of tears as she answered; it wasn't a reaction he'd expected.

Fiona said, "She says she's seen the film probably hundreds of times, between the editing process and all the screenings since, and she doesn't understand what's going on. She says she didn't make a horror movie."

Dave felt a rush of pity for Fan Chiu-yi. He knew that companies like Dragon Galaxy were talking to her because she'd made a film that had deeply affected enough of the audience to become a genuine cultural phenomenon, but she had no idea what she'd done or how to do it again.

Chiu-yi cried openly then, softly, lowering her head to the restaurant table, talking in such low tones that Fiona had to lean in to hear her. When Chiu-yi finished, Fiona leaned back in the padded booth and took a deep breath.

"What?" Dave asked.

"She says that she's asked people what they see in the film. They describe a terrifying ghost that appears in the background of shots, lurking in the dark. Although it's greenish and has a misshapen head, they say it's definitely the grandfather in the film—Fan Lung, her real grandfather."

After that, Chiu-yi wouldn't talk anymore about *Family*. They finished lunch and she left, thanking Fiona but making it clear that she didn't expect a callback from Dragon Galaxy.

When she was gone, Dave asked, "Will you hire her?"

Fiona shrugged. "She says she wants to make dramas, but those don't make money. We need horror movies. I'll talk to her."

> > >

Dave took that night away from the script for *Hard Chase* to see *Family* again. He found another theater, this one in Mong Kok, where it was playing. The evening showing was two-thirds full.

He stared hard at the screen. He was more impressed with Fan Chiu-yi's directing and writing skills this time, thought it was probably to Dragon Galaxy's detriment that they wouldn't make a dramatic film with her . . . but there was no ghost.

When a woman three seats away jerked in shock, he squinted, focusing on the parts of the image that shaded off into deeper hues.

There was nothing there. Despite the fact that two seats down a man cursed in Cantonese, upsetting his soda.

By the time the film was over, he'd never felt like such an outsider before.

> > >

An hour later, in his hotel room, Dave looked again for online information on *Family*. He found some grainy photos someone had shot during a showing of the film, purporting to have captured the "ghost." He saw a slight distortion in the photos, but nothing like the horrific specter that had been reported by those who found the film frightening. He chalked it up to power of suggestion, the human tendency to see what you wanted to see.

He was reminded of a paranormal investigation he'd once attended as research for a horror screenplay he'd been hired to develop. The investigation had taken place inside a house on the edge of Hollywood that was supposedly haunted; he'd been present with an investigator, a medium, and five others who'd each paid handsomely (as he had) to attend. They'd met at the house, a rental currently empty, at ten p.m. By two a.m., the investigator had demonstrated the use of K2 meters (to measure fluctuations in electromagnetic energy), voice recorders, and even dowsing rods, claiming varying levels of success in "contacting the spirits who are present here." At three a.m., he'd sat with the others in a completely darkened room on the ground floor, next to a seemingly levelheaded college professor who'd abruptly blurted out that something was touching him.

Dave had felt nothing. When he'd listened to the audio recordings later on, where others said they heard voices, he heard only the uneven thrum of white noise, sounding like an electronic wind rustling unreal trees. The professor had been sincerely unnerved, as had a secretary and a special effects expert, and he believed them all; he just didn't believe they'd been contacted by spirits of the dead. He couldn't explain what they *had* experienced.

Now, three years after that night, feeling lonely and hungry and curious, he made his way out of his hotel room to the bakery and was pleased to find it still open and Anita working. He ordered a *yuenyeung* and two French baguettes. As he paid, he asked Anita, "What you were telling me yesterday, about being scared by that movie . . ."

"Yes. With the *gui*."

"Right. I was wondering . . . have you ever seen ghosts anywhere else?"

"Yes. When I am twelve, my auntie die, and one week after I see her. And last year, during *Yu Lan*, I see *shui gui*—water ghost—in ocean where man drown."

Dave thought for a second. "*Yu Lan* . . . that's . . ."

"Hungry Ghost Festival. When *gui* come home."

Dave nodded, thanked Anita, and started to leave with his purchases. She called after him just before he reached the shop's door. "There are many *gui*. Some do not haunt in houses."

"*Do jeh*," Dave said, thanking her before making his way out into the damp Hong Kong night.

> > >

When he saw Fiona at work the next day, he asked her if Dragon Galaxy was going to work with Fan Chiu-yi.

"I don't think so. I talked to her after lunch yesterday and told her we'd love to make another horror film with her, but she said, 'I didn't make a horror film. My brothers did.'"

"Her brothers?" Dave thought back to the meeting yesterday. "The ones who didn't come back from Canada and Beijing for Fan Lung's funeral?"

Fiona nodded. "Yes."

"Why would she say that?"

Fiona sipped from her cup of tea, considering her answer. "Chinese people believe that sometimes ghosts come about if they haven't been properly honored at the funeral and burial."

Dave asked, "Do the Chinese believe everyone can see ghosts? Or only some people?"

Fiona eyed him quizzically. "I think all people, but . . . maybe it is only some. What do you think?"

"What if it's something we're either born with or not, like eye color or musical skills?"

"But can't you learn to play music?" Fiona asked. Her phone rang then, and she excused herself to answer.

When she came back, she had some new script notes for *Hard Chase*. There was no more time to talk about *Family*.

> > >

Two days later, he was at the offices trying to wrestle the last act of *Hard Chase* into shape when his phone rang. He saw his mother's name on the screen, felt the dread in his gut before he answered.

"Dave, it's Mom." Her voice hitched. "It's Dad . . . he had a massive stroke this morning, and he—he's gone." She burst into tears.

All the strength went out of Dave's body. He even dropped the phone for a second before finding enough energy to lift it to his ear again. His mother was saying something about how it had been quick, he hadn't suffered, the funeral—

"I'll be home tomorrow, Mom."

"Can you try to call your brother? I haven't been able to get through to him."

"I will."

He wasn't scheduled to leave Hong Kong for another three days, but when he told Fiona what had happened, she made arrangements and got him on a flight out of Hong Kong in three hours. He'd have just enough time to grab his things at the hotel and get to the airport.

Numb, feeling drained and leaden, he haphazardly stuffed his clothes into his suitcase, dropped his key at the front desk, and fell into the car Fiona had arranged to take him to the airport. "Don't worry about the script," she'd told him, "we'll pick it up again when you're settled. I'm so sorry, Dave."

On the ride to the airport, he texted his brother, Matt, but got no immediate answer. He put his phone away and thought about the last time he'd seen his father. It'd been three months ago, when he'd visited the family home in Sacramento. His father had asked him how the screenwriting business was going; Dave could sense the disappointment when he said there were a lot of irons out there but no fires yet.

Last week when Dave had called from Hong Kong, his dad had been impressed when told that the company was covering his travel *and* paying him. "That's great, Davey."

Dave tried to grasp life without his father, and felt disconnected, shut down. He barely made it through airport security and onto his flight.

An hour out from Hong Kong, Dave turned on the screen mounted on the seat back before him. Flicking through the movie selections, he stopped when he saw it:

Family.

His fingers were shaking when he plugged in the headset and started the movie. Even on the small, muddy airplane screen, Fan Lung's performance seemed poignant now, though his character was stern, unyielding in his devotion to bygone traditions and beliefs.

Then he died.

Dave leaned forward in his seat, peering into the pixels on the small monitor. He remembered where audience members had first gasped and uttered, "*Gui,*" and as that point approached he felt a knot form in his stomach.

The granddaughter and mother were in the kitchen talking...

There. What had he just seen? That flash, in the unlit far corner ... had it been an aberration of static, or a form, a glow, an awful, eyeless face?

Dave turned the movie off and ripped the headset away, so

cold he was quivering. He unwrapped the thin airplane blanket, tugged it around himself, and imagined being in his own kitchen at home, hugging Mom while something watched from the darkness, roiling with cold fury at how it had been dishonored.

He didn't want to think about the funeral without Matt.

NIGHT OF THE LIVING

Paul Cornell

ANDY HAS DREAMS that aren't appropriate for his age. Or that's the weird thought he has when he wakes at four a.m., needing to go to the toilet. The words in that thought fall away as he heads to the bathroom. His mum had been in his dreams. She died when he was ten. Dad died when he was nineteen. Now he's twenty-three. And a manager. But his brain, he thinks as he pisses, is saying he's doing it wrong, even in his dreams. Some part of him is still in the box of his family home, long gone. That part is safe there. No, 'safe' isn't the right word. As he heads back to his bed, back to sleep, he thinks, and it's an uneasy thought, that he wishes the old house would sell, not just because he needs the money. He doesn't like the idea of his family home standing empty. Then he's asleep again.

> > >

Morning. Reset. He remembers some of the thoughts of the night before as he drives to work. He discards them. Meaningless. He's the one who uses the master key card to open the doors at the multiplex. No morning shows on a Monday. He can get there when he likes, as long as everything is done before the matinee. He gets there early.

Monday matinee is the Gold slot, the pensioners slot, when over-65s pay half price. It's one of the slots the company has been pushing on local radio, and the only one where that seems to have worked, because they now have a core group who always shows up and the audience is getting bigger, the only slot where that's the case. Andy is worried about today. He finally went with Callum's choice of movie. He's not sure why. Andy has a policy of trying to include the staff in the handful of decisions that can be taken at the local level. Callum, whose job was to check the tickets and make sure customers went to the right screens, had been suggesting ridiculous choices for Gold, every week. Andy sometimes thought himself too stiff, too dull. Callum is the opposite. He's always saying and doing stupid, attention-seeking shit. And he has such a sackable face. But Andy can never find a sensible reason to let him go. Callum had suggested *Fifty Shades* for the Gold slot, that shark movie with Jason Statham, a live *Titus Andronicus* from Stratford, one of those cheap *Thomas the Tank Engine* children's features. He always makes the suggestion to Andy in private. And he always has the same slightly desperate look on his face. So Andy isn't sure if the suggestions are jokes or attempts to trick him or just a weird way of reaching out, some honest uselessness. That last possibility keeps luring him, keeps getting him to sincerely ask Callum to try again. Every time he does, after Callum leaves the room, he feels he can hear the others laughing at him. One day it'll work, that's what Callum might be saying to them. One day I'll trick him into doing it. It's true the Gold slot is a tough one to pick for. You don't want anything extreme, but at the same time you don't want to patronize the old folks. When there's a classic to download from Central it's easy, but mostly it's a question of picking something from the main rotation. Last week, on his latest attempt, Callum, while not quite hitting a hole in one, had at least got on the green. "What about *Weyward House?*" he'd said. *Weyward House* is an option that third-tier cinemas like Andy's can take up. It's the sort of thing that's not really suited to an out-of-town multiplex, that only really plays well in city center locations, a cult folk horror movie from the 1970s, restored and extended, on a limited theatrical run. Crucially, it's only explicit enough these days to merit a 15 rating. Which had tipped the balance in Andy's on-the-spot decision making.

But now it's the day of the Gold slot, Andy wonders if he's just given in. If he's finally been made a fool of. He says hello to Chloe and Megan as he opens the doors for them, looking maybe a bit too carefully at their smiles, seeing if they're in on a big joke. How many punters were they going to get today? Would dozens of empty seats be a good punch line for Callum's joke? A certain number of regulars will show up for anything. They told him that when criticizing what they'd just watched. Chloe and Megan work the main counter, so they have to take the hot dogs out of the freezer and have them steaming an hour or so before kickoff. Not that the oldsters eat many hot dogs. For some reason. Andy does a quick mental calculation, based on his vague supposition of when the hot dog was invented. Yeah, these guys probably ate them when they were young, but . . . this was a thing he was never going to get to ask and would never learn.

Mikey, the projectionist, hurries in. "Love it, love it," he says, pointing at Andy. "We've actually got a classic here. Just for once. Site says it's downloaded. Aspect ratio's a little different, so we'll be doing a little bit of the old . . ." He moves his hands out horizontally and vertically like he's doing those old dance moves.

"Love it." He pats Andy on the shoulder before heading off to the locked room where he spends much of his time. Nobody likes Mikey much. When he first got here, Andy had wondered why, but he's sort of getting it now.

Here's Josh, with the beard, who works the coffee and ice cream. He gets most of the concession business for the Gold matinee. Josh is a few years older than Andy, and always looks like there's someplace he would rather be. He nods. "Boss." Which Andy had never asked anyone to call him.

From the doors comes a shout. Callum is there, waving. Andy lets him in. "Any of them here yet?"

"You're eager!" calls Chloe.

"They'll be swarming in, you be ready!" Callum gives Andy a wink that feels more aggressive than conspiratorial and heads over to grab a coffee before taking up his place at the ticket-check stand.

Andy looks at his watch, then goes and opens the doors. Sophie rushes in as he does so. "Sorry, sorry."

"You're fine." Actually, she's now officially late, but he tries not to count small infractions. Still, this has been her fourth time in two weeks. "But don't make a habit of this, okay?"

Sophie is the only . . . person of color? His brain trips over the description. That might be the right thing to call her. "Black," his old mum would have said, or worse. Sophie's the only one working here. There weren't many in the regular audience, either, and none among the oldsters, though the town center is . . . diverse, is that the word?

Sophie stops, closes her eyes for a second, raises her hand for a moment's pause. Andy wonders if he's being disrespected. But when she opens her eyes again, it looks like she really needed that moment. "Yes. Don't worry. Sir."

She actually means the "sir," which makes him feel ridiculously awful. But he doesn't quite know how to continue the conversation, especially with the others all looking at them now, so he just nods and puts on what he hopes is an encouraging smile.

> > >

Soon the old folks start arriving. And they *are* all old folks. Andy had wondered if maybe they'd get a couple of cinephiles. The numbers are actually pretty good. He makes eye contact with Callum and gives him an appreciative nod. Callum bites his lip as he nods back. Then Andy watches him return to scanning the crowd. Is this maybe not what Callum's been hoping for? Is the joke maybe that they'd all stay away?

After a couple of minutes, as is his habit when he's gauged the attendance is high enough, Andy goes to join Chloe, Megan, and Sophie on the ticket and food counter and opens up another till.

"I don't know how you stay warm, look at you," one old lady is saying to Megan, looking through her purse for exact change. Megan has a look on her face in return that asks why they always get into conversations with her. Andy kind of wonders why, too. Chloe is genuinely friendly toward the pensioners; she's chatting away right now. Megan, though, can only go through the motions. Andy wonders if it's something like cats going to sit on people they know are allergic. He finds that, while she's looking in her purse, he's been staring at the old lady's face. He never knew his grandparents. His parents were never old enough to be like this. Her skin seems to have separated from what's underneath like she's a roast chicken. Her facial blemishes are so obvious they look like minor wounds. There's no attempt to conceal them. She wears whiskers on her chin, in public. Can't she shave them? Doesn't she want to? What's it like to be inside that? He can't imagine she's just like him underneath, that she hasn't noticed getting old. The way these people talk says they're different. They spend a lot of the time actually telling his employees that they're different.

"Do you mind?" says the old man Andy should be serving. He's looking at him with an expression somehow half anger, half humor. "When you reach her age, you'll take a while to find the right change, too."

"But why is she bothering?" murmurs Megan, way too quietly for this lot to hear. She, like Andy, must have seen the credit card in the purse.

"Not at all, sir," says Andy in his bright, meet-the-public voice, getting on with selling the man his ticket. "Nobody's in a rush today."

If he said that to the normal queue he'd get eye-rolling and people calling out from further back, but with this lot it seems to meet with general approval. The old lady, oblivious, finds her last coin and puts it on the counter.

Andy feels Megan's hand tapping him on the arm. He looks across to see Sophie being accosted by one old man who's speaking very loudly into her face. "Black coffee," he's saying. "I like it black. I can't say that, can I, not to you! I like a bit of black!"

Sophie would normally be stoically getting through all this, but today she looks like she's about to cry or answer back. Andy tells his queue he'll return in a moment, goes over there, and lets Sophie make the coffee while he once more switches to forward facing. "No milk for you then, sir?"

The old man laughs and shakes his head. "You can't say anything these days."

"No, sir, indeed you can't" is what comes out of Andy's mouth, and it sounds like he's agreeing, and he isn't quite sure if he's trying to be sarcastic or not. He takes the coffee from Sophie. Her hand is shaking. He hands it to the man. "Time for your break," he says over his shoulder, and she's off into the back without replying.

The old man now seems flustered that he might have actually done something wrong, but Andy calls Josh over to take on the till he's opened up and quickly starts serving the woman who's next in line, until the old man, still talking to himself, heads for the screens.

"And you know my friend Lucy," one old lady is saying to Chloe in the queue beside him, "she's just been on a cruise! Where do you get the money?!"

"I know," says Chloe, smiling.

"And can I have a bag of those sweets, please? Oh, you know my friend Lucy I tell you about? She's just been on a cruise!"

"I know," Chloe says, and keeps smiling.

Andy looks at her, and they share slightly different sorts of smiles.

> > >

When the oldsters have all bought their tickets and snacks, and the brunt of them are being dealt with by Josh, who's back on the coffee, and Callum at the entrance to the screens, Andy takes a moment to go into the back and find Sophie.

She's slumped on a plastic chair in the staff area where the lockers with all the stickers on them are. She has her feet up on the table. She's drinking some of the proper coffee. From the locked door at the back, which goes through to the projection booth, come the noises of the advertisement playing on Screen 12, where the Gold movie is. Mikey's in the booth, but he won't be able to hear them through all the padding. "Sorry," says Sophie.

"Not at all," says Andy, with his personnel voice, "I'm sorry you went through that experience."

"I haven't been doing great, I know. I need this job."

Andy sits down. "You're not expected to put up with abuse."

"Being late, though."

"Well, yeah. That might become an issue. Are there any ways you could improve your timekeeping about leaving home on a workday? Maybe you could change something?" This comes straight from a seminar Andy attended. The title of the seminar had been "Positive Enforcement: The Hidden Boss."

Sophie closes her eyes again. "It's my housemate. He . . . I think maybe I should say she now . . . they are going through so much shit. They just needed someone to talk to. But I was on my way out the door. I was the only other one left in the house."

"If you want to go back home, I can give you a leave day."

"No. I'm here now. I've done it now. Either way. I hope they'll be okay when I get home. I guess."

"Have you called . . . them?"

"There's just the voice mail. She takes such shit. There was something new online this morning, it's over and over, you know, people who don't think she should . . ."

Andy is enormously out of his depth now. He keeps his serious face on and nods. "I'll keep that in mind about you coming in. If you want to switch to evenings it'd be fine."

"Can't. I have my . . . I go to therapy on some evenings. For my PTSD. And I don't want it to be like I'm running away from the old folks."

"Nobody would think that."

"I'm diagnosed autistic, I can't really tell sometimes about people's faces. Are you being as okay about this as I think you are?"

Andy wants to say he has no idea. But he settles on "yes." Which seems to be the right answer. And results in a smile from her. He nods, gets up, and leaves it at that. He feels pretty sure Sophie will reappear in time for the end of the movie.

> > >

As soon as Andy heads back out into the foyer, Callum is immediately in his face. "Bunch of racist cunts," he says. "Is she okay?"

"First off, safe-for-work language. Secondly, yeah, she'll be fine." Andy is surprised at this reaction. And pleased, kind of. He doesn't want to give Callum time to bridle at the telling off. "Hey, your choice of movie really worked out."

Callum looks away, shakes his head, walks off.

What is that about? He hears the door to the back opening and looks over to see Sophie coming out to her station, head down. The other women note this with wry smiles to each other, which Andy doesn't really like.

The sound from the screen changes, a noise they all know in their bones, as the trailers stop and the movie comes on. Andy decides he should go and have a look. Callum is obviously up to something, but it's vastly unlikely Mikey would be in on it, so it isn't like he's going to go and find porn playing or something, but . . .

He enters carefully, letting the padded door fall back against his shoulder first before it closes so it makes the least possible noise. The screening is packed. He always loves this feeling, being slightly back from an audience who are all looking forward. Mostly, they were silent. Sometimes he'd had to enter when there was too much noise and they'd had a complaint and he had to put on his sternest business face to warn a patron. Today is a weird combination of the two. This is a largely quiet and entirely well-behaved audience, members of whom, nonetheless, are talking quite loudly, and other members of which are equally loudly telling them to stop. That's pretty standard for Gold audiences. He remembers the previous time he did this, on the first occasion he'd run one of these, just to get a feel for what this audience is like. Some of the talking is solo, whispered, repetitive. That could be a bit spooky, if it took you by surprise. Put this lot here in the dark and the voices came out. They were like the smallest kids, who also needed to talk their way through a movie.

On the screen, the opening scenes of *Weyward House* are playing out, idyllic images of a 1970s summer. Quite weird for a horror movie, quite relaxing. This is from years before Andy was born. But he can still feel a powerful sense of . . . what? Nostalgia? It sucks him in so quickly. This is good direction, good music, too. He's feeling a longing for somewhere he's never been.

The house he's seeing on-screen is like his parents' place. There's a cloudless, perfect, summer sky. Children in sleeveless jumpers and shorts are running through wheat.

Andy decides he's seen enough. No, he's decided it's harmless enough. For this audience. Soon the horror must start, but the kind of movie this is tells him it can only go so far, be only so intense. Surely. And there's the 15 rating. That's the official verdict on the nature of life displayed on this screen.

It's a bit much for Andy himself, though, for some reason. He heads out.

> > >

Robert De Haviland had been slightly apprehensive about today's choice of film for his weekly cinema visit. And yet he'd given scant thought to not going. He likes the people he's got to know on these afternoon excursions, and, dear God, it's a chance to get out of his flat. The local newspaper had featured the poster for the film, a skull made from fresh vegetables, in a style recognizable from when he'd been a regular cinema-goer. And yet he didn't recognize the title and could find only the smallest of references in his film guides. He's hoping that, should things get too fraught on-screen, he'll just be able to close his eyes and open them again for any sexy bits. This strategy has been successful for him many times in his life, a life in which things had become too fraught quite often. In the side of his memory, as it does once in a while, comes the smell of a burning car and the screaming of his boy. He takes a deep breath in through his nose. Long ago. All gone now. Downstream. That nice cinema smell instead. He loved scary movies as a teenager but became worse and worse with them as he grew up, increasingly afraid of being taken back to moments of terror. But what's on-screen now is pleasant, well shot, peaceful. These are scenes of a world he knows. Every now and then in his daily life he catches glimpses of current music and fashions. He actually sat down to watch the Christmas Day *Top of the Pops*, and found it all much of a muchness, all blandly pleasant, but with all the acts obviously meaning things with their fashions, their makeup, their lyrics, that went past him. He's smart enough to know when a meaning is present, and too old now to know what it is. When, with Sandie Shaw, for instance, back in the day, he'd been swooning at every inch on or off her mini or her haircut.

So this film, this film, oh, it's the most perfect encapsulation of what he misses these days, it's a parade of images he understands, throwing meaning at him. These kids are in a countryside he knows, of pylons and footpaths, and now they're at the seaside, with so many smokers, and those penny falls machines, where coins endlessly fell over the edge and might drop slight value into your hands. The quality of light is what he remembers from back then, too. Had the summers literally been more golden? Have his eyes changed? Have everybody's? Or have the summers since been spoiled?

Robert watches the plot of the film, slight so far, start to unfold, and knows these children and their lost accents, and finds himself lulled and gripped and yearning. Slowly it starts to get a little too much. But he's not going to close his eyes. No way.

> ⟩ ⟩ ⟩

"It's pretty good," says Mikey, watching the movie from inside the projection booth. "It's really pretty effing great. Makes a change."

Andy is walking back and forth in the booth, his arms wrapped around himself as if it's cold in here. Which it isn't. They put the heat up for the oldsters, and the projector itself gives out warmth. He'd wanted to hear Mikey's reaction to the movie, but for some reason he hasn't wanted to join him at the window. "Good choice, then? Reasonable choice?"

"What? Yeah. Hugely. Callum. Phew. Weird." Mikey isn't even looking at him.

"It's a bit all over the place from what I've seen. What's it even about?"

"What *isn't* it about? Decay. The end of the world. The night arriving and the day never coming back. Critics are only just starting to write about it. Kim Newman for *The Guardian*. There's going to be a special edition Blu-ray. Hence the rerelease."

"I don't recognize the name of the director."

"He only did *Weyward House*. Well, and one movie that wasn't finished. The writer had worked on all sorts of things. Then he lost his children—a son and a daughter—within a year of each other, and he couldn't keep working, but then he met the director, who'd just discovered . . . well, he had a year to live. He stretched it to nearly two, in the end. He made this and tried for something else, but . . ."

Andy turns away so Mikey can't see the look on his face. "They made a horror movie about this stuff? About their lives?"

"They never said it was, but yeah."

"That's terrible."

"It's a pity people have only heard of this movie before now because of the urban legend."

"What urban legend?"

"You see it on movie-buff Twitter. Someone did some sort of survey in the 1970s about major life events in cinemas in the US. You know, which films killed people, which films had women giving birth in the cinema. Small samples, obviously. Bloody statistics. And it was this one, by a long way."

"What was?"

"The movie that most people died while watching. I suppose because for this movie it was about five people and for the rest of them it was one here and one there, something like that. Coincidence."

"Was it?" Andy now has a thought in his head that has made his day slightly worse. "When the movie was rereleased, did you tell Callum all this?"

"Maybe. Yeah. I think I did." Mikey's face falls as he realizes. "Oh. Shit. Disappointing. I thought he was into it."

"Yeah." But still, what can Andy really accuse Callum of? Not trying to get their patrons killed, not really. The movie doesn't carry any warning about flashing lights or anything else that causes seizures. This must be why Callum had been so weird this morning. Because they were in the middle of something he'd thought was going to be the raw material for a funny story he could tell about a joke he'd played on Andy, but it had turned out to be just something everyday that was happening to him. Can Andy even have a word with him about this? Maybe just let it play out?

Andy shakes his head, annoyed at his indecision, and heads back into the lobby.

> > >

He sees Callum watching him as he enters.

"This is weird," says Chloe, smiling.

But is it him or is there something nervous about her expression, too? Why is he feeling like this?

"What?"

"None of them have come out to go to the toilet. Normally we get a lot of sales like that. They have a wee, then they want more sweets. Today: nothing at all."

Andy's about to say something noncommittal when the muted sound of the movie suddenly changes. They all react together, all of them attuned to the noise that is always part of their lives at work. That drone of speech, music, and sound effects, normally on the edge of audibility, has suddenly leapt up in volume. Only the voices still aren't quite audible, the music is still muted, it's all, somehow, impossibly, just . . . bigger. "What the hell?" says Andy. He runs into the back and bangs on the door of the projection booth. "Mikey, what's going on?"

He hears a reply, a puzzled question. He uses his card to unlock the door and hauls it open. In the dark, his face illuminated by the controls, Mikey is staring at him. "Who are you? How did you get in here?"

"Stop pissing about. Did you turn the sound levels up?" Andy still doesn't want to look out at the screen, for some reason. But he does. The movie still looks normal. But he can hear the same effect he did in the lobby, that the sound is as muted as one would expect, but that it's also somehow more intrusive, more demanding.

"I'll call the police," says Mikey. "I will. They can tell me why I'm here."

Andy turns and sees the expression on Mikey's face. He's glaring like Andy's the one at fault. Like Mikey is a proud defender of something he's certain of. Fuck, is this drugs or some shit? Maybe a stroke? He seemed fine earlier. "What's wrong?"

Mikey just folds his arms, like he's won the argument, and looks away, shaking his head. It's the oddest response Andy's ever seen from an adult. It's like something a toddler would do. So . . . okay, call the police? Yeah, that's where they were. He'll keep it local, no need to tell Central. Josh has some experience with the projector. He'll bring him in here to shut it down, check the settings, restart the movie for the angry customers who are doubtless now filling the lobby to complain about the sound, and see if he can get medical help in here.

"Okay, buddy, you stay there, we'll make sure you're sorted out." He heads quickly out into the lobby again, and is surprised to find no annoyed customers, just his staff, gathered together in the middle now, as weirded out as he is. The sound of the movie continues, as strange as before. He starts to ask Chloe to call for an ambulance when there's the sound of the screen door slamming, very fast, and then suddenly, by the ticket checkpoint, there's a figure. And then, instantly, several more.

It's several of the old folk from the screening. How had they got there so fast? There's kind of a blur around them. As if—

And then they're right among them. Andy takes a single step forward, a thought forming in his head like this is going to be a public relations nightmare, but in that second he sees something blurred by speed coming at him and reflexively ducks aside.

The blur reforms into an old man, standing by the coffee stall, hunched and looking as scared as Andy is feeling now. Other blurs resolve themselves into other old folk, who are staggering and yelling, appearing and disappearing all over the foyer as they blur in and out. Andy's team are rocked by sudden impacts as the blurs come at them and strike them and knock them over. They're surrounded.

"Andy, come on!" That's Sophie, yelling from the door to the back. Everyone starts running toward her. Andy sees blurs of motion all around him. Some of them head for the main doors and form a line. Are they stopping his people from leaving? It's weirdly still afternoon out there, still normal out there, if he could just get out there. He hesitates. Are these blurs as scared as he is or aren't they?

A blur comes straight at him from the doors, and he jumps aside again, slips on the polished floor, starts staggering, gaining momentum, in a nightmare, toward where Sophie is fighting with Megan just inside the doorway to the locker room. Sophie is trying to get her body into the gap, to keep the door open. Megan is trying to slam it shut, screaming at her to get out of the way. Andy leaps over the counter, grabs the edge of the door, heaves it open, shoves Sophie and Megan in front of him, then throws himself inside and slams the door after him.

They all stand in the room with the lockers, panting. The weird noise of the movie seems impossibly louder still in here, the metal of the sink and kettle vibrating with it. "What the fuck?!" Callum has his hands held up like it's everyone else's fault and could they do something about it, please?

"I had to." Megan steps into Andy's face. "They were trying to get in. I'm sorry."

Andy doesn't know how to deal. He looks to Sophie. "Thanks."

"Oh like fuck!" shouts Megan. "Oh God, oh God!"

There's a noise from the door to the lobby. It isn't like organized thumping, like they were in a zombie movie, although it really is now like they're in a zombie movie; it's like random blurs are hitting the door. Thump. Pause. Thump, thump. It's somehow worse than a determined assault. This doesn't feel like a story. "What's happening?" Josh is fumbling with his phone. "I can't get a signal."

"You never *can* back here!" Chloe yells at him.

Andy goes over to the door to the projection booth and makes to open it. His card doesn't work. He pulls at the handle and finds something is physically holding it back. What's doing that? Mikey himself? "Mikey, are you okay?" No reply.

"*We're* not okay!" That's Chloe.

Andy looks to Callum. "Tell me everything. Tell me why you did this."

"You think I did this?"

"I don't mean—this! I mean why did you want this movie? I heard about the urban legend from Mikey, but what's it got to do with this?"

Callum spends a moment looking at him like he's mad to be treating this like it's a story. But then he visibly decides this *is* like that. "I don't know! Mikey told me about it. I thought it'd be a laugh. We could see if it was true."

"So you wanted one of the old folk to die?" Andy's aware the others are looking between them in puzzlement.

"My nan comes to these things, okay? I talk to her about the movies after. If it was this one, I could have had a laugh with her about it. And you agreed to this movie—this is your fault!"

"Is your nan one of them out there doing this to us?" asks Megan.

"No! She didn't come today! So I thought 'oh well' and just wanted it to go okay and then maybe Andy would stop looking down his fucking nose at me."

Andy doesn't have time to process that. "Did Mikey tell you much about the movie?"

"Yeah. And I read up about it. There are these kids growing up and it's all great, but there's this empty house. It's supposed to be haunted. The kids go there and they see some shit which nobody seems to understand, and they think they've got away, but then, as they leave the house, it ages them, in a blur, like that, and it varies by how far they got from the house, so you think one of them that the film's been about is going to be okay, but he isn't, either. They go back to their homes and they start passing this stuff on to their families. It doesn't make much sense. Everyone ages to death."

"Blurs, right!" Sophie is nodding.

"How do they win?" Andy asks. "How do they stop it?"

"I think . . . maybe someone burns down the house?"

"Could we burn the movie?" says Chloe.

"The movie's a digital download," says Josh. "Maybe we could burn, I don't know, the projector, the computer?"

"We're going to set something on fire," says Chloe, "while we're trapped in here?" There's a sudden flurry of battering at the door, as maybe three of whatever those things are hit it in close succession. Everyone yells. Andy sees the door bulge like it's literally about to come off its hinges.

He goes back to the projection booth door. "Mikey," he shouts, "it's us! You have to—!"

The door to the lobby bursts open, the lock flying across the room. The blurs are among them. Andy has time to see one rush at him.

Then it's on him.

> > >

He takes a deep breath, in shock . . . and then realizes everything is peaceful. He's somewhere else. Everything about where he is feels familiar, but, like in a dream, it takes him a moment to get it.

He's at home. At his family home. He's alone. He's standing in the middle of the living room. All the furniture of his childhood is here. There's the vase he'd broken, that Mum had angrily glued back together. The shape of the crack had always reminded him of her anger. There's the sofa cover he ripped.

Oh God. His parents are in here. He can hear them talking, through the wall. He goes to the window. He sees the blurs swirling in the corn outside like the tornadoes that are only in films. They're all around the house. There's no getting out of here.

He goes to find the voices. Every door he opens is familiar. He can hear his dad louder than his mum. He finds the correct doorknob. He goes in to see him. There he is, in the bedroom that smells of him. He's lying on the bed, his mouth open. His eyes are open, too. The pills are all over his pyjama top. Andy sits down beside him, like he did on the day he found him. He'd come back in after working at the print shop, expecting to talk to Dad about his day, about his memories of Mum. Dad is half in pyjamas and half-dressed. The television is on. It's showing some nothing shit. Someone talking and talking.

Andy stands up, like he'd stood up then. There had been grief. Such grief. For weeks. But he'd got past it. His back had straightened. And stiffened. He goes to change the channel on the television. He sees on it the date of his own death. There's his name. There's the date. He knows what that is. The television announcer tells him, to make sure he gets it. It's still decades away. But real. He nods at it.

He goes to kiss his father, though he doesn't have to. He did this at the time, and that had ended a thing, and this is just for his pleasure, not his need.

Then he heads for the kitchen, where the front door is. He finds Mum hanging there. As he had before. He'd expected it. He doesn't close his eyes. Like last time. He looked. He looks long and hard once again and then he nods again.

He goes to the front door and opens it and goes back.

> > >

The blur rushes away from Andy. He's back in the locker room. He sees what's happened to the others. The blurs seem to be avoiding them now. Oh. Because they've all been inside one. They've all been changed, in a way he hasn't. Chloe is kneeling, weeping, staring off into space and stroking her own shoulder with bent fingers, saying, "Listen, I forgot to say, before I go . . ." over and over again. Megan is muttering and glaring, making faces at the others, faces that are almost ridiculously angry.

"Someone's taken my money," says Callum, taking notes from his own pocket and letting them fall to the floor as if they aren't the money he was looking for. "We need to call the police." Josh is walking like an animal in a bad zoo, from one side of the room to the other, then immediately back the other way.

Sophie comes up to him. There's a much more stable look on her face. "You can't trust them," she says. "The Canadians. They all stick together. They say they're poor, but they look after each other. They're given all the jobs. You switch on the BBC, always a Canadian, never one of us. Kids these days hear those accents in school and they come home copying them. If we're not careful, we'll all become Canadian."

Andy takes a step back, not able to cope with the look in her eyes that demands agreement or the world will fall apart. If this is a horror movie he's in, is this, like, meant to be these people getting what they deserve? He doesn't see how. Some of it seems to mean something, but most of it seems random. It all just . . .

is. He finds himself thinking about the dream he just had while he was in the blur, and he can't find anything in it to hold on to. The thought falls away. Why isn't he like the others are? He has no idea.

He doesn't want to wait to see if he's going to get another dose. From inside the projection booth, the sounds of the movie are increasing, even more, still distant in that weird way, as always, moving toward a climax. The blurs seem to be ignoring him for now. He runs through the remains of the door into the foyer. The blurs suddenly flood out behind him, like he's their leader now. And he realizes, with horror, what's ahead. The first punters for the evening movies are approaching the main doors, the ones who wanted to print their tickets before going for a meal. They have puzzled expressions on their faces. Where is everyone? What are they seeing in there? The blurs speed for the doors, hungry for them.

What can Andy do? He can still hear the sounds of the movie out here. And that gives him a thought, a save-the-day horror-movie-hero thought.

He sprints back into the room with the lockers. There are a couple of blurs left in here. He dives at one of them, grabs at it, finds something solid inside, and pushes it in the direction he wants it to go.

It hits the projection booth door at full speed. The door buckles and flies aside. The blur spins off. Andy leaps in.

Mikey sits beside the projector, drooling and sobbing. Andy goes to look out at the screen, on which he sees a havoc of no meaning and crying people all dying of old age. He turns back and sees the power button on the projector. He reaches for it.

But as he does the music changes. He looks back and sees the words "The End" have appeared on the screen. And as is the way with old movies, they dissolve into blackness almost instantly. The lights come on automatically.

Andy stands there with his finger above the button.

> > >

The foyer turned out to be full of the corpses of very old people. Their paperwork said they were all a couple of decades younger than they looked. They had all died of old age. One of them was named Robert De Haviland, and he was dead like all the rest. The staff, apart from Andy, were suffering from the early onset of various geriatric conditions. None of them ever recovered. They spent the rest of their lives in institutions.

It was left to Andy to explain, and he could not. He didn't try. In the end he wasn't arrested for anything and the cinema chain couldn't dismiss him. Many explanations were offered. Andy was often asked, but he never answered, and he never volunteered any thoughts on the subject. He remained a manager for forty years. He never married. He never had children. He lived alone. He retired when he was forced to. There was no mention of the inexplicable at his retirement dinner, where he was presented with a long ser-vice certificate and a clock. He stared at the clock as if insulted and made no speech. He went home. The world changed around him. In later years, as Canadian refugees started to arrive in Britain, he grew strangely angry, but he took it out on himself. Mostly.

Eventually, being part of a mystery was the only thing left to him, and he did start to talk, to anyone who wanted to interview him. He came up with all sorts of elaborate theories. He made a plot out of what had happened. He blamed people. He got to appear at conferences and have boxes of books sent to his door. It didn't matter. He hated that it didn't matter.

He started to forget who he was and how things worked. He tried to hide it. Neighbors noticed. Health visitors noticed. Every now and then he tried to mention to people that he knew the day he was going to die. Nobody paid much attention. One little girl wrote it down.

One day he was sitting on his own sofa listening to someone explain something that was making him angry. Then he was having breakfast somewhere that was not his home. He angrily asked how to get out of there. Nobody seemed to want to tell him. But it all turned out to be okay. He grew steadily more sure that today he'd be going home. And today. And today. And today.

Eventually he forgot what he'd always known: that he was going to die.

He started living his life again, in bits and pieces, all out of order. It all seemed like now to him. But there were some times when people were insisting to him that this was now and the other times were not, and some times when nobody was insisting anything.

And then there was one afternoon when it was the Gold matinee again, and he had to open the doors to let his staff in. The terrible movie played. The noise rose up. The blurs came. He went into the house of his childhood. But this time it was different, because his mum and dad were waiting.

THE ONE WE TELL BAD CHILDREN

Laird Barron

America is not a young land: it is old and dirty and evil before
the settlers, before the Indians. The evil is there waiting.
—WILLIAM S. BURROUGHS, poet

Two millennia into its decline, the empire spreads west like
a bloodstain. The wilderness gives naught a whit for the
depredations of callow men—it sees them coming, and grins.
—W. S. BURROWS, beggar

Beware *Ardor of the Damned*, for even as you watch it,
it watches you.
—ANONYMOUS CRITIC

AT DUSK, someone knocked on the cottage door. A single leaden
thump.

The nine of us (me and my eight younger siblings) flinched
where we gathered at the table with our bowls of gruel and musty

root and tuber sides. I'd lowered the oak bar before ladling supper, as one does, and shuttered the small windows tight. Weasels
and bloodsucking bats infested these woods. The cottage walls
were thick-hewn logs; the ceiling was made of timber, slate, and
moss. Dirt was packed beneath our bare feet. We were proofed
against beasts and also beastly men in that snug wilderness
holdfast.

Fear will creep through any seam or notch, regardless.

The knock was particularly disquieting, as our home lay in the
hinterlands. Visitors were rare and unwelcome. We didn't have
any neighbors unless you counted squirrels; rabbits; and the
bones of pets, a dear deceased uncle, and possibly an ambitious
census taker or two. Mom and Dad enjoyed their privacy.

Three days ago, our parents had embarked on their annual
trek to the city (with Dan the mule lugging a cartload of herbs,
pelts, and carved madrone staves for trade at the market), leaving
me and my wee brothers and sisters to fend for ourselves as best
we could. They promised to be home within a week, depending
on how it went. Dad took his trusty flintlock rifle. Mom carried
an antique blunderbuss. However, we kids weren't defenseless.
Great-Granddad's boar spear leaned in the corner, in case.

Between this rib and this rib. Dad once demonstrated the proper
thrusting technique with a glint in his eye that reflected the shine
of the spearhead, dusky as wine, and pitted and cold. *See, this
crossbar keeps the blade from sliding too deep. This groove channels
the blood so you can wrench the blade free and have another go. Lean
into it, son, hips and back. The animal's life will travel along the haft
and into you with a killing stroke. You'll feel the last flutter of its heart.*

In better days, our loyal hounds would've guarded the entrance
like two heads of Cerberus. Fluffy lived a long life, but he died
three years ago, as did his littermate Atticus the very next winter.
After they trotted off to play fetch with Hades, Dad didn't get

around to replacing them. Lean times, lean times. Herbs, pelts, and madrone staves weren't selling fast enough to feed eleven mouths and counting.

The kids stared fearfully at the door, then turned their grubby, earnest faces to me. Dad himself often exhorted all concerned to memorize a critical rule, *Never ever answer the door after sundown.*

Gods save me, I couldn't reveal to the innocents that I'd grimly anticipated the knock for hours. It was a warning of sorts; a signal to me alone. I kept calm and played the role of an attentive big brother (nearing fifteen winters, which made me eldest by four) who'd not permit any harm to befall my charges no matter the inducement.

"This is the day we die," Little Johnny said; a coincidence or precognition. Our brothers and sisters echoed those words in a chorus, except for Lazy Eye Larry, who glared at his emptied bowl (and, simultaneously, the door).

"I will definitely murder the lot of you if you break into song," I said to ease the tension.

"Is it a wolf?" Salamanca said. Allegedly named for the night she was conceived in the Midnight Grotto while Mom and Dad visited on a vacation. Resources were plentiful (such as friends willing to babysit) before the fourth or fifth child.

"No, Sally," I said.

"Ms. Petals! What about Ms. Petals?"

"Not to worry, she's safe." Ms. Petals, our cow, was locked away with the chickens and geese. The shed's walls were almost as thick as the cottage's.

"Is it a bandit?" Marlon said. "I bet it's a bandit. Ten bandits."

"Wolves don't knock, you idiot," Theodora said to Salamanca.

"Neither do bandits, Teddy," Constantine said. "A bandit would kick in the door and have our guts."

"No," Flynn said. "Bandits would burn the house and stab us

when we ran outside. That's how we did it in the old days." He'd come into the world as the last of triplets (behind Theodora and Larry); caul over his head, an ominous alignment of stars, the whole bit. While performing mind-numbing drudgery around the homestead, he regaled us with tales of a previous life wherein civilization fell into ruin and he'd roamed a postapocalyptic land-scape accompanied by a vicious clockwork dog. He and the dog spent their days looting and fighting, on the run from the servi-tors of some black god. We humored him. It seemed best.

"I wanna be a bandit," Marlon said under his breath, but loudly.

Doug said nothing. Like Mom, he preferred his own counsel.

I didn't voice the obvious fact—bandits were too smart to go abroad in these woods after dark. At any rate, the knock wasn't repeated.

"Seconds, anyone? Then we'll have a show."

The kids went for more tubers. They'd have gone for a second helping of dirt.

Friday was traditionally Moving Pictures Night. In our par-ents' absence, the youngsters expected a magick lanthorn story. I'd spin the lanthorn to project colored lights upon a screen and lackadaisically perform a rote retelling (my impressions were awful at best, despite Mom's occasional tutelage) of Grendel's val-iant slaughter of Beowulf and his merry men, or how Hercules met his fate at the knives of his wife and children, or the comedic demise of the Greek commandos when the Trojans (instead of lugging it home) set fire to the giant wooden horse the invaders left on the beach. Entertaining as these standbys might be, I had something far more exciting in mind.

I put on a happy face while Fluffy and Atticus curled up in the corner of my mind, growling and grumbling their spectral discontent.

> > >

Before disappearing into the hinterlands to lie low (and raise a brood of children), Mom was an actress trained by the Royal Academy of Performing Arts. Theater and cinema ran in the family blood—her great-grandmother starred for Muybridge the Crazed Photographer as a model in his groundbreaking stop-motion sequences that segued into the first moving pictures.

Mom rode the whole starlet arc further. She shared a stage with Clint Eastwood and danced with Gregory Hines at the court of King Dick. She'd even headlined a major film production, called *Marion's Regard*, an "erotic" critique of King Dick's life and rule. Therein lay the seeds of her downfall. Let us say the king was eminently displeased to be the subject of profane mockery. My parents made themselves scarce rather than entertain a date with the royal headsman.

The padlocked trunk at the foot of their bed contained several clothbound books: an abridged encyclopedia of flora and fauna, the unabridged plays of Marlowe and Webber, and a two-volume treasury of ancient mythology, from which she'd taught us to read and write. The trunk also held her favorite dresses and hats she'd retrieved upon expeditiously vacating the capital so long ago. She seldom donned any of her costumes; not even the hats during the holidays, when hat wearing is practically mandatory.

Dad, as a beardless youth, soldiered in the king's army and received a dire, nonspecific injury while campaigning against the hostile western realms. He'd been remanded into the care of a physician who also knew something of stagecraft and motion pictures. The physician befriended my father and after the war, taught him to operate magick lanthorns and projectors.

The aforementioned magick lanthorn hung from the cottage center beam, erstwhile property of the kindly physician. Tonight, my interest lay with Dad's projector stored under a bearskin next to Mom's ironbound trunk. This projector was modest of size and design, and utterly utilitarian compared (so I'd been told) to the baroque monstrosities housed at the Shakespeare Theatre (those were carved from the skulls of elephants and saltwater crocodiles and prodigious men).

Dad cranked it up every Friday night, certain holidays, or when he got drunker and more sentimental than usual, and screened a film from his collection squirreled away in a recess carved into the cottage wall. He'd sealed the niche with a hefty stone I'd only recently grown strong enough to lift. Family favorites tended toward dramatic reenactments of historical events: *Starry Night in Hades*; *Bronson the Killer*; *Once Upon a Time in the West Part III*; *Night of the Psychopomp*; *Red Fang*; and *Birth of an Empire*.

He'd executed the principal photography on Mom's (and his) last film, *Marion's Regard*. A set of the reels from this feature was wrapped in sealskin and bound with a complicated knot. Dad referred to it as the Death Knot because he would instantly spot if anybody messed with his handiwork and take precipitous action. We were all too young to view anything so violent and lewd.

Even I, the eldest?

Especially you! Dad said, slamming his fists on the table.

In any event, prohibitions against screening *Marion's Regard* were effectively redundant, since the projector itself was off-limits on pain of a thrashing. His admonitions notwithstanding, I'd paid close attention on Moving Pictures Night and warranted I could successfully operate the projector without undue difficulty.

The kids begged me to break the rules, since life was short and bandits might burst in at any moment. They tugged at my sleeves and entreated me with the wily skills of hardened street urchins. Marlon reasoned that surely, if we exercised caution, our parents would be none the wiser. As I feigned a wavering countenance,

Theodora chimed in with her own assessment in regard to the risk of my probable punishment: I hauled enough water and chopped enough wood to indemnify myself against an overly severe beating.

He's worth two mules was Dad's highest compliment of my contributions around the homestead. He wasn't free with compliments, sentimentality, or compassion.

Once, in a moment of reckless abandon, I asked Mom if Dad's military service had embittered him. She was peeling potatoes when I blurted my query. Her flat expression didn't change, although her peeling tempo increased dramatically. She said, *Your father is more temperate than when we first married.*

I shuddered to think.

Before his agonizing death, Mom's brother, Lucio, had come to live with us. Uncle Lucio, a veteran of taproom anti-royalist pontification, complained that an unfortunate by-product of the romanticizing of the Westward Expansion was that numerous execrable plays were written to commemorate the slaughter. Worse, John Wayne and Clint Eastwood (who'd served as imperial foot soldiers in the ebbing years of the war effort) rose to fame for assuming lead roles in the productions.

Dad, quite proud of his own participation in the wars, and also a huge admirer of the actors, rolled his eyes in response to Lucio's frequent monologues. Only Mom's presence kept the men from coming to blows. One afternoon, while gathering wood, Uncle Lucio surprised a black bear and got mauled for his troubles. He expired after much suffering on a pallet near the hearth. Happily ever after: Dad's jolly mood lasted a solid fortnight.

In the here and now, I cleared my throat and pretended to arrive at a weighty decision.

"Ask and ye shall receive." I uttered a full-throated *mwahahaha!*

The children scattered in mock terror and made themselves comfortable on their straw mats, waiting with scarcely restrained eagerness. They'd apparently banished thoughts of nightwalkers and bandits. Even Doug and Larry were intently focused on the coming attractions.

"What are we watching?" Theodora said.

"Tonight, is the night of . . . *Ardor of the Damned*," I said with dramatic emphasis. The children gasped. This sounded suspiciously adult and therefore forbidden. They gasped louder when I reached under my pillow (hell of a place to stash contraband, but there were limited hidey-holes in cramped quarters) and produced film reels wrapped in a hide. The hide was matted in dirt and gore. It reeked of musk, dead roots, and animal sickness. Maggots dripped from the folds of the hide as I extracted the reels, which were in comparatively pristine condition.

Point of fact: my parents didn't own a copy of this exceedingly rare work. One might then inquire how it had fallen into my clutches. A fair question that will have to wait. Suffice to say, agents of Fate are ever prowling, even in the wilderness.

I'd read an uneasy description of *Ardor of the Damned* in dad's black guide (a manual he stashed with a cob pipe and special tobacco) to banned films. *Ardor* was an animated feature composed by the beloved and reviled artist K. M. Wanatabe. Wanatabe vanished after a hushed scandal at the imperial court, where he'd gone to instruct the empress's heirs in the art of animation. Even the most diligent biographers neglected to list *Ardor of the Damned* in his filmography.

I stretched a beaver hide across the drying rack, flesh side up. Dad had scraped it smooth, or nearly so, with a stone blade. Veins and bruises and coagulated suet formed a constellation of subterranean stars. A satisfactory projection screen indeed. Next, I rolled the projector into position, opened a panel, and lit a diminutive lantern. Then came the reels of specially cured and coated intestine, which I painstakingly situated within their niche. A myriad of discrete, sequential images was burned into the coils of sheep gut, and by some sorcerous alchemy formed an illusion of continuous, uninterrupted motion once the machine engaged. Finally, I adjusted various widgets to my satisfaction, sealed the panel, and wound a crank. Inner gears clanked, winding a series of springs. Upon release of tension, the unwinding springs would empower the entire device. I flipped the switch. The projector's internal mechanisms clicked and clacked. A pale ray emitted through the aperture lens and struck the screen. The ray broadened and blurred against imperfect fossil records of a mammalian life; it obscured dead flesh with the artifice of man-made light and color.

Cursive letters of the title card read: *Adapted from an old, old tale we tell bad children.* Permit me to attest, those responsible for this virtually unknown production were not fond of children in the slightest. Some knave also paraphrased a great philosopher: *When one gazes long into the abyss, one is altered.* Followed by: *Youngblood is the best to sup.*

In the beginning, the kids oohed and aahed. The grand vistas of a wilderness far lusher and lovelier than our own beguiled them and invited them to drop their defenses.

Darkness and evil seep into the frame oh-so-gently on teeny-tiny centipede feet. A phantom landscape coalesces, its geography peopled by silhouettes of men and beasts whose eyes burn crimson, reflecting the febrile sun sinking face-first into its grave. Then rises the black castle, perched on its hollow fang of a mountain peak. Then the prehistoric leeches, the robed supplicants, the rusted throne crouched upon a mound of rotting skulls, and the alluring woman in white, Lady Carling, doomed mistress of Baron Need.

So true to life were the painted characters, I recognized the heroine (tragic villainess?) at once. Depicted in the blush of youth,

Mom was radiant and cold as the February snows. It could be reasonably assumed that Wanatabe admired her and paid homage with his artistry. It was also possible that the film's evil glamour twisted my perceptions. According to Dad's guide to banned films, a critic (and defrocked priest) had referred to *Ardor of the Damned* as the Devil's Hand Mirror—it showed viewers what it wished them to see and thus opened them to demonic manipulation.

As the tale unspooled, I crouched in the shadows providing sound effects and musical accompaniment with empty pots and jars, a cup of nails, a bag of blocks, and Mom's washboard. This was a story obsessed with the ideal of child sacrifices as sublime provender for Those Who Wait. Only bad children, naturally. Except, what child isn't at least somewhat mischievous? A mischievous child is halfway to being a brat and a brat isn't generally scribed on the good list.

Intertitle cards supplied written narration to the more baroque subtext of the narrative. I intoned the following passages as they occurred:

> *Troglodytes squat in the depths, blackness lit by red torches as they congregate before an altar to Old Leech. In those primordial times their rude tongues could not, would not approximate his true name, and thus exclaimed him as a glottal bleat of abject horror. They are the wiser. Old Leech is the father to all soft, crawling predators. Best to slur, and murmur, and thus deflect the depredations of his baleful attention. Those who act in his name are either damned or damnable. The latter are ever on the prowl for innocent, squalling provender. In modern times, they extend their thoughts to the surface world, seeking the soft minds of wicked men to warp and command . . .*

And:

Baron Need's wig fit a tad sloppily. Need stitched together scalps he'd taken from screaming rebel officers. Off-white filthy, matted, it listed when he slapped it on, high as Franklin's kite and wroth. Always pissed in both senses of the word. Opponents feared him on the battlefield. They feared him in the ballroom. He stole the wives of his enemies and murdered the cuckolded gentlemen in duels or drowned them in ornamental punch bowls. Blood bubbling amidst blood. Ultimately, his contact with They Who Wait completed his corruption and transformed him into an engine of malevolence. He became the Eyes and Ears of Old Leech, the Mouth . . .

I orated the monologues of Baron Need the Blood Eater himself, a shapeshifting disciple in service of the cult of a sleeping god and lover/tormentor of Carling, the Lady in White:

When you rise upon the wind and the world flattens, purple black above the western blaze, the red gash of the universe herself, men become fleas and their whining chorus bleeds into the gelid, granular nothingness of the void. You are unable to believe, at first. Later, when the proof mounts and becomes irrefutable, you refuse to cede what your eyes behold and what your heart grasps, because the hindbrain and beating heart are ancient as blood.

Small wonder that Lady Carling (who'd presumably been sold a bill of goods regarding the baron's true nature) and Baron Need's arranged romance soon crashed upon the rocks:

Later, Lady Carling crawls through a tower window. She clings to a patch of ivy as the stone ledge crumbles beneath her bare feet. Her gown shimmers by the fire of a yellow moon. Wispy clouds race across the inverted oubliette of the dark sky; the hem of her gown flutters, a trailing shadow. Her eyes are large and black, the moon

sunk within their center as if reflected upon pools of stony mid-
night water. She releases her grip and gracefully plummets, arms
extended toward the indifferent gods in their heaven.

Poor, trapped Lady Carling; poor trapped Mom. Lady Carling's
chosen means of escape from a poisonous love affair was suicide
(she'd soon discover her error; some unlucky folk who died in
the baron's castle rose again as thralls of the Great Dark). If there
was some supernatural parallel between *Ardor of the Damned*
and the narrative of our own material reality, Mom was no less
doomed.

As the film progressed into its third act, Baron Need lamented
the "death" of his mistress and the extinguishment of his own
humanity:

The curse assumes manifold forms. Your fangs, your claws, your
coal black pelt that does not shine under a midnight moon are no
more singular than milady's gray face and long, spoiled tongue, her
talons that rend the wood and enamel of coffins. Nay, you are an
asymmetrical match. Sometimes, in a flattering light, she is comely
once again. In such moments you recall her as she was the night
she plummeted from the walls of your stronghold. You imagine the
beautiful shapes of the sons and daughters she would have given
you. Instead, you gather the children of peasants and freeholders
and jettison their unfinished souls into the maw of the Great Dark.
You supplicate They Who Wait and the One whom They serve in
hopes of a reward or release . . .

. . . and so forth until an oblique, crushingly nihilistic finale
transpired, everyone was dead or worse, and the credits (written in an indecipherable text) rolled. Chilling silence filled the

cottage until Constantine whimpered. A couple of the youngest joined in. Otherwise, they remained eerily quiet.

After I packed the projector and snuffed the lamps, our miserable clan had lain in the faint glow of the hearth coals. I practically heard my brothers and sisters blinking, pop-eyed, as each digested the phantasmagoric terrors he or she had witnessed. Most terrible must have been the sinking realization that the faces of the children in the film were strikingly similar to their own.

In my dreams, Baron Need and Lady Carling fled as the castle blazed against the midnight sky. The ruined couple wandered the forest until they discovered a humble cottage. The baron raised his fist to hammer upon the door. He called to its inhabitants in Dad's voice. The door creaked open and revealed walls embedded with skulls and a dirt floor that crumbled into an abyss. A choir of children sang from the bottom of the pit amid flickers of lightning and the sullen glare of lava beds.

> > >

The next dawn, after milking Ms. Petals, I trudged into the deeper forest. This day I didn't venture forth to gather kindling wood or to forage for our supper. I carried the boar spear at my side and glanced neither left nor right, stoic as a prison guard, or mayhap a prisoner marching for the scaffold.

The spitting image of Sir Gregory Peck slipped from a patch of shadows, agile as an eel.

Despite his startling entrance, this was scarcely a surprise. I'd previously encountered him the day after Mom and Dad departed the homestead. However, the beloved actor had died in a carriage accident several years before my birth and this semblance, or affectation, filled me with dread. Which was doubtless his aim.

He meant to suggest his power over life and death, the ability to subtly distort laws of physics that lowly men presumed to be immutable.

Thus, upon our prior meeting, I'd immediately dubbed him Not-Peck, whilst nodding and behaving agreeably, rest assured. He'd claimed admiration for Mom and Dad as artists, albeit he lamented their dismal lack of parental instincts. Not-Peck was dead-on, but at least my parents hadn't raised a fool.

When mommies and daddies are desperately unhappy, we come to them, he'd said. *They've thrown you lambs to the wolves. All is not lost. You I may be able to save . . .* Upon concluding that conversation, he'd presented me with *Ardor of the Damned* and an admonishment to handle the reels with care. Beyond its dangerous hypnagogic properties, *Ardor* was virtually extinct. Two copies had survived the inquisitorial purges of outraged critics—this and K. M. Wanatabe's personal cut. Not-Peck referred to the film as the catalyst of an alchemical process that might transform the minds and bodies of young viewers to something . . . palatable.

Today, the "actor" wore a silk shirt and breeches beneath a fine wolf pelt cloak. He appeared in the guise of himself during middle age when he'd chewed scenery in *The Dark Omen* and *Cape Terror*. Black hair grayed at the crown and temples; square of jaw and broad through the shoulders. A priest or a sinner; a hero or a villain, as the script required.

"Hi, kid. Where are you going with that spear?" Not-Peck rested his hands on his hips and looked me over. His rich, sonorous speaking voice lagged ever so slightly behind the movement of his lips.

"About our arrangement . . . ," I said.

"A deal is a deal, son. We spit on our palms and everything."

"We did—"

"All you must do is leave the door unbarred tonight and take a powder. Why are you glancing around like a yokel? Your parents can't bail you out. Halfway to a sunny beach in the East Indies by now, I'd wager."

The legends were explicit—demons and devils spoke with forked tongues. Contrarily, when it came to unholy pacts, they were bound by unassailable tradition to cleave to the exact letter of the law. This creature desired the blood of my blood and required my consent to swoop upon his (its?) prey. Surely, I could gain leverage if I knew where to pry.

"How can I be certain?" I said.

"Trust me, lad, you're in the lurch," he said. "Go into your mother's trunk. She doubtless removed a keepsake. Her favorite dress, a flattering hat. Items none of you would miss before it was too late."

To my chagrin, Not-Peck's doppelgänger had it right. I'd already tossed the chest and discovered that Mom absconded with two dresses and matching hats. A pretty fantasy suggested itself—my parents hadn't run away. No, they'd merely paint the town red, she, dressed to kill, on his arm the way they'd done it up ages ago. Soon, they'd be stumbling home with a handful of coppers and a bag of beans, hungover from a detour into fabulous extravagance and extravagant sentimentality.

And yet, and yet . . .

"Mom and Dad made a bargain with you," I said to taste the betrayal, to weigh its merit. "A bargain to leave their children alone in the wilderness."

"Bargain, pact, call it what you will. Your parents agreed to abdicate their familial obligations. The rest is on your shoulders. In your father's absence, you are the man of the house."

"You didn't say why they made their bargain."

"Didn't I?"

"Fortune? Fame?"

"Door Number Three," Not-Peck said.

"To escape." I reconsidered. "Freedom."

"A stripling youth, yet wise as pharaoh. You've read the fairy tales, yes? Blueprints of a murderous truth. Oafish fathers, wicked stepmothers, unwanted kiddies—"

"She's our real mother. I know that much."

"She's a woman with thwarted ambitions. Starring in a propaganda film mocking the king tends to be a career impediment. A warren of mewling brats is the icing on that dung cake. People love to fuck; they aren't always sanguine regarding the consequences. Nine is a hell of a litter."

Nine? Oh, our cozy abode could've been even cozier. Two more babes were stillborn and toddling Elmer was bitten by a tick and succumbed to fever. I'd overheard a whispered conversation with Dad; she'd enlisted the aid of an apothecary's various herbs and elixirs to no avail—the babies kept on arriving sure as the seasons. Who needed a melodramatic affliction such as lycanthropy or vampirism? Fecundity was my parents' curse.

He plucked a flower from the brambles, meticulously shredded the petals, and extended his tongue to lick the thorns until his flesh abraded. He didn't bleed.

"I'm fresh out of vitreous humor," he said upon noting my morbidly attentive expression. "We are lacking the other kinds of humors, too. That's what I've been trying to explain. Your brothers and sisters can help us with that."

"We" and "us" cued the arrival of a man and woman who emerged from the undergrowth with nary a rustle. These worthies bore the likenesses of supporting actors I'd often seen, yet couldn't name. Lord X and Lady Y.

"Meet the fellow members of my, ah, troupe," Not-Peck said.

"Why does he come to us armed?" Lady Y said. She wore a ballroom gown cut so low I might've blushed had the greediness of her gaze and the dullness of her bared teeth not taken me aback.

"Frightful pointy spear you have there," Lord X said. Decked in a fancy suit, he, too, seemed tarnished beneath the finery and powder. Eager, the pair of them. Very eager.

"Easy, comrades, no reason to excite a delicate moment," Not-Peck said. "The young master and I were discussing his future." He sidled closer and rested his limp, heavy hand upon my shoulder. The breeze hissing among the leaves sounded the same as his sigh. "Last night, I knocked to remind you of our pact. Did you play the film? Did you expose their sweet, innocent consciousnesses to unalloyed horror?"

"Was there a choice?"

"Was there a choice, it asks. The path most certainly forked. You merrily skipped down the left-hand trail and here we stand, albeit your feet are cold. Again, I say, cold footed or not, uphold your end of the bargain and leave the door unbarred tonight."

"Else one lonely day here in the desolate wood, we'll exact our vengeance," Lord X said, and Lady Y tittered, happy with either outcome, judging by her grin.

The air darkened as the forest canopy shivered and blocked the wan sunbeams. He became one of the silhouette characters from *Ardor of the Damned*; his eyes shone crimson.

I nodded and glanced away to hide my emotion.

"Now, that's better." His voice softened into cajoling mockery. "Tell us, compliant lad, did our little critics enjoy cruel Wanatabe's finest effort?"

What had the actor said? *When mommies and daddies are desperately unhappy, we come to them.*

Predators come running when they scent helpless babes in the wood. As frigid reality seeped into my bones, I doubted that even these sly gremlins who flitted in the shadowy niches of the frontier could rectify grim fate. Mom and Dad were permanently excommunicated from the ranks of privilege and adoration. If fairy tales had taught me anything, it was that the blackest-hearted wish granters possessed limits . . . and that wishes generally had a nasty catch.

The canopy shifted again and the sun poured its light through a notch above us. Sunlight is the natural enemy of that which slithers in the dark. No silver, holy water, or eldritch steel proved necessary. Since primordial times, men have successfully massacred every furred, scaled, and feathered creature that walked or crawled across the earth, and we did it with nothing more than a sharpened stick. That morning in the woods was no exception.

"On second thought, I bet you're a big, fat liar, Sir Gregory."

Some heroes succeed by dint of cunning and treachery. Dad had taught me to deal with problems the old-fashioned way—run like hell or resort to violence. I jabbed the spear into Not-Peck's breast just the way I'd practiced a thousand times on hay bales. He leaped backward off the spearhead, spun on his heel, and pitched headfirst into the bushes. Some vital portion of him ejected with a flatulent gush and left behind a wrinkled, empty sack not unlike the shed chrysalis of an overlarge insect. The skin smoked where sunlight touched it, and evaporated.

Lord X and Lady Y observed this turn of events with smirking distaste rather than alarm. Neither offered resistance to my shrieking onslaught; they stepped into the underbrush and vanished. As I ran pell-mell for home, the troupe's laughter followed me through the trees in the screams of the jays.

So close! So close!

> > >

"Vlad?" Constantine glanced up from making mud pies as I stumbled into the clearing where our cottage hunkered. She took scant notice of my disheveled appearance. In fairness, dirt, twigs, and dead leaves were common embellishments of my work attire. I patted her head. The rest of my siblings were scattered around the yard, tormenting the chickens and one another. Their shouts of joy and malice were subdued. The resiliency of children allowed them to shuffle their nightmares to the bottom of the deck and proceed with their trivial endeavors.

Lazy Eye Larry and Doug gave me reproachful looks as I strode into the cottage. Therein, I fetched a jug of wine from the cabinet (among Dad's few luxuries), slumped at the table, and started drinking with earnestness.

Afternoon slid sideways into evening. Flynn, old soul that he was, took over my duties and bade the others to leave me in peace. Under his instruction, they battened down the hatches, served themselves lukewarm gruel, and eventually tucked in for sleep on the heels of a long, tedious day.

Eventually I resurfaced from my sojourn in the arms of wine-soaked oblivion. As the children tossed upon their mats, I burned *Ardor of the Damned* in the hearth, poking the reels until they crumbled to coals, then ashes. I regretted this course of action and could not fathom why. I imagined souls were released as the loops of film charred, rising with the smoke that disappeared up the chimney. This didn't help. My skull felt enormous and full of a howling void. A primitive part of me wanted to replay the film, to savor the dread, to luxuriate in its wanton cruelty, to gorge upon nihilism.

Oh, you've done it now, Not-Peck said, a dancing shadow thrown by the flames.

I spent the remainder of the night in Dad's favorite chair,

watching the door and waiting for a knock that didn't come. Sleep overtook me and in nightmares the disembodied heads of Not-Peck and his cohorts floated in a void, jeering my callow impetuousness.

> > >

Mom and Dad arrived on the sixth morning while the rest of us were barely roused for breakfast and chores. She could sing like an angel, our mother. Her voice echoed along the winding trail and into our meadow. I peered out the window and witnessed Dad sweep her into his arms for a brief song-and-dance number. Both of them were restored to carefree youth, especially Mom. Radiant and free. *Free*. Dan the mule followed in dumb bemusement.

The kids scurried to meet them. Our parents froze momentarily. Their jaws hung slack enough to draw flies. Then it was hugs and kisses (gruff ones in Dad's case) all around, and later, pancakes with honest-to-goodness maple syrup. The children celebrated their windfall of food and cheer because such occasions were fleeting.

Inevitably, Dad noticed I'd drunk his wine (he upended the empty jug while frowning ominously). Worse, he detected my fiddling with the projector. I'd striven to replace everything precisely as he'd left it. A fool's game. He roared with furious indignation, caressing the machine with the tenderness some men show a prize hunting dog, or the love of their life. He glared at me with the promise of an imminent thrashing. Theodora and Salamanca cried, hoping to soften his heart. Marlon offered to fetch a whipping stick (a big one!), and Flynn muttered that he knew this would happen, we should've stuck with the magick lanthorn, et cetera. Mom shook her head once and Dad swallowed whatever curse he'd intended to utter and stormed outside to chop firewood. Chopping firewood served as his go-to stress reliever besides batting me like a wicket ball.

Mom smiled wanly and kissed my cheek. Her lips were cool. Age and melancholy had descended upon her. Other than that, our household was a temporary bastion of love and light. There was even semi-fresh fruit and a chunk of beef from the market to reinforce the usual roots and tubers for supper. Truly, the horn of plenty overflowed.

Dad, despite professing road weariness, rolled out the projector and played *The Old Woman in the Hobnail Boot*, a grim comedy satirizing the famine of 1320 and the plight of harried moms with far too many mouths to feed. Work camps, brothels, and academies of experimental medicine were apparently ready, willing, and able to deal with surplus offspring. Beneath the comedic veneer, it dealt with similar themes as *Ardor of the Damned*, except without laying man's cruelty to man at the foot of monsters or generational curses.

Was it a coincidence that Dad selected a scathing commentary on poverty and the burdens of large families the first night back from a venture to the bright lights of town? Was it, on the other hand, a (rather sharp) message?

We retired to bed. I lay awake, fretting.

Then I dreamed that far below the cottage foundation, far below the rocks and farthest-slithering roots of the entire forest, abominations congregated in a pitchy cavern, black save for a bloom of aqueous light on a dank wall. *Ardor of the Damned* played on and on to gibbering applause. My family knelt in manacles at the fore of the assembly, shrieking and laughing. A vast, half-glimpsed monstrosity coiled among the stalactites. Its slavering maw dripped glaucous slime upon them and befouled their tortured countenances. Flesh deliquesced and bone blackened, yet they harmonized in agony.

Voices woke me. I pretended to snore and observed Mom and Dad in repose. They whispered, and by some trick of the hearth embers, their eyes shone in the gloom. Dad spoke my name. I kept on with the fake snoring. Soon, the fire died and so did their secretive conversation.

I crept away before dawn with a knapsack of food and the boar spear.

A decent man would've snatched one of his smaller siblings, taken the hapless child out of the black forest and given him or her a chance at a life. My flight was over and through inhospitable terrain. It deviated from the well-trod paths Dad would follow, were he to give chase—and were he to come after me, bent on fulfilling his pledge to the demons of the wood, or from pure spite, a kid on my back wasn't a handicap I was willing to accept.

> > >

Years passed. I sought my fortune as a remarkably well-read soldier (later, a mercenary freebooter) and so doing, endured violence, privation, and suffering for coppers on the pound. How convenient that my childhood indemnified me against such petty travails! Incidentally, I aver from experience that maidens dig scars.

My moods were strange, alas. These moods, and a murderous temper, tended to isolate me from gentler folk. I spent many nights alone, huddled near a campfire and complaining to the shadows that plagued me in ever greater numbers. When I finally yielded to sleep, my dreams manifested as dreadful, animated visions of my abandoned family in dire extremis. Frequently, the baron and his lady beckoned my astral self with knowing smiles. These visions compelled me to circle back to the homestead as a dog will to its own vomit.

I returned on a bright spring day to find the cottage in ruins. Fire and time had reduced the structure (and that of the shed) to charred timbers and soot-caked stones. Wildflowers sprang from the ashen soil. An eagle nested in a dead tree nearby. The bird glared and cried for its mate, disturbed by my presence. In trudging the edges of the property, I stumbled across a long, barren depression in the earth; a shallow trench lined with the intact skeletons of eight children and two adults. Wind had scoured the soil and planed it so the bones were partially exposed.

The grave confused my sense of time and objective reality.

During my travels, I swore I'd glimpsed several of the kids fully grown. At those crucial moments, I quickly turned and fled, lest our gazes meet and they recognize the elder brother who'd deserted them. And if I'd deftly avoided Salamanca and Marlon one enchanted evening during the Fire Festival, or ducked aside in the nick of time as Lazy Eye Larry (his large, boisterous family in tow) lumbered along the lane of a village at the edge of this benighted wood not two winters gone, how could all eight of their fragile, moldering skeletons be entombed here? The worst part was that years of drink and anguish had taken a savage toll upon my mind. I could not, no matter how much I racked my conscience, remember if it had been me who'd committed this massacre.

I lay among them under the stars. Fluffy and Atticus kissed my face and I sat bolt upright in the gray dawn, and it was raining.

> > >

Tormented by relentless nightmares, I went hunting for K. M. Wanatabe. Although it stood to reason he'd long since perished at the hands of his detractors, if not old age, I proceeded, bolstered by faith in the adages that the devil protects his own and only the good die young.

The Fates were kind—the filmmaker proved elusive rather than dead.

This land may seem endless, but there are only so many hiding places that aren't under a rock or in the hollow of a rotten tree. Assuming one is infinitely patient, and also willing to employ red-hot pincers to the tender bits of less-than-forthcoming witnesses, one will usually succeed in running quarry to earth.

Intelligence provided by a minor actor who'd starred in several of Wanatabe's films, and a cousin who'd shared Wanatabe's confidence once upon a time, brought me at last to a stinking, muddy city on the edge of the sea. I took residence at a sty passing for an inn and curled into myself, like a spider drawing down tight, to watch and wait.

Wanatabe dwelt in a hovel at the end of an alley and received no visitors. He frequented bathhouses and a decrepit theater that hosted third-rate stage productions and obscure, unpopular films. Those who knew him were apparently ignorant of his past, nor would they have likely cared. He was just another toothless, spindly senior citizen who'd outlived family, friends, and usefulness.

Late one night, the ancient filmmaker (practically mummified) blinked awake in his narrow bed. He focused on me. I patiently crouched, my spear point hovering a gnat's hair from his eyeball. Mummy or not, his brain remained agile; he took in the situation expeditiously.

"My coin purse hangs from the back of yon chair. There is nothing else of value." The latter was not entirely true.

"Mr. K. M. Wanatabe?" My spear point didn't waver. "The Mr. K. M. Wanatabe?"

"It warms my heart that someone cares." His lip twitched with a trace of reflexive conceit. No artist wants to be forgotten, not even an artist who's gone to pains to ensure that very outcome.

"Why did you unleash *Ardor* upon the world?" I said.

"Bitterness," he said without hesitation. "Youth is wasted on the young, and so on."

"Some say the devil wrote the script."

The ubiquitous "they" had many theories about the occult provenance of *Ardor*. The emulsion formula contained the blood of innocents. Phantoms are trapped within the frames. The spirits call, they beckon, they hypnotize, they implant nightmares and visions. The most passionate conspiracists posited that Wanatabe was no filmmaker, but rather a black magician in league with the Great Dark.

"Did the Church send you?" He spoke carefully, soothingly, as one might to a rabid animal. "Trust me, superstitious drivel notwithstanding, it's merely a film. I'll confess to artistic wizardry. No black magic was necessary, however."

He studied my face, searching for a clue to my identity. I saved him the suspense and explained in brief, concise detail.

"Oh!" The old vulture actually cracked a smile. "Your mother was a beautiful woman," he said right before I drove the spear through his eye and deep into the headboard. His body trembled as he feebly pawed at the haft.

I left him pinned there as I ransacked his chamber. Locked away in a cheap armoire, tucked under soiled linen, lay the sole existing copy of *Ardor of the Damned*. I cradled the reels to my breast. Tears of joy (it shames me to say) streamed down my cheeks. Reunited, at last!

Behind me, Wanatabe wheezed and choked and proceeded to mutter his life story, which, of course, began with the recounting of a terrible childhood.

SNUFF IN SIX SCENES

Richard Kadrey

Scene 1

FADE IN

We see a basement or a room in a warehouse. The walls are old, scarred metal. The floor is concrete. Fluorescent lights illuminate the space in a greenish glow. There are two chairs and a metal meat hook hanging by a chain from the ceiling. The walls, floor, and edges of the room are covered in transparent plastic held neatly in place by identical segments of gray duct tape. A rolling table stands nearby. It's piled high with tools: hammers, carpet knives, saws of various kinds.

A man in white Tyvek coveralls, a hood, gloves, and booties is in the foreground, making adjustments to the white balance on the camera. We look straight into his face through the lens. He is middle-aged, with fine crow's-feet around his eyes. In the background is a young-looking woman. She has a blond Mohawk and is dressed in boots, shorts, and a torn EAT THE RICH T-shirt. The young woman rubs her arms as if she's cold.

Finally, the white-suited man nods and steps away from the camera. He turns to the young woman. "Say something so I can see if the audio levels are right."

"What should I say?"

"Why don't you start by saying why you're here today?"

She nods and looks down at her boots. "I'm Jenny . . ."

"Careful. No last names."

"Right. Hi. I'm Jenny. I'm here today to get murdered by Ward over there." She holds her hands out to the side, like a model on a game show indicating a prize. "Is that all right?"

The man looks at something off-screen. "It's perfect. The levels all look good."

"Now you introduce yourself?"

"Indeed I do." Ward beams into the camera. "I'm Ward. No last names, like I said earlier. And I'm here today to murder Jenny. It's important you know that what we're doing is entirely consensual. Isn't that right?"

Jenny purses her lips, uncomfortable. "It's true. I volunteered to let him kill me."

Ward looks at her. "Should we talk about how we met?"

Jenny shrugs. "It's your movie."

"That's true. Okay. Jenny and I met through an online app called—"

"Maybe you shouldn't say the name. You might lose your membership."

"Good idea." Ward stands next to Jenny with a hand on her shoulder. She rubs her arms again, trying to warm them. "Let me just say that I recently became aware of a certain phone app—not unlike Tinder—on which people with exotic needs and desires can meet. In my case, I wanted to kill someone. In Jenny's case, she wanted to die."

She holds up a finger and says, "For a price. I'm not dumb."

"And a pretty price, too. Fifty thousand dollars. Who's that money going to, by the way?"

"My mom. She's kind of an asshole, but she's sick and Dad left. Fifty grand will help a lot."

"That's sweet of you."

"Thanks."

Ward thinks for a moment. "Is there anything else we should say?"

"Um," Jenny says as she ponders this. "I know. I was wondering why we're doing this today and not, say, last week or next? You were very specific about the time."

"Right. I almost forgot," said Ward. He walks to the tool table and picks up a long steel cylinder with two prongs on the end. When he presses a button, there's an electric buzzing sound. "I kill people every ten years. It's kind of my thing. But this year is special. I just turned fifty. It's why I'm recording this session. I figured that I needed to get in one more big kill before I'm too old for this stuff anymore."

Smiling, Jenny says, "I'm your midlife crisis."

Ward laughs. "Exactly. It was get a Corvette or kill you."

Jenny laughs, too, and says, "That's funny. You're funny."

"Thank you. Anyway, I think it's about time to wrap up this first chat. I'll be getting to know Jenny more throughout the session. We're going to talk about all kinds of things before I let her die."

"I have one more question," Jenny says.

"Hold it for later."

Ward jabs the metal cylinder—a cattle prod—into Jenny's side. She screams and writhes in pain.

CUT TO BLACK

> > >

Scene 2

FADE IN

Jenny is blindfolded and bound to the chair with duct tape on her wrists and ankles. She's sweating and breathing hard. Ward slaps her and she jumps in surprise. When he walks around behind her she cranes her head back and forth trying to figure out where he is.

Ward has something in his hand. When he turns we see that it's a circular saw. He puts it close to Jenny's ear and turns it on for a second. She jumps in her seat, frightened by the sound.

"Fuck!" she yells.

"Are you scared?" says Ward.

"Of course I'm scared, you bastard."

He sets the saw on the tool table and rolls the whole thing in front of Jenny so that when he takes off her blindfold, she can see what he has in store for her.

Quietly Jenny begins to cry.

Ward says, "It's a bit more than you bargained for, isn't it?"

"Yeah," she says and looks up at him. "Tell me about yourself, Ward. Please? It will help."

"Why should I help you?"

Jenny tries to wipe the tears from her eyes with her shoulder, but can't reach. "My life sucks. I bet yours is great. Tell me about it. Please?"

He picks up a curved carpet knife, drops it. "I know your life sucks, you fucking idiot." When he finds a hacksaw, Ward weighs it in his hand. "Who else would volunteer for this?"

"Don't be mean," whispers Jenny.

Ward takes a breath and lets it out. "Unlike you, I come from a good family and I've gotten pretty much everything I ever wanted. I'm a partner at work. I have a great wife and a smart, lovely daughter. A nice home, too. Even a motor boat where Carla and I go fishing on weekends at the lake. Carla is my daughter."

Jenny opens her mouth, then closes it.

"Go ahead. Say what you want," says Ward.

"It's going to sound weird."

"That's okay. You'll be dead soon, so it won't matter."

She bites her lip and in a rush of words says, "I wish I had a dad like you when I was growing up. Mine didn't give a shit about any of us. You know, he tried to fuck me once. He only stopped because Mom came home."

Ward frowns. "That's awful."

"Yeah. It was."

"Well, thank for your kind thoughts about me as a father. I tell you what. Seeing how much your life stinks and how fulfilling mine is, when I kill you, I'll do it fast."

Jenny sits up. "You promise?"

"I promise."

"You know," she says. "Your ad didn't really specify that you were going to torture me. You just wanted to kill someone."

He comes over and sets the blade of the hacksaw on Jenny's arm. "I guess I lied."

She turns and says, "Did you ever consider that maybe I lied, too? Maybe I'm a pain freak. Maybe I'm getting off on this. Would that ruin things for you?"

Ward chuckles. "I saw your face. You were scared shitless."

"That's what I mean. Maybe I get off on being scared."

"Oh yeah?" Ward moves in front of her, blocking Jenny. He tosses the saw away and grabs something else from the tool table, but we can't see what. "You get off on scared? Well, try this."

All we can see is Ward's back. Jenny screams.

CUT TO BLACK

> > >

Scene 3

FADE IN

Ward's frowning face fills the screen. The camera tilts back and forth as he shakes it. "Damn thing. I should never buy used equipment. You missed some great stuff."

He steps back. Jenny is slumped in the chair. Blood trickles from her mouth and nose. Her arms and legs are bruised. "Say it," he says. "Say how a lot of great stuff just happened. Tell the me in the future just how goddamn magnificent I am."

"You're the worst," Jenny screams. "You're a monster!"

Standing beside her, he tousles her short hair. Jenny lurches for his hand, trying to bite him. Ward stays just out of her range. Finally, he takes the circular saw off the table and walks behind Jenny, turning the saw on and off. She cringes but can't move away. Leaning over her, he whispers in her ear, "What should I cut off first, I wonder? Should we start with a leg?"

Jenny sniffs and says, "Wait! What kind of medical supplies do you have?"

A puzzled expression spreads across his face. "For you?"

"Of course," she says. "Cut off my leg and I'm going to go into shock and bleed out. Trust me. My sister-in-law is a nurse. It's not like in the movies. You hack off too much too soon, there's no more fun for you."

Ward walks around her and lowers the saw. "I hadn't thought of that."

Jenny cocks her head at him. "I thought you'd done this before."

"It was always quick. Not like this."

She leans back in the chair, a faint smile on her lips. "Holy shit. You're a virgin. You've never killed anyone."

"Yes I have," he shouts.

"Then you should have thought this through better," says Jenny. "I bet you hear that a lot at home."

Ward slaps her hard across the face. "Don't talk to me like that."

"My mom had me young and she said it screwed up her whole life. She had to settle down. Take any shitty job. No more fun for her. Did you have a kid young?"

"Well, aren't you little miss know-it-all?" Ward says. "You're not as dumb as I thought you'd be. After I've had some more fun, I'm going to cut off the top of your head and scoop out your brains."

"I love that idea," says Jenny happily. "But don't get excited and finish too quick. Do you have that problem with your wife? Finishing too quick?"

Ward balls up his fist and swings at her.

CUT TO BLACK

> > >

Scene 4

FADE IN

Jenny hangs from the overhead hook by her bound wrists. She's stripped down to her panties. Ward hits her repeatedly with a heavy flogger. Jenny screams and squirms with every blow.

Finally, Ward lowers his arm to his side. He slumps into one of the chairs, breathing hard. He flexes and rubs his flogging arm.

From the hook, the bruised and sweating Jenny says, "You okay?"

"Shut up," says Ward.

"Look, if it's any consolation, if you die down there, I don't think I can get down. I'll probably starve or freeze. Isn't that comforting? Even if you stroke out, I'll die."

Ward flexes his arm. "A little, I suppose."

"You should exercise more."

He nods, sweat on his brow. "I know. Like I said, that's why you're going to die. I'll be too old and used up before long."

Jenny wipes blood off her face onto her arm. "Don't feel bad. Lots of older people do great things. Henry Miller didn't publish *Tropic of Cancer* until he was forty-two. Ray Kroc didn't start McDonald's until he was fifty-two. Grandma Moses was seventy-seven before she started painting."

"I'm going to gag you," says Ward.

"Don't you want to hear me scream? Here. Listen." Jenny shrieks at the top of her lungs. Over and over again.

Ward clamps his hands over his ears. "Stop that!"

CUT TO BLACK

> > >

Scene 5

FADE IN

Jenny is back in the chair, but this time she isn't bound. Ward holds her in place, weakly, slapping and punching her. She laughs the whole time.

CUT TO BLACK

> > >

Scene 6

FADE IN

Ward is sitting on the chair next to Jenny. He's sweating heavily and softly crying. She has an arm around him. Gently, Jenny says, "Can I tell you a secret?"

"Sure. I guess."

"I was fibbing earlier. Remember when I said I was a pain freak?"

Ward drops his head into his hands. "Oh shit. You really were getting off the whole time?"

Jenny shakes her head. "It's worse than that."

"How could it be worse?"

"Have you ever heard of CIP?"

Ward lurches away from her. "Oh god. Is that like AIDS? Did you infect me?"

Jenny laughs. "No, stupid. CIP is congenital insensitivity to pain, aka congenital analgesia. I don't feel pain. All your so-called torture was a joke. I know it's sad, but you're a failure, Ward. A complete and total failure."

He shakes his head. "Don't say that." Ward reaches for her, but Jenny shoves him away. Exhausted, he falls back in his chair and weeps quietly.

"Remember how you were afraid of being old and useless one day?" says Jenny. "I'm afraid today is that day."

"This is so humiliating."

Jenny puts an arm around him again. "Don't take it so hard. There's still someone you can kill."

He pulls away and looks at her through narrowed eyes. "Who? Not you. The moment's over. I blew it. All the money. All the planning. Worse, it's all on video. Shit. I have to destroy it."

Ward starts to get up, but Jenny grabs his hand and pulls him to the tool table. "You don't have to go out a failure. Think about it. There's still time to go out a winner."

Jenny puts a box cutter in Ward's hand. He wraps his fingers around it and sighs. "Thank you," he says wistfully.

Slowly, his eyes on the box cutter the whole time, he walks to the camera and kneels so that his upper body fills the frame.

"My name is Edward Thomas Jensen," he says. "And I'm a winner." He puts the box cutter to his throat and slashes himself deeply from ear to ear. His body shakes as blood pours onto his white Tyvek coveralls. He gurgles and his hands claw at his throat as he chokes. Soon, Ward's eyes roll back in his head. A few seconds later, he collapses onto the concrete floor.

For a minute, all that's in the frame is the plastic-covered room. One of the chairs has fallen over. Then Jenny's face fills the screen. Her EAT THE RICH T-shirt is back on. She lowers her head, then looks up. "I have one more confession." She looks around, as if making sure no one is there to hear. Then, beaming at the camera, she says, "Hi. My real name is Samantha. And I always wanted to kill someone."

She moves out of frame. All we see is Ward on the floor, then Samantha's hand as she turns off the recorder.

CUT TO BLACK

INSANITY AMONG PENGUINS

Brian Hodge

I believe the common denominator of the universe
is not harmony, but chaos, hostility, and murder.
—WERNER HERZOG, *Grizzly Man*

IT'S THE LITTLE THINGS that can stick with you the longest . . .
the fates of small and seemingly insignificant creatures lost
beneath the vault of heaven.

If I'd seen this when I was a boy, I would've cried. To my
father's shame, I was a sensitive one growing up. *Bambi* left
scars. But the documentary isn't that old, so I just take in the
scene and feel sad in my grown-up way.

The on-screen world is all white ice and rocky ground and a
milky sky dissolving into the haze of the horizon. It's populated
by little tuxedoed characters. The documentarian has come to
Antarctica to chronicle the lives of various weirdos and misfits
who have rolled down the globe to work at the bottom of the
world, in one of the harshest environments on the planet. He's

found some avian researchers, but the camera is mainly interested in the penguins. They all have someplace to go: colony and penguin society toward the left, open water and bountiful feeding on the right. Life is good.

Except there's this one lingering in the middle. He? She? It's a he to me. We all see ourselves in the penguin.

The moment is preceded by the most absurd question in movie history: "Is there such a thing as insanity among penguins?"

This one spends awhile refusing to move. He could be contemplating his options. He could be listening to a call beyond the hearing of humans and microphones. He could already be fixing his gaze on his distant goal.

With his back turned on the life-giving sea, he eventually sets off waddling toward the mountains of the interior.

There's more disturbing footage from polar regions, but it's the implications that needle at me. The penguin's journey is certain death. Were they to catch him and bring him back, the biologist explains, he would only head for the mountains again. It sounds like the voice of experience, as if they've tried and failed. The penguins refuse to be saved.

"But why?" the documentarian asks.

Nobody asks *why* like Werner Herzog in *Encounters at the End of the World*.

Nobody else could sound more resigned to the fact that there is no answer.

> > >

Even deep into the age of Netflix and On Demand, once or twice a week I visited the Video Maven. Because it was still there, and a part of me refused to let go of what places like this once meant to me.

By now, with the name of Blockbuster a joke, synonymous with extinction, the Video Maven shouldn't have existed. You couldn't even call it the last of a dying breed, because the breed was dead already, chain stores and independents alike, their wares clogging landfills and gathering dust on the loneliest shelves of charity shops.

Lydia Appleton was its founder, owner, curator, and, for the past decade, sole employee. She stayed in business through stubbornness and an iron will to refuse to surrender. Plus she'd moved from the original location to where the rent was cheaper, holding on behind a steel door in a sheer brick wall, inside a windowless rectangular space in a renovated factory off Belmont currently rocking 25 percent occupancy. Here, there was no pedestrian or drive-by traffic for impulse stops. To come here, you had to know about the place—you had to mean to.

Outside, it had the look of someplace you weren't supposed to be. Inside, it was a time capsule, with walls of purple-painted brick and exposed pipes. It was crowded the way submarines are crowded, every cubic foot stuffed with movies and memorabilia, and just enough room to walk the rows.

I waved hello to Lydia at the front counter and made the dive. Something would call to me. Something always did, a fresh discovery in a stale wrapper. This was the magic that kept me coming back, along with just enough other nostalgia fans to keep Lydia hanging on. Those of us Of A Certain Age for whom picking out a movie meant inspecting an artifact on a shelf before it ever meant clicking a thumbnail on a screen.

I wasn't alone, which was good to see. A subsegment of the hipster crowd kept her going, too. They'd rediscovered vinyl and cassettes, so who was to say they couldn't spearhead a resurrection of VHS tapes? The Video Maven was just retro enough to lure them in to ogle the packaging on movies made before they were born, back when the special effects were cheesy and *Be kind, rewind* was our code of honor.

A pair of corporals from the man-bun-and-beard army was scrutinizing the empty DVD case for . . . I strained to see . . . *Revenge of Billy the Kid*. Nice. Deformed goat-man seeks his gory retribution. They were in the deep end of schlock, playing along in the proper spirit of it all.

You didn't come to the Video Maven for the latest plug-and-play module in the Marvel universe. No, you came for the goods Netflix would never touch. You came for vintage splatter and cyberpunk and vigilantes. You came for Italian zombies and Asian creature features. You came for *Terminator* rip-offs and *Rambo* clones.

Iron Man 3? Get the fuck out. *Tetsuo: The Iron Man*? Welcome home, brother. *The Pumaman*? Welcome, sister. You're among friends.

On a random glance up I caught Lydia, still behind the counter, staring at me with exasperation, like, when was I ever going to notice? She twitched her finger in a come-hither waggle.

We'd known each other forever, from my perspective. Back when she'd first opened the shop, Lydia was a girl geek before girl geeks were cool, out and unrepentant decades before her kind became an affront to territorial manbabies and neckbeards. At the time I was halfway through high school, and girl geeks seemed as rare as unicorns, even though late-blooming dorks like me dreamed of them just the same.

Now? Now she'd reached that stage where women with strong enough features start to get called handsome. Her hair had turned a magnificent shade of gray, still long, still lustrous, just not as poofy. Beneath a tailored thrift shop jacket, she wore a Cramps T-shirt that somehow still looked as fresh as it had twenty-five years ago.

"I could've texted," she said, "but I wasn't going to miss seeing the look on your face."

At the moment, the look on my face had to have been wholly blank.

"Your white whale? I have it on good authority . . . it's not a myth."

"I've had lots of white whales. Which one are we talking about?"

She pause-blinked, summoning patience to deal with the slow kid. "Come on, Troy. There are all the others, and there's this one," she said. "*Todestriebe*. It really does exist after all. Wanna be my date?"

> > >

Wait a minute. How old are you? Experience matters.

If you grew up with the Internet, every musical and cinematic desire just a few clicks away, then you have no working concept of how things used to be. Today, if you have an itch for the latest lo-fi obscurity by some band of misanthropes recording in an Oslo basement, or a prerelease peek at the new superhero epic, or the dregs of adult-baby-diaper porn, it's yours for the taking. You stream it. You pirate it. You order it. You lack for nothing, you spoiled brat.

And you love it that way. I love it that way.

At the same time, there's a primal hunter-gatherer inside me, fresh off the savannas, who still hungers for the thrill of the hunt. There's an entire content-satiated demographic of you who've never experienced this. Never ordered a rare bootleg from a cheaply printed catalog and hoped what arrived wasn't a total con job. Never known what it was like to haunt dingy labor-of-love shops, flipping through racks of new and used with a weary, wary prayer in your heart, figuring yeah, you'll probably leave disappointed . . . but just maybe, *this* will be the place where your fingers freeze and your pulse quickens and, hardly daring to believe it's finally happened, you pull out the elusive quarry that's obsessed you for months, maybe years. Vinyl. Tape. CDs and DVDs, before ripping software. Japanese laser disc. Whatever— *the old ways.*

But when it happens? My god, the triumph, a fanfare of choirs and trumpets in your head. The endorphin rush, as for a few rapturous moments time and space have folded just right, to bring you and your prize together. Snap it up quick, before the universe changes its mind.

I missed that.

I've always missed that.

But she brought it back. With her enigmatic grin, Lydia brought it avalanching back . . . and through the chaos, hostility, and murder, I thought I caught a glimpse of some divine underlying harmony.

> > >

A week later, I arranged for three days of personal time off from the courier warehouse I managed. Lydia left the Video Maven in the hands of a trusted barnacle from back when she could afford to hire employees. Responsibilities cast aside, we plunged into the kind of impulse craziness neither of us had indulged in for twenty years: flying across a continent, from Chicago to Vancouver, to see a film most people didn't believe existed.

Given the fate of brick-and-mortar outlets, no one would've blamed her if she'd opted to spend the last decade sitting on her existing video stock, eking out a living from the shrinking pool of nostalgia fans who didn't mind paying $1.99 to rent the likes of *The Evil Dead* for old times' sake. But that wasn't Lydia. She cared too much about her tribe to neglect them, or take them for granted.

Instead, she never stopped refreshing her shelves. She scoured the world for rarities and lost gems and releases that had never had North American distribution, so she could give them, like kittens, a forever home. She performed eBay searches with righteous diligence. She subscribed to collector newsletters. She had contacts at home and abroad. You want *The Terminator* in a Tamil dub, or a no-budget Nigerian rip-off of the original? She knew a guy who knew a guy who—you get the picture.

She'd never stopped putting out feelers for *Todestriebe*, the rumored lost documentary by Werner Herzog. I hadn't known this until she got a legitimate hit. As always, a guy who knows a guy. Supposedly, a print was in private hands, with rare showings that might pop up anywhere in the world. It wasn't a commercial endeavor. You couldn't buy your way in. You just had to be invited. And another was coming up. A bit of back-and-forthing with some anonymous gatekeeper, and Lydia managed it.

In the world of Willy Wonka, we would've been waving a couple of golden tickets. Instead, what we had was . . . well, I wasn't sure.

"On a scale of one to ten," I said somewhere over Minnesota, "how weird is this?"

"I'd give it a five-point-five."

"That's all?"

She stretched back in her coach-class seat and kept her voice low. "By now, I'm pretty confident the film is authentic. Nobody seems to be making money off this. And you don't bring people from all over and show them a hoax, not if you don't want a roomful of angry strangers and don't know how they'll react. So whoever is behind this is probably an obsessive collector who somehow got his paws on this amaze-balls prize. And you know what *they* can be like."

Not as well as Lydia, surely. You sit behind the counter of a shop like hers, you become a magnet for pasty-faced hoarders who can deliver enraptured monologues about their collections until your eyes glaze over.

"With some of them, the best part of having something no one else does is the chance to lord it over everybody else. It's not enough to have it . . . they need *you* to see they have it. They feed off your envy."

"So, scale of one to ten," I said. "What are the odds—"

As Lydia grinned and cut me off, I felt a flash of the old mind meld you develop with someone you've known in so many different ways, over so many years.

"Nine," she said, "that you could count the number of times this guy's been laid on one hand or less."

> > >

Antarctica again. Same film, different researcher, this one a polar biologist in a shack around the frigid waters of a diving hole blown through the sea ice. Until I saw this, I'd never considered evolution in quite such terrifying terms.

He speaks of the hideous ways to die in this deceptively tranquil aquatic world, if you were small enough. He tells of worms with mandibles designed to rend flesh. He describes becoming ensnared in the tendrils of predatory blobs, and how you would exhaust yourself as you struggled to escape, until the creature drew you in and began breaking you down into compliant, digestible bits.

It's a horrible and violent place to be, to live, to grow, your existence defined as something else's food. It is, the biologist observes, a world that developed eons earlier than human beings.

Herzog's question is as long-ranging as it gets: "Do you think that the human race and other mammals fled in panic from the oceans, and crawled on solid land to get out of this?"

He does indeed. The biologist regards this as the primary impetus for our most ancient ancestors to flee to someplace where they could evolve into larger life-forms. To leave the horrors behind, he says.

It sounds good. For a few moments, it sounds reassuring.

Until I realized the conversation didn't proceed to what seemed obvious: even if nothing was waiting for us on dry land, something would be, eventually. The principles had already been established, and life was destined to abide by them. Old predators might rejoin us on land, because they missed the taste of us and enjoyed the challenge of a new hunt. Some among us would evolve into hunters themselves, advanced and unprecedented.

The horrors would follow, their paths laid down in the light of a younger sun.

> > >

Out the plane's window, flatlands had given way to the rough and rumpled chaos of mountain peaks and alpine valleys.

I realized this was the act of an obsessed fan, but I didn't feel like one. True, I'd admired Werner Herzog's work for decades. I found him fascinating as a creative force, someone who could be a madman in service to a mission, in search of what he called "ecstatic truth." I couldn't imagine the resolve it had taken to subject himself to such endeavors as supervising a crew dragging a 320-ton steamship over a jungle-covered mountain for *Fitzcarraldo*. I couldn't fathom where he'd come up with the idea to film most of the cast of *Heart of Glass* under hypnosis.

And I could scarcely conceive of maintaining the kind of artistic partnership he'd had with Klaus Kinski, a madman of a different sort. "To see Kinski," wrote critic Roger Ebert, was "to be convinced of his ruling angers and demons." Over the course of five films, they brought out the best and worst in each other. Great art, but more than once, one had schemed to murder the other.

Eventually, though, it was Herzog the documentarian who came to fascinate me the most. I knew of no other filmmaker so intent on working both sides of the narrative divide. No other filmmaker who seemed so deeply humane, yet so dour about the universe humans inhabit. Plus I liked how much Herzog *wasn't* one of those documentarians who believed the filmmaker's presence should not intrude into the documentary. He was all over them. They couldn't have come from anyone else.

And Lydia was into almost none of it. Herzog just wasn't in her cult wheelhouse.

"Why are you doing this?" I asked her. The question had gnawed at me for days, but I'd been afraid to bring it up until now. Over the Rockies, it was too late for her to change her mind.

"I passed muster. I was invited. Lydia Appleton, plus one. You're just my tagalong."

"Seriously."

"Oh. *Seriously.* Well, that's different, then." She slid her reading glasses down her nose and looked me eye to eye. "I seriously want you to have this. It's a once-in-a-lifetime opportunity. I wouldn't be able to live with myself if I hadn't made it happen. Plus I get bragging rights too, so those *and* good karma. Win-win."

"And you're okay with being away from the store for three days?"

Lydia rolled her eyes and sank back in her seat. "Oh, good god, you don't think I need a little time off once every few years? The place cost me two husbands, you know. I don't do well with ulti-matums, but there are still mornings I walk in and look around and say to myself, 'Really? All that, for *this*?' So a break from each other does me and it some good."

Again, the ache, as I wished it could have worked out between us, when we'd given it a try one tentative time, after I, too, learned what it was like for a marriage to implode. Lydia had been empa-thetic and understanding, and knew how to make great popcorn and buy ice cream and pour shots of tequila, and for sure she had a god-tier movie collection. It could've been a rom-com from the eighties: geeky late bloomer grows up and finally gets his chance with the dream girl who was out of his league when they met, because she was nine years his senior.

By the time we took our short-lived tumble, the age gap didn't seem nearly as prominent, but the dynamic still wasn't quite right, and maybe never could be. There was no shaking free of the worry over what Lydia saw when she looked at me. She would always remember the bruises, the confessions. She would always remember how back then my dad kept insisting he was only try-ing to knock the fag out of me, and I'd thank him someday. She would always remember why I got into schlocky videos in the first place: I thought if he came through and saw I was watching something with lots of boobs, he'd leave me alone. Only it didn't work that way. The world is full of carnivores intent on devour-ing their young, and if one rationale gets invalidated, they find another.

Lydia would remember it all, along with my adolescent ado-ration and puppy-dog eyes. How could she ever look at me and respect one thing she saw?

But she was here, now, next to me, and we were over the mountains, and I couldn't think of anyplace I'd rather be. There was that. There would always be that.

"So don't worry, I'm doing this just as much for myself as for you," she said. "I feel compelled to do this. I really do. I heard the call and I answered."

> > >

Which brings us to Timothy Treadwell, maybe the most doomed figure in the history of documentaries. At some point early in his life, or along a cumulative series of points, something broke him, left him not entirely fit to exist in human society anymore. The case could be made this was a sane reaction. His unique response, not so much.

Because the man in the blond mop-top loved grizzly bears. For thirteen years he followed some call he heard, to go to Alaska to live each summer in proximity to them. He filmed the bears. He felt accepted by the bears. He scolded the bears when they acted up. While wintering back in civilization, he advocated on their behalf.

He loved grizzly bears so much he got himself and his too-trusting girlfriend eaten by one. He'd spent years fatalistically forecasting the possibility of such an end, if not that he would take Amie Huguenard with him. Or condemn one of his beloved bears to execution and a gut pile.

"We hauled away four garbage bags of people out of that bear," says the pilot who had to help with the aftermath.

In so many ways, Treadwell was a classic Herzog protagonist. That the story came with such a definitive end, a debate partner embracing a diametrically opposed view of nature, and over one hundred hours of footage already shot, must have been irresistible to the documentarian in him.

Treadwell may even have filmed his killer a few hours before the situation went bad. He definitely recorded the audio of his demise, the video camera switched on but with no time to remove the lens cap. We the viewers don't get to hear the attack, but don't have to wonder about its specifics, thanks to the coroner who accepted delivery of the garbage bags. He takes a queasily theatrical delight in recounting the details constructed from the recording and forensics.

As deaths go, these weren't quick and they weren't clean.

Treadwell spends several minutes very much alive and aware. He has time to yell for help. The man who, for years, was at peace with the idea of ending up as bear shit changes his mind, now that the moment has come and it's no longer theoretical. Who wouldn't? Spending a while with your head being gnawed on would realign anyone's priorities. But by then you've already made all the decisions necessary to put your head in the jaws.

"What haunts me is that in all the faces of all the bears that Treadwell ever filmed, I discover no kinship, no understanding, no mercy. I see only the overwhelming indifference of nature," Herzog says in voice-over, while the likely perpetrator lifts his ursine muzzle, time for his close-up. "To me, there is no such thing as a secret world of the bears. And this blank stare speaks only of a half-bored interest in food."

> > >

After touchdown at Vancouver International it was low-grade cloak-and-dagger stuff, as though we were playing a spy game for middle-aged adults who needed more excitement in their lives but didn't want to put their necks on the line to get it. Lydia had already sent the showing's organizer our flight data, and now she texted to inform him of our arrival.

We'd been given three lodging options: low-budget, midrange, and luxury hotel, and went with the cheapest, just like our Kia rental car, because that's life. I'd stayed in worse motels, but the place still smelled of cleaners and musty carpets. We would be here only two nights. Until tomorrow: sit tight, enjoy the city, await further instructions.

If the Chicago we'd left behind was all lake-frozen winds, Vancouver was wet springtime chill, with swirls of rain drizzling from banks of black clouds that scraped over the coast with the ponderous density of tectonic plates. When we woke the next morning, Lydia yanked open the curtains and it was more of the same.

After a time, she seemed to be peering out the window too intently.

"What are you looking for?"

"Cameras," she said. "Wouldn't it be just what we deserve if this whole thing was a setup and *we* were the subject of the documentary?"

Deserve? Ouch. "That would be . . . cruel."

"Haven't you been paying attention, Troy? The Theater of Cruelty moved over to cameras a long time ago." She gave the wet asphalt world outside our window a final inspection, then turned her back on it. "Find some pants, we need coffee."

The whole day was like this—waiting, watching, not entirely sure for what. We'd flown 1,800 miles to sit around anticipating texts. This was who we were, really—small people with small lives letting someone else dictate our next move—and I hated the feel of it. We may have been on one of the most exclusive guest lists in the world tonight, but nothing about it felt privileged. We were still being operated by remote control.

While passing the time, Lydia and I debated which of us had believed less in the film's reality. We both, for different reasons, always loved the idea that a lost Herzog documentary could be out there. But the biggest challenge to our faith wasn't that the man himself disavowed *Todestriebe*'s existence. It was because such a thing no longer seemed possible.

Once, maybe, but not now.

Todestriebe had come along much too late to be another *The Day the Clown Cried*, whose few prints had been locked away since 1972, after Jerry Lewis reconsidered why he'd ever thought it was a good idea for the world to see him as a circus clown leading Jewish children into Hitler's gas chambers.

I'd only been hearing rumors of Herzog's lost documentary for the past ten or twelve years. Digital age, easily. If the thing had gotten sufficiently far along in editing and postproduction to be considered complete enough to be lost at all, then it should've leaked. It should have been available on pirate sites and through BitTorrent clients.

Can't trust anybody these days. That's what the system counts on now.

> > >

The final text came late in the afternoon, informing us showtime was in ninety minutes, with a link to a live map. Until now, we hadn't had a clue where this was being held. By the look of it, a fair drive to the east—suburbs, or maybe beyond, where suburbs gave way to the old coastal forests. We merged with a rain-smeared red river of taillights on the other side of the glass.

"We've come full circle, you and me," I said.

"I don't think I follow."

"You helped me bag my very first white whale. Remember?"

Lydia groped to recall it but finally shook her head no. "It had to be a lot of years ago. And there have been a lot of whales."

"Nine Inch Nails. The *Broken* video."

She groaned. "I probably shouldn't have done that. I wouldn't, if I'd known."

I was a kid back then, defenseless at home and with the bruises to prove it. For a time, when they were new to the world, Nine Inch Nails spoke to me like nothing else, giving voice to all the fear and loathing I couldn't articulate.

Apparently front man, everything man, Trent Reznor had a few things to work through, too. More success than he'd wanted. Accusations of being a sellout, a poseur. Record company woes. Too much, too soon. So he recorded an EP, *Broken*, the angriest, ugliest thing he could conjure. It wasn't enough. He made videos. It still wasn't enough. The project needed something more. A framing device for the videos, maybe. So he hired a fellow musician and filmmaker to conceptualize and shoot it.

Then they stepped back and took a hard look at what they had: a twenty-minute snuff film. Grainy footage of a guy luring another guy off the street, then torturing him to death while forcing him to watch the videos.

The surprise consensus: *Maybe we shouldn't release this after all.* Jerry Lewis, all over again. *What have I made?*

So they set it aside, never to be seen, except for a few videotape copies Reznor dubbed for friends. Which was how it escaped into the wild. Can't trust anybody, remember? It was viral video, analog style, years before YouTube, until it landed on the bootleg black market. No context, just this *thing* . . . this raw, screaming, misbegotten thing.

In no time, people came to believe it was real. Every generation of copies downstream from the originals became that much grainier, more degraded, more authentic-looking. It was found footage before there was such a genre. You were never supposed to see this.

I had to, of course. Thirty bucks was a lot of money to a high school kid in the nineties. But totally worth it, because for a few weeks, I was the fucking man. I was the one with the unicorn, and the power to decide if you were worthy of seeing it.

So I thought I had a solid understanding of the kind of person we'd find at the end of this trip, while Lydia was still mulling over our early history. *I probably shouldn't have done that.*

I'm glad she did, but what I never told her, and never would: that shit does damage. Back then, it wasn't make-believe splatter. It was the real thing. There were kids I showed it to who on the surface were all enthusiasm—awesome, coolest thing they'd ever seen—then they didn't sleep well for days, weeks. They turned jumpy, fearful they could be snatched off the street. Because it happened, they'd seen proof. They were so much closer to imagining what they looked like on the inside, and how their heads would look on a refrigerator shelf.

"Contributing to your delinquency even then," Lydia said, seemingly joking, but she didn't sound pleased with herself.

> > >

The map led us over civilization's ragged rim, to the edge of the Northwest's boreal forests. Evening came on all at once, the sky's last light choked out by old growth pines and cypress lining the roads like shaggy towers.

Our route ended at a turnoff onto a long, wood-chipped drive that led to a house invisible from the road. Cedar and glass and stone, the estate had the look of a weekend getaway that was hardly ever used, bought because it was a good investment and the owner had to put his seven-figure salary somewhere.

We improvised a parking place on a semicircular asphalt pad along with eight other vehicles. Around us, the trees dripped heavy with rain. At the door, a couple of burly guys in suits screened our admittance by inspecting the data trail on our phones, then confiscated them and did a pat down to make sure we weren't bringing in anything else we could use to pirate the showing. Can't trust anybody, right.

Under a dimming skylight, we milled about the atrium with a dozen other guests and counting, as more continued to arrive. One pair had flown in from Japan. Two others had crossed Canada entirely, coming from eastern Quebec. We were free to help ourselves from a self-serve bar and snack platters set up on a narrow table topped with green glass. I wanted bourbon but stuck with sparkling water, doing a double take at the bottle. Penguin Ice—really? What, somebody's idea of a morbid joke?

When everyone had arrived, the security duo led us through a house unable to decide whether it was a hunting lodge or a five-star hotel. Behind a pair of double doors waited a theater in miniature, with five rows of six plush seats. I would've been happy to see *Todestriebe* crowded around a laptop monitor, but the screen took up an entire wall, with speakers for seven-channel surround.

Lydia tipped her head against mine, her torrent of gray hair brushing my cheek. "This is what I need. Expand into the space next door and host movie nights," she said flatly. "That'll save the business for sure."

"Put me down for season tickets."

She snorted. "Dream on. I couldn't afford to build a jerk-off booth in a smut shop."

Once we were seated, a man I hadn't noticed with us outside took his place between the seats and the screen. Casual dress, but he fought the springtime chill with a pullover sweater that reeked of a staggering price tag. He was well into his middle years, and maybe older than he looked, with the kind of rejuvenated skin stem cell treatments could buy.

"Thank you for coming," he said, and opened his arms in welcome. "Thank you for answering the call."

Intriguing way to put it. Already he wasn't quite what I was expecting.

He introduced himself as Tobias Woodbury, and assured us he didn't expect anyone to recognize it now, or remember it in the future. Captain of industry? Media mogul? Third-generation wealth? Did it matter?

He took a self-conscious glance around. "I know how this is going to sound here . . . but after enough time, money ceases to be anything other than the most superficial way of keeping a meaningless score."

I felt Lydia squirm beside me, her bullshit detector on high alert, maybe hearing *It's a Wonderful Life*'s George Bailey: "Comes in pretty handy down here, bub."

We had a quote for everything. I wondered how many of our thoughts were embeds left by generations of screenwriters.

Woodbury went on. "These last years of my life have been devoted to coming to terms with this. There should still be things that can't be bought for any price. There should be thresholds accessible to only those who are open to finding their own way across them. It's a self-selecting, self-anointing, group . . . and you're here.

"Like most of you, probably, I first heard of *Todestriebe* years ago. Like many of you may have reacted, the more I tried to learn, the less I believed it was anything but a baseless rumor."

Murmurs of agreement rippled through the two dozen of us in his audience.

"Now that I've seen it—tonight will be the seventy-third time—I have come to believe it is a film entirely unlike any other in existence. It's a film that insisted on being made. Although it carries familiar fingerprints left by its creator, it is not truly his creation. He was simply chosen."

As Woodbury let this sink in, Lydia again squirmed beside me, a different feeling to it this time, as she leaned forward in rapt attention.

"How many times have we heard our beloved artists—painters, sculptors, authors, composers, and yes, filmmakers, too—claim a work they've finished seemed to exist already, and they were only the conduit it passed through? This has never been more true than with the film you're about to see. *Todestriebe* has always existed. Werner Herzog was merely chosen to bring it into the world. Its central figure was chosen. Its events were chosen. All by the film itself. *Todestriebe* willed itself into being as a statement of principle."

I felt another ripple through the audience, an urge to ask, *A principle of what?*, but no one wanting to be first.

"There is only one copy in existence. I'm not its owner," Woodbury said. "All I have been is its custodian for a while. And its student. The only difference between me and you is how I'm now in the fortunate position to share."

Because . . . that's what the film wanted? Just following his version of logic.

As Woodbury took his seat in the front row, to watch for the seventy-third time, the lights dimmed and a digital projector behind the back wall came to life. The screen lit up and my decade of searching arrived at its zenith.

Todestriebe.

In English, if you must, *Death Drives*. The title sounds scarier in German.

Most things do.

> > >

It opens on an endless expanse of white, stark against distant mountains, with no sign of the polar sea. A bird's-eye view, from a helicopter or drone. We've been here before. Maybe Herzog came back. Maybe he never left, and it's from the same trip.

"Is there such a thing as insanity among penguins?"

He's occasionally recycled when revisiting his past, but it's a surprise for the redux to come so soon. The link to *Encounters at the End of the World* is immediate, even before the camera drifts toward a tiny figure trudging across the most pitiless landscape on earth. The same penguin? A different penguin? It can never matter.

"I don't mean that a penguin might believe he or she is Lenin, Napoleon Bonaparte . . ." Against the soundtrack of a mournful choir, Herzog's voice is hollow, reverberant, a faraway echo from the past. "But could they just go crazy, because they've had enough of their colony?"

The penguin slows, stops. When it moves again, it shuffles erratically, as if trying to find the tenacity to continue, until there's nothing left to draw on. It topples forward into the snow and doesn't move again.

"These questions have never left me," says Herzog, now fully in the present. Or someone who sounds just like him. He's a popular one to mimic. But I want to believe. "I accept that survival is the first impulse that drives all living creatures, even those whose eyes show little more than overwhelming stupidity. But I also believe survival is capable of being overruled by a force which may be even more powerful. *Todestrieb* . . . the drive toward death."

Lydia leans in to whisper in my ear. "He sounds like the scariest grandfather imaginable. This soothing voice telling you terrible things."

Not even the brush of her lips can break me from the spell. As the camera moves in to linger and the choir blends with the Antarctic wind, it takes several moments for me to grasp what I'm seeing. I see, but don't comprehend. I can't comprehend because what I'm seeing makes no sense.

A fixed, ground-level camera captures a time-lapse view of the penguin. A carcass shouldn't decay here. The cold, dry air should create a natural mummy. Even so, over time, the penguin comes apart. It doesn't rot. It . . . dissolves, becoming as crystalline as the snow. How many passings of the midnight sun watch this happen? Unknown. Irrelevant. Time has no meaning here.

"Nothing grows in this place but despair. There is nothing for death to nourish." Herzog sounds as perplexed as he did when asking why penguins head for the interior in the first place. "And yet, even here, beneath the blankness of this ancient ice, an unsatisfied hunger seems to roar."

The penguin vanishes a granule at a time, until the view pulls back on the barren wastes. In their colossal silence, it may be my imagination that they seem temporarily sated . . . even by the fate of so small and seemingly insignificant a creature lost beneath the vault of heaven.

A title sequence comes next, more of the somber choral music he likes so much, beneath a montage of clips shot by seasoned pros and panicked amateurs.

Animals first. A pod of whales lolls beached and dying along a shoreline. A flock of birds circles overhead, then plunges to smash itself against the stone of a campus bell tower.

Now human beings enter the picture, to challenge the animal kingdom. A man leaps from a retaining wall into a zoo enclosure, taunting the nearest tiger until it takes him down. An ecstatic preacher jitter-dances at the front of his church, until he staggers after being bitten in the face by the snakes he waves in each hand.

Finally it's just us, Homo sapiens left to our own suicidal

devices. An oblivious driver on a cell phone preens at her dash-cam at the precise moment her car is T-boned and her head snaps toward the impact. A scab-pocked young woman spikes a syringe into her thigh; the abscesses in her lower leg are so deep, bone is visible. On a religious pilgrimage, thousands begin to stampede, trampling the hundreds who can't keep up.

By the time the montage ends, I'm already feeling exhausted.

Then all is quiet, except for a chorus of evening insects. The camera lingers on a man half obscured by shadows that fall over him like cage bars.

"It isn't true, what they always end up saying about me." His accent is German, his English impeccable. "But none of it is true. I never have hunted anybody. I never needed to."

From close off-screen, that unmistakable voice: "Is it possible this is because of your name, and there is no way to avoid it? Is this your destiny?"

A caption gives his name as Rolf Jaeger. Ah. I get it now. I've seen *Pacific Rim*. I know *jaeger* is German for *hunter*.

"My name, yes. Jaeger would be my name, wouldn't it? It's the little joke played on me before I even was conceived."

"Who would play such a joke on an unconceived child?"

"Who has the most to gain from me? Who can take the longest view?"

Jaeger dawdles in the shadows, waiting for an answer, but Herzog isn't biting. This early, he still thinks it's his movie. He doesn't want to say he has no idea.

Maybe Jaeger smiles. It's so hard to tell. "My maker."

"And who is it you consider your maker?"

No, he's not in a cage, even if maybe he should be. When Jaeger moves out of the shadows of the branches and into the light—my god, he looks like Klaus Kinski. Not from one angle, not in the right light, no, he really looks like the five-film collaborator Herzog was nearly driven to kill. The blond hair, the high cheekbones, the sensual mouth, the blue eyes so easily given to disdain, the air of arrogance and cruelty . . . they're all there. Whatever small differences there may be are overpowered by the rest.

How irresistible it must've been once Herzog learned of this man. A career spent searching for ecstatic truth in a universe of chaos, hostility, and murder, and one day this is what it brings him: a doppelgänger of the man he'd called his best fiend.

What else could that be but harmony?

"Who is *my* maker? Who is the maker of teeth?" Jaeger seems annoyed. "I am a sentient tooth in the jaw of the cosmos."

Backstory, yes, and not a moment too soon.

Shades of *Into the Abyss*, Herzog's documentary on crime and punishment, and the generational legacy of violence in violent families. Rolf Jaeger may be a notorious figure in Germany, but no one has heard of him here. He is, I'm not surprised to learn, a person of interest in the disappearances of thirty-seven people across Germany and Austria, Switzerland and Belgium. He's the one thing they all have in common. He's rumored to be some sort of cult figure to them.

He exists and they find him, it's as simple as that. Then some are never seen again. He doesn't bother denying it. But there are no bodies, ever. Bones, in a few cases, but bones often tell frustratingly incomplete tales. These show no tool marks to reveal how they came to be bereft of flesh.

Arrests, he's been through many of those, yielding a rogue's gallery of mug shots. Interrogations, too. They always end in his release. When pressed to explain how such a thing could be, he's scornful of simply proclaiming his innocence.

"The maker of teeth prefers to see me free," he says.

"I have heard authorities claim you draw people to you as some kind of guru, even though I myself dislike the word. Is this true, as you see it?"

Jaeger appears amused. "No. I don't like the word either. All I am is a superficial yogi."

"What does this mean, in practice?"

"It means I am stuck." Haughtiness overcomes him as he seizes the chance to lecture. "An ancient Vedic text of the Upanishads gives us five dimensions, five layers, of being. The highest of these is bliss. Then comes wisdom. Then the dimensions of mind and energy. The lowest . . . the outermost . . . is the physical. They called it the food layer." When Jaeger smiles, even his teeth are Kinski's, strong and even and white. "I am stuck, but I'm happy here. It is a happiness of purpose. This is where I belong."

Herzog is playing with fire here. He has to know it. Has to be as curious as the rest of us why Rolf Jaeger isn't behind actual bars. He has to be wondering what this man will do in front of him, perhaps even to him, because Jaeger is convinced he can do it with impunity.

We're none of us safe—that's what Herzog appears to be saying here. For each of us, it's out there: some beacon, some irresistible lure, pulling us toward it whether we realize it or not. It waits, and in its service we will choose to do things we'll regret, things we might never be able to turn away from, things that may end us entirely.

And he's as susceptible as any of us.

If it's even really him. I don't know anymore. If this universe of chaos, hostility, and murder could deliver up another Kinski, might it not manifest a second Herzog?

> > >

Years I spent, looking for this thing. Not constantly, but every so often I would resume the hunt for any newer evidence to settle its legitimacy. All that ever awaited was more frustration.

It wasn't hard to find the occasional *Todestriebe* thread on obscure film forums. Someone was always claiming to have seen it, but vague on details and defensive when pressed. Know-it-all skeptics, too, presenting their theories: "Actually, this is no more than an inept attempt at creating viral interest in an upcoming commercial project, by someone who doesn't understand viral marketing. Quite pathetic, really."

Only one post, from years ago, stuck with me. I don't know why. There were no details, no reason to give the author the benefit of the doubt. There was just something about it that felt . . . credible.

"If you ever get the chance to see it, pass. Don't. Just don't. It will take you an hour and forty-three minutes to see it, and the rest of your life trying to unsee it."

When has a warning like that ever worked?

> > >

For a thematic side trip to hell, Herzog—if this is truly his doing—folds in the sordid case of Armin Meiwes. I remember hearing about him, the Rotenberg cannibal who found, first, an online fetish forum to advertise for a well-built man who wished to be killed and eaten, and then, just such a man.

Herzog employs archival footage from a prison interview and snippets of the four-hour video Meiwes shot that long, gruesome night at his farmhouse.

"I decorated the table with nice candles," he says while seated at a different table. He looks so ordinary in his blue shirt and thinning hair. "I took out my best dinner service and fried a piece of rump steak . . . a piece from his back . . . made what I call princess potatoes and sprouts. After I prepared my meal, I ate it."

The visuals don't stay long with Meiwes himself. His voice continues over scenes from his home movie.

"The first bite was, of course, very strange. It was a feeling I can't really describe. I'd spent over forty years longing for it, dreaming about it. And now I was getting the feeling that I was actually achieving this perfect inner connection through his flesh."

I'm astonished by how much Herzog chooses to show. Some might see prurient provocation, but I don't think that's it. Maybe he was annoyed by the criticism he got for the scene in *Grizzly Man* during which he listens to Timothy Treadwell's death over headphones: *Why should he get to hear it and we don't?* There was no need—the coroner had already given a play-by-play account. The voyeurs still wanted more. They wanted to hear raw mortality.

Fine, he seems to be saying in response. You wish to see? Then look and see. See this emasculated man bleeding in a bathtub with a look of gratitude in his eyes. See his bisected carcass hanging from its ankles in a makeshift butcher shed. Seen enough yet? No? Look closer, then, see the curve of his ribs inside his gutted-out body cavity.

See, and know this is love.

All around me, people gasp and groan. That shit does damage, remember.

Who could want such a thing? It's easier to understand the cannibal—there can be no greater act of domination. But who could yearn to be on the wrong end of the knife and fork? That's his real interest here.

They're out there . . . and dear god, he finds them.

"I've always lost myself in other people," says a nervous young woman in an empty room with peeling windowsills. "It's never enough. Why not carry it all the way?"

A middle-aged man on a park bench leers into the camera, something lascivious in his gaze, as if he's filming for a dating profile. He squeezes his thigh. "I'm thick. I'm meaty. Juicy. Who wouldn't want me?"

A couple, too. The man looks smaller than the Amazonian woman to begin with, the contrast exaggerated by the way he hunches on the floor beside her wrought iron chair. He strokes the leather of her knee-high boots. She stokes his hair the way she would a favored pet.

"I want to be in her belly," he whispers. "I want to pass through her. I want to become a part of her. Then neither of us will ever have to be lonely again."

Herzog sounds surprisingly gentle: "You find the prospect of death preferable to loneliness, even though death is the only state certain to be permanent?"

The man continues to fawn at the woman's knee. Behind big, dark bug-shades, she smiles. Her voice is throaty. "Our kind of togetherness is permanent, too."

"Are you not afraid of speaking your intentions so candidly, when your own words could be used against you?"

"They could only put me on trial," she says. "They can never take him out of me."

There's no way these people could find each other without the fiber-optic cables and wireless signals wrapped around the globe. Herzog's voiceover knows this, too: "I question whether, underneath all its utility and emptiness, the Internet has become a necessary tool of self-annihilation."

Their stories unfold alongside his deeper exploration of Rolf Jaeger, and Herzog is curious to know what he makes of them. The inquiry triggers another titanic rant, withering in its contempt, that must have been familiar from the Kinski era. It's all a grotesque pathology of sex gone wrong, Jaeger shouts. He despises them—pathetic people who don't really want to die; they just want to bond with some other pathetic person and have exhausted all other options for how to go about it. They yearn to be told what to do by someone who has no boundaries left.

Such distinctions still seem little different from the devotees Jaeger draws as the film follows him between city and country-side. He exists, and they find him, yes. *But why?* He has insights. He has answers. He's accessed realms, in time and space, his admirers have no idea how to find. How can they be so certain of this? A few seem embarrassed because they have no better answer than they can just tell.

Jaeger isn't without charisma. He's sure of himself. He never shows doubt. He careens from loving to paternal to tyrannical. And he listens. He listens a lot. It's his hold on them. I bet most of these gullible people just wanted someone to listen awhile.

Yet the camera is allowed only so far. It has to remain at a distance when he meets with five of them in a tight circle beside a campfire behind a cabin on an Austrian hillside. He could be telling them anything over there. They could be promising him anything in return.

Stop, I want to yell at them. *Don't you know where this is going? Can't you see what he is?*

I know his shape-shifting type—eager to replace anything he's said before with something else that sounds better now. I know it before he proves it, when Herzog, during another campfire retreat, revisits their earlier conversation in which Jaeger called himself a superficial yogi.

"That was all wrong. What I am is a shaman, in the most uni-versal sense."

"Forgive me," Herzog says, sounding as though he's had enough and is ready to spar, "if I have noticed a consistent lack of drums this entire time."

His jab incites another tantrum. It has nothing to do with drums, Jaeger bellows. It has everything to do with the journey, one's answer to the call for initiation. The one commonality to shamans across the world's cultures, through time, is a vivid visionary experience of their own death. Torn to pieces by whirlwinds or wolves, swallowed by snakes, chewed to dirt by beetles and worms.

"You begin as useless! Your life is useless!" Jaeger shouts. "To be remade, to become something able to walk the tides between worlds, you must first be broken down."

He spins from the camera and stalks back to the fire, calling out to ask if there's one among them who is ready. When he stomps toward the camera again he's never appeared more unhinged. I am thoroughly convinced of his ruling angers and his demons.

"Do you know why I don't hesitate to do this in front of you, in front of your silly camera?" he demands. "Because no one will ever believe you."

He returns to his volunteer, whom I remember from earlier— Stefan, his name, young enough to be impressionable, old enough to know better. Drifter by choice, poet by inclination, and living in the wrong century by accident of birth. There's nothing for him in the vulgarity of the present.

The camera observes from a middle distance as Jaeger and Stefan stand facing each other. They exchange words only the observers lingering at the fireside can hear, with rapt and upturned faces. Leisurely, Jaeger unbuttons Stefan's shirt, then his own. He caresses a hand up Stefan's slat-ribbed side, then turns rough as he yanks them together. Jaeger cranes his neck and cups the back of Stefan's head.

We've been in this disoriented zone before. The camera sees too much and not enough. Maybe Jaeger understands light and shadow and silhouette as well as any cinematographer, and lets the camera see only as much as he wants it to see.

Wait. No. What . . . what are those? And where did they all come from?

I can't breathe. I've forgotten to. Is anyone here breathing? Is Lydia?

I wonder if the rest of the audience has viewed the works that have come before, so they can contextualize what we're witnessing. Have they watched the polar biologist speak with horror of what it would be like to become ensnared in the tendrils of the predator? Do they recall his description of struggling to exhaustion, of being broken down and rent to bits? Did they ever ponder how the horrors would follow us onto land, and how we would evolve into our own?

Except . . . there's no struggle here. In this squirming mass of tendrils, there is only acceptance.

There is only the *todestrieb*.

I've heard agony and I've heard ecstasy, but I can't tell what I'm hearing from Stefan now. I only know I've never heard anything like it, and hope to never hear it again, a jubilant keening that warbles and wails to a point no human voice could go without breaking, except his continues onward, upward.

He folds in half, backward, no longer able to hold himself upright—only Jaeger is keeping him standing. On his upside-down face is a wide-eyed look of transcendence and awe. Yogis spend their entire lives hoping for one peek at whatever he's seeing.

It's a lie, it's a lie, I'm screaming inside. I think of paralyzing venoms and morphine dreams. *You're only seeing what will keep you docile . . .*

But try telling him that.

As Stefan sags further, a gap opens between them, and in the hostile interplay of firelight and shadow, I catch a glimpse of the network of gnashing maws at the chaotic center of Jaeger's being.

> > >

I couldn't remember seeing the end of the movie, or if it even had one.

It was simply over, and the lights came up, and I was sitting in the midst of an audience that looked bludgeoned into submission. Crying, sick, stunned into silence . . . any response was valid. It was art. It was supposed to provoke a reaction.

Beside me, Lydia was the silent type. I moved to hold her hand and found it cold and inert. It hurt me to wonder which of us, in the future, would blame the other more for this. *You were the one who wanted to go. Yeah, but you made it possible.*

Please, now the reveal that it was all an elaborate hoax. Remember Lydia at the motel this morning, asking what if we were the subjects of a documentary? *Come on, just tell us.* I wanted to laugh at myself. To feel stupid for daring to believe any of this.

When our host, Tobias Woodbury, returned to the front of the room, he wasn't alone this time. Okay, *now* the reveal, even better with the rest of us looking at him in the flesh: this actor who'd played Rolf Jaeger to perfection, and was still so committed to the role that in his presence I was more convinced than ever of his ruling angers and demons. I was willing to concede he'd seen things beyond the veil of everyday none of the rest of us could.

"If you are here, you were meant to be here," Jaeger said. "If you watched, then you were called to see."

I could believe there was only one copy of *Todestriebe* in existence, whether Jaeger had fabricated it, stolen it, or procured it by threats.

"Some more than others tonight. You are welcome to join us out back when you are ready."

As Jaeger peered out over us with his polar-blue eyes, I wondered if this was what it was like for Timothy Treadwell at the end, face-to-face with his final bear. No kinship, no mercy, just a half-bored interest in food.

"As for the rest of you? The years are long. I exist, and you may find me yet."

And Tobias Woodbury? Only the eyes of a man who'd watched *Todestriebe* seventy-three times could look so enraptured. No one else could appear so ready.

They left together.

In time, another four followed.

Before Lydia and I could make it to the car, that keening I'd hoped to never hear again began to shred the night air, rising in pitch beyond the range of human ears.

> > >

Free to leave? Sure. We retraced our route in reverse, returning to the city and our shitty motel in a silence of fog and empty distances. What was there to say: Thanks for an interesting evening out? How about coffee and pie?

Lydia and I didn't much sleep, and couldn't feel clean no matter how long we stayed in the shower. We were stuck counting the hours to a return flight I had no idea how to disembark, because . . . what, just go home? Then what? Tomorrow is the first day of the rest of our lives, trying to unsee this thing?

That shit does damage.

Even I had no idea how much.

The irony I've always found most haunting about *Grizzly Man* was how close it came to avoiding its ending, thus never being made at all. How close Timothy Treadwell and Amie Huguenard came to going home. They'd called it a season, packed up their gear, and got as far as the airport ticket counter before deciding to return to the Alaskan bush awhile longer. As if they'd heard a call to go back.

Had Lydia seen this, and never told me? She would know I had. And trusted I would understand exactly what it meant when, after a trip to the bathroom at Vancouver International, I found her seat in our gate's waiting area empty. Or if not right away, I'd get the message eventually.

When I missed our flight, too, I couldn't say if it was because I was still waiting for her to come back. Or because I wasn't aware of when everyone else started to board. Or because I was trying to work up the courage to go after her, but couldn't get past my fear of the mess that might be waiting.

Mostly I wished I'd paid more attention to how much of herself Lydia must have seen in Stefan—alive in the wrong time, unable to see anything more ahead for her.

All I'd ever wanted was someone to watch movies with, and talk about what they meant before we went to bed. Profound ones. Silly ones. All the ones in between. It seemed so simple, so little to ask for.

So why couldn't I have reached out a hand's length farther, and accepted it?

But as I sat transfixed by the sky, by the clouds and all they concealed, the maker of teeth made it clear. That's not how this universe works. That's not how any of this works.

FROM THE BALCONY OF THE IDAWOLF ARMS

Jeffrey Ford

WILLA HATED SATURDAY NIGHTS. She had to leave the kids home alone with no babysitter. She knew they weren't old enough to be on their own, but there was no one nearby to help her. Their father was three states away and she wasn't unhappy about that. Every cent she made waitressing was apportioned before she even served the drinks and meals at Walsh's Diner. Only when the tips were great did she have enough to stow a few dollars away for an emergency. She'd never been a churchgoer growing up but now she prayed every night, primarily for the kids to stay healthy and to get to a better place and time. It had nothing to do with religion. Leaving them on their own was taking a big chance, but there wasn't any aspect of their life now that wasn't.

Landing the unexpected diner job was a godsend and with it she just managed, before the start of winter, to get out of the mothers and children shelter they'd landed in and into a crazy old apartment. It was at least warm and had a door that locked. The electricity and the water were erratic, the TV was dead, there was no shower in the bathroom, just an old tub with lion claw-feet, and the furniture smelled like a dog on a rainy day. Still, in its way, the old place was magnificent. The ceilings were ten feet or more, affording plenty of room to dream of a better future. And it was cheap—a redbrick leviathan from the early 1900s. Four stories with a tile roof. Some of the brick was chipping, a few of the windows on the bottom floor were cracked, the bannisters were splintery, but otherwise, the place looked pretty good for an old wreck. There were three-story wooden buildings on either side, both ramshackle and abandoned.

A copper plaque above the tall front door, its letters gone green, announced *The Idawolf Arms*. The real estate person told her that the owner, who lived on the top floor, a Mr. Susi, had just opened the place up for rentals and was renting only the middle two floors. The first floor was a dusty lobby from way back when the place had been a small, upscale hotel—dim lighting, sheets thrown over the furniture and front desk. It was spooky to walk through at night on the way up to the third floor. As of yet, there were no other boarders, but the owner had hopes to rent the remaining available rooms. Willa never met Mr. Susi, and the real estate woman told her he was "somewhat reclusive."

Whereas Willa hated Saturday night, the kids, Olen and Dottie, looked forward to it. With Willa not there to scold or hug, there were any number of opportunities to be bad. They weren't, though. Even Dottie, the younger at eight, knew what was at stake. They perfectly grasped the dilemma their mother was in with work and not always being able to be there; how everything in their lives balanced on a knife blade. Willa cared so much and they could feel it. They wanted for it to be always like that. So, instead of running roughshod, breaking things and eating badly, they behaved and channeled their energy into a ritual built around a miracle of chance.

At the door, before leaving, Willa knelt down in front of the kids and once again went through the list of things they were absolutely not allowed to do—leave the apartment, open the door to strangers, cook anything on the stove. They could use the microwave to heat up their dinner, spaghetti in the refrigerator from two nights earlier.

"What if it's the cops at the door?" asked Dottie.

Willa remained patient and said, "Get a chair, stand on it, and look through the peephole. If it's someone saying they are the cops and they're not dressed like cops, go and get in the bathroom and lock the door behind you."

"We'll be okay," said Dottie, sensing that even the thought of someone breaking in made her mother a nervous wreck.

Willa reached into the pocket of her blue-striped uniform and brought out a small bag of M&M's in each hand. "You can only eat these after dinner and if you're good," she said, and they all laughed at the absurdity of it. Then she slipped her coat on, kissed and hugged them, and went out the door. She waited to hear it lock behind her and then the kids listened to her footsteps on the creaky stairway heading down to the dark lobby. They bolted into the living room at the front of the apartment to look out the tall window. In the twilight they saw her heading up Rose Street, away from the dilapidated end of the city.

Olen went through the apartment and turned on all of the lights. Then he settled on the couch with the paperback he'd recently gotten at the local library used-book sale—*Watership Down*. Next to him, sitting on the floor, Dottie drew a portrait of a robot with a head like a lightning bolt, eyes, and a square mouth.

"What's that one's name?" her brother asked her. He loved the things she called her robots. There were dozens of the pictures lying around the apartment. After the drawing and the naming, there seemed nothing in it for her.

"This one is going to be Mrs. Shakes," she said, concentrating on keeping the pink crayon in the circle of the right eye. "She shakes and then electricity shoots out her ears."

"I don't see any ears on her," he said.

While looking him in the eye, she drew a *C* and a backward *C* on either side of the robot's head. She laughed and gave him the finger.

An hour later, night had fallen and the children knew they had to get moving so as not to be late for the show. Olen put the spaghetti in the microwave and Dottie poured the milk. "Cheese?" she asked, putting the milk back in the fridge.

"You mean that white stuff in the shaker?" asked Olen. "That's not really cheese. That's the shaved-off calluses of old men's feet."

"I used to eat it," said Dottie.

"What happened?"

"You."

Dinner was served. The spaghetti was partially cold, but they were so hungry they didn't even bother to put it back in the microwave. While they ate, they discussed the new school they were in. They'd been in a number of them in the two years since their father had left. "What's your teacher's name?" he asked her.

"Mrs. Beaglestretch."

"No way."

"That's her name," said Dottie. "Every day after lunch she goes in the coat closet at the back of the room and farts. We all hear her in there and everybody tries not to laugh."

"You're making that up."

She shook her head. "Who's yours?"

"Mr. Mace. The kids call him Mace Cut and Paste 'cause all he does is hand out sheets he makes on the copier that we have to fill out. He never teaches us anything, he just hands out sheets. He sits at his desk while we fill out the sheets and looks at his iPhone."

When they were finished with dinner, they scraped the plates into the kitchen garbage and set them in the sink. Sometimes they washed them and cleaned up the kitchen, but as it was, they were running a little late. By seven thirty, they were back at the front window looking down and scanning the sidewalks, watching for any movement beneath the only two streetlights in the neighborhood that still worked. "Like usual, you watch on the right and I'll watch on the left," he said.

"I always get the right," she said, disappointed.

"I always get the left. What difference does it make?"

"None, I guess," she said. A moment later she pointed quickly and said, "What's that?" But in an instant, they saw it was a kid on his bike, going in the opposite direction. Then there was a long spell of silent anticipation.

Around quarter to eight, Dottie spotted the black dog only a second before her brother did. Their mother had it from the real estate lady that the animal's name was Nox. "He'll be coming soon," Olen whispered as if the person they expected in the street could hear her. Through the glass, above the wind and the rustling of the leaves in the giant sycamore that shaded the Idawolf Arms, they could hear the high-pitched whistle that flew up from the shadowy street and caused the dog to freeze in midstep. Its master emerged out of the dark and into the glow of the streetlight in a black overcoat and black wide-brimmed hat. The ends of a long scarf were lifted behind him in the wind. Olen thought of him as a part of the night that stepped out of itself in the form of a man. Dottie thought of him only as Mr. Susi. They knew he was their upstairs neighbor. That simple name, though, had over the course of the last four Saturday nights come to inspire fear and wonder.

"Get the flashlight. I'll turn the lights out," he said. They scurried through the apartment and met at their mother's bedroom door in the dark, a thin pen light illuminating Dottie's face. Olen moved around the bed to the big window that looked out at the abandoned wooden building next door. Dottie followed. The sill for that window was a seat, with a ledge that came out four feet and a cushion on top. Olen noticed that Dottie had her blanket wrapped around her. He thought it a great idea and wished he'd gotten his, but the show was soon to start and he didn't want to miss a moment of it. She sat always on the right and he on the left, each with their back pressed against the wide frame.

"Okay," he said when they were both in place. She turned off the flashlight and there came the sound of M&M's bags being torn open. All else was silent, and from where they sat, they could hear Mr. Susi use his key on the door in the lobby. They heard him on the steps, up all three flights, and heard the door to his place open and close. A moment later, they breathed deeply and a large circle of light appeared on the side of the old building not but ten yards away. A crisp bright circumference six feet wide and high. Following the light came music filtering down through the heating duct system, "Mr. Susi's symphony music" their mother called it when she heard it whispering in the kitchen.

Olen and Dottie understood how it worked. After the first night they'd witnessed it, they were on the street the next day and happened to be in a position to see the upper story of the Idawolf Arms. On the top floor, in one of its rooms, there was a circular window, floor to ceiling. Olen explained to Dottie the effect. It all had to do with the way the room was lit. The bulb, no doubt set near the ceiling, projected whatever stood or moved in front of it as a silhouette, which appeared one story down on the worn gray wood of the building across the alley. The silhouettes came through so clearly in the circle, the detail amazingly precise. After the first few glimpses of Mr. Susi's shadow passing by, the music somehow always took over and coordinated its slow, smooth rhythms to whatever was happening in the bright circle. It was only then that he appeared in full silhouette, standing at the center of the light in a shirt with long, puffy sleeves and a high collar. His hair was a tall wave about to break. They heard, very faintly from behind the music, the whistle that called the dog to him.

A thin, pointed stick appeared in his hand and he held it up like a maestro's baton and turned slowly in circles. Dottie realized for the first time, from his profile, that Mr. Susi had a beard. Nox followed him around, carefully watching the stick as if his master was about to throw it. Somewhere the music jumped to a faster pace just as the dog jumped to his hind legs. He bounced around and Susi held the baton up high just out of the reach of the creature's jaws. When he brought the baton down to his side, the music rolled slower, and as it devolved into a lullaby, it was as if the dog had gotten used to walking on its hind legs. He strode slowly back and forth in front of his master, stepping like a dainty clothes model. Both Olen and Dottie stopped chewing M&M's as the face of Nox seemed to stretch and deform and then snap back into the silhouette of someone with long hair piled atop their head. In fact, the dog had transformed into the figure of a woman in a long dress. She opened her mouth wide and leaning toward Mr. Susi's left ear vomited a torrent of tiny butterflies that came like a raging creek and after swamping him from view swarmed upward and around the room like a murmuration of sparrows.

The music swept along in an elegant discordant waltz. Olen and Dottie had seen all this before, saw the tendrils grow from the woman's skin, saw the flowers blossom and their vines reach out for Mr. Susi, who, producing a scissor from his pocket, cut each feeler as it drew near. With every cut, agony registered in the woman's body with a jerk, a heaving of the chest and the head thrown back to utter a whimper of toads that appeared on her lips and then leaped to the floor. Mr. Susi raised the scissor like a knife and stuck it in the side of the woman's head. Smoke puffed out and as it did she shrank back into a dog with human legs and arms. The kids had no words to describe what the meaning of it was, though they'd seen the same before on other Saturday nights. An icy ball of confusion spun behind their eyes. All through the weeks the strange imagery of these movies twisted through their day and surfaced in their dreams. What came next, though, was something new.

Nox lunged, his teeth bared and snapping. Susi's arms went up in the air and the dog-man took hold of his master's throat. There was a lightning jerk of the snout and dripping blackness as if a bottle of ink had spilled everywhere. In profile you could tell that not only did Mr. Susi have a beard but that also his throat had been ripped out. It was Olen who screamed. At the sound of it, Nox's head snapped to attention, and he dropped the lifeless body of his master to the floor. He undoubtedly drew toward the circular window, his shadow form gigantic in the bright circumference. "It's looking down here," whispered Dottie. "It heard you." With those words, the light upstairs went out, the music went off, and the alley fell back into darkness.

Neither Olen nor Dottie had anything to say. Their hearts were beating so loud they wondered if Nox could hear. They moved to the bed and huddled there, numb with fear, listening for the sound of the floorboards upstairs. Instead of footsteps, they heard the *tap tap tap* of dog claws. A stillness settled in and lasted so long their immediate fears melted slightly before there came a soft knocking at the apartment door. They held each other's hands and squeezed tight. Eventually, Olen moved, dragging Dottie along. He inched cautiously to the edge of the bed. They stepped down onto the floor as softly as possible. Neither wore shoes, only socks. They left their mother's room and made for the safety of the bathroom. In their journey through the dark, they had to pass the apartment door. They heard the thing breathing heavily. In a quiet but resonating voice it called, "Children, open up."

Dottie ran ahead to the bathroom and held the door, ready to slam it shut if she had to. Olen stopped in his tracks and turned to the dog-man's voice. "What are you?" he asked.

There was a low growling sound and the answer came back: "Different . . . and hungry."

A spark of fear shot through Olen and he sprinted to the bathroom. Dottie closed the door fast and locked it. Luckily the lights were working. They got in the tub and listened. Hours passed before they heard the *tap tap tap* of the dog claws on the way back up to the fourth floor. Mr. Susi's door opened and closed and there descended a perfect stillness. It was only then that they dozed off to sleep.

They woke to the sound of their mother's voice at the door. Olen got up and unlocked it. Dottie was close behind him. They hugged her as hard as they could. Willa begged them to tell her everything. She led the way into the kitchen and they took turns as she made coffee. They told about the movies, they told about Nox and Mr. Susi. They didn't tell about that one night when Susi in silhouette appeared to be having sex with an octopus. Nobody mentioned that, or the one scene where a cat was devoured by master and dog. Otherwise they told her everything. She sat at the table with her cup and lit a cigarette. Olen and Dottie sat across from her.

"Are you sure this is real?" said Willa. "It sounds like a monster movie." She took a long drag, coughed, and a tiny yellow butterfly fell out of her mouth into her coffee.

LORDS OF THE MATINEE

Stephen Graham Jones

IT'S NOT THAT my seventy-two-year-old father-in-law is actually going deaf, it's that he's a, in my former mother-in-law's words, "lazy-ass listener." I say "former" for her because she passed three years ago, kind of right on schedule as far as I'm concerned, but my wife Sheila's still kind of torn up . . . not so much about her mom being gone, her insides chewed up, bubbling up red down her chin, as that the two of them never made up proper before she went. Which, again: nothing all that surprising, this is the way things go about 99 percent of the time between moms and daughters, as far as I can tell.

Either way, the result of all *this* is that, with his wife gone, Sheila's dad's been kind of letting their apartment go to hell. Crusty dishes tottering on every flat surface, newspapers and engineering journals stacking up into fire hazard after fire hazard, the whole place an ashtray, pretty much. So, to pick up her dead mom's slack—though it's also her two brothers' slack if you ask me—Sheila commits to cleaning her dad's place up one Sunday. I offer to help, of course, it's what you do when you're married, when you're shouldering burdens together, when it's a team effort, and then it turns out that the best way I can help out is by ushering her father out of the apartment for the afternoon.

"So what do I do with him?" I say to Sheila. We're standing before the open hatchback of her car, her mentally going through the two tubs of cleaning supplies arrayed before us. I haul one up, swing it onto my hip, and she takes the other, shuts the hatchback and beeps the lock in one efficient motion.

"He just can't be there," she says, already getting her grim attitude on for the coming mess.

I look out into the haze of the city, trying to imagine her father and me muttering to each other over a Chinese food buffet for four or five hours, or the two of us doddering through a museum or art gallery, neither of which we'd know what to really do with.

"Does he like movies?" I ask, some fake cheer to my delivery.

I should say here, he and my mother-in-law were at the wedding, of course, but that was sixteen years ago. I shook their hands and called them Mom and Dad and took all the necessary pictures that day, but, since then, I've successfully avoided any meaningful interactions with them. Just the usual holiday stuff, here's a pot roast, thanks for the shoeshine kit I love it, no we don't have any secret kids yet ha ha, yeah I like my new job too, your daughter's the best, sure I can install that new washing machine, thanks, thanks.

Which is to say: Who was this musty geezer I was now to spend an afternoon with?

All the same, my time for this had probably come. You can only dodge bullets for so long. And, I told myself, it's not like he's completely checked in anymore, right? I might even just be a nurse to him, a helper, some shadowy presence holding him by the elbow, steering him away from traffic, saying completely unintelligible bullshit to him.

"He used to like action movies, yeah," Sheila answers, a tinge of unexpected hopefulness to her voice, to match my fake cheer. It's not for the afternoon I'm about to lead her father through, I don't think, but for the father he used to be, who probably played his action movies too loud too late, his way of having the last word for the day.

It's settled, then.

I haul my assigned tub of cleaning supplies up, Sheila keys us in, announcing our presence until her father creaks forward in his chair, his whole face squinting about us, and, after taking inventory, Sheila says back to me, "A *long* movie?"

"A loud one," I tell her, since maybe her father *is* going deaf— I'm pretty sure he didn't turn his head to the sound we are, but to the flurry of motion we were in his peripheral vision.

"Nothing scary," she tells me, doing her important eyes.

"Luck," I say, one hand to her shoulder, and kiss her on the side of her face, her eyes hard for the coming work.

Next I'm guiding her father down the dark hall of his building, to the elevator, and right before we get there he chicken-wings his arm out, the one I'm holding, effectively telling me he doesn't need me to keep him from falling.

Still, when he's stepping over that thin deep chasm between the carpet of the hall and the hard floor of the elevator car, I hover close, ready to be there should he need me.

"Where's she having us go, then?" he says, aiming the unsteady rubber foot of his cane at the pad of buttons, which can't be anything like hygienic for anyone else who might have to touch those buttons. Instead of helping, though—instead of *interfering*—I hang back, wait for him to find the L by himself, which is, I guess, both the third and fourth letters of *hell*.

Not that I'm thinking like that.

Yet.

"We're going to the *movies*," I tell him loud enough that he can hopefully catch at least part of it, and like that we're descending down into the afternoon, which is where him being a lazy-ass listener comes into play.

> > >

By the second trailer—we're sitting in the handicapped seats—he's leaning forward to the screen, like that's where all the sound is coming from. He turns his head to the side to better funnel these voices in, and the way his cane is spiked down in front of him, both hands on the handle to pull forward with, it's like he's hauling back on a big lever.

The theater is a four-screen job, kind of on the backside of thirty. It's seen better days; the same sixteen-year-old who sold us the ticket also filled my popcorn bucket, and the carpet is all threadbare in the middle of the halls from thousands of shoes scraping, and the urinals are the kind that are those big yawning porcelain mouths that stretch all the way to the floor, so you're practically standing in them.

We're forty minutes early for the movie, but it's the first showing too, so we sit there and wait, me crunching popcorn and watching the slideshow commercials and quizzes cycling on-screen, him nodding off since I'm guessing he can only see the static ads and questions up there, not hear them so well.

I don't mean to make fun. Someday that's me, I know. I already find myself sleeping through parts of television shows I would have been awake for ten years ago. It's the natural progression, and so what. Bring it. I'm ready.

Not that I'll ever have a son-in-law to dodder me down to the movies, but oh well. If I'm any indication, we're overrated.

Anyway, if there was an usher making the rounds through

the theater to keep everything kosher, I'd flag him or her down for assistance about this hearing problem, but as it is, I have to pat my father-in-law on the shoulder like telling him to stay put, then go to the concession stand to solve it myself, see if they have something to get him to hear the movie as well as see it.

When I come back, it's to an empty house, an old-man-less house, and my heart thumps once in my chest, kind of lurches to a soft stop, my head already reeling excuses out to Sheila, a future version of myself already scouring the men's restrooms and the other theaters for her father, then widening the search out to all the concrete and sidewalks of the city, and finally, inevitably, the hospitals and morgues.

But then I'm just standing in the wrong theater, because this action movie's playing on half the screens here. I exhale from deep in my chest and rush fast to the right theater, where the next trailer is already booming.

My father-in-law's sitting there squinting up at the screen in a way that tells me this is a bad idea, that taking him to a movie at this stage of his life, and a modern action movie at that, the third installment of a series geared for thirteen-year-old boys, is an exercise in stupidity. There's nothing for him here, and there won't be.

Still, it's where we are.

I settle into my seat and offer him the assisted listening device they had behind the counter. He takes it, holds it up against the light of the screen to properly inspect it, then recognizes it as a version of the wireless television headphones Sheila got for him a couple of years ago, so he could blare his news at whatever volume he wanted, without including his neighbors.

He grunts thanks, ducks into the rig and looks up at the screen, waiting for the magic to happen. When it doesn't, I reach over under his chin, click the green light on, and it must start receiving then, since his eyes change like he's hearing something.

What his wife meant by "lazy listener" was, I have to think, pretty much the same thing Sheila says about me: that I check out a few words in, start thinking my own thoughts, only staying involved enough in whatever she's saying to nod at the appropriate moments, pretend to play along. She's right, I guess. Maybe it's a man-woman thing, maybe it's a husband-wife thing, or maybe she just, as happens, married a minor version of the asshole she grew up with.

Either way, with the movie piping directly into his ears now, my father-in-law is pacified. I can tell because the cane he's still holding under both hands angles back and back, the curved handle at his chest now, which is kind of like a visual definition for "contentment," which, to me, translates across as "success," or, in the mental checklist I've got going, "two hours."

After this it'll be me swinging us by the corner store for any groceries he might need, which I trust will take another forty minutes *and* involve a carton of the cigarettes he's not supposed to have. Taking travel time into account between here and there and his place, if we're moving slow and careful like I plan to, that's a whole afternoon, ta-daaa. We'll come back to a rejuvenated apartment, a tired but satisfied woman, and then I'll be free.

Right on schedule, then, twenty, twenty-five minutes into the movie, I'm watching the movie alone, my father-in-law's head lolled forward in sleep, the green light glowing against his throat like a visible heartbeat.

By now I'm as into the movie as it's possible to get, considering the fare. It's all car chases followed by car wrecks, with sporadic gunfire and bikinis stitching it all together in the least likely ways. Not complaining, it's not like it was false advertising or anything, you get what you're paying for, but still, it could be in another language and I'd be watching the same movie.

Just because it's one of my assigned duties to conserve any and all battery life whenever I encounter it—Sheila says I'm the battery police, the hall monitor for charging—I contort myself to reach over, into my father-in-law's sleeping space, to turn that green light off. At which point, my fingers having to see by feel, I discover a notch that turns out to be a headphone jack.

It makes sense, I guess. If you and your movie date are sitting together, then one unit can receive for the both of you, if the kid at concessions can supply you with an auxiliary set of headphones to string between the two of you.

Instead of turning the unit off, I untangle my own headphones from my jacket pocket, reach across with both hands to hold the assisted listening device steady while I plug in.

Why not, right?

I lean back, want to chock my knees up on the seat in front of me except this is handicapped, there's just open space before us. I tilt my head over to thumb one earbud in, then the other.

Thirty seconds later, my face goes slack with wonder.

I'd assumed, the way anybody would, that what piped into a device like this would be the same thing coming through the surround sound.

Wrong.

It's—it's so much better, so much fuller. And of course it is. This isn't for hearing-*impaired* people, dummy, this is for the blind, who want to experience the movie the only way they can: through running description, while still hearing everything coming through the speakers mounted all around.

This description, though, it's . . . I've never heard anything quite like it. It's not that it's a woman's voice, an older woman it sounds like, one I guess I would call "Mom-class," as in, the kind I'd expect to be reading to the boy I still am inside, it's what she's saying, and how she's saying it. I lean up, to be closer to the screen, but then, finally, I close my eyes like I'm supposed to.

What the woman in my head is telling me is "A white convertible Jaguar skids in from the left, from a road that's suddenly just there, and it's already sliding, it's going to hit our red Charger, but the driver, whoever she is, she's hauling the wheel back over hard, she's shifting down, and from right above we can see the passenger-side door handle of the Jag just touching the driver's-side door handle of the Charger, slow motion, and in that moment the two evenly matched drivers look across into each other's eyes and smile, each knowing how many miles of open road are waiting before them."

At which point the speakers in the *theater* deliver the Charger driver's line, "Welcome to the party, babe," and then the narrator is back, saying, "the Charger's rear tires smoke, his hand guides the shifter deep into the next gear, and we stay in place behind the two cars as they race away."

And, the thing is, with my eyes closed, I can see this *so*, so clearly, so much better than if I was just watching it with my eyes. Which, I know, it's not quite cool of me to say "look how the other half lives" when I'm doing it by choice, not by accident or birth or whatever—I'm just a tourist in the land of the blind, of course it's fun if I can leave whenever I want—but still, this woman painting the scene for me, all the sounds of the movie still coming in, it's a way of watching I'd never considered, a way of seeing I'd never guessed was possible.

I close my eyes tighter and suck air in deep, to relish this.

The bar fight at the strip club is something else, but I don't even peek, just surreptitiously guide my popcorn bucket onto my lap, in case other moviegoers have filtered in.

At the high-rise scene I already saw in the trailer, my chest actually hollows out to be this high, and when the gold Lamborghini is crashing through the golden window in even slower motion, the narrator practically showing me each piece of flying glass, I cue in to a sound that . . . what *is* that? Kind of an undertone, that I guess must have been there the whole time, since I started this.

It's like . . . it's not steady, but it's constant. A grinding? Metal on metal?

I open my eyes to the comparatively bright theater, to see if, I don't know, to see if some woman is standing before me, filing her fingernails on an emery board, her *metal* fingernails, and using a file, not sandpaper and cardboard, but there's no one. I chance a look around, and we're alone in here in the middle of the day.

Beside me, my father-in-law is still sleeping.

I pull my left earbud out, listen to the theater, but there's only those shards of glass whistling down along the side of the highrise, whuffing down onto the white umbrellas set up around the pool, so many stories below the action.

It's an old device, I tell myself. An old device at a crappy, soon-to-be-retired theater, and we're probably the first person to use it in years. There's dust in the transmitter, there's bleed over from a competing signal, or—or the headphones for this particular jack are *proprietary*, that must be it. Whatever I'm hearing, it's because the grooves in my plug don't line up perfect with the internal ridges in the device. I'm not even supposed to be listening like this. Of course something's going to sound a little off. What was I thinking?

Mystery solved, I thumb my earbuds back in, lean back, close my eyes to try to make this movie not so terrible.

After the pool scene, which the visual-assist somehow makes believable—it's all about if you want to enjoy or not—in a moment of comparative silence when the hero is just cruising along in what turns out to be an electric car, which means a *quiet* car, I hear it again, that undertone of metal on metal.

This time when I turn my head toward it, toward my father-in-law, I keep my eyes closed, and my whole body goes cold.

I'm in his apartment with him.

And—and I haven't been actually hearing that sound, it's that, this woman's voice, it's split in half somehow, has a top level, the stuff she's supposed to be saying, the stuff she's reading from her script, but somehow she's whispering under that, asking me, "Can't I *hear* that, can't I hear that metal-on-metal grinding?"

My first impulse, my almost reaction, it's to open my eyes and push away from whatever this is, what this can't possibly be, but, but—I *do* push away, both my hands firmly on the armrest, the cable between us tightening, but I don't open my eyes.

This . . . I'm with him, somehow, my sleeping father-in-law. Like, his memory, his mind, his self, it's leaking out through his ears, it's infecting the device, it's crawling across the headphone cable into my mind's eye.

I shake my head no, no, but at the same time, in a sort of wonder, I *look*.

> > >

He's standing in the kitchen, the television blaring from the living room. It's the Turner Classic stuff Sheila's mother was always so in love with, that she always insisted on instead of my father-in-law's blarey news programs. Meaning this is from then, from before, from when she was alive. Before she died.

Why I keep watching now, it's because I want to see how old she is in this. And, because, I don't know, maybe we're all voyeurs? Or we all have that tendency, will all sneak a look if given the chance, if there's no real risk involved? If there's no way to get caught doing the Peeping Tom thing?

All I'm doing is listening to a movie through a pair of earbuds, man. Completely innocent, here.

I close my eyes even more, to see better.

Judging by my father-in-law's gnarled, liver-spotted hands, this can't be more than five years ago. What he's doing in the kitchen is . . . it's dinner? Sort of. Maybe. Which, I never knew he was capable of that, of dinner, of being the one to prepare the food, of bringing it instead of having it brought.

But, what this means, what I know it has to mean, it's that Sheila's mom is already sick, that she's already been coughing up blood for a few months.

That grinding sound, though, that metal-tearing sound, I can finally attach it to something that completely makes sense, now that I'm seeing it: a can opener, one of the old-fashioned wall-mount electric ones, that slowly turn the can around, biting perforations into its top. I guess I've maybe even seen it there in their kitchen tucked under the counter right by the doorway to the living room, the wallpaper all stained under it, I just never actually *noticed* it. And I assume its motor or chassis or whatever must be mostly in the wall, since all that's showing is a square white plate and then the silver arm that holds the can while the little saw blade teeth chew into it.

Sheila's father is opening a can of generic creamed corn, holding it with his right hand to keep it from dropping when it's done, I guess—to keep more splashes from happening. But it's not built to be guided like that. The pressure he's applying to the side of the can is changing the tilt of the can, is slowing it down, is making the sharp teeth dig in at a slightly different angle, and maybe into the same place in the lid, even.

In the living room, the music swells for some romantic moment or another.

Next door, the action movie roars on, as if on the neighbor's incredibly up-to-date sound system.

I start to turn that way, to the bright lights and screeching tires, but I come back to this slowly rotating can of corn, and the visual-assist narrator says, as if speaking just and only to me, for me, "And we can see what his hand on that rotating can of corn is resulting in, can't we?"

I look closer, can't, no.

Not until my father-in-law lowers the can from the magnet that stays latched onto the lid.

"Glittering there in the yellow kernels," the narrator says, rapt on this detail, highlighting it for me, "are little . . . are those metal *shavings?*"

They are.

The ancient can opener would have worked fine, done its job like it's supposed to, probably works just like advertised every time my father-in-law uses it for his own meals, but by angling the can over just enough, and slowing it down, he's turned it into a weapon.

He sees these metal shavings, too, I mean. And he nods about them, humming in his mouth contentedly.

They're so obvious, now that I've seen them. Before he stirs them in.

Then he's walking into the living room but "We stay behind, don't we?" the narrator says right into my mind. "We stay behind, and we look over to the pantry. The door's open, isn't it? Go on, lean in, see what's there."

It's the trash can, overflowing with the torn-open cans of food my father-in-law's been feeding my wife's mother for weeks now, it looks like. For months. That he's been killing her with.

I suck a harsh chestful of air in and open my eyes, find myself staring right into my father-in-law's face, his saggy eyes wide open.

He smiles at me, then chuckles, turns back to the screen, clapping me once on the thigh and leaving his hand there, like initiating me into a new place. Like ushering me in and keeping me there.

On-screen, a car explodes on landing from an impossible jump and the sound of the explosion is muted and distant for me, is happening in some land far, far away from where I am now.

> > >

Walking down the sidewalk when the movie's over, ready to catch my father-in-law should he stumble, what I'm really doing is rewinding through my mother-in-law's last couple of years. The doctors diagnosing ulcers and "nonspecific intestinal hemorrhaging" or whatever it was. It didn't matter then. What mattered was that she eat only bland foods. What mattered was all the prescriptions meant to quell the digestive storm raging inside her.

What she was doing was watching TCM and eating tiny slivers of metal. If her health plan paid for more or better imaging, maybe the jig would have been up, and it all could have been an accident, bad luck, one failing kitchen appliance trying to kill her, her husband unwittingly involved.

As it was, she just kept getting chewed up from the inside.

And nobody suspected anything, least of all Sheila. Her mom was the right age for her body to be failing in unexpected ways, wasn't she? It was a tragedy, it was sad, but it wasn't any kind of real surprise. It's what we all have waiting for us, surely.

Only, it didn't have to be. Not for my mother-in-law.

Did she know right at the end, too? Did she finally see a glittering shard in her corn or peas and look up to her husband, watching her spoon this in?

At that point, coughing up blood, blood in the toilet, her stomach and intestines in revolt, all failing, did she just guide that next bite in anyway and turn back to her classic movie?

I don't know.

She was from that long-suffering generation, though. The one that would rather hide a thing like this than involve her own daughter. The one that would rather her daughter keep a father she could believe in.

"And now he's walking along the sidewalk close to the building," the narrator now whispering in my head says, "reaching forward with his brown cane as if pulling the sidewalk to him rather than pulling himself forward on the sidewalk."

And no one knows, I add, my heart beating in my throat, nearly choking me.

Do I tell Sheila, though?

I mean, first, before that, how do I even say I know this, right? I "saw" it in the audio description for that car movie I took your father to? A woman reading a script in a sound booth months ago whispered it to me?

More like I dreamed it. More like I zoned out in the movie as a form of self-defense, and in that zoned-out state I worked up this grand story for how your father, he *killed your mother*, Sheel, really, serious, I solved the case. Also, there *is* a case.

As proof, of course, I could take a can from the pantry, it doesn't matter what, and mess with its angle in the can opener until it leaves sharp little slivers of metal behind.

At which point Sheila would look up from the bowl I've just poured, study me long and hard.

"Are you accusing him?" she would say to me. "Do you really think my father's capable of this?"

It's as unlikely a scenario as a car crashing out the high window of a building, landing in the pool in a way that doesn't kill everybody involved.

It doesn't mean I don't believe it with every fiber of my being, though.

I saw it. With my ears, sure, but in a more pure way, too: in my head, leaked across through a headphone cable.

Whenever my father-in-law is sitting in the room with us, nodding like catching his head from falling over and over again, now I know that what he's doing is congratulating himself on having gotten away with it, with killing his wife of forty-five years. And for no reason I can come up with other than that one day he saw that he *could*.

Can that happen, at the end of your life? Can you become a killer in your dotage, in your golden years? Can you want control of the remote enough that murder's your best option?

Nobody will suspect you. There's no motivation anybody can claim, there's no first attempt, there's no bad history, there's no evidence anybody can find. Just, one day you saw a bright, curled piece of silver in some sliced pears you'd just opened, and you looked up from them to the horrible old movie filling the living room, and you nodded maybe. Maybe.

It can happen, I think. It *did* happen.

I've never considered doing anything even remotely like that to Sheila, but I'd be lying if I said I hadn't imagined her dying in a car crash or a mall shooting. Not just imagining it, but fantasizing over it. Not like I wanted it to happen, but like . . . I don't know. Like the pity that would result after that, for me, and how I wasn't involved at all in this, could just start over now, start clean, it was attractive somehow. In a dull, never-going-to-happen, please-never-happen way.

I love Sheila, I mean. I want us to grow old together, to watch our television shows together until the end. I want it to be her and me, a team. We'll be the ones who make it, together. That's what I've always intended, what I've always dreamed.

But if this ever surfaces, what her father did to her mother, I don't know.

It'll send her into a spiral, I know. One she might never pull out of all the way. One that might take me down with her.

And I can't have that.

> > >

"He punches the button for the third floor with his cane on the third try," the visual-assist in my head narrates when we're back to the building.

We stopped at the store and went up and down every aisle, so now I have two paper bags of groceries, *not* including a secret carton of smokes, thank you.

"Did you two have a good afternoon?" Sheila asks, opening the door while I'm still trying to get the key into the lock.

"Lords of the matinee," I tell her, stepping aside to present her father, safe and sound.

Sheila's hair is in a scarf, her sleeves rolled high up her arms like Rosie the Riveter. The stringent scent of cleaner washes out past us.

While she gets her father settled I quietly haul all the trash bags down to the trash. When I get back, Sheila's unfolding a blanket over her father's lap and working the big-button television remote into his right hand. There's not an ashtray in the room, not a newspaper left. For him it has to feel like his life's been dialed back to five, ten years ago. Sheila's beaming, glowing, bright and smiling. It's been a successful Sunday for her. She's a good daughter.

The television comes on under her father's trembling index finger and the commercial that blares into the room is for the movie we just sat through. The one we just listened to.

"What did the two of you see?" Sheila asks, her face somehow blank, as if there's no wrong answer.

"Period piece," I say with a shrug, lying for no reason I can claim, "that one with that one girl with the hair?"

Sheila considers tracking this down with me but then shrugs it away, looks around the place as if proud.

"Looks great," I tell her. "You found the way it used to be."

"I give it two weeks," she says back, and that's probably about right. "See the kitchen?"

I pretend I didn't, go back in. The counters are gleaming, the handles of everything catching the light.

"Couldn't be better," I tell her, and she proceeds to unpack the groceries we just got, line them in the pantry, and, while she's doing that, I find myself studying the wall-mounted can opener.

It's an ugly, unwieldy appliance, one I can't imagine was ever considered normal. It's like—it's like those old hatches or flaps or whatever that you still find in old houses, that you can plug a vacuum cleaner hose into, that are connected to some sucker-pump in another part of the house, that are supposed to make keeping the carpets clean so much easier.

Can openers should just be something you stash in the drawer, twist with your hand.

"Did you like it?" Sheila says, half in the pantry.

The movie.

"Love story," I say, "turned into murder, you know," and now my hand's to this wall-mounted can opener.

All it takes is a slight push to bend the top arm down not even five degrees, two or three of which it still has enough spring to recover on its own. It'll still function, will still open cans. Just, well. I'm not going to be here every meal like he was for his wife. I can't guide every can. Except like this, by messing with the machine, making it where it doesn't even know how to open a can without turning it into a weapon.

Thirty minutes later, being the good son-in-law, I use it on some canned beets, my father-in-law's professed favorite, what we just bought twenty-four of in a flat box.

He's watching his news, his headphones on so we don't have to hear it.

"He looks so good," Sheila says, speaking freely, since there's no chance of him tuning us in.

"I liked spending time with him," I say back, guiding the bowl of beets in, stirring the clumps with the spoon, hiding the bright slivers in deep. "I wish—I mean, I should have been doing it all along."

"You know," Sheila says, absolving me, "life."

It's our usual call-and-response.

I settle the dark purple beets down into my father-in-law's left hand.

I reach past him, pull the chain on the lamp beside him off, in case the silver in his meaty purple might try to glint, give away what's going on here.

The look he gives me about the light going away is hard, uncompromising, and that it lasts one bit longer than it should that tells me he probably also turned the lamp off on his wife, didn't he? Of course he did. Otherwise she might have seen what he was doing. Otherwise she might have known how he was killing her.

I hold his eyes, trying not to tell him anything, trying to just make him guess, because I imagine that has to be worse, more what he deserves, but then Sheila's there at my side, her hand on my shoulder, her voice up on tippy-toes because she's being a good daughter, because I'm such a perfect son-in-law.

"Do you need anything else?" she's asking her father.

Her father looks from her to me, and then to his beets, and then he stabs his spoon in, brings it up to his mouth, and by the time we're leaving, I'm the last one in the room with him, the one carrying his empty bowl back to the kitchen.

His mouth is purple, the juice leaking down his chin.

I come back with a napkin, dab that color away, and the assist in my head settles back in, says, "And after the son-in-law leaves the room, the deadbolt clicking over, the grinding undertone comes back, doesn't it? That metal-on-metal sound, and when the old man on the chair chocks his headphones back and looks into the kitchen, what he sees, just partially, is *me*, standing at the can opener, bringing him his next meal, and his next, because his wife loves him enough to feed him, and keep feeding him, even when he tells her he's full, even when he tells her it hurts. "Just one more bite, dear," she'll tell him, holding her hand under the spoon as she guides it to his mouth. "Just one more bite, and then you'll be all done, won't you?"

On the way out, balancing a tub of cleaning supplies on my hip, I reach back in, switch the overhead light off with finality.

"It was a good time this afternoon, wasn't it?" Sheila says to me on the elevator.

"I should go to the movies more often," I tell her, and use my knee to push the button to deliver us down, away from this, into whatever wonders our old age might have waiting for us.

A BEN EVANS FILM

Josh Malerman

THE FIRST PART of the movie was terrible because he didn't know a thing about editing yet. He was doing it all "in-camera," a phrase he'd never heard in his forty-one years of life. After stealing the camcorder (down his pants; much easier than he thought it'd be) he learned a great many terms like it. "Film terms," he called them. And every one of them tickled Ben Evans pink.

"Continuity."

"Backlighting."

"Jump cut."

He worked on a learning curve, no doubt, and those first fourteen minutes took a lot longer to do than the latter forty. Example: he'd dressed his dead mother up like Mary the Homeowner (one of Ben's favorite characters) and filmed her until the knock on Mary's door (Ben tapping the TV tray closest to him with his free hand), then he hit pause, removed the Mary makeup from mother, dressed her up like Mary's Friend Andrea (another of Ben's favorites), put her outside the door, and rolled the camcorder again. After this shot of Andrea, he paused again, dressed Mother up like Mary once more, put her back inside, and called action. Because Mary had to answer the door, of course. And because Mother played both roles, of course. Makeup on Mother, makeup off Mother. New makeup on Mother. New makeup off. This particular conversation between Mary and Andrea took nine hours to film. Ben didn't notice that the sun went down through- out the course of the scene, an interaction that, on tape, lasted all of forty seconds.

In the beginning, Ben shot the movie in order. Because that's how movies look when they're done. And because Ben was mak- ing a movie, after all.

The same learning curve occurred with the dialogue and sound, as Ben had no knowledge of overdubbing and no means to do it if he had. For the first half of the movie, the voices (all Ben's) are much louder than they get later, as his lips were so close to the camcorder he held. He spoke for both his dead mother and his dead father and all the people they played, trying his hardest to give each character a different accent. This process changed mightily once he stole the Tascam unit from RadioShack (up his sleeve; easier than he thought it'd be) and watched a YouTube tutorial on syncing audio with video. Yet, being dead, his parents didn't move their lips at all, so there was nothing to sync and only the duration of the shot to worry about. Long enough for Ben to say their lines for them.

"Principal photography" began on January 1 of that year. A New Year's resolution, indeed. He let the cold in every time he carried Mother or Father to the backyard. He fell twice on the ice while filming them through the kitchen windows of their home. Once he thought he broke his wrist.

No matter.

He came to call the movie just that, *No Matter*, for how many

times he had to repeat the two words, what with all the unforeseen problems that occurred while making his movie.

Ben liked the idea of "unforeseen problems." He'd read of
similar things happening on movie sets all through history. It
was exactly the sort of thing the screenwriter who had come to
town told Ben and a crowd of ten others, gathered in the Samhattan Library.

You must get rid of the words "good" and "bad," the writer (a fellow Michigander!) said. *It's the doing that matters.*

Ben almost called his movie *The Doing.*

And what a way of looking at it! You must make do with what
you have, of course! Use the tools at hand! Involve the people
around you!

Ben involved the only two people he lived with.

No Matter was finished in late July of the same year, and
Mother and Father looked different by the end of it. They looked
darker. Thinner. Sunken. For this, Ben rewrote the script often.
He thought of the screenwriter Jim Bradley and how he would've
said yes, make it work, yes, go forth, yes rewrite the script, give
your parents new characters to play, evolve.

No matter.

None! Not when Ben ran out of makeup and had to steal more
from the mall. Not when he dressed his dead father in his own
unwashed suit and strode around the house nude, camera in
hand. Not when he found himself hungry and exhausted for having expended so much energy in the name of his film.

No matter.

Once it was done (and what a day that was) Ben carried his
dead parents back up to their bedroom. He watched his movie
a dozen times. He set the VCR to repeat and slept in the living
room. When he woke, his forty-one-year-old bones cramped from
the couch, the movie was still playing.

Dead mother dolled up like Mary. Dead father as the nosy neighbor John.

The feeling was overwhelming.

It was time to start calling himself a filmmaker.

It was time to start thinking of himself as an artist.

It was time to show someone else the movie.

Like Jim Bradley said, the day comes when you have to send your work out into the world. A time comes when you have to *share*.

So, on an August afternoon in Samhattan, with the sun so bright he hung a blanket over the living room window, Ben Evans took the first step toward sharing.

He invited someone over to watch his movie.

> > >

Roger came over around noon that day but didn't stay inside the house for more than five minutes. He told Ben he couldn't stand the smell. The actual word he used was *stench*. It bothered Ben deeply. The pair had gone to middle school together, high school, and kept in touch for the twenty-four years since. Ben saw Roger all the time at Melanie's Grocery, at the Fountain Pen Theater, even once at RadioShack. He'd prepared the house for Roger's viewing. He'd bought chips and dip.

But Roger simply wouldn't stay.

So Ben suggested showing him the film on his camcorder outside in the yard. Roger agreed, but it was frustrating when he said he couldn't see anything on the tiny screen, that the sun was making it hard to tell what was going on. Is that your mom and dad? Those dolls kinda look like your mom and dad. No offense. And sorry for the loss.

It bothered Ben, the way Roger talked about his mother and father. Like he was calling the movie amateur because Ben didn't have "real" actors. Like he was saying the makeup was bad, since they really only looked like themselves. Like Roger was nay-saying the film.

What would Jim Bradley say to that? He'd say you did it, Ben. And that's all that matters.

The doing.

No Matter.

Ben and Roger ended up in a shouting match. Roger told Ben he had to clean his house. Then he left the yard and drove home.

Ben called his friend Hugh to come watch it instead.

Hugh didn't say anything about a "stench" and this only forti-fied Ben's idea that Roger was jealous of what Ben had done. Jim Bradley talked a little about that kind of thing. But Hugh . . . Hugh walked into the house, sat in Ben's dead father's easy chair, crossed his legs, pointed at the television, and said, "Let's see it."

For Ben, pressing play, starting the movie, was a very big deal.

Hugh cracked a beer and snorted some white powder as the title came on the screen.

Then he watched the whole thing. Oftentimes his eyes grew wide, other times he seemed to squint. Ben wondered if it was because of the lighting. Sometimes the sun did go down during the course of a single scene. Ultimately, it didn't seem to matter. Hugh popped a second beer, then a third. He didn't laugh at the parts Ben knew to be funny, but he didn't seem bored by the lengthy, more sorrowful stretches, either. Hugh even watched the credits.

"Good movie," he said when it was over. Then he leapt up out of the easy chair the way Hugh always moved, and made for the door. He turned and said to Ben, "I'd love to be in your next one. Hell, I'd even just hold a light."

Ben had never felt better in his life. The way Hugh said it. It felt like something had gotten started.

A career.

But minutes after Hugh left, Ben had to get dressed for his other career. His job. Line cook at a chain restaurant downtown. That night was a company party.

Ben wore the same suit Hugh had just seen Ben's dead father wearing, as the old man was propped outside the kitchen window, peering in on his dead, made-up wife.

> > >

Cathy was a hostess at the same restaurant. She and Ben couldn't have been farther apart during their shifts than they were. Cathy almost never came into the kitchen and Ben had absolutely no reason to go out into the lobby. For this, it wasn't until the holiday party at John John's that they spoke for the first time.

"You seem like you have more pep in your step than you used to," Cathy said to Ben as the two stood in the buffet line with empty plates in their hands.

Ben didn't know what to say. He thought maybe she was kidding. He thought maybe she was talking to someone else. But no, this woman, five years his senior, was intimating that she'd noticed him at least twice in her life.

"Me?" Ben asked. But by then he was only buying time. He knew she was talking to him.

"You," Cathy said. She punched him softly on the arm. "What's your secret? Have you been eating better?"

"What do you mean?"

"You seem happy."

"I am happy."

"Good."

They didn't speak again, as Ben turned his back to her, unsure what more could be said. But the night was long from over. And Cathy found him again later in the bar area of the restaurant neither of them worked at.

Ben drank a beer. He liked how Hugh drank his beers while watching *No Matter*.

"You again," Cathy said. She smiled and her eyes shined beneath the bangs of her wiry hair.

"Hello. Still happy."

Cathy laughed and Ben was surprised. He hadn't meant to make a joke. Yet, here he was, basking in the afterglow.

"You're cuter in person," Cathy said.

Ben pretended she meant that he looked different on-screen. As if she'd maybe seen a documentary on the making of his movie.

"What about me?" Cathy asked. "Don't I look different than when I'm standing at the hostess stand?"

"Yes," Ben said.

Then he fell in love with Cathy. As she shrugged a silent thank-you.

"Do you like movies?" she asked.

"Yes. I made one."

Cathy looked genuinely surprised.

"Really? That's amazing. I want to know all about it."

"Okay."

"What's it about?"

How many times had Ben answered this very question in interviews he pretended were real?

"It's about a woman who is lonely and her friend comes over and helps her out. And there's a neighbor who watches her through the window."

Oh boy did the idea sound small. So small!

"Cool," Cathy said. "I'd love to see it sometime."

To Ben's great relief, Cathy took up conversation with other coworkers. He watched her flutter from person to person as friends do. He saw the way she laughed so easily with the others and he understood they knew each other much better than he did. She'd said she wanted to see his movie.

Might this mean more people would want to?

He looked into his beer then. He didn't like the feeling in his stomach. A little twist. Like he'd been fantasizing wrong. If that was possible to do. Like he'd been imagining all these people loving *No Matter* and talking about it and exchanging theories, but in reality he didn't want anybody to see it.

That night, Ben didn't sleep much. He thought of that twist in his stomach and how it hurt to imagine Cathy watching his movie. He'd heard of a "fear of failure" before, but this felt different. Like he might be exposing a part of himself he shouldn't be exposing if he showed his movie to her. Like if he'd gone to work without his shirt on and it wasn't the nudity that made him race back out to the parking lot, but the tattoo he had.

Ben didn't have a tattoo. But that was the idea. That was the feeling.

Like he had a tattoo that admitted something bad he'd done. Something maybe Cathy shouldn't see.

> > >

But Cathy liked Ben and so the relationship went somewhere. Somewhere good.

On Ben's second shift following the company party, Cathy came back into the kitchen looking for him. He heard her voice before he saw her, bright and sparkling, and he hid in the mop closet. It was his first reaction and it felt like something he should do. But when the other cook, Jasper, called out for him, Ben had to step out into the light.

"Hello, you," Cathy said. She smiled his way and Ben had a faint feeling that he was supposed to smile back.

"Hi, Cathy."

"So you do remember me."

Ben nodded. "Of course."

"What are you doing tonight?" Suddenly it felt to Ben like the two of them were very alone. As if all the staff and all the customers knew this moment was coming and had quietly snuck out the front door to wait in the parking lot until it was over.

"I'm not sure," Ben said. He'd planned to go home. Watch his movie.

"Let's go out," Cathy said. She was taking charge. Even Ben's inexperienced mind was able to glean that much. It felt good and bad at once.

"Okay, sure. When?"

"Anytime."

"Okay. Where?"

Cathy shrugged. "We close in two hours. Figure it out by then."

She winked and walked away. Ben saw the black swinging door swallow her up like a dead mother's tongue and he turned away from it.

Then the kitchen came back to vivid life and Ben wondered when everybody had snuck back in.

"Way to go, tiger," Jasper said, slapping Ben on the shoulder. "No offense, but I honestly didn't think you had this in you."

Ben wasn't offended. He smiled. He thought of Jim Bradley. The screenwriter was coming back to town for another talk.

He would take Cathy to see him.

> > >

On the way to Samhattan Books, Cathy said:

"I've never met someone like you. Here we are, in our forties, and it's easy to think love has passed us by. You see your friends getting married when you're not even twenty-five and you hear they're having kids and suddenly everybody in the world has a family but you. You learn to accept it after a while. I did anyway. Around thirty-three I started saying forget it, I haven't settled yet and I'm just not going to. But years later . . . years! . . . I run into you. It's incredible. *You're* incredible. You're so kind. So open. So real. And so I wanted to thank you, Ben."

She put her hand on Ben's forearm as he drove to the bookstore.

"Thank you for showing up in my life."

She gave his arm a little squeeze.

"Here it is," Ben said.

He pulled into the parking lot of a strip mall. About a dozen cars were parked near Samhattan Books.

Ben turned to Cathy and said, "I hope he inspires you like he did me."

Cathy smiled.

"See?" she said. "You're always thinking of others."

> > >

Inside, Jim Bradley had already begun talking to the crowd of twenty. He paused for a beat when he saw Ben and Cathy sitting down.

Cathy noted it. She smiled because she knew how much Ben liked this man. Yet, she couldn't help but wonder at the unease that flickered in Jim Bradley's eyes. She chalked it up to the screenwriter not remembering Ben's name. That was fine. He would learn it again today when Ben introduced her following the lecture.

Which Ben did. Or tried to, anyway, but the people were gathered by the table Jim Bradley was signing books at. What books? She wasn't sure exactly. Looked like the guy had written a "how-to" book about writing films. Ben stood near the table for a while, just kinda staring at the writer.

"That was interesting," Cathy said. Because it was. The man talked about how it's silly to wait for inspiration. How what it really takes is getting in front of the typewriter every day and how a little bit every day really adds up. Truth be told, Cathy almost fell asleep at one point. But she could feel the electricity coming from Ben. As if she were in proximity to a dream realized.

She'd thought many times during the lecture how it was time for her to see Ben's movie.

"I like his approach," Cathy said. But Ben wasn't really listening. He was half smiling, still staring at Jim Bradley behind the fold-out table, as the screenwriter made the locals laugh.

"Cathy Bettman?"

Cathy recognized the voice before her last name was spoken. She turned to see her ex-boyfriend Kevin standing behind her in the bookstore.

Her stomach sank a little. But, one of the by-products of meeting a man later in life was that he would end up meeting some ex-boyfriends along the way. She didn't think Ben would mind. It was a part of life. Part of being forty.

"Kevin," she said. He looked older. Wrinkles at the corners of his blue eyes. A lot of white in his beard. "Are you a Jim Bradley fan?"

It was the first thing she could think to say. Kevin shrugged and half rolled his eyes.

"It was something to do," he said.

Cathy felt the familiar pang of disappointment. Of course Kevin didn't get anything out of the lecture. She suddenly wished he wasn't here.

"What are you doing in Samhattan?" Kevin asked.

"Here to see him speak."

"Really? You still living in Glover?"

"Yes," she said. Then she heard a ruckus near the fold-out table.

"Get out of here," Jim Bradley said. "Please leave the store *now*."

Cathy couldn't totally believe what she was seeing. The writer was talking to Ben. Ben who looked a little pale. A little like a boy who just realized Santa Claus is real, yes, but he doesn't like you.

A bookstore clerk came over and took Ben by the arm.

"Looks like your friend said something fucked-up," Kevin said.

Cathy heard the laughter in Kevin's voice without turning to look at him. And she didn't look at him again, as she was already walking toward Ben.

"What's up?" she asked.

Jim Bradley looked to her with pleading in his eyes. *Do you know this guy? Can you help please before this gets weirder?*

"What happened?"

The clerk began escorting Ben out.

"Jim Bradley—" Ben began. But the writer cut him off.

"Hey, man, I don't know you. And you don't just say what you said to someone you don't know."

Ben was past Cathy now. Before following him out, she stepped to the fold-out table and said, "You're an asshole. He came here to see you."

Jim Bradley shook his head. Cathy didn't want to admit it, but he had the unmistakable look of someone who was in the right.

She hurried to the exit, where Ben already was.

Outside, standing on the strip mall sidewalk, she asked him what happened.

"Not much," Ben said. "Let's go home."

Cathy thought of Kevin in the store. Kevin who no doubt was now talking to Jim Bradley about how weird Ben seemed. No doubt ripping her, too.

"Ben Evans," Cathy said. Then she said the first thing that came to mind, the only thing that made sense to her then, a way to prove to him that he was loved despite being rejected by someone he'd admired. "Ben Evans, if this is going to go anywhere, I'll have to meet your parents."

Ben stopped walking to the car. He turned to her and held her eyes a beat.

"I got a better idea," he said. He smiled then. A warm, genuine smile that had Cathy believing he was feeling good again. That she had done the very thing all partners want so desperately to do: she had stopped him from feeling bad.

"Oh yeah?" she asked.

Ben took her by the hand.

"I'll show you the movie I made with them."

> > >

The drive home was wonderful. Ben felt great. He hardly thought of the scene at Samhattan Books at all. Felt more like something that happened a few years ago. More than that. A middle school snafu. They were going to his house to watch his movie. He thought of Hugh and how much Hugh liked it.

At the 7-Eleven, he got chips, flavored water, and wine. Cathy liked those things. He asked her if she was excited and she said sure she was. Ben was, too.

In the driveway at home, he got out and went straight to the door. Almost there, he looked back and saw her carrying the wine bottle by the neck.

"Are they expecting us?" Cathy asked.

But the question was lost in the clatter of Ben opening the screen door and stepping into the house.

Cathy followed him in.

> > >

Immediately her mood changed.

It was the smell of the place. It wasn't like standing downwind when your dog took a shit in the yard. It was more like when the rain broke up a pile someone had forgotten to pick up.

A bad smell from a little while ago.

"Oh," she said, unable to stop herself from covering her nose and mouth with her open hand.

"The movie's in here," Ben said.

Cathy looked to the staircase before following Ben to the living room. It didn't sound like anybody else was home. Didn't he say he lived with his parents? Didn't he say they were a little older? Needed his help around the house?

It smelled like Ben needed a little help around the house.

When she entered the living room, he was already on one knee, fingering a knob on the VCR on top of the TV. She saw a flash of a shot, a yard through a window maybe, before he hit stop and rewound it.

She looked over her shoulder to a kitchen doorway. She thought there might be cleaning supplies in there. Should she go get some? Should she help out with this smell?

"Take the easy chair," Ben said. "It's good luck."

It didn't feel like the right time. Of course it didn't. Here she'd gotten Ben to forget the weird scene at the bookstore and now what? She was going to tell him his house stunk like a wet graveyard?

"Okay," she said. She gave the chair a quick swipe to remove some crumbs and sat down.

The tape was done rewinding.

"Okay," Ben said. He was facing the TV, a finger on the VCR. "I hope you like my movie."

> > >

For Ben it felt like the first time. Maybe it was because he was seeing it through the eyes of someone who was seeing it for the first time. That made sense. He'd heard of things like that before.

Cathy said something. About the makeup? Asked him who made this. Is that what she said? He wasn't sure. Sounded like she was asking who made his mother!

Ben answered as best he could. Told Cathy how great his mother and father were throughout. Wanted to tell her how much work the first fourteen minutes or so took. That was the stuff of legend. When one scene of a movie took a lot longer than the rest of it.

By the time his father was on-screen, Ben was positively overwhelmed. Here he was, showing Cathy the movie! And there was Father with the mustache Ben had painted above his lip. He wished he'd stood his dead father up a little more erect. The way he was leaning wasn't great "composition."

No matter.

Cathy asked something else. Sounded like she asked when his mother and father were going to be in the movie. Ben didn't respond to that one. Obviously she couldn't have asked that. There were a lot of things she asked that she couldn't have asked.

At one point he looked over to her and saw she was looking back at him. This made Ben feel bad. He looked back to the screen and wanted to tell her to do the same but he'd read about people being overbearing when they show their own art and how you were supposed to let people "come to the movie" at their own pace.

Cathy was asking more questions. Sounded like she was getting serious. Ben didn't mind. He would love to talk about the movie all day and night. But would she watch it all first?

"This part," Ben said. It wasn't an answer. He just particularly loved the part where he'd stood his mother and father up in the kitchen and talked for both of them. He'd done a really good job here. The only problem was the edit, perhaps, and how, if you caught it, you'd see his father begin to fall to the right. Ben had to pick his father back up that day, the day they filmed, but he thought he'd done a better job of getting rid of the beginning of that fall. Still, the last word of his mother's sentence landed right as his father began to move, so . . . Ben guessed it was an artistic decision. He thought he'd made the right one.

Cathy's voice was getting higher. At some point Ben thought maybe she'd gotten up and was in the kitchen? Maybe she wanted to see where certain scenes were shot? That was cool. That idea. But when he looked back at her, he saw Cathy standing next to the easy chair, looking to the ceiling.

Ben watched the movie. He heard something like pleading in Cathy's voice. Like she wanted an answer to her question. But Ben wasn't going to go into the meaning of the film until it was over. So he watched. And watched. Ignoring the rest of the world, all the world that surrounded the square of the TV. Even when he saw Cathy was no longer in the room. Even when he thought he heard creaking upstairs. Where was Cathy? Had she gone upstairs? Why? And had she come back down? He figured she was standing behind the couch. Maybe she had been the whole time. Why would she be interested in his mother and father upstairs? Whatever it was, it was okay. People had to come to the movie at their own pace.

When he heard the front door open and close (quiet, like someone was trying to be quiet), boy did it work perfectly with the movie. He wished he'd added a sound just like it. It was incredible the things you noticed when you watched a movie so many times. Even one you made yourself.

A similar thing occurred a little later. The unmistakable sound of a siren grew louder and louder. Ben wished he'd added the sound to the movie. Had he actually? When did he add this? He wasn't sure. But boy did it work. His dead mother was looking out her bedroom window, head cocked to the left, her face done up with a lot of makeup that Ben had put a lot of care into. And the siren? It absolutely added to the feel of a city. It suggested an entire world was going on outside the story of the made-up woman on the screen.

Cathy hadn't asked a question in a long time and Ben only looked to the empty easy chair once more as he heard the front door again, a door he just did not remember overdubbing. Must be real? Really happening? Either way, it went so well with the movie. The scene where Mother and Father stood in the very living room Ben sat in now, as the strings fastened to the bolts in the ceiling held them erect and standing and as Ben spoke for them both. He heard the creaking of the front door opening and clapped his hands for how perfect it was.

Because, as the door opened, his mother (Ben) said,

It's windy out there, Ben Sr.!

And his father (Ben) responded with,

Strong enough to blow the house down, dear! Strong enough to blow the whole dream apart!

Someone said, "Mr. Evans? Are you in there?"

And Ben clapped again because it was just so perfect. The audio, the visuals, Mother and Father.

And the voices, too. Getting louder. Like they were coming up the front hall to the very room he sat in.

"I'm right here!" he said.

That's how real it was. That's how good a job he did.

That's how good the movie was. So realistic that when he felt hands upon his shoulders, he thought, *Oh, Mom, oh, Dad, we did it. And it's the doing that matters!*

A film for the ages.

Made by Ben himself.

A Ben Evans film.

THE FACE IS A MASK

Christopher Golden

"WHAT DO YOU MEAN you're going to burn it?" Massarsky asked. "It's a lot of money to shell out for something you're planning to set on fire."

The younger man, Timothy Ridley, perched on the edge of the worn, burgundy leather sofa as if he might make a run for it. He swirled the ice in his glass of pomegranate juice but never seemed to take so much as a sip.

"You know the story behind the mask?" Ridley asked.

Massarsky leaned back in his chair, its matching leather crinkling loudly. "You think I'd have bought the thing if I didn't know the story? Its 'provenance,' as collectors say?"

Ridley nodded. "I've heard about your collection."

"You say that like you've got something sour in your mouth, Mr. Ridley. You come here and tell me you want to buy an item from my collection, tell me you intend to burn it, and then you talk to me like you feel dirty even being in my house."

This last part troubled him most deeply. James Massarsky had worked tirelessly with designers and contractors to get this house built. He had spent decades in the film business, first kissing ass and then making sure everyone else had to kiss *his*, and goddamn if he didn't deserve this house. A man's home was his castle and he had built one worthy of its king. Seven bedrooms, sprawling lawns, central house with two wings and two cottages on the property. Now here comes Ridley, wanting to buy the mask from *Chapel of Darkness* but acting like Massarsky is somehow beneath him.

"I'm sorry," Ridley said. "I just . . . . this isn't a pleasant errand for me."

Massarsky wanted to punch him in the throat. "I've tried to make you comfortable because you're a guest in my home. If you find it so unpleasant—"

"No, wait," Ridley said as Massarsky began to rise. "I'm not explaining this well."

"That's for sure." Massarsky settled back into his chair. "Tell me again how you ended up calling me. How did you even know I owned the mask?"

"A friend of my family's came to your Christmas party last year—"

"This friend have a name?"

"I'd rather not say. Particularly as you don't seem very happy about it," Ridley admitted. "But apparently she told my mother that the mask was in your collection, and that you said it gave you the creeps and you were thinking you might sell it one day. My mother asked me to track down your number. I called you, and here I am."

Massarsky sipped his scotch. "You an actor? Writer?"

"I'm a history teacher in San Diego," Ridley said. "My mother was an actress. Her name is Athena Ridley."

"Doesn't ring a bell."

This was a lie. Massarsky had a fairly encyclopedic knowledge of cinema, both the great films and the trash, but Ridley had been rude, and so he wasn't going to give the guy the satisfaction.

Over his career as a studio executive and then as a producer, Massarsky had been involved in dozens of hugely successful films, including several that had earned Oscar nominations and one that had won Best Picture. The walls of his home were festooned with framed photos of himself with some of the great actors and directors of the past forty years, everyone from Robert De Niro to Denzel Washington to Meryl Streep and Jennifer Lawrence. In most of those photos, he had cropped out everyone who wasn't either famous or his own family. His collection of Hollywood memorabilia—Hollywood ephemera—was a motley selection of rarities and one-of-a-kind items, many with particular significance to him. *Chapel of Darkness* was neither. The film had never been completed, but he knew the name Athena Ridley.

"You've seen the unfinished reels of the film, I assume," Ridley said.

Massarsky sipped his scotch. "Of course. They showed up on YouTube years ago."

"My mother is the woman strapped to the table in the ritual scene at the end of act two. I was born the same night. They hired her because she was nearly full-term in her pregnancy and they wouldn't have to use makeup effects to make her look pregnant. I guess they didn't expect her to go into labor in the middle of shooting, three weeks early."

"No. I guess they didn't." Massarsky hesitated. "Did they really try to kill her on camera?"

> > >

Ridley had been warned about Massarsky. His legend painted him as a ruthless snake, drunk on power he hadn't yet realized had begun to fade. Ridley didn't care—all he knew was that he couldn't leave here without the mask, and that meant pretending the question hadn't made him want to knock Massarsky on his ass.

"This stuff is all fairly personal, Mr. Massarsky—"

"Call me James."

"James. You can imagine that it's painful to talk about," Ridley went on. "I've never really known my mother, not the woman she was before she gave birth to me. The woman who filmed *Chapel of Darkness*. She's been in and out of mental health facilities since 1961, the year they shot the film. All I know about the original Athena Ridley are things I've learned from relatives and family friends."

He paused. How much could he share? How much, without making a man like Massarsky decide to double the price for the mask? Ridley saw a strange glint in the other man's eyes and wondered how much he might already know.

"My mother had a psychotic break while filming that scene," he went on. "You must know part of this. An actor named George Sumner was one of the masked cultists in the ritual scene. My mother went into labor, probably set a world record, gave birth to me in just over an hour. They kept shooting while she was screaming, sweating. Filming as if it were all part of the ritual. Later, she said they were really going to sacrifice her. That the ritual had been real, that the cult of Belial was real."

"But George Sumner interfered," Massarsky said.

Ridley paused. How much did he really know? He said he had investigated the provenance of the mask, and it seemed he really had.

"Yes, Sumner interfered. He fled the set and called the police. A camera operator named Olmos helped him get away and he was stabbed to death on set for his trouble. With Sumner gone, they didn't have enough people to complete the ritual—the requisite number, according to my mother's ravings, is thirteen. By the time the police arrived, the whole set was in flames. Several people died in the fire, including the director, but most escaped, my mother among them. Sumner did not die in the fire, but several months later he was struck by a car on Pico Boulevard and killed instantly."

Massarsky tapped a finger against his chin in contemplation. "This is all fascinating, Tim. You mind me calling you Tim?"

"Of course not."

"Good. Tim. It's all fascinating, but it doesn't tell me why your mother wants the mask."

"It doesn't matter, does it? I heard you were interested in selling."

"Oh, I am. The thing gives me the fucking creeps. At first, I liked that, but I've owned it for eighteen months and every week it gets under my skin a little more. But satisfy my curiosity, if you don't mind."

"I told you—"

"Your mother wants to burn it. Yes. Now tell me why."

Massarsky tossed back the rest of his scotch. Ridley's mouth felt parched but he didn't want to drink any more of this asshole's pomegranate juice. He could taste only resentment now.

"You know all the other masks were destroyed in the fire."

"Yes. That's what makes this one valuable. According to police reports, it was the one George Sumner had been wearing."

Ridley nodded. "So I've been told. Blythewood was a small UK company. They financed a ton of these trashy B movies in those days, but they worked on a lean budget. Shutting down *Chapel of Darkness* and never releasing it caused a financial burden that nearly ruined them. Some of the footage was used in other films, but most of it vanished into the vaults until the company was sold to Warner Brothers in 1992. Nobody knows what became of the surviving reels of *Chapel of Darkness* after that. I can't show my mother any of that film, nothing to convince her that—"

"Convince her what? That it wasn't real?" Massarsky asked.

"She's an old woman. Forgotten by everyone but her family and diagnosed with schizophrenia. She wanted me to bring her the mask but she wouldn't say why. I guess she thinks somehow it'll prove to everyone she's not as unstable as she seems. Athena's not the one who wants to burn it, Mr. Massarsky. That's my idea. I figure if I burn it in front of her maybe she'll finally be able to put some of those old fears behind her. Even if the cult of Belial was real, they can't hurt her anymore."

Massarsky sat back in his chair, nodding slowly. "Wow. That's just . . . Tim, that's really sad. I'm honestly sorry."

Ridley blinked in surprise. "Thank you. I do appreciate that. And I appreciate you letting me come here."

They sat together in silence until Massarsky seemed to remember that the next move belonged to him.

"Right. Okay, well, let's have a look at it," he said, lumbering his awkward bulk up from the chair and ambling toward the door. "I should warn you, though, that there's part of the story you don't seem to know."

Ridley followed him into the hall and down the corridor. "What do you mean?"

Massarsky stopped at a thick wooden door and tugged a key ring out of his pocket. "I'll explain in a minute."

He selected a key and slid it into the lock.

As they walked into the vast room, motion-sensitive lights flickered on. The illumination had a softness to it that could not have been accidental, and as Ridley glanced around, he realized just how seriously Massarsky took his collection. There were museum-quality displays inside clear cubes and behind locked glass cabinets. Some items were individually lit from within. Ridley spotted the rare poster for *Revenge of the Jedi*, the original name for the third *Star Wars* film, but based on what he saw displayed, he figured that was the least unique item in Massarsky's collection.

"This is impressive," he said, barely aware he'd spoken aloud.

"It's my passion. Almost as much as making films. Sometimes even more so."

Ridley glanced around, spotting a red balloon floating atop its string inside one case and a blood-encrusted sword inside another. He saw a car steering wheel mounted beside a photo of James Dean and didn't dare ask. Rumor suggested Massarsky's collection tended toward the morbid, and Ridley preferred not to know.

"Would you like a tour?" Massarsky asked.

"Maybe another time. For now, I'd just like to see the mask."

"I understand. You must be anxious to try this experiment with your mother."

"I think of it as therapy."

Massarsky nodded as he led Ridley up one aisle and then turned into a short, wide hallway that housed part of the collection. Overhead lights flickered on in this little annex. There were masks, pieces of costume wardrobe, and even a full-size head of the actor who had played a cyborg in the first *Alien* film. Oh, what was his name? Ridley couldn't bring it to mind.

"Here it is," Massarsky said, gesturing toward a glass case about waist high. Inside, stretched over a plastic mannequin head, George Sumner's cult of Belial mask gazed out at them, eyeless but still somehow ominous.

For a second, Ridley thought it had seen him, and he shuddered.

"You're sure this is it?" he asked.

Massarsky scowled as he used another key to open the glass case. "I can show you the paperwork. It's been verified by the top Blythewood Studios scholar. More than that, it matches some of the still photos I've acquired from the shoot."

The thing seemed dreadfully ordinary, reminiscent of one of those Carnival masks sold in Venice, but with a lovely simplicity. Its bone-white hue had been inscribed with black and red symbols that might have been runes or some kind of occult sigils.

"It doesn't look like much."

"And yet," Massarsky said, "it's what you came for. Now, please, Tim, I have work to do. If you don't want a tour, that's fine, but let's wrap this up."

Ridley approached the case. His breath froze in his chest as he reached out with both hands to retrieve the mask.

"The price we discussed?" he asked.

"Yes. Let's just get it done," Massarsky said, practically barking the words.

Ridley narrowed his eyes and studied the man. For the first time he realized that Massarsky hadn't been lying. The mask really did unsettle him.

"What's the matter?" he asked. "What the hell are you afraid of?"

Massarsky smiled thinly. "Just don't put it on. I've let several people put it on, and it's been a mistake every time. They've ended up with nightmares."

"That's ridiculous," Ridley said.

But as he drew the mask from its case and felt the rough, dry-leather texture of the thing, he felt his pulse quicken. His heart thumped a bit harder. Unbidden, his hands lifted the mask toward his face and he bent his neck slightly.

"Ridley, wait," Massarsky said, reaching for his arm. "I know how it sounds, but several people have had odd experiences. Said they'd seen—"

Somehow, Ridley managed to pause with the mask only inches from his face. He could see through the eyeholes, could make out a display case containing the derby hat Peter Lorre had worn as Moriarty in the ill-fated, never-completed 1933 German-language version of *The Adventures of Sherlock Holmes*. The hat had caught Ridley's attention in the instant before Massarsky had shown him the mask.

"What did they see?" Ridley asked.

"I don't know. It's hard to explain."

"Have you ever put the mask on?"

"Once," Massarsky admitted.

"And what did you see?"

"Nothing," he said, but Ridley thought he might be lying.

The urge to don the mask felt so strong that his hands trembled until he surrendered. With a breath of relief, Ridley placed the mask over his face, tying its silk ribbons at the back of his head.

Massarsky and his collection were gone.

Ridley's hands fell to his sides. His breathing sounded impossibly loud behind the mask. He felt the urge to turn and run, but his body would not obey. Instead he froze, a whispered profanity slithering inside the mask, and slowly scanned the darkened space around him. He had never been on the set of a movie before, but he saw the camera operator and the people swinging microphone booms around and adjusting lighting rigs and knew this couldn't be anything but that.

Not just any movie, either.

The world seemed to tilt beneath him. Ridley nearly collapsed when he allowed his gaze to focus on the stone altar. A much younger version of his mother lay there, head thrown back in a silent cry of agony. A hooded man knelt between her splayed legs as a woman stood over her, an officiant with her arms lifted in mock ecstasy, chanting some guttural gibberish. The woman wore the mask of the cult of Belial, as did the robed extras gathered around the set. The young and beautiful Athena Ridley let out a roar, a kind of battle cry, and her face turned bright red beneath her cinema makeup. She was an actress, but this could not be a performance.

The whole cast took up the chant.

Even Ridley found himself chanting, his mouth moving of its own volition. His mind did not know these words or this language, yet he spoke all the same. A rare exultation soared in his heart, his skin felt flush, and if there had been any doubt that this ritual must be genuine, that joy erased it. The camera kept rolling.

The hooded man received the infant into his arms. Timothy Ridley stared at the newborn, its pink skin smeared with blood and birth fluids. When the hooded man turned, Ridley saw his mask, and the glint of silver from the blade of the ceremonial dagger in his hand. He wanted to scream.

Thoughts collided, fear battling reason. Here he stood, impossibly and yet inarguably viewing the past through the mask of a dead man.

The blade severed the umbilical cord. Robed figures moved into a circle around mother and child. Ridley found himself moving, too. From the corner of his eye, he saw the camera operator shift position—saw the director signaling with his hands, saw the boom microphone swing lower.

The officiant behind the altar reached into her robe and produced a dagger identical to the first. One by one, the cultists drew their blades and raised them high. Ridley's own fingers slithered inside the folds of his robe and found a sheathed dagger. He felt the unaccountably icy cold of its handle, and he drew the blade out, against his will.

His eyes welled with tears.

"No," he managed to whisper, even as this body stepped toward the altar. Toward his mother, and toward the newborn that already had his brown eyes, already had the little furrow of the brow that would mark his every adult expression.

Within the vault of his thoughts, Ridley fought back. Mustering his will, he forced his eyes closed. For a moment he felt torn between worlds, times, realities. He could hear, as if from the bottom of a well, Massarsky's voice speaking his name. "Mr. Ridley. Mr. Ridley, are you all right?" Even the temperature of the room shifted, turning into the cool of Massarsky's air-conditioned palace in the Hollywood Hills instead of the warm, close, nearly suffocating air on that long-forgotten film set, with its choreographed spotlights and strategic shadows.

Wake up, he thought, even though he knew this was no dream.

Steeling himself, he forced his hands to rise. If he could untie the mask, tear it from his face, he could step away from this. George Sumner had been the actor wearing this mask, all those years ago, and he'd found the courage and strength to break away from the scene, to flee the ritual. Ridley had to do the same. Then Olmos, the man behind the camera, would step in to protect the infant.

His left hand touched the silk ribbons tied behind his head, but then he felt a sharp pain on the right side of his neck . . . the tip of the ceremonial dagger puncturing the skin, drawing his blood. His hand clenched around the hilt and he opened his eyes.

Opened George Sumner's eyes.

"No!" he shouted again, but this time he stumbled forward, and his heartbeat was his own. It thrummed, the wings of a caged bird, and he shoved two of the cultists aside.

A woman pointed her dagger at his sternum and he knocked her hand away, then tore off her mask. Beneath the painted sigils of the cult of Belial was a familiar face, some starlet or other, but with her identity bared she drew away from him—from the altar—as if she could not proceed with what came next without the mask.

By this time, in reality—in history—George Sumner had run. What did it mean that Ridley wore George Sumner's mask, wore his body, and had not run?

"Cut!" the director barked.

In the scrum of people, Ridley saw and felt everything at once.

The infant in the arms of the hooded man—the bloody, smeared infant with his brow furrowed, about to launch his first plaintive wail in this world.

The strange, sickly glint of light in the eyes of the crew all around them in the dark, beyond the booms and the camera, their silhouettes strangely misshapen, hunched and crooked and waiting like predators full of anticipation.

The actors in their masks, these actors who were not acting, closing in around the altar ever tighter, suffocating.

The hooded man who had delivered baby Timothy Ridley, the man who now held him up as an offering.

The raised daggers.

"Cut!" the director shouted again.

The officiant chanted louder to drown the director out, and the others followed suit.

But it was Ridley's own mother, the young ingenue, half-naked and draped in silk, belly partly deflated, who raised her head and sneered across the set at the director.

"Don't you fucking dare stop shooting," Athena Ridley snarled.

The first dagger swept down, but it did not plunge into her flesh. Instead, the officiant dragged the blade across Athena's belly, splitting the skin so that blood began to seep and run and stain white silk.

"The blood of the mother!" the officiant cried.

The chant was echoed from behind a dozen masks . . . including Ridley's own. He was himself, but he was also George Sumner. A George Sumner whose moment to flee had passed.

Another blade rose, and Ridley could not let it fall. He bent low and drove his shoulder into a cultist, knocked the actor aside, and threw himself to the stone floor beside the altar. On his knees, he found himself eye to eye with Athena.

"Mom, please," he said quietly. "What do I do?"

"Speak the words," his mother said. "Summon him."

The circle erupted with chanting. Ridley joined them. He felt the name Belial on his lips without understanding the rest, and could only watch as the hooded man set the infant back between its mother's legs, still smeared in blood and birth fluids. Again voices called out to Belial.

Ridley couldn't breathe. The room darkened, as if the whole world had dimmed. The film crew were truly only shadows now, shadows and gleaming eyes. Time had frozen between one heartbeat and the next. He felt a loss that cut to the bone, grief pouring into him. Another dagger swept down, this one in the grip of the hooded man, and sliced across the infant's chest, just above his heart, only deep enough to draw blood.

The burn of that cut sliced across Ridley's own chest. He could feel the wicked bite of the blade and the trickle of blood down his skin, though no blade had touched him.

He screamed and lunged for the baby, but an enormous man struck him in the temple and hurled him against the stone base of the altar. A booted foot crunched down on his throat, pinning him to the floor. Inside George Sumner's mask, Ridley began to suffocate.

He still clutched Sumner's dagger, but as he raised his hand, another cultist dropped upon him, a blond woman whose mask seemed partly askew. He glimpsed the corner of her smile under the mask as she trapped his arm against the floor with her knees.

Her dagger was the first to cut him. She lifted it with both hands and rammed it through the meat of his shoulder, cleaving muscle. Blood sprayed and he screamed with the voices of two men, decades apart. Another blade bit into his thigh. The third plunged into his abdomen, the fourth into his side, the fifth into his right arm, scraping bone as it jammed between ulna and radius. After that, Ridley could no longer scream. Numbness flooded into his veins to replace the blood that spilled out. The blade that thrust into the side of his face, shattering teeth, might have been the tenth or eleventh. He felt that one, though he was no longer capable of screaming. He could weep, though, and he did.

When they were finished, there had been twelve wounds. Twelve daggers. Twelve murderers in their Belial masks on the set of *Chapel of Darkness*, every moment preserved on celluloid.

His mother, Athena, slipped off the altar. Had the afterbirth come? He wasn't sure, but she was there beside him nevertheless, kneeling with the infant Timothy in her arms, still smeared with their shared fluids. The baby suckled at her breast in quiet contentment as Ridley's blood pooled on the stone floor. The officiant raised her arms and began a prayer to gods of pain and cruelty.

Athena bent to whisper in his ear. "He is close. So near to us now. But only you can complete the ritual. Only you can bring him into our midst."

One hand cradling the babe, she reached the other to touch his arm. She took his right wrist and lifted it, and his fingers began to open but she clasped hers around them, making sure he kept his grip on the dagger. The last dagger. The thirteenth.

As the baby nursed quietly, she helped him bring the dagger to his own throat and she kissed his temple.

"This part must be yours," she said.

Ridley would have laughed if he could have. Lunacy. It was lunacy. He would never . . .

But in the shadows overhead, something breathed. The shadows themselves had form and awareness and they waited impatiently, urgent with desire. The chanting rose into a sensual crescendo and it seemed to caress him. This body knew what it had to do.

He drew the blade across his throat and a wave of blissful relief swept over him. It lasted only a moment before a chill seized him, icy needles of pain. Ridley inhaled sharply and his eyes went wide. The shadows roiled and coalesced around him, enveloping him, and as he sipped his last breath, he drew the shadows into George Sumner's lungs.

As his life ebbed, he heard the baby crying, and the voice was his own.

> > >

Massarsky felt the room go cold. He always had the air-conditioning up too high, but this was something else. A glaze of frost settled on Ridley's skin. At one point the man had been talking behind the mask, a quiet chant in some language Massarsky could not make out. He'd even reached up to untie the mask, but something had stopped him. Ridley had dropped his hands to his sides again and hadn't moved since. Massarsky had moved, though, backing first a few steps and then a good eight or nine feet away. He hadn't lied about the three people he had allowed to try on the mask before. All of them had seen something when they'd put the mask on, something that had given them hideous dreams, but none had reacted the way Ridley had.

"Jesus," he muttered. He could see his own breath. With a shiver, he crossed his arms, trying to keep warm.

Frost had formed on the mask now, and somehow it no longer really looked like a mask. Instead, Ridley appeared to have a
caul over his face, a thin membrane with blue veins just below
the surface, veins whose patterns matched the symbols that had
been drawn there before.

Ridley turned to look at him, the movement so abrupt that
Massarsky let out a tiny squeak of fear. Behind that mask, that
caul, Ridley's eyes glittered with flecks like embers, as if they
reflected some celestial hell.

"The circle is complete," a woman's voice said, making Massarsky squeak once more.

He exhaled, watching his breath mist in front of him. Massarsky did not turn around. He did not know how she had gotten
into the room, though he had known she would come. She had
promised, after all, that she would be there.

"You brought payment?" he asked.

Athena Ridley, aged and riddled with cancer, had a rough,
rasping laugh. "You are bold," she said. "I've always liked that in
a man. And yes, of course. I've left the money on your pillow, the
way men like you have always done for whores."

She walked to her son. Or whatever now lived behind that
mask, inside those glittering eyes.

"Come, my love," the dying woman whispered, taking the
silent thing by its hand. "At last, we may begin."

When they'd left, Massarsky locked the door behind them.

Then he wept.

And then he counted his money.

FOLIE À DEUX, OR THE TICKING HOURGLASS

Usman T. Malik

I WANTED TO MAKE a hundred mothers cry.

In Shahdara was his villa. A pretty, spacious thing with an artificial pond set in the enormous basement and a gym filled with benches, barbells, and training equipment bought at Loha Bazaar. He was such a good neighbor, indulgent, generous, and the street was filled with urchins and runaways. They were received there, anyone who needed food and succor. He welcomed them with open arms. Fish swam in his pond, bright orange and blue green turned misty-magical by the play of light and shadows in the basement. After the older boys had worked out and a masseur oiled and rubbed and pressed open their knots, he and his boys, young and old, walked downstairs to watch the fish with wide-eyed wonder. Together they dropped feed into the pond and sang children's songs. They especially loved singing "Machlee ka bacha Pani mai se nikla":

> The fish's son jumped out of the water
> Father caught it. Mother cooked it.

We all ate it. Had so muuuch fuuunnn.
So muuuch fuuuun.

In Shahdara was his video game arcade. A nine-year-old boy in a colorless shalwar kameez slammed the token slot, fished around in his pocket, cursed, looked around. He caught sight of a one-hundred-rupee note curled on the floor like a Gold Leaf wrapper, Jinnah's unforgiving face peering at the ceiling. Eyes lit up, the boy ambled across the shop.

I swear to God, the boy would say later, I never stole the money. It was just *there*.

In Shahdara next to the video game arcade was a room dusty and windowless. Thieves were sent there for disciplining. The room was mostly quiet. Occasionally a moaning sound might cut through the machine gun, beeping, and laser sounds of the arcade.

In Shahdara adjacent to his villa was a concrete godown. It had huge double doors and rust on the padlock. Sometimes a chemical smell spilled out from beneath the doors, eye-watering and acrid.

I could have killed more, could have killed five hundred, but I didn't. I didn't want to break my vow. One hundred was the promise.

The sentence would be commensurate to the crimes, said the local magistrate. He would be taken to Iqbal Park; in the shadow of the majestic Minar-e-Pakistan, before a blue lake, he would be hanged to death. His body would be chopped into one hundred pieces, dissolved in acid in front of the parents, and cast into the Ravi River.

The sentence was immediately challenged by the provincial government, condemned by human rights organizations, and denounced by a local sharia court, but each passing day brings it closer to fruition.

And we will film it all. The butchering of a butcher.

> > >

You have an hour, they say. I am amazed Amina managed even that.

He sits straight in his chair, his dirty salt-and-pepper hair parted to the right. He is smaller than on TV. "You two," he says. He looks so ordinary.

Amina stares into his eyes. She wears a pretty mauve head scarf that is knotted around her chin and flutters a bit when she speaks, "Aap jantay hain hum kyoon aye hain?"

"I know why you're here."

"Khalid sahib will help us with the taping and, later, filming," Amina says, nodding at me. I click the tape recorder on. "Can you identify yourself for the record?" He does. Amina goes on, "This is an extraordinary sentence. It is possible they might not move forward with it."

"You know what they say isn't true, but this isn't a sham, either. Art never is. Did they tell you I went to NCA—yes, the college—and almost graduated before I opened the game arcade?" He looks at her, tugs at the collar of his sweater. He has a soft chin, and the thick turtleneck holds it aloft like an egg. "Doesn't matter what they say. Doesn't matter what they do but I'm glad everyone will watch and hear my story." He lowers his head and his square plastic glasses slide down his piggish nose. He could pass as a schoolteacher. A child could look into those soft hazel eyes, find them friendly and comforting.

"No one has ever cared. For too long the world has stayed silently complicit. No more. It should know what it did to me, what it plans to do to me."

The electric fan of the police station whirs above us. The room smells like sweat and cigarettes. Amina sits still.

"What it does all the time to my orphans, my runaways."

"And what *has* the world done to you or those orphans?" Amina says.

He laughs. "Have you ever read the papers? How many children disappear off the streets of Lahore daily? How many cops and waderas and judges are involved in those trafficking rings? Me, I have been saving them for years. Taking them off the streets. Homing them."

"A wonderful homing that included rape and murder, sure." Amina raises an arm, brushes a stray hair away from her eyes. She was an acne-prone teen now left with pockmarks. I've seen her touch them sometimes, but not today.

I say, "They want your blood."

He licks the left corner of his lips, then the right, quick darts. I saw him do that in the first interview. There is even a grainy paparazzi shot: his dark snaillike tongue worrying the pencil-line mustache, his mocking gaze fixed sidelong at the crowd of onlookers and policemen—a macabre snapshot picked up by hundreds of media outlets and shot around the world in a matter of hours. "They are garbage and they want garbage things. This video, though, after it's done—"

"Do you have any family?" Amina doesn't use his name, won't. "It will be tough on them."

"Just my boys."

"Your boys?"

"My beautiful boys."

"Your father?"

"Passed away two years ago."

"There is a chance," Amina says, "we could put a halt to the filming. A court order—"

"No."

"So be it. Theek hai. We'll make sure we're ready."

He shows yellow teeth. "I'm sure you will."

Amina is staring at his teeth. She has hidden her hands away from him under the table. Her left, closer to me, is a fist. What does she see? An image of those teeth gently biting down on a brown nipple. A filthy godown in Shahdara, bare yellow bulbs dangling from the wood-slatted ceiling, smell of dust and wheat chaff; and between the dozens of wheat sacks, arms and legs moving languorously.

Acid-Walla they call him, I think, and squeeze my eyes shut briefly.

"We will be in touch with the Inspector sahib." Amina is standing. She moved so softly it is unnerving. "Tell me something."

He waits with all the patience in the world.

"Why give yourself up? Why send the letter?"

He pushes his glasses up his nose and squints at her. "What's your name again?"

She tenses.

"Amina Swati, *Daily Jang*," he reads from her ID card. His tongue sweeps out and in. "As God is my witness, Amina dear, we will become *frands*. One day you will know what that means. Then you will understand the true nature of the *frandship* I gave my boys." He says the word in English, stretching it out like wet taffy, sweetmeat put away for later consumption. "But if you can get me the hourglass, I'll tell you more."

"What?"

He leans across the table. "My mother's ticking hourglass. Find out what they did with it and everything you want to know—yours."

There is a look in her eyes; Amina turns and walks out. I follow her and we cross the courtyard under the warm late-afternoon sun to the main gate of Kot Lakhpat Jail. A group of prisoners are playing badminton. They eye us as we pass but say nothing.

I glance at Amina. Her face is white as the walls of his cell.

"Monster," she says. "Crazy, filthy son of a whore. He should be raped by a dozen men and dumped in the gutter." She won't look at me when she says those words. "They played right into his hands. He wanted this."

"Wanted what?"

"For his final act to be as public as possible."

"Why do you think?"

"Because he's nuts and all psychopathic nuts want the world to know them. Acknowledge them. Validate their miserable, worthless existence."

It is eleven a.m. on Friday, October 12. The sentence, we've been told, will be carried out in exactly a month.

> > >

I first heard about House Number-100 from our family tutor Sir Akram the Terrifier, who gave private tuition to us all. He rode his bicycle from one cousin's home to another, oiled hair curled and glistening beneath his dusky wool cap, and special-knocked on our doors. We hated that cap. We hated his bicycle. He used to have a motorbike, but after receiving a particularly nasty beating, Khan Bhai took a cricket bat to it, smashed it into a misshapen hunk. Threw the hunk in the empty parking lot behind our joint-family home. (A school now stands in that lot.) Gul Uncle had to pay Sir Akram for a new bike and my cousin was grounded for months.

Khan Bhai still grins when he talks about that. "It was a glorious day," he says. "A win for us kids." In hindsight he respects our tutor, brings Sir Akram's kids presents—real conscientious is my cousin—but back then he was pissed. "Told Sir not to touch my face but he didn't listen, did he?"

House Number-100 near Kabootar Poora. Sir Akram tutored the children who lived there: two boys bright and courteous who worshipped their teacher, he said. So hospitable that he never had to punish them. Cardamom tea and buttered toast served each time he went to their house. Their grandmother was a *visitant*—a pahunchi-hui-khatoon. Everyone knew she commanded jinn; they fell in with her, silent and vaporous. A body of a man glimpsed prostrate on a prayer mat, vanished in the flick of the eye, then back in that meem shape, his hair limp and heavy like tarred straw, arms outstretched before the deity.

Sir Akram insisted the deity was God.

Her grandchildren, he said, were told to tread lightly at dusk, to be careful, respectful. Respect goes a long way (especially toward one's teachers). Dusk belongs to the jinn, and the house unfolds at night.

I last met Khan Bhai a few years ago after a road altercation left him bed-bound for a week. His leg was broken in four different places; he had fractured three fingers. "Happens," he said. I admired his restraint, his indifference. His unsmiling wife brought us tea and left the room. We sat and sipped. Life really had grounded him well.

"Do you remember the Parhai-Ka-Neelam-Ghar Sir Akram used to hold?" Khan Bhai said.

"Yes!" I cried. "I haven't thought of it in years."

"Education Jeopardy." He slapped his thigh, laughing. "My God. Those sweets. Remember how he'd give out sweets to the winners? Or if you could pronounce all the prayers correctly?"

I smiled. "I remember. You used to win all the time."

"You did, too. At least for a while." Khan Bhai coughed up a bit of tea. "Later, I think, you got behind a bit, no? Got belted a few times."

"Yes, me and Salman, both. Remember when he was beaten with that stick, the one with rusted nails in it? God, we thought he wouldn't stop bleeding. Would die of tetanus or something."

He looked at me, frowning. "Who? I thought it was you." He dipped a cake rusk in his tea. "I do remember that day. Kind of. It still find it amazing that, even though they knew, our parents never said anything besides, 'Sir jee, please be careful next time.' What the fuck, right?" It was eerie, a bit discomfiting, seeing Khan Bhai mimic Sal's mother. He was good at that, always had been. Mimicking, pretending, surviving. "To top it off, if you complained too much, your parents would beat you up as well. I mean, so where does one go? It's such a trap." He tapped a bandaged finger on his tea saucer. "You know, it's funny: I don't remember half of that time. I'm sure I'm not the only one who wants that shit behind me. You hang out recently with any other cousin?"

"It's been a while."

"Hasn't it?" He grimaced and shifted his leg. "These bahanchod pins. They told me they don't hurt after the first few days, but my leg is on fire."

"Maybe put a little salt on the dressing," I suggested.

"Oh, fuck off now." He chuckled. His face was a bit pale, a sheen of sweat on his forehead. "I hope the leg's not infected."

I told him it wasn't. The leg looked fine, it really did. Nice and healthy, warm and pink. It was a surprise when three days later Khan Bhai was hospitalized.

On the fourth they took the leg.

> > >

I tell her he is crazy, no point in wasting time, but Amina is bent upon due diligence.

She goes to the police, she asks around. She harangues the forensics team until they issue her a permit allowing her to revisit the villa and the godown in Shahdara. The bloodstains have been scrubbed, the piles of tiny clothing removed, the tagged plastic bags with earrings and bracelets and warding amulets long submitted as evidence; but the metal chain, polished until it shines, still hangs from the ceiling. The rich coppery smell lingers.

Amina tries to enter the basement. The door is locked.

In the godown she upends the few remaining gunnysacks. A thin sprinkle of grain, wheat dust, nothing else, she tells me later.

No hourglass anywhere.

"The man is delusional," I repeat. "You *do* you see that, no?"

Amina and I go to the newspaper office to discuss potential interviews with the two boys hiding in his villa when he was arrested. Both have been sentenced as accomplices to several years in prison. We are told it would take a week to get security clearance for either to talk to us.

"There have been threats against the three of them," Nadeem Bhai says. He is a tall, lanky man with wild Manto hair and round horn-rimmed glasses. "That is the reason he turned himself in publicly, you know, after the letter he sent. Matter of time before he was found and lynched. Maybe killed extrajudicially by a cop."

"Folks in Shahdara knew him well. His history of violence. Sexual abuse of minors. An incident from years ago when he was nearly beaten to death by a mob," Amina says. "This wasn't his first play."

"No," Nadeem Bhai says. "It wasn't."

"We all know much of what he's saying is bullshit," Amina says. "We have normal, healthy kids who lead normal, healthy lives. We all went to regular schools with regular kids and their regular, normal parents. What I'm wondering—what has been keeping me up at night—is"—she leans forward—"how could've things come to a head like this? How come no one in that neighborhood figured out what was going on in that house and that godown? Are we that blind to what's right in front of us?"

Nadeem Bhai looks at her and says nothing.

> > >

Everybody knew a cannibal lived in the graveyard near Kabootar Poora. He was tall and graceless with long shaggy hair, his body covered in black oil, maybe it was tar. His teeth were crooked (but very sharp); his eyes, slit and peeled like the inside of an onion. At dusk if you walked near the market wall of the graveyard—a broil of branches bore down on the sidewalk there—a shadow would swoop and drop on you, an oily weight, and you'd never be seen again.

Stories of its seizures of little children were rampant. Hadi, the chowkidar's son, had seen one with his own eyes.

I was never seized, even though I walked those streets at night. The day would end, the sun would slink away, its weak orange tail between its legs, and I would sneak out of the house and race to Kabootar Poora, where Sheeda the shopkeeper would give me leftover soda from a prior customer. I would tip the bottle

What is the meal prayer?

In the name of Allah the Beneficent and Merciful

and chug it, letting the iced liquid soothe my parched and raw throat. *Lub lub lub. Dub dub.*

The graveyard near Kabootar Poora was hauntingly beautiful. Marble tombstones dappled with sunlight surrounded by solemn peepul, banyan, and neem. Mounds of baked earth beneath a web of ancient branches and limbs, leaves drifting in still air. Is there a mystery more charming than the calligraphy on ancient gravestones?

A barbecue vendor had set up shop by the eastern wall of the graveyard. We often joked his kebabs were the best in the city for a reason. I remember one night vaulting the wall of our home, Salman in the lead—he always was the brave one—his eyes gleaming like a cat's, racing to the bazaar. We swigged Coke, smoked a couple cigarettes, kicked over a brand-new bicycle near the video game arcade, then fled to the graveyard, where we stole a couple seekhs from the vendor and munched kebabs all the way home. Or were they leg pieces? Sometimes I suppose it's difficult for children to remember, even if they were paid sweets to remember, or sometimes to forget, and in the spaces between remembering and forgetting are—

I think there was a rustle in the bushes, a shadow that had followed us. I saw it rush at Salman, but we got lucky because there was a muhallah chowkidar making his rounds and Salman yelled and the chowkidar came running, and that was that.

What is the Proclamation of Faith?

I bear witness that there is no god but God, and Muhammad is His messenger.

We could have been witness to so much more but we weren't. We were lucky that night. No cannibal ever dragged us into an old house where jinns lived harmoniously with mad old ladies. No one *ever* seized me, or knocked me about, seriously hurt me. I was fortunate that way.

Lub lub lub. Tap tap. Tick tick.

Tick tick go my earliest memories, dim-lit, colorless. Certain smells—laddoo, black plum, coconut oil—may flood some of them with color for the briefest instant, then like the aftermath of a lightning crack, they return to lifelessness.

In one I sit in our room in the old family house with a tall chador-clad maid next to me. Fiercely I grip her hands, my eyes locked with hers. I am small, no more than four, and I gaze up at her and say, "This world is nothing. What comes after it's done ticking is the real thing." She is silent, looming, ink-faced. I can't tell if she listens raptly or is somewhere far away. "I have seen this clearly," I say. "So clearly."

No color, no sound, no stirring of life in this memory, this room, our old house, in the comfortless proximity of this tall, brooding maid toward whom I have no feelings. I don't remember her face, her name, the feel of her hands, her gaze, her shadow on me. I cannot smell that chador, although I have smelled dozens like it since.

"I know it," I say. "I *know* it."

Sometimes I can hold this memory in my hand. I try to feel its ends and follow them, but here remembrance breaks and I find myself in mazing corridors.

The next thing I remember is a dream I dreamed a few times as a boy:

Salman and I are walking home from the graveyard, gnawing on pink-red chicken legs, large as a baby's. The moon is full and then it's not, and from the bower of banyan and peepul limbs overhead a shadow drops and we startle and run. This time no chowkidar shows up with a lantern in one hand and a large whistle in the other, no sharp warning sound: *Fleee Fleeee*. Instead the shadow, oil-limbed and glistening, chases after us. We sprint, panting, until Salman trips over a cluster of bushes and drops, and the shadow falls over him.

Terrified, I scramble up a tree and watch them wrestle. The boy twists and thrashes; the shadow pins the boy's arms behind his back. A twinkle of moonlight on metal on the shadow's forearm; it turns him around, fumbling with his shorts. The boy screams and the shadow shoves its fist into the boy's back. *Tick* goes the metal-thing on the shadow's forearm

It's a Rolex, a beautiful, expensive Rolex, I think

and the boy's vision is filled with dirt and bramble. Above him is the ink face of the sky pressing itself into the boy's neck and back, an urgent paucity of moonlight, any light, and the boy stops moaning even as the shadow begins.

Tap tap. Tick tick. Tick tick. TICK TICK!

The frequency of the ticking, the tapping by the boy's head increases; as if someone is hammering on a giant iron door. So fast now, as if there is a gurgle in the earth.

Sometime later the shadow is up and gone. Salman staggers from the bushes, his chest hitching. I climb down and we try to walk home, but we are confused; around us darkness has swept in deeper and more palpable than we have ever known. The roads, streets, and alleys don't make sense, the gutters are overflowing. I look at Salman but his face is a watery mirror of mine; his eyes are like holes in an old, withered tree. Soon we come upon the doorstep of a small, narrow two-storied house near Kabootar Poora. A large marble plaque proclaims a terse message that glitters, suddenly moonlit:

100

We fumble with the door handle and pile in when the door opens.

> > >

"Did you find it?"

"No."

"They took it when they searched my house."

"No one saw it. No one has it." Amina watches him tilt his chin and scratch it with a dirty, uneven fingernail. His beard has grown out in a salt-and-pepper fuzz. "If you tell me where you hid it, maybe I can try again or have someone else look."

He leans back in his chair, studying her. He has the same turtleneck on he wore the last time we came. "The hourglass has sat on top of my cupboard for years. I've never allowed anyone to touch it. After sending the letter, when I had to go underground for a few weeks, I took it with me to a friend's haweli inside Delhi Gate but I brought it back later. It was in my bedroom when I went to your paper. It was in my bedroom when they called the police. You cannot miss it. It isn't exactly dead, you know."

"It ticks?"

"Yes."

"The hourglass? Your mother's hourglass ticks?"

"Yes. Quite loudly, too."

Amina tongues the inside of her upper lip, gives me a side-long glance. I raise my eyebrows. "Do you know how long it has been ticking? Does it have batteries?" I say.

He smiles at me with his teeth. "You think I'm crazy."

"What do *you* think?"

"You think I don't know how hourglasses work? I do, you smug chootiyay. But this one is different. My mother, she—" He fidgets in his chair, pulls up the edge of his sweater so it cushions his chin. "My mother, my grandparents weren't ordinary people. We've had miracles in our family for generations. That hourglass, it has been ticking for as long as I can remember. It is a wonderful thing, a fabulous thing. It told me my destiny, it has comforted me for years and years. It has comforted my boys, my poor hungry boys. It has called—"

Soft like silk, Amina says, "I'd say you're full of shit."

He goes still. Amina's pockmarks are flushed, the red imbuing deep shadows to them. I think I see them tremble with her heartbeat.

"I spoke to the policeman who questioned your boys. Your boys don't remember seeing an hourglass or a clock in your house. They said you hated timepieces, that there was none in the villa—"

"The hourglass is not that—"

"—That you told them *not* to go near a cupboard in your bedroom, but they thought it was because you kept all your money there—"

"—Easy to see. It can hide itself from the wrong sort—"

"—And the police found some of the tagged plastic packets in that cupboard. They were filled with . . . souvenirs from the dead children."

Silence. Amina pincers the edge of the table between her thumb and index and leans forward. "Suppose I believe you for a moment. Suppose there is a ticking hourglass and I find it and bring it to you. What do you plan to do with it?"

He moves his head from left to right, his gaze fixed on Amina. He begins to tap a knuckle on the table. Fixed intervals, patient, ceaseless. *Tap tap tap tap.* His eyes shine, those friendly soft eyes. "You know I hear it ticking every night, even though I can't see it? It misses me as much as I miss it." His tongue flicks in and out. "I would listen to it. Every remaining moment of my life till they took me to the gallows. I would ask them to have it next to my body as the TV stations stream your masters mutilating me so the entire world can listen to my mother's hourglass. It doesn't tick for everyone, but there must be someone like me out there who can hear it, who will understand."

Amina's face is contorted with disgust.

"Who will know what it is like to be my one of my boys, to be *me*. My mother's hourglass will draw them to their destiny, just as it drew me."

"So you'd like someone to assume your mantle. A copycat."

"I love the fact that you're my frand in all this. My partner in getting this message out to the world. More people need to hear about the punishment this naked, guilty society doles out to kids like my boys."

"If it were up to me, I would let you rot in prison forever. This debacle of a public execution"—she shakes her head—"you would have none of it."

"I believe I told you I was at NCA? I'm an artist. Think of this as body art of a sort, and now you will stream"—he tap tap taps away—"the metamorphosis of my body, its disassembly to every corner of the planet. This cunt of a country—the whole world, really—will bear witness to its crimes toward us."

Amina looks like she wants to say something, but our time is up.

As we leave, she says, "I can't do this. I'm telling Nadeem Bhai to find someone else."

"I don't blame you—"

"His art? He raped and molested dozens of children, killed God knows how many street kids, and now he wants airtime? I won't be a part of his games, his delusions."

"You might want to think about this for a second. We're the only official channel to be allowed to stream it. Public executions such as this can be deterrents—"

"Says who?" She points a finger at me. "All evidence points to the contrary. Anytime an asshole like him is turned into a TV celebrity, five more crawl out of the woodwork. It's a never-ending cycle."

This is true. Carefully I say, "It's a public event. The filming will happen whether we do it or an onlooker does with his personal camera. Think about it for a second. Once we have it on tape, once we've had time to clean it up, add interviews with the parents and witnesses, we could have the docu-film of the decade. "

"The film of the century, the recording of a lifetime. Don't you understand what we're doing?" We're past the police checkpoint at the main gate, and a cyclist, wheeling up the road, turns to watch us. He has a camouflage cap on his head. "The filthy permission we are giving to the world by putting something like this on tape?"

"Someone has to."

She looks at me, startled. "He isn't wrong, then, is he? We're all complicit." She runs a hand through her hair, knocks off her hijab, carelessly fixes it, stares at the cyclist who whirls left and pedals leisurely past us. "Where were we when he molested those boys? All these bloodthirsty, righteous mobs?"

A shiver runs through her, twisting her features, slumping her shoulders. It is as if the world has taken ahold of her, wrung out all that energy, that fervor. "All our filming," she says at last, her voice low, "and capturing and streaming of this is a communal crime, a shared psychotic breakdown. We are shit, aren't we. As a nation and as a species." She turns and begins walking away from me. "And I hate this duplicity."

I watch her stride down the street to her car. Behind me two guards in navy shirts, bulletproof vests, and khaki pants beckon to a motorcyclist without a helmet. Scaling the terraced rooftops on my left is a bare-chested boy who runs with a kite string in hand, the huge patang following him like a predator in the heights. The evening sun has bloodied the horizon. Limned in red, the boy and his patang glow, then sink and vanish behind a jagged brick wall.

I get on my bike and set off for the villa in Shahdara.

> > >

For a long time now I've despised the stories of Alif Laila Wa Laila.

Likely I never developed a taste for fairy tales, such fabular stories of *The Thousand and One Nights*. Perhaps I have realized that the worst thing about them is not the lie they tell us about ourselves but the heedless workmanship, the fragility of the lie. One scratch and you find the real story secreted in the belly of the false.

I find such callousness distasteful and arrogant.

The embryonic truth of one tale (told otherwise for centuries) goes like this:

Once upon a time a fisher boy cast his dragnet into the ocean. Up came seaweed and limpets, short dresses and long hair. Disgusted, he flung them and cast his net again. This time he netted a pale girl face and a wool chador that assumed the shape of things he didn't like. Angry, he ripped the chador and bloodied the face with fishhooks. Back in they went.

He threw his net a third time, for three is also a magic number, and up came gurgling a dozen golden tokens, a weighing scale, and an antique hourglass with brass bases that twinkled in the sun.

Squinting, the fisher boy picked up this last, freed it from the net, turned it upside down. A sandy substance, not quite the color of tar, began to trickle the opposite way. The boy shook the hourglass back and forth, rubbed the verdigris on its bottom.

The sandy substance ceased its ceaseless fall. A shadow fell over the hourglass.

"What is your command, my lord?" the tall, fiery-haired creature—a jinn, the boy realized—said gravely before bursting into laughter.

The boy said, uneasy, "Do I get three wishes?"

The jinn shook his head, still laughing. "No, lordling."

He explained how he'd been trapped in the hourglass and thrown in the sea by a clever sorcerer, destined to trickle forever and forever, and for the first hundred years he vowed to give all the riches in the world to his rescuer.

None came.

Two hundred years passed and he grew cold in his trickling and afraid. He vowed to grant immortality and everlasting beauty to his would-be rescuer, yet luck did not favor him.

Another hundred years passed—

"And by now I'd curved a part of me into a meem shape. I went inside myself. I dreamed of looming towers and lush gardens, the taste of first love and the smell of Paristan and Mount Kaf, how I once chased a young pari down to her fae hole by the river; and I told myself this time I would not be released. This time I would take the man who upends me, removes me, pours me out—and cut him into a hundred pieces. I would dissolve the pieces in acid, then pour it all out into the Ravi River.

"And right on cue, you came along. Only thing is, lordling," the jinn said, looking troubled, "you're not a man."

The boy faced the creature bravely. "Don't mock me, jinn. I am, too."

"Besides," said the jinn, "you don't look like you have enough meat for a hundred pieces."

"Well, you don't look like you could fit in an hourglass, either, but appearances can be deceiving, can't they." The boy had a sly look in his eyes. "In fact, I don't believe you were ever in yonder tiny thing to begin with."

"No?"

"I bet you're all smoke and screen and no real jinn-magic. Prove me wrong if you wish."

"And how do you propose," said the jinn, "I should prove myself?"

"Why," cried the boy, "show me how a grown body could fit into that hourglass!"

The jinn nodded, thoughtful. "As you wish."

He reached forward and grabbed the boy.

The fisher boy screamed.

The jinn snapped his fingers together.

A vat of boiling liquid appeared on the shore. The jinn *hoed* and hummed and clamped his hands around the boy's torso. He wrung him like a washcloth and rinsed him out, and all the while he held him above the vat to catch the seepage, then crumpled him. Into the vat he dropped the soft tail of blood clot that was the fisher boy, lifted the mixture, and chugged it.

Done, he placed the hourglass on the sand, swirled back in, went to sleep.

And dreamed.

> > >

Amina is joyful. She cannot breathe for delight.

The nightmare, she tells me on the phone, is over.

It takes me a moment to get the specifics out of her: Pressured by human rights organizations, the Supreme Court has taken suo moto notice of the "inhumane sentencing." There would be no public hanging, dismemberment, or acidic dissolution; just a plain, good old-fashioned hanging till death.

And there would be no filming.

It really isn't surprising, we tell each other. The local magistrate had become too senti, too dramatic when he passed that verdict. Of course, it was going to be stopped.

He has much to do with it, of course. Relentless visits by human rights workers and activists painting ghastly pictures of his final moments; our killer got scared, caved in, let his lawyer make phone calls, use the egregiousness of the sentence to whip up public anger.

I walk around with the phone receiver cradled between my head and shoulder. Amina jokes that she can hear the grin in my voice. We talk for a bit. It is something of an anticlimax, she admits, but she is tremendously relieved, nevertheless. No streaming of the execution, no viral videos, no duplicity on *her* conscience. "I don't know how I would have faced my own children had I gone through with it," she says.

She finally hangs up. I press the phone once into its cradle, lift it, and make a call. I walk outside, breathe in the night air. I think of Amina and smile at her wonderful innocence, look at the moon and sigh at its beauty. What a blessing it is to have time, I think, and such beautiful sights to spend it on.

The package is to be delivered after midnight.

> > >

Khan Bhai's father had a film shop on Hall Road. Even as a kid I suspected that was why my parents disapproved of my hanging out with Khan Bhai (that and probably the motorbike incident), why Uncle Faris and Father didn't quite get along. Films are haram, photography is haram, we were told. Pictures render living objects into eternal idols and idolatry is haram. Throw in lurid buxom Bollywood and Lollywood heroines humping the air in mango groves and grassy fields and you were talking an all-expenses-paid trip straight to the fires of Jahannam.

One Friday, after school was out, Salman and I hitched a ride to Hall Road with his brother. We got dropped off at Habeeb's Milk Shop, where we bought two bowls of doodh khoya filled with ice cubes swirling in caramelized milk, a layer of tukhm balanga and dry fruit on top. We lapped it all up, then walked to the film shop, where we watched the shop tech clean the video drum of an old VCR. Uncle Faris was out, the shop was mostly empty, and it was a soft spring day. Salman yawned, shook himself, and declared he was going to go explore other shops in the building. The doodh khoya was heavy in my belly. In the back of the shop on a dusty old couch secreted behind half a dozen TV and VCR sets I lay my head down on my schoolbag and went to sleep.

A loud bang startled me awake. I sat up, rubbing the soreness from my neck. The room was lit from a large TV switched on and tuned to a dead channel, the hissing powdery gray squirming on the screen. It had been off when I went to sleep. I got up and walked over. A VCR sat atop the TV with a VHS in its maw. I peered at it, but the title space was blank.

I nudged the VHS in, stepped back, settled on the couch.

Bright rainbow lines fluttered and crackled on the screen. The light and pixels contracted into a tiny fist, then bloomed into Technicolor:

The scene is set at night. Two boys crouch in front of a closed door, their backs to the camera. One tumbles forward as the door swings open, the other quickly glances back—his eyes roll large and white—and follows his friend, slamming the door behind them.

The voice of the narrator comes at the audience: "You watch them enter and at once you are filled with terror. It is as if a boiling vat of vitriol has overturned inside you, the contents frothing their way past the coils in you into your deepest recesses, brightening the edges, jolting your fulcrums."

The boys stand sweating in a halo of light from an overhead chandelier, a jagged beast of a thing hanging above them—one snap and they might be driven from their vessels. Their hearts thump loudly. They're in a wood-floored hall. Odors of incense, jasmine, and coconut oil haunt the air.

The taller of the two hesitates, then steps forward.

"And thus the brave boys go within and not without," proclaims the voice of the narrator.

The camera follows.

They tread softly down the hall lined with frames on either side. The camera pans across some of them: Mughal miniature art replicas, Arabic verses in calligraphy, numbered magic squares, frowning men and children. A portrait of an erect brooding woman seated in a gold-armed chair, shoulders gripped by a pale man with a black beard and kohl-drawn eyes standing behind her.

His is the darkest presence in the house, the boys think, and so thinking hurry on.

Strange the front door was unlocked. Surreal no one has accosted them yet. Where are the residents of the house? A door on their left is wide open. They peer in to see a dim-lit drawing room with plush sofas, a large dinner table, side tables with lovely vases, and sconces on the walls—except the sofas have been moved, the large mahogany dinner table and side tables pushed against the walls.

On a large bedsheet spread on the marble floor in the middle of the room a silent congregation sits kneeling, straight as if in tashahhud. Perhaps a dozen, clad in pristine white.

The boys hang on to the doorframe. Their mouths are open.

Flowers are arranged before the kneelers in bunches and vases that smoke with incense. Clover sticks, half-drained bowls of milk, and jars of honey sit next to the flowers. Faces pallid and perfectly symmetrical, they may as well have been chiseled from ancient stone, loom over them. The congregation is so quiet and still the boys imagine they can hear their pulse resound through the drawing room.

"The house unfolds at night," says the narrator.

A scratching in the walls, in the ceiling. The room shivers once.

The congregation jolts forward. They slam their foreheads

into the floor, one by one, staccato collisions that sound like birds hitting a windowpane. Milk bowls are upended, the vases topple. The lines of heads now lie limp, prostate, bleeding.

The floor gurgles.

The taller of the two boys breaks. He turns and dashes blindly back through the hall, his feet clattering on the wooden floor.

The other boy stands riveted. He is looking at the wall the congregation had been facing.

The camera does not swivel in that direction.

Slow the hands of the congregants as they rise and float in the air in a gesture of obeisance. The torsos remain prone, the bodies curled in comma. Gentle the forward motion of the boy as he steps inside the room and begins walking to the head of the congregation.

"Dusk belongs to the jinns," says the narrator, "and the ones filled with dusk, too."

Darkness falls and the door of the drawing room slams shut.

> > >

The hissing electric gray returned on the TV screen. I got up and turned the TV off, returned to the couch, and went to sleep.

I remember waking in the dark later, screaming my mother's name. Uncle Faris rushed into the back room and, finding no immediate threat, yelled at me. I remember nausea and lethargy and feeling feverish. I remember the rickshaw he hailed for us (day wasn't over yet for him) and Salman and me lurching home through the traffic on Mall Road, Jail Road, and Main Boulevard past Firdous Market with its jalebi and paan khokas and barbecue vendors, me dozing with my head against the green plastic swing door, which had a bright parrot with flamingo plumage painted on it.

I dreamed on the ride home; of this I am certain. I don't remember the dreams.

But even in waking hours, for years and years and years, the vapor and essence of them would hang to the edges of our house, our street, our muhallah. Even Salman noticed there was something wrong with our world; it made him vertiginous, look around him askance, he said, but I could be equally brave and strong sometimes and would wipe the fog away, as if with the edge of my sleeve.

What else was a friend good for, Salman would say, wink and smile; and his eyes would glow bright, dark, and old.

> > >

In Shahdara is a spacious, pretty villa with tall brick walls and a brass gate. I meet my new friends in the street outside.

"Done?"

They nod.

"Trouble?"

"Not much."

I pause for effect. "And the two accomplices?"

"Cared for. A guard will find them tomorrow morning."

I smile broadly to make sure they see it in my eyes through the mask. "Wonderful."

"May Allah bless you," one says. He is beginning to tear up, but his lips are pressed tight together when he doesn't speak. Red rages in his cheeks. "Make sure you—"

"I will take care of it, I assure you, in the most auspicious way inshallah."

The other hesitates. The first nudges him, and they climb into the van and speed away. What they return to remains uncertain. Some will say the loss of a child is a permanent sundering of the heart, and the way theirs went at the hands of a monster . . . a sorrow greater than mountains could bear, or so I read in the Quran as a boy.

Or was it another book?

So little I remember of that boy.

I walk to the entrance of the villa, caress the broken padlock on the gate, and quicken my steps toward the house.

The pond in the basement is black with algae, fetid with the smell of dead fish. Light from a cluster of sixty-watt bulbs set into the ceiling cuts golden swathes into the water. Next to the bulbs is a ceiling hook from which dangles a metal chain, one end of it clamped in the teeth of a cranking mechanism placed next to a tripod and a large vat. A gleaming butcher knife hangs from a hook on the mechanism.

I make for the tripod. Once the angle and camera settings satisfy me I go to him.

He is curled up naked on the marble floor in the center of the basement, hands and feet bound with thick jute rope that loops up and through a metal square pressed against his back. Blood darkens his nostril and the corner of his lips. Tape marks glisten around his mouth. His glasses are cracked and streaked with red. When he parts his lips to sneer, a wheeze escapes them. I'm quite sure the word it carries is "sisterfucker."

A dusty cupboard stands at the far end of the basement. I smile at him brightly before walking over to it and returning.

"Your wish is my command. Here," I say, squatting, and place the hourglass before him.

The sneer disappears. His eyes flash to the hourglass and stay there. We sit in respectful silence for a while.

He whispers, "Who are you?"

I shake my head.

"You can see it?"

I smile and rise to my feet.

He tries to wriggle toward the hourglass. "You can hear it?"

I pause to block his sight line, look him in the eye. "Can you?"

Uncertainty, surprise, fear sit coiled in him. "No, not anymore."

I nod. I reach forward, grab his trussed feet, and begin dragging him toward the hanging chain.

He squirms and tries to roll. "What the fuck are you doing?"

I hook the chain to the clip on his back and begin cranking. Thrashing, he jerks up into the air, twisting higher with every seesaw of the crank. When he's high enough, I stop and fetch the hourglass.

What a thing of beauty it is with its brass bases and the glass bulbs that have not stopped twinkling. Passed down dozens of generations, it has glowed like a beacon, calling some, disappointing others. The dark sands have not stopped falling since the last time I upended it when I visited the villa alone; the trickle ticks. To others the paradox between the seen and the heard might be fatal. The countdown it measures, a period accrued by grains of sand so ancient the desert it was collected from disappeared millennia ago, is exactly one hundred.

One hundred what? That depends on the listener.

I turn it over, noting the tremor that susurrates through its body as the sand begins to fall the other way. On the bottom base whirls the wolf etched in dervish wool, its left index pointed to the heavens, right toward the earth. The wrong configuration. Or the right. Who defines either?

He is spasming on the metal chain, spit and blood flying from his mouth. "Put me down, madarchod."

"You were correct about one thing at least. It was biding its time for the perfect master to claim its mystery." I put the hourglass on the ground, this hereditary beast of his. I carefully feel across the edges of the mask to ensure my features are perfectly obscured. I return to the tripod and fiddle so the angles are just right. "What does an hourglass do, you think?"

That stops him. He hangs, swaying in a circle, his eyes bulging and red with gravity.

"What purpose does it serve?"

Sweat pours down his forehead. He twitches. "My . . . my mother's hourglass is special. It has spoken to—"

"It bears witness to the passage of everything. You did so well with ninety-nine but you failed with the hundredth. The last sacrifice should have been you. Had you consummated the process and procured the righteous testimony of millions as they watched your elevation, your dislocation from the mundane, you would have been His holiest and all of us, including me, your subject. But now that completion falls to me."

"Whose holiest?" He stammers, then louder he screams. "Please let me down. Please."

"He is a hidden treasure. He remade you, reshaped you, to find Himself." I drag the vat below him, position it perfectly. "Now, for the greatest film the world will ever see. A record of His reverence, His emergence."

"What are you talking about? My God, I didn't mean anyone harm. I just wanted to protect my boys. The hourglass told me, it promised—"

"You really never knew." I laugh and click the red Record button.

Begins the final cut.

"There is no greater being but He, and I am his messenger." I recite the holy declaration of faith as I bend and upend the hourglass for the final time.

The sand begins to trickle and tick.

I go to him with the knife in hand and start skinning.

The hourglass ticks. And ticks and ticks.

His screams fill the basement as I cut and peel him. Carefully I slice and turn my instrument, run it up and down until I've freed him of his burdensome covering. I scratch my head, I judge the best angles. I take pains not to block the camera's vision.

There once was a boy who was a walking wound, I think. Filled with bleeding holes and needed patching.

This is the easy part. Once it's done, I will have to redesign the movements of his blood. I will nick and sew and ligate till all his human highways come together into one perfectly synchronized dripping blood clock, which will tick down our insignificance, tick up to what is greater than the sum of all our parts.

I hum as I work.

Needed patching for a long time, this boy; he saw and knew and swallowed a secret and didn't tell anyone, and one day in an old, waiting house dusk walked up to him and claimed him as its own.

The shadows stir on my left. I turn just a little as Salman crawls out of the dimness and squats next to our handiwork. He is small and as thin as I remember, hasn't aged a bit. I nod to him, and his dark eyes glitter back at me.

Somewhere someone is shuddering and moaning, a sound like gurgles in the dark. We envy the moaner and the millions who will watch later.

Silent, we work. Reverent, we wait.

The lights in the basement flicker. A ripple goes through the pond.

Such a pity, I think sadly, that I don't remember *that* boy. His little life.

The dead fish rock suddenly in the water, sending fresh vapors of stench everywhere; the web of algae parts.

Then again I must not blame myself. *I* was never taken.

Dark like tar, a head, maybe human, rises from the gloaming.

Never claimed.

The towering thing steps dripping from the pond, soft and deliberate and utterly, irrevocably, beautifully curlicued. A perfect vessel of meat and memory.

Never filled with holes.

HUNGRY GIRLS

Cassandra Khaw

Avoid using cameras during the Hungry Ghost Festival.
The dead can be trapped there.

Emil

Her mouth was a red word of worship. I remember that. Red like she'd lipsticked it with blood. I stared at the petaling of her lips, the way she pursed them, incisors briefly lettering the plush flesh. Unlike the rest of them, she could sing: big operatic notes. A little rough along the higher registers, sure, but her voice when it plunged was smoky as the belly of an old whiskey cask.

I stared at her and all I could think is *what a fucking shame.* So much potential, every drop of it wrung out on a stage for the dead. Roger knew where to find them. Maria, he carved out of a burlesque club on the border of Hell's Kitchen. This one, he was going to wrench from the getais, which, as far as I could tell, were like Mardi Gras for ghosts except with more cover bands and less nudity.

Still, I liked Kuala Lumpur and its rat warrens of neighborhoods, its roundabouts going nowhere, highways spiraling in figure eights, as though they were talismans to constrain the damned.

Or to keep them out.

"Look at all the ah peks." Maria sucked at her teeth, glaring at the old men. She was a proper Brooklynite, accent and everything, the big-shouldered '80s jacket over a black-sequined corset, jeans torn and painted-on, fingernails jeweled. Gold on black. Always gold on black. Asian American but only barely, according to how she tells it. "I wonder how many of them *won't* be jerking off to her tonight?"

I couldn't stop staring at the girl on the stage. None of us had the willpower to look away. Maria could sneer as much as she liked, but I knew she was only doing it because she was just as mesmerized. The girl shines despite the smoke lifting from the joss sticks, and the *expression* carved on her face: it was something for a church, a chapel, a temple rotten with offerings. It was holy, that's what it was. I shivered in echo of her ecstasy, her eyes enormous and strange and, for a moment, salt white under the overhead glare.

"May's perfect," Roger said. He was five ten and lean as a rod of sculpted bone. Just as pale, too, the transparency of his complexion magnified by all the black he's wearing. Didn't matter that we were in Malaysia, or that the weather here *dripped* like sweat. Roger had to have his Steve Jobs regalia. I guess I understand it. The wardrobe was a costume. It made him singular, visibly the auteur he aspired to be. Anything less and he'd be another white guy, come to commoditize the Hungry Ghost Festival.

The night smoldered orange along the city line, an unnatural flame eating at the dark. The getai couldn't have been less impressive: rickety roadside stage, a back wall of dirty canvas, bored hosts, and girls who wore their sequins like someone else's forgotten shine. But the dead didn't see cause to complain, so who were the living to argue different?

A lone Prius rolled past the performance, its tenants invisible behind smoked windows.

"Sure," says Maria, "if you like jailbait."

We tried a few times, but Roger said Maria didn't have it in her to be a leading lady. Too much grit in her lopsided grin, too much nose to her raw-boned face. Killer as the foil to the sweetheart, sure, but too saw-toothed for a happy ending. He casts her as the femme fatale, the big bad, and it works: Maria's expressions were a broken heart caulked with bitter pride, vulnerable and crystalline. If you ask me, we didn't need the girl. Maria could have done it, played the wounded thing come home to a country full of someone else's ghosts.

Roger shot her a look over a shoulder. "Are you *jealous*?"

"I'm not jealous." Maria lit up a spliff, hand cupped over the flame. The light canyoned her cheeks, left her gaunter than she really was. "Jealous implies I give a shit about you."

"And you don't?"

"Sure, I do." A rough-throated laugh. She hacked smog into the air, scowling. "I care about the fact you're going to make me famous one day. Or at least, get me close to the motherfucker who can do that shit. At this point, I will fuck all of these ah peks for a shot to do something with my life."

Maria said the last half too loud, the word *fuck* a gunshot from her mouth, her lips rosy and human. One of the bow-legged old men—every one of them in uniform: wifebeater, loose shorts, sandals, receding hairline—leered at Maria, who fixed him with upraised brows and a don't-mess-with-me grimace. I winced.

"Then go hang out with the people who make blockbusters.

You got their number, right? Their agents talk to you, *right*? The fuck you doing with an indie filmmaker?"

She exhaled, sharp and silent. Maria wasn't, isn't into theatrics. Another woman might have stubbed out her joint in the webbing between Roger's fingers, called him an asshole, told him to get lost and book it business class on his dime. But not Maria. Because Daddy's little hellcats? That's their damage. They're into codependent salvation. She'd put in too much time to call it quits now.

Instead, Maria thins her mouth, inhales again: deep, deeper, until her eyes water from the fumes, but she won't let it go. Same way she won't let Roger go, no matter how many times I remind her it's how the story goes. He won't change. She won't, either.

Onstage, the girl cleared her lungs and belted out a note, perfect as anything—a sound like the world cracked into halves.

But there was nothing strange about her.

I swear.

Maria

The first four years were good.

Roger and me, we were Pygmalion and Galatea, the magic-man and his muse. He said he hadn't seen anything like me before. I was perfect, Roger told me the first night we fucked, sweat curling his black hair into cowlicks. Under the moonlight, I could see where I'd left a road of bruises along his neck, down to the divot of his collarbone. Roger liked it rough, he said. *It helps me remember I can feel.*

We made a few movies together. Short things. Artsy. There was nudity and old-world visual effect. None of that digitized flash. Plastic, plaster, and old-fashioned paint. Roger killed me for his canvas a hundred times over: skewered me, opened me like an orchid, while I shivered under a wet wreathing of fake blood.

I liked it. I won't lie. I liked how hands-on he was, every detail of the gore something to be tuned like the dial of an old radio, teased like a nipple or a new idea. Roger's pillow talk was as avant-garde as the rest of him. It felt like beginnings, like worship.

Then, we made a mistake.

The threesome shouldn't have happened. We weren't ready. I remember, though, how we'd applauded our maturity then, legs knotted: mine over the slope of his calf, her knee hooked over my ass. She made us breakfast in my cramped Williamsburg kitchen: eggs Benedict with andouille, hollandaise sauce the color of champagne, duck-fat potatoes. I remember the morning sunlight and counting the fine hairs along her ballerina arms.

"This is us," Roger whispered to me, conspiratorial, his arm thrown over my shoulder. As with everything else, he's precise with the eggs, too: a motion of the spoon, and the yolk bloomed across the china like a small sun. "We got this. I got you."

The axle of our recent pleasures said nothing. Just smiled. Crossed her legs at the ankles as she sipped coffee in my sundress, and her mouth was red, red, red.

Things rolled downhill from there.

> > >

"Does she even fucking speak English?" I stared at the girl as she curled on the edge of the sidewalk where we'd been filming half an hour ago, one of Roger's glossy black cigarettes pinned between her fingers, her mouth red as worship and glistening. Roger wanted *authenticity*, wanted his new star to *flower* in a place she'd become accustomed to. So, there we were: half-awake at four a.m., amid the trash left behind by the getai's audience, pretending Roger's latest obsession was a jiangshi, one of those "hopping vampires" from old Hong Kong cinema, and she didn't remind me of that girl who upturned my world.

Tremors ran from her scalp to the floor of her hips as she raised her arm, teeth clenched against the exertion. Fucking junkies. A starved coil of smoke twitched up into the gloom.

The girl inhaled, those unblinking doll eyes of hers obscured behind a fake yellow talisman. Sweat gleamed on her ceramic skin, mauve veins like logograms. Under the orange light, the red dome of her hat looked like a flayed skull cupped in a black bowl.

"This is the fifth goddamned time I had to tell her to not *grab* me," I said. She was only meant to jump out at me, not lunge, not grope and claw like a fucking zombie.

"You're supposed to be a professional. Act like one." Roger's eyes metronomed over the girl, restless, lingering longest on the spade of her crotch, nearly visible under her cheap black robes. The girl was *thin*. Chopstick thin without the barest netting of fat. I remember thinking, with some kind of sororal regret, that she'd shrivel in a few years. Just like I had. Not that it mattered. Not that this mattered. When we wrapped up this project, I was gone. Back to New York and its skyscrapers and its smiling, shining, successful, dead-eyed hopefuls. "Use it to motivate your performance, or whatever it is actors are supposed to do."

"Hell of a director." I pinched the wad of flesh that the girl had burrowed her nails into when she lunged at me, and winced. It would bruise by tomorrow, I was sure of it, flower black and indigo where the pressure of her hand broke through capillaries. I remember being surprised by how strong she was, how much force she carried in her wire-frame body. "You don't even know how your actors work."

Roger didn't even blink. "Jealousy's ugly on older women, Maria."

The way he kicked my name from his mouth, it was like I was someone else's drunken mistake. I ran my tongue over my teeth. "Fuck you."

The girl jackknifed her head up, tongue lolled out, the tip touched to the talisman. A wet spot spread across the paper. I'm still amazed to this day at the work Sophia did on the girl. Roger didn't believe in budgets, wouldn't buy into the practice of crowd-funding, said it diluted the film to whore out the credits to so many nameless benefactors. Genius shouldn't be sold for a dol-lar. So he made us make do.

And Sophia, Jesus, now she was a talent. She could come up with miracles for a buck and some change. Despite the fact we had nothing, she made that girl look . . . *unsettling*, ghostly in her Qing dynasty regalia.

Yeah.

That's the word I wanted.

Unsettling.

The girl—what the *fuck* was her name? May, Madeline, Maggie, it all blends together, their names like someone else's pleasure—made a noise, and I glanced over to her. Smoke bled from her nostrils, the hinge of her parted lips. There was dust floating from her mouth, motes of silver in the filthy air. Her eyes had a rim of frost. Like cataracts. Like she was going blind. She blinked at me once, slow, and soaked in the backwash of Emil's lighting, she didn't seem completely real.

Sophia

They fucked. Like, there was no way they didn't. When the girl came back into makeup after the first ten takes, she reeked of hours-old semen and someone else's sweat, a man's musk under a cover of cheap cologne. Roger's. I don't know where they could have gone to do it. There wasn't anywhere to go. It was my trailer and Maria's, and I don't think she would have allowed them privacy. Maybe he took her into the jungle outside the parking lot.

"You okay?"

She blinked at me, amber eyes and a full mouth that wouldn't entirely close, red as worship, red as a bullet's kiss. The girl sat down on her appointed bench, hands rested on her lap. The cheap black robe we'd ferried out of Goodwill was water-stained, its hems heavy with mud. There were wet leaves in her hair and white petals. She stared at me.

"I don't know if you have unions down here, but if Roger did anything you didn't want, you tell me."

That was my bargain with the devil. I wouldn't tell on Roger's affairs, wouldn't judge, wouldn't ask questions, would blot out hickeys and dab away evidence of his bacchanals, wouldn't do anything that'd jeopardize my professional relationship with him. Unless one of his debutantes squealed. And if they did, I'd take their testimony global. I did six months of makeup for a television company in New Jersey. There were folks who still owed me.

But that girl.

I peeled back her collar while she sat there, suddenly frightened for her. I didn't know what I was going to find. But I know I hadn't been expecting *that*. The skin underneath was the same color and texture of petroleum jelly. No blemishes, no bite marks, no discolorations. No veins. Only an off-white creaminess glimmering like she'd bathed herself in oil.

"Did he hurt you?" I was sure. I was so sure. And I think my certainty was scaffolded on guilt. Maria had sat in the same chair once, vacant, body humming with grief. But I had said nothing then.

The girl looked up at those words, like she'd heard me, eyes becoming massive and alive. Her mouth opened as the door did, and Roger came sweeping inside from the green-smelling dark, ushering his star away.

Emil

I was with Maria when it happened.

Roger walked the girl out of Sophia's trailer, one arm draped across the small of her back, the other held out. She placed her hand in the cup of his palm, allowed him to lead her down the rusted steps. He couldn't look away. I couldn't blame him. Even in her cadaver makeup, she was striking.

"I'm so done with him." Maria passed her spliff over. I took a drag and tried to pretend I was one of the hungry dead, and I didn't need to breathe. "She's, what, eighteen? Fucking pervert."

"What are you going to do after this?" I said when I'd stopped coughing, every thought mired in spirals, weighted down by the weed. That Maria could stay so furious all the time, despite all the pot she smoked, was testimony to something but I wasn't sure what. I still am not. But what I remember was the hungry angles of her face, the moonlight working shadows into the sockets of her eyes. "Are you going to stay in show business?"

Maria said nothing.

"I don't know," she whispered after a while. "Everything about show business reminds me of him."

There wasn't any need to say who.

"I have a degree in accounting. I could do that. Go home. Go back to school. See what happens when I apply myself." Her lips curled at the last half of the sentence, her expression withering, the scorn inward-facing. "I don't know, I don't know."

She shook herself like a dog ridding itself of the rain.

Roger sloped past us, eyes abstract, the pupils blown out. Beside him, the girl looked even smaller than she was, reduced by the dark-fabricked breadth of him, her face like something hand-molded from a candle. I don't remember her features. There'd been shapes, sure, but all I can call up now is that mouth of hers, red and wet and glistening like a fresh heart, the color bleeding at the edges.

"Asshole," Maria said, blowing smoke at them.

Neither of them spoke. Without an opponent to ricochet off, Maria's fury had no propulsion, no momentum to keep going. She squeezed her blunt into her palm, gasping as the skin cooked in the embers, a sweet smell lifting from her fist. I swore at her and tried to peel her fingers open, while unscrewing a bottle of water at the same time. Cold fluid splattered us. Maria jerked her hand from my grip, cursing.

As I staggered back, I felt a small hand on my spine, curving up my back to take hold of a shoulder. I swiveled at the touch. It was the girl, leaning up on tiptoe and halfway out of Roger's embrace. She kissed me, tongue crowbarring my teeth apart somehow, a slab of thick muscle reaching in to trace my molars. Long, impossibly long.

"What the—" I pulled away, drool stretching between our mouths like a payment of silver.

"Fucking asshole. You men are all the same." A clatter of heels told me Maria had fled. When I finally orientated, every last one of them was gone, melted into the dark.

Last time I saw any of them, swear to God.

Maria

Wherever the asshole is, I hope he's dead.

Fuck him.

I hope she ate his heart.

Sophia

We waited for a week.

We thought that, maybe, Roger was on a bender. It wouldn't be the first time. When we shot his last film in Cuba, he vanished for three weeks and came back, hair beaded and skin tanned, complaining about how someone tried to falsify his involvement with a pregnancy. But this time, Roger didn't return.

Maria went back to Williamsburg and became an accountant like she told Emil she would. She was good at it. At least that's what I heard. We haven't talked since.

Emil shot up a convenience store two weeks later in Berkeley, screaming about ghosts.

I went home.

Home to small-town nowhere, working in a salon, away from Hollywood and its dreams of faceless hungry girls with bright red mouths.

That was it.

You have to believe us.

We have nothing else left.

CUT FRAME

Gemma Files

Old movies are the dreams of dead people.
—NIALL QUENT to BARRY JENKINSON,
   CanCon on CanCon (1995, First Hand Waving Press)

Transcript of file recorded 12/05/18 by R. Puget / T. Jankiewicz
Filed under Case #C23-1972, Freihoeven Parapsychological Institute,
   Toronto
Reported: Intern L. Jankiewicz 11/17/18
Cross-saved at www.noetichealth.org/interviews/torcdusk.mp3

RP: —test, test, test. Excellent. This is Ross Puget for Noetic
   Health, here with Dr. Tadeusz Jankiewicz of Toronto, who's
   consented to be interviewed at the encouragement of his
   granddaughter Lily, our favourite intern. Say a few words into
   the mike, Doc?

TJ: Like this?

RP: Perfect. I don't suppose you had a chance to sign the paper-work we sent you yet?

TJ: Yes, all done. I'll admit I was surprised at the amount of releases you require. Lily made this sound very much a . . . hmmm, what? Hobby, I think is how she put it.

RP: I'd use the word "vocation," myself.

TJ: Have you had legal troubles before?

RP: (PAUSE) Nothing significant.

TJ: And you'd like to keep it that way, right? It's okay, Mr. Puget. I've had patients minded to be—unpleasant, from time to time; a little posterior-covering never goes amiss, eh?

RP: You're very understanding.

TJ: Well, this isn't a story I would have told if I was still practicing. I should also warn you, the material I *can* show you doesn't offer much proof of . . . anything. Not as much as I'm guessing you'd prefer to have.

RP: Well, we'll get to that when we get to it.

> > >

Supplementary Notes

Subject: Dr. Tadeusz Jankiewicz
(Photograph attached: 5'8", 172 lb., Polish Caucasian, white hair, blue eyes)
Bio: DOB 2/15/1941, Morges, Switzerland
Immigrated to Toronto with family August 1943
Graduated U of T Faculty of Dentistry June 1965
Retired April 2008
Location: Subject's residence, 132 Fermanagh Avenue, Toronto, Ontario
Notes: *(Transcript of voice recording, R. Puget)*

Home looks like it was built in the '20s, but really well maintained. Floors mostly hardwood. Front parlour's been converted
into a single-patient dental treatment suite, apparently no longer
used. Wall decor's very much film-buff paradise: instead of paint-
ings or photos, framed lobby cards, posters, alternate artwork—
the classic concept art poster for *Star Wars* is here, some modern
Hitchcock reworkings, looks like a complete run of Cronenberg's
'70s and '80s stuff . . . one bookshelf's full of film reference
stuff, too—books by Ebert, Kael, all three of Danny Peary's *Cult
Movies*—wow, he's even got *Weird Sex and Snowshoes*. Bet it's
been a while since anyone took *that* down. Oh. Just noticed—one
spot on the wall outside the dental suite looks like a frame's been
removed. Remember to ask what that was.

> > >

Transcript torcdusk.mp3 *continued:*

RP: We should probably start with the basics. You're the primary
    investor and only currently living producer credited on IMDb
    for *The Torc*, directed by Niall Quent and released in 1973.
TJ: Sounds impressive, doesn't it? All it meant was that I signed
    cheques and got to visit the set, wherever it was that week.
RP: How did you become an investor?
TJ: One of my patients at the time was a producer, a real one,
    and he'd worked with Quent before. My practice was becom-
    ing successful enough that I was thinking about tax-protective
    investments, and Oleg told me the film industry was an excel-
    lent place to park my money.
RP: This was the beginning of the tax-shelter era of Canadian
    film, of course. I saw your collection, in the living room.
TJ: Ah, well, that's all 20/20 hindsight, isn't it? I have to admit,

even at the beginning, Oleg was telling me all about the ways I could hide even more money if I'd wanted to, at a hundred percent return, so it didn't surprise me when it all came crashing down in the '80s. Did you know that of the sixty-six feature films officially produced in Canada in 1979, more than half of them were never released at all? And this was the year before their internally notorious "Canada Can and Does" campaign, at Cannes—the one that Lawrence O'Toole wrote about in *Maclean's* (article referenced can be found by searching under June 2, 1980, at http://archive.macleans.ca), under the headline "Canada Can't." A hundred percent became fifty, and all the Hollywood North types ran back home like their, eh . . .

RP: Asses were on fire? Wow, no, I did *not* know all that. This Oleg sounds like he was a real, um—

TJ: Oh, he was a sleazebucket, without question. Not that my own motives were more honourable, I suppose.

RP: The tax returns.

TJ: Only partly. The rest . . . that was for *her*. Tamar.

RP: Tamar Dusk. (BEAT) Did you ever get to meet her? Maybe on set?

TJ: Once. But I'm getting ahead of myself. It's important that you understand things as I came to understand them. The— situation. Have you ever seen *The Torc*?

RP: Yes, actually. I probably didn't have the intended audience reaction; I just remember that booming narration, and the catchphrase—"*Don't! Put! On! The Torc!*" (LAUGHS)

TJ: (LAUGHS) Well, don't feel too bad. I'm not sure even Quent knew what reaction he was going for. That wasn't his, what's the word, his *process*. Oleg once told me Quent's method was simply to film as much as possible with "any recognizable American," as he said it, and then to do the pickup shooting afterward—and only *then* would he figure out what the film was "about." Sometimes, Quent wouldn't even have much more than a title, or even a poster—nothing so coherent as a script.

RP: And this didn't put you off? It sounded like a good idea?

TJ: It was the only film I'd ever been personally involved with. It still is. I wasn't a director, I was a dentist. And a fan.

RP: Of Niall Quent?

TJ: Of Tamar Dusk.

> > >

Supplementary Notes: Tamar Dusk

Tamar Dusk

From Wikipedia, the free encyclopedia

Tamar Dusk, born[?? confirm] **Tamar Janika Duzhneskaya** (January 6, 1917–????), is a Slavic American actress best known for her "exotic" roles in several noor and horror B movies between 1936 and 1960, all directed by Nicholas Ryback, as well for the controversies surrounding her personal history that emerged during the era of the Hollywood blacklist and, in latter years, apocryphal rumours about the "Dusk Curse." This controversy has continued in part into the modern day following Dusk's last appearance in the little-known Canadian horror film *The Torc* (dir. Niall Quent, 1973), after which Dusk and her husband began an extended campaign to render Dusk's personal information as legally inaccessible as possible, to the extent that even Dusk's date of death cannot presently be verified. Her most well-known roles include Mara in *Under the Bridge* (1937), "The Woman" in *Woman without a Name* (1940), Ingrid in *Kiss of the Succubus* (1945), Eriska in

Blood Mirror (1953), and Mrs. Larkwood in _The Whispering Widow_ (1957), all directed by Nicholas Ryback.

<<Attached file: Tamar-Dusk-1953.jpg>>
<<Attached file: BLOOD-MIRROR-poland-1953.jpg>>

From IMDb.com:

"I never had the opportunity to work with Tamar myself; there is no doubt that her refusal to work with anyone other than Nicholas Ryback did her career no favors. I was lucky enough to meet her once or twice, and if there is any substance to the 'Dusk Curse' rumors, it only proves how any beautiful yet remote woman can provoke destructive obsession in others simply by existing. She had the remarkable gift of making you feel as if merely by joining her company you had rescued her from some great sadness, yet when you left her, you took some of that sadness with you—and it seemed a gift. Had she chosen to work with any other director, she would have been one of the great tragic actresses of her generation." —_Alfred Hitchcock_

"Dusk had talent. Can't argue with that. Her problem was, she never really stopped performing. That's nothing unusual in Hollywood, but she took it over the top. The whole business with only shooting at night, hiding her real name, her home country—she let the press make too much out of it, probably to get the publicity, and it shot her in the foot. She was no more a Communist than my cat. But between all the questions she wouldn't answer and her lack of friends, it didn't surprise me how it ended. She put all her eggs in Nicky Ryback's basket. Once his eyes were gone, so was she." —_Elia Kazan_

"I do not talk about myself, because I do not consider it a subject of appropriate interest. The audience is here to watch the characters I create. My task is to disappear." —*Tamar Dusk*

> > >

Transcript torcdusk.mp3 *continued:*

RP: Tell me about the first time you saw Tamar Dusk.

TJ: On-screen? It was 1955, I was twelve. One of my friends had persuaded his big brother to act as the "accompanying adult" so we could all go to a late-night showing of *Blood Mirror* at a repertory theatre. I remember the smell of the popcorn—too much fake butter—the feel of the velvet cushions on the seats. If I close my eyes, I can still see all her scenes.

RP: Do you remember which version of *Blood Mirror* you saw?

TJ: You're thinking about the lost final scene, aren't you?* No, I'd never heard about any of that; like I said, I was a fan, not a film student. Not that it would have made a difference. Young men are never put off by stories like that, are they? Rather the reverse.

RP: Some of the books say Nick Ryback deliberately spread the rumour about a lost ending, to make up for the fact he didn't

---

* The only Hollywood director with whom Tamar Dusk ever worked, Nicholas Ryback (born Nikolai Rybakov in Petrograd in 1922), was known for prescreening his films to small private audiences before general theatrical release, often conducting final and sometimes radical edits alone after this feedback. *Blood Mirror* (1953) in particular was rumoured to have had its entire final scene removed and destroyed after the studio saw it in rushes, with a replacement denouement supposedly assembled from already-cut segments. Apocryphal reports pop up from time to time of the intact original version being broadcast late at night on local television channels, but this is considered to be an urban legend.

really *have* an ending. The blacklist was into full swing by then, he was already getting pressure over working with Tamar at all, and since he was a Russian émigré himself, he wasn't in any place to protect anyone else.

TJ: But better bad publicity than no publicity? That sounds much more like Quent, to be honest.

RP: You know, some people believe Tamar Dusk literally never worked with anybody but Nick Ryback in her entire career. The idea that she'd come up here and make some crappy Can-Con project, with Niall Quent of all people . . .

TJ: Well, she *did* only work with Ryback, in Hollywood. But this was Hollywood North, one time, for one picture. Quent counted himself a very lucky man, in that respect.

RP: And what was he like, to work with?

TJ: Hmmm. Well, I didn't speak with him a great deal, on set or off, but he didn't strike me as, let's say, the most organized of men. At the time, I thought he was just as starstruck as the rest of us. I remember being quite angry about it, in fact—he was hogging Tamar, her presence. Getting the chance to meet her was the entire reason I became involved, but whenever I brought it up, Quent always had a reason why it wasn't a good time. She was feeling under the weather, she had a meeting and had to leave the moment shooting was done, they had to review script changes . . .

RP: You thought he was bullshitting you? Pardon my French.

TJ: Well, I didn't have proof. It was all very plausible. She was not a young woman; she'd gone through her share of tragedy. Her career had mostly ended around 1960, when her director friend, Ryback, contracted retinal cancer and had to have his eyes removed, and then her first husband died—supposedly due to alcoholism, they say, but . . .

RP: Yeah, the rumours were all that it was suicide via OD. Pathological jealousy.

TJ: Indeed. And her second marriage wasn't exactly . . . oh, let's tell the truth and shame the devil, why don't we? She married for money. He was a decade her senior, a financier who owned a chain of fur and leather coat warehouse outlets throughout Ontario—I don't remember the name, I think they're out of business now. That was how she came to live up here. He built her a private cabin of her own somewhere in Muskoka, the size of a mansion, fully staffed, all the luxuries. Even an in-house movie theatre. Though . . . I don't think she ever watched anything there. (PAUSE) I don't think she could have.

RP: What do you mean?

TJ: We'll come to that. This has to be in the right order, Mr. Puget. (PAUSE)

RP: So . . . what was it about her, exactly? Back in the day?

TJ: Huh. (LAUGHS) Have you *seen* her?

RP: In pictures, sure. Photos, stills . . .

TJ: But the films?

RP: I've seen clips.

TJ: Not enough. You had to see her in motion, but, um—also everything around her, all the rest? Ryback built his whole film to show her off, like a . . . jewel case. A stage. You needed to see how other people looked at her, how they reacted when she wasn't there anymore. Even all the empty places where she might eventually be—it was a kind of suspense. She might turn up anywhere, any moment. It was like, eh . . . scratching a raw place just after the scab comes off, so sensitive, a memory of pain. All the nerves on fire, half-healed but still wounded. Like an itch. You were always looking for her, desperately, even after the movie stopped.

Besides which, she was *sexy*. I didn't even know that word, the first time, but I felt it. In *Blood Mirror*, she was that first figure of complete, untrammeled eroticism every young boy encounters, sooner or later—the person, the face and body you can't even *think* about without, ah . . . reaction, decades later. Will you think less of me if I admit that every woman I've ever been with, even Lily's grandmother, looked like her, to some extent?

RP: Well, uh—I guess everyone has a type.

TJ: I've made you uncomfortable; I apologize. But please believe me, this isn't just prurience; I was far from the only man to have that reaction.

One of the elements of the so-called Dusk Curse was the fact that Tamar had so many, they call them "stalkers" now, I think—far more than a comparatively minor B-list actress should have had. Security on her movie sets was eventually something like twice the industry norm. Which you'd think would make for good headlines, but most producers recognized the increased expense and insurance risk as counterproductive—only one mistake, one mad fan, and they'd have a disaster on their hands. That was the real reason she worked exclusively with Ryback: he was the only one willing to underwrite her costs. Which most people never think about, but when your own funds are at stake, that sort of research becomes critical. Film runs on cash. Once you've seen for yourself how money affects literally every decision in the process, you learn how to follow it.

RP: Is that why she married the rich Canadian guy? For money, security?

TJ: Difficult to say. I think he did make her feel safe . . . safer. She needed that.

RP: Because of her stalkers.

TJ: (SIGHS) We think we understand how bad things can get,

because we lived through the 1960s, the 1970s . . . I remember someone inviting me and Lily's grandmother out to *Deep Throat*, you know? Dinner and a movie, like a double date; "high-toned," mainstream pornography. We sat there holding hands, trying to look anywhere but at the screen, as our hosts dry-humped each other next to us. Or your generation, growing up with the Internet—every one of you saturated in blatantly sexual imagery, from childhood on. But, nevertheless . . .

. . . try to imagine being Tamar Dusk, as a young woman, in 1936. To be, without effort or even intent, a figure of such raw attractiveness that more than half the people you speak to become stupid with it, while far too many of the rest turn vicious, jealous, petty, spiteful, suspicious, resentful. You think things might get better if you go to a place so full of other beautiful people, surely some of them can perhaps see past that glamour and be friends with who you *are*, instead of obsessed with what you look like; it doesn't, though. Because the people there still just want to use you, to package you like a drug and sell you to addicts. So what you thought would be your salvation becomes, instead, just another marketplace, another pit full of dogs eating each other for the same scraps. Another hell.

RP: Doesn't sound all that unusual so far, for Hollywood.

TJ: No. Most people on the same track, though—Greta Garbo, Hedy Lamarr, Rita Hayworth, Merle Oberon, Dorothy Dandridge . . . no, not even poor Marlene Dietrich, fleeing Germany one step ahead of *her* biggest fan—

RP: Hitler, right?

TJ: That was the rumour. And Garbo liked girls, and Lamarr swam nude but wanted to practice science; Merle could pass but Dandridge couldn't, and Rita was a Mexican dancer too young to drink alone, who had to have her hairline raised with electrolysis so no one would know she wasn't Irish. But none of them had to deal with what Tamar Dusk had to deal with, for which I'm sure they thanked their various versions of God. Or *should* have thanked Him.

RP: Wait a minute. Are you telling me the Dusk Curse was *real*?

TJ: What everybody *thought* was "the Dusk Curse" was only a side effect, essentially. The truth of it, the full phenomenon, is what I promised Lily to tell about you today.

> > >

Supplementary Notes: The "Dusk Curse"

Tamar Dusk

From Wikipedia, the free encyclopedia

The "Dusk Curse" [edit]

Following public backlash after Dusk's testimony before HUAC, rumors about the existence of a "Dusk curse" began to circulate among film crew who had worked on Ryback's productions with Dusk. Much like the "*Exorcist* curse"[14] or "*Poltergeist* curse"[15] of later decades, where a statistically unusual concentration of on-set misfortunes were attributed to supernatural influence supposedly arising from the subject matter of the films, any accident or disruptive event was retroactively blamed on Dusk's presence, even on days where she had not been on set. However, film researchers during the 1960s documented and verified a number of statistical oddities in the history of Dusk's productions[16]:

- Incidence of <u>suicides</u> among on-set crew, averaged over the body of Dusk's work, was approximately 25% higher than normal (the median range).
- Reports of <u>violent behavior</u> and assault on the part of crew members were nearly 50% higher than normal.
- Incidence of <u>divorces</u> among on-set crew was approximately 40% higher than normal, with an exceptional pattern—over 75% of proceedings were initiated by the male partner.
- The number of on-set crew who later went into therapy for significant psychological problems, ranging from <u>major depressive disorder</u> to <u>drug addiction</u> and <u>antisocial personality breakdown</u>, was approximately 30% higher than normal.

Skeptics have explained this discrepancy by noting Ryback's production company was known for saving money via deliberately waiving industry hiring standards, something for which Ryback faced several union sanctions in his career.[17] It is also true that despite the supposed danger of Dusk's presence on set, very few staff ever resigned from a Ryback production once principal photography had begun; the statistical patterns observed above did *not* hold true for anyone actually performing on camera during the production, whether they shared scenes with Dusk or not. Nonetheless, rumours of a "Dusk curse" have continued to circulate ever since filming wrapped on Dusk's first major role, and persist to this day.

> > >

Transcript torcdusk.mp3 *continued:*

RP: You say it was a side effect? A side effect of what?
TJ: Tamar didn't have a word for it. If I had to come up with the

kind of term you'd use on your website, Mr. Puget, I'd probably call it "psychosynthesis" or something like that. But even that's misleading, because it suggests that what was happening was natural for her. It wasn't.

RP: What are you talking about?

TJ: The effect she had on other people, and the effect that . . . other people, their attention, their . . . worship . . . had on her.

RP: Okay. Which was?

TJ: (SIGHS) That what they wanted from her inevitably ended up making her into something else, something which would fill a very particular hunger. Something . . . inhuman. (PAUSE) Less so in person, or so she said; if she'd only been a theatrical actress, then perhaps the effect might have—scattered among the crowd she evoked it from, somehow. Dissipated. What really changed things, however, was the camera's lens, the camera's *eye*. The camera's ability to fix her image as a sort of . . . moving idol to be played and replayed at will, as a literal object of worship.

RP: Worship. For who?

TJ: Her fans, of course, and the filmmakers who fed them. People like Ryback, like Quent—though I don't think Quent really knew what he was cooperating with, whereas Ryback knew *exactly* what he was doing. (ANOTHER PAUSE) People like them . . . or like me.

RP: And—I'm sorry, I'm lost. *How* did you know about all this, again?

TJ: Tamar told me, of course. (BEAT) Ah, I've buried the lede . . . that's the term, yes? Lily's grandmother always told me I couldn't ever keep to the point of a story. (ANOTHER BEAT) Give me a moment, please; I'll show you the proofs I was saving for the end.

  When I finally got Quent to agree to a set visit, I went out and bought myself a Polaroid camera. I was hoping for some shots of myself and Tamar, of course, but I was genuinely fascinated by everything else, too. You said you'd seen *The Torc*; you should recognize a number of the faces.

RP: Wow. There's Quent—holy crap, he looks young. This guy played the lead, right?

TJ: Steven Paulson, yes. And Bill Walker, he played the villain, the would-be modern-day Druid—"busiest actor in Canada," they used to call him, for a while. That's Claudette Beecroft, the love interest. This was the day we filmed in High Park. Look at the skyline.

RP: No CN Tower, Jesus. So weird. Wait, is that—?

TJ: Yes. That's her.

RP: Are you sure? I'm sorry, it's just—she looked a lot younger, in the film.

TJ: I took that shot when she arrived, at the start of the evening's shooting. I was lucky enough to catch her again when she left, later that night. Let me find it. Here—there she is, getting into her town car.

RP: (PAUSE) I don't understand. Didn't she bother taking her makeup off?

TJ: That's what everybody assumed. But I was the principal investor; I got to look at the budget, their production schedule. There were two American films shooting in town and they'd already gone through five DOPs—directors of photography. People just kept quitting, jumping ship. They had one makeup assistant, plus barely enough money to cover basic blood effects. Nowhere near enough time, or skill, to shave forty years off someone's face, not even for the ostensible star.

RP: What are you saying?

TJ: I'm saying that when Oleg knocked my camera off a table and broke it next time I visited the set, it wasn't an accident, and we both knew it wasn't an accident. Which was why I didn't bother buying another one.

RP: Did Quent know?

TJ: Honestly, I don't know what Quent knew, or didn't. Or when he figured it out for himself, if he did; he had his own problems, lots of them. Rewriting the script every night, for one. Feeding Tamar her lines from behind the camera. But I watched and I learned, and one evening I came by when both he and Oleg were away, just in time to overhear one of the PAs saying Ms. Dusk's dinner had arrived. I jumped in and said I'd take it to her, in her trailer, and nobody saw anything wrong with that. I remember that when I lifted my hand to knock on her door, I could actually see it shaking . . . my God. I'm shaking now.

She looked up when the door opened. She smiled at me. I don't think anyone else in my entire life smiled at me the way Tamar did, not even my wife on our wedding day. Does that sound terrible? It should.

I expected her to be different, in person. But she wasn't. She wasn't different, at all. Things . . . bent, around her. All the light in the room went in her direction. Like a halo. But her eyes . . . her eyes. So dark. I don't . . . I can't possibly . . .

RP: (AFTER A MOMENT) Doc?

TJ: Yes. I'm sorry.

I served her, like a waiter. She told me to sit down. Took a bite, chewed it, swallowed. Then she looked back up, and said, in that husky voice: "You know, don't you?"

RP: Know what?

TJ: That's what I asked. She just shook her head, and sighed. Said something like: "No, it's better that way. Even suspecting protects you, for a little while, as acting out the story protects me, and them—the other performers. The flow only ever goes one way, Nikolai told me; those who feed can't be fed upon." I asked: "Nicholas Ryback, you mean?" and she said, "Yes." Was that why she'd only ever worked with him? And at this she actually laughed, and I would have felt stupid, except by then, I had no room left to think of myself.

She laughed, and she said: "He knew before I did. They were the ones who told me where I come from, what I was . . . Nikolai and the little secret church he belonged to, back in Los Angeles. That city is full of cults, always, like Rome before the fall. All the names they gave me—*nocnitca, gorska majka, plachky, mrake*. They told me what I would become, what they *wanted* me to become, but Nikolai only went along with it so far. He knew a good thing when he saw it, after all; he had plans for me, for himself. So he taught me how to use the movies to stave it off, slow it down. Suspend it, perhaps even for good."

RP: . . . What?

TJ: I think you heard me, Mr. Puget.

> > >

Supplementary Notes: Terminology

(from the Freihoeven Institute files, compiled and written by Dr. Guilden Abbott)

Nocnitca (Polish), *Gorska Majka* (Bulgarian), *Plachky* or *Kricksy-Plaksy* (Slavic), *Mrake* (Croatian)—the night flyer, night moth, night hag, night maiden. All versions of this archetype seem to trace back to the phenomenon known as night terrors, the *Mára* or night-Mare, an apparent confusion in the hypnagogic stage of pre-REM sleep during which the conscious mind snaps awake but the body remains functionally paralyzed. Very specific hallucinations will then ensue, along with a literally pressing sense of dread, anxiety, and immediate physical danger. Sufferers often speak of a dark figure standing over them, a woman who trails her long hair down their bodies, a beautiful but faceless figure whose appearance shifts from attractiveness to awfulness almost at random.

Sometimes, in its "night moth" form, the *Mara* is seen to hover above the sleeper, borne on filmy, insectile wings which also appear spun from her own hair. At other times, it crawls on the floor like a caterpillar or larva, rising to suck at the sleeper's face with a circular mouth full of lamprey-esque teeth. Sometimes, in its "night flyer" form, the *Mara* unfurls itself ritualistically from a standing cocoon whose outer skin is often described either as stiff and peeling, much like the bandages of an Egyptian mummy, or soft and folded in on itself yet knotted at the top, like an Elizabethan-era burial shroud. In this last form her face is "blank as the moon yet set with two great black jewels for eyes, its expression impossible to read and her hair a glittering swarm about her, floating in every direction like a mist." (Hélas Manzynski, *Grandmother's Tales* [Hope & Gershwin, 1922], translated by Morden Jegado.)

Theosophically speaking, the moth is both a psychopomp and a symbol of the soul. Similarly, just as the moth was once said to subsist on tears sipped from the corners of sleeping nightmare-sufferers' eyes, the *Mara* is said to both siphon off and inspire its victim's dreams. A secondary stream of mythology suggests that—night terrors aside—these dreams can't possibly be entirely nightmarish, since the point of the exercise is to keep the sufferer as much asleep as possible while still allowing the *Mara* to conjure the emotions she supposedly feeds upon. This clearly seems to align the *Mara* with stories of incubi and succubi, first found in Roman tradition—male and female daimons who lie full-length upon sleepers of the opposite sex, arousing them with fantasies of passionate activity, then sucking out the resultant yin-yang energy. Repeated visits from an incubus or succubus will eventually bring about deterioration of the sleeper's health and mental state, or even death; in *The Hammer of Witches*, mediaeval tales have been collected that imply these creatures can shift form from male to female at will and vice versa, sucking sperm from male victims in order to impregnate female victims with parasitic phantom babies.

In some tales, the *Nocnitca* is known to visit when one sleeps on one's back, hands folded on the chest (a position allegedly called "sleeping with the dead"). According to some folklore, night hags are made of shadow, may also have a horrible screeching voice, and might allegedly also smell of the moss and dirt from her forest of origin. Finally, a stone with a hole in its centre is said to be protection from the *Nocnitca*, since she can only be glimpsed while awake by looking through such a lens or frame. Otherwise, she will remain perfectly invisible, subsumed into the body of her unlucky mortal host.

> > >

RP: So . . . Nick Ryback was in a cult. A Hollywood cult.

TJ: So Tamar Dusk said.

RP: I mean—there's a lot of those, right? Tom Cruise, that kind of—

TJ: Oh, you're thinking of Scientology? Nothing that recent. I think she meant older things, odder things. And as to whether or not Ryback was *in* the cult or simply associated with them somehow, well—I think he had been, yes. That he might even have been looking for someone like her, for them. But when he found her, I think things must have changed for him. I can't see how they wouldn't have.

At any rate, when I asked Tamar what she meant, her face went through a . . . transfiguration, is the only word. All her mouth did was turn down the slightest degree, and suddenly I had to fight to keep from sobbing, even though her own eyes were absolutely dry. And she said, so quietly I could barely hear her: "I am a person, still, you know. Like anyone else. I want to live, to love—but it is hard, so hard, to do either. And when an alternative is offered, no matter how deeply you may suspect it might be a mistake, you *have* to try. You cannot . . . not."

And then it was as if she'd woken up, and she looked at me and said, "You are Oleg's friend, the dentist. The one with the money." And I said yes, I was, and she leaned forward and grabbed my hands—I literally lost the ability to breathe—and she said, "If you love me, take the money away. Stop paying for this. If they cannot pay the crew, they cannot finish." And I said I'd given my word, and she said, "It is not you who will pay the price for keeping it. I beg you. Go."

And then her expression changed again, and her voice got deeper. And her hands were moving in mine. And—somehow, I don't know how—she was suddenly speaking perfect Polish, with the accent of my parents. And she said, "If you need another reason, I can . . . encourage you." And she was leaning toward me, closing her eyes, and I was closing mine, and—

I don't know what would have happened if the PA hadn't knocked on the trailer door right that second. Logically, why would I have been in danger, after all? She had just begged me in sheer desperation to do something only I could do. Doing anything that might . . . damage me . . . would have made no sense, and yet. I got the feeling that she was not entirely in control of herself, in those last moments. That something, some—instinct—had taken her over. And when the PA's knock broke that trance, I don't even remember fleeing. I only remember finding myself in my own car, shuddering and gasping, like I'd climbed out of a bath of ice.

RP: Jesus.

TJ: (PAUSE) The next day, I called Oleg. I told him I was pulling my funding. That he was no longer welcome as a patient at my practice. Well, he was extremely unhappy, and made some unpleasant suggestions about how he could change my mind, until I pointed out that I'd been his dentist for a year and a half and could make sure the police learned everything they'd need to know to find him, right down to his Social Insurance Number, his birth certificate, and his dental records. And that was the end of my involvement with *The Torc*, the last time I ever saw any of them in person.

RP: But it didn't work. The movie came out anyway.

TJ: (DEEP SIGH) I know. I went to see it; I was one of the few who did, in its very brief and limited run. Somehow, Quent had found just enough resources to produce that final sequence, along with whatever interstitial material he needed to fill in the gaps to his satisfaction. I suspect he did most of the final photography himself.

RP: What makes you say that?

TJ: Well, it's pure speculation, at this point. But . . . in epidemiology, the term "natural immunity" refers to people who are born with the antibodies to a particular disease already in their system. There are people who are tone-deaf, who literally can't hear the difference between music and noise; there are those who can't tell red from green, and those who can't see colour at all. So it has always seemed to me that if certain . . . influences existed, certain . . . methods of exchanging metaphysical energies, let's say—then some people would also be naturally insensitive to those, as well. Whatever . . . effect Tamar had on most around her would simply roll off them.

RP: You think Ryback might've been like that?

TJ: Oh, I don't know. I don't even know if what happened to him was related to Tamar at all; people do just get cancer. But if he was—and if Quent was another one—it would explain why Quent was able to finish the film without any . . . issues. Especially if he did everything himself.

RP: (PAUSE) But he couldn't have, could he? Not if *The Torc*'s final sequence wasn't shot until after you left the production. There's too much F/X work in that scene for it to be a solo job. Too many extras, for that matter—there's like, what, thirty, forty people in the glade, not including Tamar? No way Quent did the aging makeup on all of them himself. Or the lighting, for that night shoot. And Tamar herself, the perspective changes, the distortions, the way he makes her look, like, twelve feet tall near the end, that's not—

Jesus.

Oh, you're not—Doc, tell me you aren't serious.

TJ: Like I said, Mr. Puget, pure speculation.

Still. I've been an amateur student of Canadian film for over forty years now; I've read dozens of articles about Niall Quent, and seen all his interviews. He's not a man shy of talking about himself. Yet *The Torc* is one film he's never discussed in detail. He's never even said much about working with Tamar Dusk, beyond the usual rote phrases about what an honour it was, how wonderful a person she was, all that . . . bullshit. (PAUSE) If you play this for Lily, can you cut that out?

RP: No. Look, Doc, if what you're talking about really happened, how the hell could Quent—and Oleg, I guess—get away with it? Forty people dead, or disappeared? I don't care how much money you throw at something, you can't cover that up!

TJ: Can't you? This was the early '70s, no cellphones, no Internet, no GPS satellites or surveillance drones. And when I stopped the funding, Quent and Oleg lost any obligation to report production expenses to anyone, let alone involve ACTRA or the CLC. If anything, I think about how *incredibly* easy it would be to find a few dozen young, hungry people on the streets of Toronto, people with no families or resources, desperate dreamers who'd do anything to be in an honest-to-God *movie*. . . . People who wouldn't balk at being driven out to someplace in the Ontario backwoods, so long as they went together. Perhaps the buses were hired by Tamar's husband, a man who'd find it a lot easier to hide a few under-the-table payments than an official production investment he'd have to claim on his tax returns. A man who's since spent the rest of his life erasing as much record as he can of himself . . . *and* his wife.

After all, Mr. Puget, consider how much strangeness you yourself have seen, in all the stages of your work. Your vocation, you said to me. Strangeness that others have reported, eyewitnesses with no evidence of madness, no reason to lie. Your Institute has photographs, videos, sound recordings—a veritable library of the stuff. Yet people, in general, *still do not believe.*

RP: (LONG PAUSE, THEN) Look. Ectoplasm and psychic decontamination is one thing—even death, when it happens. But there's a *body*. There are *records*. People *know*. You're telling me that over forty years ago, one of Canada's most respected filmmakers not only participated in an act of fucking mass human sacrifice to turn a retired B-list actress into some kind of pagan night goddess, but *filmed* it and *released* it? As a goddam *feature-length movie*?!

TJ: Why not?

Some secrets are far easier to keep than others, Mr. Puget. Some are so incredible people will simply laugh them off; others are terrible enough that no one *wants* to believe them, if given any choice at all. And some are so ghastly that by the time you are certain of them, they have already tainted you for good—drawn you in so deep you cannot betray them without being destroyed as a coconspirator, a fellow monster. Tell me you haven't seen proof of this, not just yesterday but right now, in so very many places.

RP: (PAUSE) That's different.

TJ: Of course it is.

But as I said, this is all just inference. Filling in the gaps. Like astronomers, spotting planets not by looking for the light, but for where the light disappears. By thinking not about what's *in* the film, but what's been cut from it. And why.
(LONG PAUSE)

RP: The film keeps right on playing, though, right? Canadian Content regs keep it in circulation, even if it only ever shows in the middle of the night. People keep on watching it, and . . . nothing happens.

TJ: Apparently.

RP: Why?

TJ: Maybe . . . you just had to be there, physically. No taint seems to have attached to her earlier films, after all, beyond a certain—very specific—sexual allure. But whatever her films did for Tamar, however the psychic attention of viewing them sustained her, I believe that stage of her . . . existence is over, at last. Her husband lives in her presence, alone with whatever she's become; maybe it laps him in, keeps him forever asleep like Endymion, forever alive like Tithonus, frozen in a halo of dream. I don't know whether or not to envy him, really. If there's any danger left in her image, however, I think only lies whatever the viewer brings with them, while viewing it.

RP: So . . . that's why you took down the picture outside your office suite, right? Because it was of her. A portrait, a film poster, something.

TJ: Yes. (PAUSE) She fought so hard to remain as human as she could, for as long as she could—even marrying a man for whom she felt nothing, thinking that would make them both safer. If there is anything left of who she was, I cannot think she is happy.

RP: How would you know?

TJ: Exactly.

[TRANSCRIPT ENDS]

> > >

Supplementary Correspondence

Date: January 9, 2019
To: drgabbott@freihoeveninst.ca; ross.puget@freihoeveninst.ca
From: andrew.sorenaar@geography.utoronto.ca
Re: Geolocation request

Dear Dr. Abbott and Mr. Puget,

Apologies for the delay in responding; most of my grad students were away for the Christmas break. I'm sorry to say that we weren't able to find a single conclusive candidate location for the terrain images you provided—there simply wasn't enough detail in the shots. However, based on reviewing the vegetation visible in the frames, and factoring in the information you were able to provide about likely distances from the Toronto core and accessibility to motor vehicles, we were able to isolate three possible coordinate sets—and fortunately for you, they're all relatively close to one another, up in the Lake of the North district. With a good all-terrain vehicle you should be able to visit all three in one or two days. GPS coordinates and map routes are attached. (If you do travel out to visit these coordinates, I advise caution; these locations are all very remote and emergency assistance would be very long in coming.)

Hoping this information is of use to you,

Dr. Andrew Sorenaar
University of Toronto, Faculty of Geography & Planning

> > >

From a Note Found in the Empty House of Dr. T. Jankiewicz:

Dear Mr. Puget, Lily, and Dr. Abbott:

Though it perhaps goes without saying, let me nevertheless make things clear: I apologize for misleading you all. As you noted during our interview, I had removed one of the lobby cards made for *The Torc*'s initial screening from a display on my wall—a cut frame from the film's climax, the ritual conducted at a "druidic altar" supposedly located just outside the rather literally named fictional small town of Night Worship, Ontario. You will no doubt recognize it as one of the geolocations Lily showed me, as part of our own final conversation.

The fact is that even after withdrawing my money from Oleg and Quent, I made sure to continue paying certain lesser crew members to keep me informed on all aspects of *The Torc*'s production, including location scouting. As you will no doubt have figured out by now, the particular site where the climax was filmed is located on what Overdeere residents refer to as "the

Dourvale shore," near the location of the Sidderstane family's original canning facility. It was chosen because of the central feature, a gigantic root mass growing up through the ruins of the cannery's central hub, forming what appears to be a single massive altar fashioned from weathered stone and living wood. At the time the lobby-card picture was taken, the root system was covered in fungal growth of a type that Quent wasn't able to identify.

In the years since, I've tried to match the photograph to existing species, and found that it most resembles a combination of two types of jelly fungus, "black witch's butter" and "yellow brain." Since these are most commonly found on either the dead branches of deciduous trees or living hardwoods, you wouldn't normally expect to find them on a living root system, even one as . . . exotic . . . as this one. Looking closer, however, you'll see the gelatinous mass gilding the roots that spread outward from the "altar" contains sprinkled blooms of orange yellow, in distinctive fleshy outcrops. You can also see a clear layering of folded, lobed dark orange fruit-bodies underneath both types of fresh "butter," indicating that the growth has been flourishing and dying off cyclically for some time. It's an amazing effect, and I remember the location scout describing Quent's clear pleasure at having discovered it. The only thing they had to do in order to "dress" it before shooting was to add candles and dishes of spirit, which were set alight to provide ambience during the climactic sequence.

Near the end of our interview, after you had already turned off your recording equipment, I made sure to suggest that this altar must have been an improvised construction of black yarn and hastily painted Styrofoam. The geographic experts you consulted would therefore have searched assuming it to be no longer there, which is why all three of their possible candidate sites could not fail to be wrong. By the time you read this, you will have visited them all and found nothing, while I will have gone straight to the correct site.

I leave you the lobby card, since you evinced a clear interest in it.

I don't know why I assume whatever has become of Tamar might still be there. I do not know what I will find at the site, nor whether what I find will be what *you* might have found, had I allowed you, Lily, and your Dr. Abbott go there as planned. One way or the other, however, I believe, perhaps selfishly, that I am doing you all a favour—Lily, most specifically. I certainly know I am probably doing myself one.

To die without seeing her again, you see, at least once . . . would have been—anticlimactic. To say the very least.

I remain, yours truly,
Tadeusz Jankiewicz, DDS

PS: Lily, my sweet girl, I am so sorry. Please believe that I did not mean to betray your trust. It is only that my interactions with Mr. Puget reawakened an old addiction inside me, and when I saw a way to indulge it, I took it.

I love you, child, as I loved your grandmother and mother. I will miss you, always.

Goodbye.

MANY MOUTHS TO MAKE A MEAL

Garth Nix

JORDAN HARPER was a fixer for the studio. Not a high-level fixer—the kind who sorted out problems with the stars, arranging abortions and sudden marriages and unexpected corpse removals and so on—because the studio he worked for didn't have any stars. Pharos Pictures was firmly second-rate, B movies only, and the one time they did have someone with star power, Peggy Karolobian (who the world would later know as Carole Stannard) she was only there long enough for one movie and the time it took MGM's lawyers to break her contract.

Jordan still had to arrange abortions and sudden marriages and remove unexpected corpses, but he didn't do it for stars. All the dirty work he managed was for middling actors, and hack directors and fringe-dwelling producers, and there was always a calculus involved. The studio didn't swing into action to protect everyone on the payroll. How much was that person worth to Pharos Pictures? If the studio was going to be compromised, if the perpetrator was perceived to have some future value, and their sins were not too difficult to paper over, Jordan would be called in. If not . . . let 'em twist in the wind.

That's what Sol Theakston liked to say. He was the decider, as president of the studio, son-in-law and nephew of the moneymen back East who funded the whole operation. Even B movies were expensive. It was rumored Pharos was a cash-laundering operation for Theakston's family, who were still better known as the Goldberg rum kings, since they hadn't changed their surnames like Sol.

But Jordan didn't think so. He'd know if that was the case, and besides, Sol loved movies and often talked about his ambitions to build Pharos into a first-line studio. It was possible he might even do it. The pictures they'd been making had been getting better and doing better over the past few years.

Maybe one day Jordan would be a fixer to the stars. But he knew it wasn't going to happen soon, and definitely not the Friday morning he got a call from Mrs. Hope, Sol's secretary, personal assistant, and passer-on of special jobs and bad news.

"Sol wants me to check up on an *extra*?"

"Apparently she's threatening to go to the papers," said Mrs. Hope. Her voice was old and scratchy, but everyone sounded like that over the crappy phone in the Lookout Bar, a dive with no windows on Hollywood a couple of blocks along from Grauman's Egyptian Theatre. Jordan took his breakfast at the Lookout every morning, and made the calls that were better kept out of his office at the studio.

Mrs. Hope was actually young, under thirty, and Jordan thought her better-looking than most of the actresses he knew. Or more interesting, anyway. She was also a lot tougher than anyone else on the lot, including the crowd of ex-cowboys and circus folk who did the stunts. Jordan had seen her slash the back of an importunate associate producer's hand with a straight razor, so quick neither man had seen where the razor came from, or where it went, since Mrs. Hope had just kept on walking to her car as if nothing had happened.

Jordan thought that producer was particularly stupid, not taking his cue from Sol, who always treated Mrs. Hope like she was his sister, and an older, wiser one at that.

Jordan had noticed this, first day on the job, and always behaved accordingly.

"Go to the papers? Do you know what she might go to the papers about, Mrs. Hope?"

"This is from Mr. Theakston personally this morning," said Mrs. Hope, which meant she did know but wasn't going to discuss it without permission. "He told me Amity Truelove, real name Helga Sorenson. Apartment three, One Twenty-Six Bora Bora Gardens."

"Okay. I'll go over after I sort out that business with Teddy Thorogood's ex-husband. Shouldn't take long."

"Very good, Mr. Harper. Mr. Theakston expects to see you at five, as per usual."

"You got it. Good morning, Mrs. Hope."

Jordan returned the earpiece to the wall mount, the faint sound of the operator connecting Mrs. Hope to someone else echoing out of the Bakelite receiver.

An hour later, with only a slight graze on the knuckles of his left hand testament to the sorting out of Teddy Thorogood's ex-husband, Jordan parked his green Model A two blocks short of his destination. It was a habit he kept to, even if it meant some extra walking. Better for reconnaissance, and for leaving no obvious clues.

The apartment building he was heading for was anonymous, one of a dozen two-story affairs in a row along Bora Bora Gardens.

A new street, half of it still dirt, half badly paved. The buildings were cheap, pink or white stucco over concrete. Some developer had made a lot of money. And had probably overextended and gone bust in the last four years.

Jordan paused outside One Twenty-Six for a moment to re-adjust the .45 automatic in his shoulder holster, checking for the thousandth time that it would draw easily. It was a government-issue pistol he'd never given back after returning from France in 1919, and fourteen years later it continued to serve him well. He had an almost superstitious attachment to it, and to his other lucky piece, an 1837 five-franc silver coin that he carried every-where. He'd seen the glint of it and bent down to pick it out of the mud at exactly the moment a shell had burst overhead, killing his friend Izzy and two other guys, four days before the Armistice. He'd copped some wounds to his back from the flying fragments of hot metal, but he would have been killed if he hadn't bent down for the coin.

He didn't often need a gun, but he liked to know it was there, as it had been when Jordan had first gone up the line, all blink-ered and deaf in his gas mask and the German trench-raiders had burst out of a yellow-green poison gas fog, and he'd shot them down, doing what had to be done from immediate instinct, without even thinking.

He had a lead-weighted sap in his right trouser pocket as well, and a small folding knife in a holster sewn into his belt at the back. He hardly ever had to use them, either, but like the pistol, he thought it better to have them handy than not.

Jordan noticed all the windows were shut tight, and the cur-tains closed, before he went up. That could mean anything, but it was odd, since everyone else had their windows open. Apart-ment three was the second on the left, up one flight of stairs. He could hear the family on the right-hand side arguing about lunch, a couple of kids demanding something and their weary mother telling them to shut the fuck up. It was that kind of new neighborhood, full of people feeling worn-out before their time.

All the other apartment windows were open because it was May, and starting to get warm. Jordan could feel it himself, the sweat building under his arms and in the small of his back. Soon he'd have to change to one of his lighter suits. In weight, that is. Nothing white or tan or anything stupidly light in color, because they stained too easily. It was a lot harder to see blood on a good dark blue or black suit.

No one answered his knock on the door. He hammered the knocker again, a few times, a lot harder, but there was still no response.

"Hey, Miss Sorenson!" he called. "It's Jordan Harper, from the studio!"

There was still no response. He rested his head against the door, pressed his ear to the timber. He couldn't hear anything. No quiet footsteps or the sound of someone sneaking back from the door. No harsh breathing, someone huddled against it. All things he'd heard many times before.

Jordan sighed and took a look at the keyhole. It was a three-lever ward lock, almost as useless as not having a lock at all. Jordan sighed again and took out his ring of skeleton keys, tried the one he used the most often, unlocked the door, turned the handle, and pushed it open to the extent of the safety chain.

Someone was home. Just lying doggo.

There was an odd smell emanating from the apartment. Jordan's nose itched as he smelled it. It was kind of familiar, but not. It took him a moment to realize the familiar part was the stench of death, but it was overlaid with something else, something sweet and flowery. Reminiscent of the white flowers that grew on the vine out the back of his house up in the hills. He hated that vine for its pungency and its ability to regrow no matter how many times he uprooted the damn thing.

He sniffed again. The corpse smell was unusual. That first whiff had reminded him of the trenches, the overpowering rotten stench of days-old, disemboweled, blown-apart bodies. But it wasn't strong enough, and besides, if there'd been a dead body or bodies here for any length of time, the neighbors would have noticed, closed windows or not. The apartment building wasn't that well constructed. Plenty of gaps and holes for a smell to travel . . .

Jordan thought about the situation for a few minutes, wondering if it would be best to leave this one. Call it in to one of the cops on the payroll . . . but then he didn't know what it was about, and it probably concerned Sol personally. What could an *extra* go to the papers about, concerning the studio?

"Ah, crap," he muttered to himself. He drew his pistol, worked the slide, and kicked the door in, the chain separating from the wall with a loud crack.

Jordan moved in quickly, stepping aside so he wasn't framed in the doorway, the pistol ready. It was very dim, with the curtains drawn, but he could see the little sitting room was empty. Likewise the kitchenette, which was just an alcove off the main room. There were two other doors, one to the bathroom, one to the bedroom. He knew these cookie-cutter apartments.

He kicked the bathroom door in first, moving fast. The neighbor with the hungry kids might be stupid enough to come and have a look, or maybe even run out to get a cop. They wouldn't have a telephone. None of these places had telephones.

Despite the need for haste, Jordan hesitated a moment before the bedroom door. It was the smell again, that sweet odor he didn't like, even more than the stink of rotting flesh.

He took this door differently, turning the knob slowly, easing the door open, standing off to the side. The smell intensified, but even worse than that, he heard a soft, unpleasant noise, something he couldn't identify but he instantly hated. He didn't want to hear it, wanted to run away from it.

It was a kind of card-shuffling sound, real low, lots of little sounds joined together, one after the other, but it wasn't hard-edged like with cards. It was wetter, softer around the edges, and constant.

Jordan peeked inside, his heart hammering worse than it had even when he was on the firing step, waiting for the word, for the whistles, to go over and up into the shrieking, machine-gun-drumming terror of an assault . . .

There was a body on the narrow bed. A woman. Probably. She had been wearing a nightdress, which had been white, and was now uniformly a faded pink, and shredded into fragments.

Things moved on the body. Insects, Jordan thought. Or worms. Or something . . . his eyes and brain couldn't process what he was seeing. Lots of tiny things roiling across what was now just a lump of meat, the skin long since gone, half the flesh, too, and even the bones diminished, foreshortened . . .

Eaten.

Jordan choked back the bile in his throat as he worked out what he was seeing.

They weren't insects or worms. All those tiny, fingernail-size things . . . they were mouths . . .

Tiny, toothy mouths.

And the sound was them chewing.

Jordan retreated. He eased down the hammer on his .45 and re-holstered it, trying to be methodical, even though his hands were shaking. He walked to the kitchenette, though every part of him wanted to run for the door. There was an almost new Direct Action gas stove; he'd seen it on the way in. He spun all the knobs on full, heard the gas hiss from the rings. He opened the oven door, and the hissing grew louder.

But even the smell of gas couldn't overcome the horrible sweet smell. Jordan tried to breathe shallowly as he flung open the kitchen cupboards, pulling out everything, throwing things down to the floor until he found what he'd hoped for, or close enough.

A full tin of lighter fluid.

He was working on instinct now. The kind of sixth sense that had kept him alive in the war, and in a few tight situations since.

His fingers shook as he undid the cap on the tin. He forced himself to walk steadily back to the bedroom.

The chewing sound was louder, more rasping. The mouths were working on big bones now. Jordan held his breath and tiptoed closer, the can ready. As he drew near, he saw the mouths slow, stop their work. And they began to slowly move down the remnants of the woman's legs toward her feet.

Toward him.

Jordan shook the can, spraying lighter fluid across the end of the bed and the feet. The mouths moved more swiftly, climbing on top of one another, building up a facsimile of flesh again, already obscuring the bare bone, three . . . four . . . five inches high, growing so quickly—

Jordan retreated, pouring lighter fluid in a trail behind him. He dropped the can a few feet from the door, got his Zippo in his hand, simultaneously ripping the cellophane off a thirty-cent cigar with his teeth. He pulled the door half closed, shielding himself, and flicked the lighter. It clicked but didn't ignite. He flicked it again, and again, watching the bedroom, smelling the gas from the kitchen, the stink of rot, the horrible, sweet blossom smell growing ever stronger.

The flame made him jump. For a moment he thought the next thing would be a gas explosion, and death.

But there wasn't enough gas in the room, not yet.

Something moved in the bedroom door, along the floor. It looked kind of like a tide of mud, moving slowly, only six inches high. But it wasn't mud, it was the mouths, clambering over one another, still sticky with blood and bits of flesh. Trying to climb up, to reach him . . .

Jordan lit his cigar, puffed twice, and threw it dead on the can of lighter fluid. He saw the whoosh of blue flame and felt the rush of sudden heat, even as he pulled the door shut and ran to the door across the landing.

"Fire!" he shouted, using every ounce of that command voice Sergeant Quinlan had cultivated in him at officer school. "Fire! Everyone out! Fire!"

The door swung open, revealing a child of six or seven. Jordan pushed him inside and slammed the door with his heel.

"Fire!" he shouted again. "We got to go out the windows."

A harried woman stared at him, another child on her lap, a spoon of some indigestible-looking glop halfway to her daughter's mouth.

Jordan ran to the open window. He just got to it when there was an almighty boom. The building shook, and suddenly the acrid smell of smoke banished the last of the awful sweet smell from Jordan's nose.

The older kid needed no help climbing out; he'd probably done it a hundred times. Their mother hesitated by the window, until Jordan lifted her over the sill and swung her down. He carefully passed down the little girl, dropping her the last few feet. The mother caught her.

Jordan followed straight after, and hurried them away across the lawn and down the street. Another resident, a middle-aged man, came out the front door behind them and followed, coughing and choking. His undershirt was on backward, and the belt on his trousers hung slack, unbuckled.

"Where's a telephone?" asked Jordan urgently. "I got to call the fire station."

The mother and the undershirt man stared at him, jaws slack, the fire roaring up behind them, smoke rising dark and terrible, like a living thing.

"Where's a telephone?"

"Around the corner," said the boy, pointing along the street. He could hardly bear to look away from the fire. "The store, they got one."

Jordan paused for a moment to glance at the fire himself, taking grim satisfaction from the fierceness of the flames that were leaping out of the windows of the apartment he'd been in, and already out through the tiles of the roof. Those hideous mouths would be burned to ashes, sure. He spun on his heel and started off, ignoring the cries of "Hey mister!" behind him.

He did call the fire station from the corner store, but only long enough to gabble out the address, before hanging up to call Tremont 52. The studio, where he was put through immediately to Mrs. Hope.

"This is Harper. Look, I . . . what the . . . what was Miss Sorenson going to tell the papers? When did you . . . whoever talk to her?"

"Are you all right, Mr. Harper? You don't sound like you usually do—"

"Yeah. Yeah. I know. Listen, did you talk to Sorenson?"

"I already told you Mr. Theakston simply asked me to tell you to talk to her."

What was unsaid in that sentence was when and how an extra got to talk to the head of the studio, and the likelihood that it was the usual thing, Sol seeing an attractive newcomer, calling her up to his office, promising real roles.

"Okay. I got to talk to Sol. Immediately. Is he there?"

"Yes, but he's with—"

"Put me through."

"One moment."

Jordan leaned back from the mouthpiece and took a deep breath, trying to calm himself. Mrs. Hope came back again in a few seconds.

"I have Mr. Theakston for you, Mr. Harper."

"What is it, Jordan?"

"The extra, Sorenson. Truelove, whatever. She's dead. There's something bad . . . what exactly did she say she was going to tell the papers?"

There was a moment of silence, a little self-defensive throat-clearing, and a pause followed by the click of a door. The sound of whoever had been with Sol leaving, hurried out by an urgent wave of the presidential hand.

"She sent me a letter," said Sol. "To my home, Jordan! To my home."

"Yeah, what about?"

"She wanted money. She complained the makeup she had to put on for *It Came from the Crypt* wouldn't come off, and it was hurting her skin, obviously a ruse . . . Jordan?"

"I'm here," croaked Jordan. He was seeing those mouths again, hearing the liquid rustle of their chewing. "When was the letter sent?"

"Yesterday."

"Yesterday!"

"Yeah, I got it this morning. Lucky I was there, Benton was bringing in the post as I left, so I looked through it."

Jordan shook his head. That half-eaten corpse, the smell . . . he'd thought it must have taken days . . .

"*It Came from the Crypt* is still shooting, isn't it? When was she on set?"

"How would I know? Look, I had her up at . . . you know, once. I saw her dancing at the Cocoanut Grove, I said I could use her in a film. Look, she was fine with being an extra, she didn't want more, not then, this letter was a surprise. I thought—"

"Okay, okay. Who's heading the makeup team on *Crypt*?"

"Victor, I would presume . . . No wait, he's on *Penguin Dance* . . . and Jacques is doing *Roses of Monaco*. . . . It must be someone Deville brought on, freelance."

Dreyfus Deville, or Bernie to his friends, was perhaps the worst of Pharos Pictures' directors. But he was fast and cheerful, if pedestrian in talent, and Jordan liked him.

"Okay. I got to get on it."

"You said she was dead? I mean, I was only with her once, two weeks ago—"

"I'm on it, Sol. You hang up."

The phone clicked.

"Mrs. Hope?"

He knew she'd been listening. She always listened. Mrs. Hope knew everything.

"Put me through to Bernie."

"Immediately."

Click-click-click. A bored male voice answered the phone and reported Mr. Deville could not be disturbed, as he was on sound-stage four and shooting.

"This is Jordan Harper. Go get him right now or else I'll come over there and use you as a club to get his attention. This is a studio emergency."

The voice got suddenly attentive. Everyone in the studio knew Harper.

"Yessir! I'll get him."

Jordan heard footsteps running away from the phone. He turned to look out the open store door, catching the spreading plume of smoke above the line of apartment buildings. An asthmatic siren wheezed closer, announcing the first of Engine Company 27's shiny new appliances speeding toward the fire. A ladder truck, which seemed kind of pointless for a low-rise.

"Jordan?"

"Bernie. Who you got doing makeup on *Crypt*?"

"Uh, well, Victor was busy, and Jacques—"

"Who?" shouted Jordan.

"Fellow calls himself Ozymandias," muttered Deville. "Highly recommended, and he's done good work."

"You remember an extra called Amity Truelove? Sol put her in?"

"Uh, yes."

"Okay, after this conversation you don't, right? Never heard of her. All extras look the same to you. When was she on set? What was the scene?"

"The Temple of Seth-Anthrax, she was one of the slaves who carry the—"

"She have special makeup for that?"

"Yes, yes, of course. Oz . . . I call him Oz . . . he painted these really quite horrific little mouths on her, all along her arms and . . . Jordan?"

"Yeah . . . a fly flew in my mouth. How many slaves?"

"Four."

"They all get the little mouths painted on?"

"No, only Miss . . . the one you mentioned. One had eyes, one sort of tentacle suckers—"

"Where's this Oz now. On set?"

"Well, he was. Funny thing, he was taken unwell, maybe ten minutes ago. Odd, because he'd been looking so *good* the last few days. Almost younger, but then—"

"Where'd he go?"

"His home, I suppose—"

"Mrs. Hope, you there? Call all the gates, Gower and Sunset and the Adit. This Ozymandias is *not* to be let out. Tell them he's dangerous. They're to hold him at gunpoint, don't get close, march him to the special room in my office, quiet as possible."

"Immediately," interjected Mrs. Hope, over Deville's splutterings.

"What—"

Jordan hung up, flung a bunch of nickels at the counter, and ran for his car.

> > >

"Yeah, we got him, Mr. Harper," reported Billy, the senior of the Sunset Gate guards. "Lee took him up to your office, done like Mrs. Hope told us you said. Quiet, but Lee had his gun on the feller. He didn't cause no trouble. What's he done?"

"You don't want to know," said Jordan, and the way he said it they both knew he wasn't joking. "Thanks, Billy."

He parked in his spot and strode up the path to the bungalow that housed his office. It was set apart from the other four executive buildings, and Jordan had all of it. It was his private domain. The fixer's realm. Not just his office, but also a large bathroom, a pleasantly appointed sitting room for telling people bad news, and the special room, which was actually a jail cell.

Only when he got inside, Ozymandias wasn't locked in the

special room, and Lee was slumped in the corner of Jordan's office, dead as a doornail, his empty revolver in his hand.

"I suppose people are used to the sound of gunshots here," said Ozymandias. He was sitting in Jordan's chair behind the mahogany desk. He was maybe forty. Average height, thin, and elegantly groomed, with graying hair, an unmemorable face, but striking violet-colored eyes. He was wearing the whites the studio issued the makeup artists, nurses, and bakers in the commissary. There were five obvious bullet holes in his diagonally buttoned jacket, grouped tightly around the heart, but there was no blood.

"There's nearly always an oater being shot on the saloon set, stage six," replied Jordan. "The cowboys like to unload outside from time to time. Blanks, mostly, unless they've been drinking."

He glanced at Lee, looking for the horrible, all-consuming little mouths, and then swiftly back at Ozymandias again. He thumbed back the hammer on the .45 and kept it trained on the makeup artist, even though it seemed it wouldn't do any good.

"I have seen the cowboys about the place," replied Ozymandias. "An exuberant bunch."

His voice was quite high, and he had a faint accent Jordan couldn't place. Sort of Southern, but not. . . .

"I haven't been in the movie business long, you know. It seemed to me to be a good place to find the sort of young person I needed, and so it was. But alas, not without complication."

"I guess you might say that."

He looked at Lee again. He couldn't see any mouths.

Ozymandias caught the look, and smiled, showing his teeth.

Jordan swallowed a sudden surge of bile. Ozymandias's mouth was identical to the myriad small mouths that had eaten Miss Sorenson. Or rather, those small mouths were perfect copies of the larger.

"I hear you're what they call a fixer," said Ozymandias. "I have a proposal for you."

"Okay, let's hear it," said Jordan. He was thinking furiously, trying to work out what he could do. The guy was bulletproof. He used magic. There was no other word for it. He'd killed Lee without leaving a trace . . .

"I need another young woman, and swiftly. One who won't be missed."

"What for?"

"To eat!" spat Ozymandias. He wiped his face with his sleeve and continued, more softly. "By proxy, as it were. The consumption of the actual flesh is in fact almost incidental. It is the essence of youth and beauty I consume, to restore my own, which now ebbs by the minute, thanks to you preventing the completion of my planned repast. Give me a woman, and you will live. What else can you do?"

Jordan pulled the trigger, the boom echoing through the room, acrid smoke wafting up. He winced at the ricochets, the first off Ozymandias's forehead and the second from the corner of the desk, before the bullet embedded itself with a dull thud in the wall plaster.

"Your weapons will avail you not," hissed Ozymandias, rising from his chair.

"Okay," said Jordan slowly. Fire had worked on the little mouths. If he could somehow set Ozymandias alight . . . but there was nothing at hand. . . . He had to play for time. "I had to see for myself. . . ."

"A woman. Young. Beautiful. As I was, as I have been so, so many times, as I will be again."

"Yeah . . . look, I need a drink. . . ."

There was a bottle of whiskey in the bottom drawer of the desk. If he could get that, pour it on the—

"Damn!" said Jordan, finally processing what he'd just heard. "You're a woman!"

"So observant," said Ozymandias.

Jordan stared at her.

"Get me what I need! If you will not do as I ask . . ."

She raised her hand, made a claw with her fingers, and began to whisper. At the first word, a violent pain struck Jordan in the chest. He gasped and staggered forward, clutching at the edge of the desk to keep himself upright.

"No . . . no . . . I'll do it," he gasped. "An extra, like Sorenson, no problem! I'll call one in!"

Ozymandias lowered her hand. Now he was closer, he could somehow see her more clearly, as if she couldn't be bothered doing whatever had clouded his vision before. She was no longer a middle-aged, unobtrusive man but an ancient, a crone aged and fierce, like one of the witches from Macbeth. A good version, not the one Pharos did in '26.

"I got to call, get someone sent . . . ," whispered Jordan, pointing at the telephone on the desk. "And about that drink . . ."

"No drink," said Ozymandias. She gestured for him to pick up the telephone. It was a new one, not the old candlestick he'd had for years, this had the single handpiece.

Jordan laid his .45 on the desk and picked up the telephone, his mind still furiously trying to figure out what the hell he could do. He could indeed have an extra sent over, but she . . . she would get eaten, all those little mouths *chewing* . . .

He could shoot himself, he realized suddenly. Ozymandias would get away, but she wouldn't get another victim. Not from the studio.

There was a voice on the line.

"Mr. Harper?"

Not the studio operator, as he'd expected. It was Mrs. Hope.

"Yes," he said dully, looking at the .45. "Look, I—"

"Silver will do it," said Mrs. Hope.

"Uh . . . I need an extra sent over," mumbled Jordan. He fumbled at his waistcoat pocket, feeling for the five-franc piece. "A young woman."

There was no one on the other end of the line. Mrs. Hope had hung up.

"Hurry up," ordered Ozymandias. She reached inside her robe and drew out a small ivory or bone paint box, flipping it open. The horrible, sweet scent rose from the paint inside, making Jordan gag.

She took out a brush and lifted it to her mouth, her ghastly mouth, and sucked the bristles to a point.

"The best looker on the lot," said Jordan, still talking into the phone.

"Hurry!"

Jordan dropped the telephone, swept up the .45 in his right hand, and lunged forward with his left, shoving the five-franc piece against Ozymandias's eye with thumb and forefinger, the pistol up close but not touching.

Her hand came up, fingers clawing, but he fired swiftly. One shot, blasting almost half an ounce of fine silver at 835 feet per second into the sorcerer's head.

> > >

Mrs. Hope came in a minute later, and bound up the thumb and forefinger of his left hand. He'd shot off the top joints of both, but he figured it was worth it.

"There's whiskey in the bottom drawer," he said. "We got to burn the body. And those paints. Here. Not touching either."

"Yes," said Mrs. Hope. She didn't say anything about the

imminent loss of studio property. She just got the whiskey bottle out and splashed the spirit liberally over the strangely shrunken body of Ozymandias.

"There's more whiskey in the sitting room—" Jordan started to say.

"I know. I'll get it," replied Mrs. Hope.

Jordan walked slowly to the door, cradling his hand. He watched her go and come back, bearing two opened bottles of his precious Old Overholt rye. She poured one on the body, making Ozymandias's crumpled whites sodden with alcohol, and with the other bottle filled the paint box to the brim and let the whiskey flow over, to spread across the papers on the desk.

"I got a couple of questions I wouldn't mind asking you, Mrs. Hope," said Jordan, handing her his Zippo as they both stepped back from the office door.

"Only two?" she replied gravely, flipping the wheel. The flame came at once.

Jordan nodded. He reached into his pocket and drew out two cigars, pulling the cellophane off with his teeth, handing one to Mrs. Hope.

"Two for now," he said, puffing on the cigar she lit for him. "Maybe another one later."

Mrs. Hope got her cigar actually flaming, fortunately with no aficionados there to watch.

"I can't promise any answers," she said. "On three?"

Jordan nodded.

"One . . . two . . . three."

The cigars flew across the room. There was the flash of blue flame, and the sudden heat. Mrs. Hope shut the office door behind them, and when they got outside, Jordan shut the main door to the bungalow and locked it.

They walked along the path side by side, close, but not touching.

"We must get you to Dr. Schenck, and make sure our fire department contains, but does not swiftly put out, our lovely fire," said Mrs. Hope.

"Yes," said Jordan slowly. He stopped and turned to look at Mrs. Hope.

She stopped, too, and looked at him.

"Well, Mr. Harper?"

"How did you know, Mrs. Hope? About the silver?"

"I make it my business to know everything needful in this studio," said Mrs. Hope lightly.

Jordan raised an eyebrow, inviting more. Mrs. Hope hesitated before continuing, her voice very low and confidential, kept close between the two of them.

"Like you, I have had other work, other lives, before I came here. And I also fought in a war. Not your war—one no history book will ever recount and few living folk could speak of."

Jordan nodded slowly.

"There are more things in heaven and earth—"

"Precisely," said Mrs. Hope. "And your second question?"

Jordan hesitated. He had been going to ask about the razor but reconsidered. There were far more important things, after all.

"Is there actually a Mr. Hope, Mrs. Hope?"

"Not yet," replied the most efficient secretary.

ALTERED BEAST, ALTERED ME

John Langan

From Patch.com | Arts & Entertainment

Carmilla's to Close

Local museum unable to meet challenge
of falling ticket sales and rising costs.

By Carson Roget, Patch Staff | October 1, 2018 12:03 pm ET

After more than a quarter century terrifying children and adults, Carmilla's Children of the Night, one of Stoughton's oldest continuing attractions, will be closing for good the week after Halloween. According to owner-operator Steven Barlow, a continuing drop in attendance over the last several years, combined with escalating rent and other costs, has made maintaining the museum impossible. "To tell the truth," he said via phone this morning, "I've been putting more into the place than I've been getting out of it for the last five years. I'm at the point I'm broke. Actually, I'm broker than broke. Everyone I know, I owe money to."

An updated take on the classic wax museum, Carmilla's focused on full-size replicas of famous vampires from page and screen. In just four hundred square feet, visitors to the museum came face-to-face with versions of Count Dracula starting with one based on Bram Stoker's description in the original novel and proceeding through the various film incarnations of the vampire. Patrons also encountered other characters, from Count Orlok, the villain in F. W. Murnau's famous silent film *Nosferatu*, to Bella Swan and Edward Cullen of the *Twilight* series. In addition, Barlow stocked the museum with vampire-related memorabilia, including an original inscribed edition of *Dracula*, a copy of the script for the first Spanish-language *Dracula* film signed by its director, and several movie props.

All of it was not enough, though, to generate sufficient revenue to meet the museum's mounting bills. "No one's really interested in vampires anymore," Barlow said. Over the summer, he approached Count Orlok's Nightmare Gallery in Salem about the possibility of merging the two businesses, but their talks did not lead anywhere, and in the end, he decided to shutter Carmilla's. "It's time to put a stake in it," he said with a laugh. Asked about his plans for the museum's contents, Barlow answered that he's planning to auction some of the more desirable pieces in the months ahead. "I have to do something about those debts," he said.

from: Gaetan Cornichon <otherson72@gmail.com>
to: Michael Harket <michaelthomasharket@gmail.com>
date: October 31, 2018 10:34 PM
subject: Dracula Ring!

mth—

I took a look at the listings for the Carmilla's auction and the guy put
the Dracula Ring up for sale. He didn't want as much as I expected,
so I placed a bid. I was sure some film geek would swoop in to buy
the thing at the last second, but no one did and the ring is now the
property of moi (or will be once I pay for it, heh).

—gpc

from: Michael Harket
to: Gaetan Cornichon
date: November 1, 2018 10:26 AM
subject: Re: Dracula Ring?

gpc—

You mean this?

Dracula's Ring

From Wikipedia, the free encyclopedia

> *This article does not cite any sources. Please help improve this
> article by adding citations to reliable sources. Unsourced mate-
> rial may be challenged and removed. (June 2010)*

Dracula's Ring refers to a costume prop first worn by the actor John Carradine when he played the role of Count Dracula in the 1944 film *The House of Frankenstein*. An invention of famed screenwriter Curt Siodmak, who came up with the movie's story, the ring was intended to signal the Count's aristocratic origins. (According to his memoir, *Wolf Man's Maker*, one of Siodmak's early versions of the story included a subplot centered on the ring, but it was cut from the script by screenwriter Edward T. Lowe Jr.) Subsequently, the ring became a part of the vampire's regalia, and was worn by actors including Bela Lugosi, Christopher Lee, and Frank Langella. Supposedly, three copies of the ring were fashioned for *House of Frankenstein* and supplemented with others made for later films. Forrest Ackerman claimed to own one of the original three rings, although its authenticity was never verified. The copies that remain are in the hands of private collectors.

If so, then nicely done, Mr. Big-Time Horror Author! (And on Halloween, no less!)

—mth

from: Gaetan Cornichon
to: Michael Harket
date: November 1, 2018 4:30 PM
subject: Re: Dracula Ring!

That's the one! (Sorry—I thought you were there when we went to Carmilla's last summer. Weren't you?)

from: Michael Harket
to: Gaetan Cornichon
date: November 1, 2018 4:43 PM
subject: Re: Dracula Ring?

I was—you must've looked at it when I was talking to the guy from Romania (remember, Mr. "This Is an Abomination"?).

Anyway—maybe now you'll finally write the vampire story we've kicked around . . .

from: Gaetan Cornichon
to: Michael Harket
date: November 2, 2018 6:07 PM
subject: Vampire Story

Nah—I told you, the vampire thing is all yours.

from: Michael Harket
to: Gaetan Cornichon
date: November 4, 2018 10:12 AM
subject: Re: Vampire Story

I don't know. A (maybe) vampire dad on the run with his (maybe) vampire son while they're pursued by figures who could be either FBI agents or a group of modern-day Van Helsings? Come on—that ambiguous shit is right up your alley. Plus, I like the idea we start off thinking the two of them are in some weird version of *The Road*—moving only at night, along back roads, as if they're the last survivors of some kind of apocalypse—and then we realize they're the sole remaining (maybe) vampires left in a world of people hunting for them. And I love the late-night conversations where the dad is trying to explain their experiences as if the two of them are in fact undead, but the son isn't completely convinced. Seems like it would be a good way for you to take the family thing you do in another direction, too. Not to mention, chase narratives are always fun.

I know you're busy with the move, but once you're settled in, you should jump on this.

from: Gaetan Cornichon
to: Michael Harket
date: November 5, 2018 7:19 PM
subject: Re: Vampire Story

The way I figure it, I'd wind up drawing on Porter's and my relationship, and he's already traumatized at having been a (thinly disguised) character in *Split Rock*. I don't think he'd appreciate another appearance in one of his father's novels this soon after the last . . .

And yeah, the move is all-consuming. At the moment, we're painting. Leslie wants to do the walls in eggshell with black trim. She says the kids are old enough for us to have a house with white(ish) walls. I told her fine, but I'm painting my office red (still black trim, though). Oh, and there's a wall I want to paint completely black. It's on one side of the staircase up to the bedrooms. Technically, there are two flights of stairs. The first rises left six steps to a landing, then the second climbs right seven stairs to one end of a long balcony across almost the entire second story. The bedrooms and bathrooms are on the other side of the balcony. Obviously. This whole part of the house is open, with a chandelier hanging in the middle of the space. I think it would look really cool if we were to paint the wall on the left black. Leslie isn't sure, but I'm working on her. Porter doesn't care one way or the other, but Rosemary's all in on it.

from: Gaetan Cornichon
to: Michael Harket
date: November 12, 2018 9:09 PM
subject: Housewarming Gift

Thanks for the presents! The fruit basket was waiting for the kids after school, and they fell on it like the wild beasts they are, devouring all the grapes, most of the pears, and a few of the apples before I got back from teaching. Fortunately, they didn't eat the book you sent. Curt Siodmak's memoirs, eh?

I don't think you've seen my new author photo, so I'm attaching it. It's kind of cheesy, but the ring was too cool a prop not to use.

Oh—and the black wall is a go!

<Attachment.jpeg>

from: Michael Harket
to: Gaetan Cornichon
date: November 13, 2018 9:45 AM
subject: Re: Housewarming Gift

Glad the fruit basket was a success. I thought the Siodmak might be of interest, given what it's supposed to say about the origins of the Dracula Ring. (I should probably get a copy myself.)

I tried to open the photo, but it seems to have been too much for my antiquated computer to handle. (At eight years of age, it's antediluvian.) I'm sure I'll see the pic when you post it online.

And hurrah for the black wall!

from: Gaetan Cornichon
to: Michael Harket
date: November 13, 2018 7:49 PM
subject: Re: Housewarming Gift

Funny—my agent couldn't open the attachment, either. Could be a problem on my end.

Things are pretty busy here. We're rushing to complete as much on the house as we can before this big storm hits. Fortunately, all the painting's done, including the wall. Still leaves a lot of little things . . .

from: Michael Harket
to: Gaetan Cornichon
date: November 14, 2018 10:01 AM
subject: Storm

Yes, winter storm Elizabeth: she's supposed to dump eight to twelve inches of snow on us. I gather you guys are looking at more substantial amounts.

from: Gaetan Cornichon
to: Michael Harket
date: November 14, 2018 8:04 PM
subject: Elizabeth

We are—according to the latest weather reports, we could be on the receiving end of up to two feet of snow, plus fifty-mile-an-hour winds, and temperatures below minus twenty. Good times. Might be time for me to crack open the Siodmak book you sent.

from: Michael Harket
to: Gaetan Cornichon
date: November 15, 2018 7:01 AM
subject: Odd Dream

Apropos of nothing: I had the strangest dream about your Dracula Ring the other night. Maybe this'll help pass a few minutes during the snowpocalypse.

It was one of those dreams you enter without realizing you've fallen asleep. I was in bed, lying (I thought) awake, Patty unconscious on her side of the bed, two of the dogs snoring between us. (It's a good thing we have a queen-size.) The mattress shifted at my feet and when I looked to see if another dog was trying to join us, there you were, sitting on the end of my bed fully dressed, staring at the dormer window. Despite the room being dark, I could make out you wearing your *Jaws 2* T-shirt, the one with the exaggerated shark crunching the helicopter, and a pair of black jeans. The Dracula Ring was on the middle finger of your right hand. There was a woman standing on the other side of you. At least, I think it was a woman; it could have been a mannequin. She was dressed in these gauzy clothes, like Dracula's brides in the Coppola film, and as I watched, she removed a length of silk from around her shoulders and draped it over the back of your neck (which might have settled the human/mannequin question, except her movements were stiff, mechanical). Once the cloth settled on your skin, you brought your left hand to your mouth and bit into your index finger with such force I heard the bones crack. Blood, black in the night, rushed over your lips and chin, dribbled onto one end of the piece of silk. With a jerk of your head, you tore the index finger from your hand and spat it onto the floor, then attacked your middle finger with the same ferocity. There was blood all over your hand, all over your face; the silk was soaked with it. I could feel the astonishment, the horror written on my face. The woman-mannequin lifted her blank face to regard me. Her jaw creaking, she said, "He doesn't need them. They're just props." When your teeth closed on your ring finger, I woke.

There you go: make of it what you will.

from: Gaetan Cornichon
to: Michael Harket
date: November 15, 2018 8:35 PM
subject: Odd Dream

Um, thanks. I think?

from: Gaetan Cornichon
to: Michael Harket
date: November 19, 2018 9:01 PM
subject: New Story

Well, the worst of the storm is past. It wasn't as bad as it could have been, but we still lost power for a day and half. Tried the Siodmak, but couldn't get into it. There wasn't much else to do, so I spent the time working on the beginning to something new. (Although since I couldn't use my laptop, I had to write by hand, like some kind of peasant! A peasant, I tells ya!) Thought you might like a look.

<Attachment.somewherebeyondthesea.docx>

SOMEWHERE BEYOND THE SEA

The Weather Channel has given the storm a name, Elizabeth, which Cynthia thinks is stupid, because (a) TV channels don't get to name storms, it's a privilege reserved for NOAA, one they reserve for hurricanes, not every disturbance blowing up the coast, and (b) Elizabeth is hardly an appropriate name for any kind of weather event, let alone one that's already dumped ten inches of snow in the front yard and is on track to double this amount by morning. Elizabeth makes you think of afternoon tea in china cups, with little cakes served in those trays with all the different levels. If you absolutely have to have a name for the snow sweeping down in slanted lines, the wind roaring high overhead, the cold that numbs your face when you rush Petal out for her walk, then you should choose something fitting, a name with weight, with *gravitas* (or gravy-ty, as her dad likes to say when he thinks he's being funny): Boreas, or Donner, or Vlad. (Well, maybe not Donner, because people would think of Santa's reindeer, or the Donner Party, not thunder, and Vlad's kind of over-the-top, too, but you still have Boreas, as well as the general principle that a serious storm deserves a serious name.)

Cynthia's dad, Guillaume, loves Elizabeth. Usually, he's pretty nervous in the hours leading up to a storm of this magnitude, with its potential for an extended power outage, for branches and trees down in the yard, for the driveway full of enough snow to challenge their diminutive snowblower. He wanders the house checking the kitchen drawers where they keep the flashlights, batteries, candles, and matches. He counts the cans of tuna and fruit salad stacked in the pantry, removes plastic milk jugs and soda bottles from the recycling and fills them with water, expresses his regret at not having bought a propane camp stove when the Bass Pro at Foxborough had them on sale. Once the storm is underway, he switches the TV in the living room to the Weather Channel, where it must remain for the duration of the event. Should they lose power, Guillaume has a battery-operated transistor radio the size of a pack of playing cards tucked in with whatever fruit is in the ceramic bowl on the kitchen counter. Once the house is dark, he'll remove the radio, extend its antenna, and switch it on. Its surprisingly loud speaker is set to one of the news stations out of Boston, which will deliver essentially the same information in ten-minute blocks.

Cynthia used to try to distract her father, to take him by one of his long arms and draw him away from the TV to the spot on the throw rug in front of the couches where Kevin, her older brother, and their mom would be setting up a board game, Monopoly or Clue, or a card game, gin rummy or twenty-one. But no matter how much he might attempt to join in, his attention would inevitably drift to whatever was happening on the TV, whatever new way the reporters had come up with to convey information unchanged in the last hour or two, until Mom told Cynthia to let him go, the rest of them would play his piece or his cards for him.

This storm, though—Elizabeth—is different. Dad has been giddy. It's the only word for the state he's been in. He's wearing a pair of charcoal slacks and a black turtleneck, which almost gives the impression he's dressed up to greet the one or two feet of snow and forty-to-fifty-mile-an-hour winds steaming up the coast at them. He's in his stockinged feet, black dress socks, and he's been sliding along the hallway from the kitchen to the living room and back again like a kid pretending to ice-skate. He's linked his phone to the speaker Cynthia got him for his birthday, and his Spotify app is making its way through a playlist she's never heard before. Her dad's tastes lie in that part of the musical map she calls aging-punk: loud, guitar-driven songs whose lyrics insist on the singer's integrity. Some of the bands can be a little one-note, but Cynthia doesn't mind them, not really. At least they aren't the bubble-gum pop most of her friends' parents listen to.

What booms from the speaker now is something other than self-righteous rock or empty pop. This is old music, as in, stuff her grandparents would play. Scratch that: her grandparents are reasonably cool. The piano accentuating the singer's broad voice, the horns punctuating the melody in brass blats and shouts, the whisper of brushes on the drums belong to another time altogether. This is the stuff they played in the factory where Rosie the Riveter attached the wings to the planes waiting to bomb the Nazis.

And her dad is dancing to it, turning his glide on the hardwood floor into the start of an exaggerated shuffle from one side to the next, his hands out in front of him and then retracting to his hips as he advances, as if he's pulling himself forward on invisible ropes. He might be an actor from one of those classic films where everybody breaks into song and dance at the drop of a hat, scissored from that movie and dropped into this one, a contemporary drama about a middle-class family living outside Boston. She can almost see where the edges of his figure don't fit exactly with his new surroundings. The strange way he's holding his hands, fingers down and close together, calls attention to his new piece of jewelry, his ring. ("My bling," he said, to which Cynthia immediately responded, "Please don't.") It's large, oval, its top silver set in dark wood (cherry? mahogany? Cynthia isn't sure). Dad bought it a couple of months ago, after a local wax museum went out of business and sold off a bunch of stuff from its exhibits. At first, Guillaume kept the ring inside the box it had been shipped in. To protect it, he said; although Cynthia had the sense the reason had more to do with embarrassment, as if he couldn't believe he'd spent whatever amount had been required to purchase it. From the beginning, he said he was going to wear the ring in his next author photo, which, given the kinds of books he writes, struck Cynthia as smart marketing, clever and self-aware. After the picture, however, which did something weird to his editor's computer, her father has sported the ring more and more, on the middle finger of his right hand. He says the ring fits fine, it didn't have to be resized or anything, but Cynthia thinks it looks too large, an adult's decoration on a child's hand. She asked Mom what her opinion of Dad's new ring was, but she just rolled her eyes and said at least it wasn't a sports car.

Dad approaches the breakfast bar where Cynthia is sitting with her ELA homework spread out on the gray-and-white-flecked stone surface. He's singing along with the latest track in his playlist, except he doesn't really know the lyrics, so he's mostly repeating the same words, "Somewhere beyond the sea," adapting them to the changing tune. She's doing her best not to look at him, to focus on her assignment while the lights are still on, but it's difficult. He's doing his best to distract her, to stir her to laughter, which he's always had a (sometimes infuriating) knack for. Enunciating each syllable of his song—"Some-where-be-yond-the-sea"—he slides to a stop on the other side of the counter. In the instant before she looks up from the picture of Lord Byron, out of the tops of her eyes she thinks she sees Guillaume wearing a black scarf, a ragged length of cloth wound around his neck several times, one tattered end hovering over his heart. It's an illusion, a trick of the light, because when she raises her head, there's nothing surrounding his neck but the turtleneck's snug collar.

"Hey, Cyn," he says.

"Hey, Dad."

"Whatcha doin'?"

"Homework."

"What kind of homework?"

"ELA."

"When I was a kid, we called that English."

"Fascinating."

"What's your ELA homework about?"

"Vampires."

"Really?" He leans on his elbows, raising his eyebrows.

"Yeah. Ms. Quinn's building up to having us read *Dracula*, so she gave us a packet full of information about the history of vampires in English literature."

"*Dracula*, eh? Pretty dense for ninth grade, wouldn't you say?"

"For some kids." She doesn't add "not me," because it's obvious. "That's why we have the packet. There's a lot of summary and some excerpts from different poems and stories."

"Does it mention Elizabeth Bathory?"

"I think so." Cynthia scans the pages arranged in front of her. "Here," she says, pointing at one. "The Blood Countess, right? 1560 to 1614. She was Hungarian, lived pretty close to Transylvania. She was accused of bathing in the blood of virgins. Supposedly, she killed over six hundred women and girls. Some historians think she was set up, by men who were jealous of her. She was pretty powerful—Matthias II, who was the king of Hungary and Croatia, owed her money. Of course, both things could be true. The men could have envied her, and she could have been taking regular blood baths. Once her crimes were discovered, she was sentenced to solitary confinement, walled up inside a couple of rooms in one of her castles."

"That she was. Does it say what happened to her after she died?"

"Well, her body was moved from the first place they buried it, and now no one's sure where it is."

"So it doesn't mention anything about her heart?"

"No. What about her heart?"

"It was removed from her body and taken to a monastery in France, Saint-Matthieu-des-Pyrénées-Orientales."

"Why?"

"It was a way of making a pilgrimage even if you were dead."

"That's ... odd. What was so special about this monastery?"

"There was a library of esoteric books there. Vlad III had visited the place—it must have been a hundred, a hundred and fifty years before."

"Vlad—you mean Dracula?"

"The very one."

"He wanted to look at the esoteric books, too?"

"Uh-huh."

"I hope he found what he was looking for."

Her dad shrugs. "He started a minor trend. For centuries after he journeyed to Saint-Matthieu, men and women— usually nobility, but not always—who were after certain kinds of rare knowledge followed in his footsteps."

"Wow," Cynthia says, "really?" A surge of suspicion draws her face into a frown. "Wait. Is this true? Are you making this up?" Her father is a horror writer: this is exactly the kind of story he would invent.

In reply, Guillaume grins.

"Dammit, Dad," Cynthia says, "I'm trying to study. Now I'm going to have to try not to remember Saint-Matthew-whatever-the-rest-of-his-name-was and the sinister books."

"Don't worry about it," her father says. He cocks his head to one side, almost the way Petal does if she hears a sound outside the range of your ears. "Listen," he says.

"Dad," Cynthia says, the tone of her voice a warning.

"*Listen.*" He pushes off from the breakfast bar and slides over to the counter next to the sink, where the speaker is playing what Cynthia recognizes as a Frank Sinatra song. Guillaume zeroes the volume on "I've Got You Under My Skin" and despite herself, she listens to the space this opens. From the living room, she hears the murmurs of her mother and Kevin playing whatever board game they've selected. Behind her, Petal adjusts herself in her bed and grumbles. "What?" she says.

"Don't you hear it?" he says, and she does, as if his question has tuned her ears to its answer, the storm, Elizabeth, whose raging Cynthia has registered for the last several hours and ignored for almost as long. Now she hears the steady roar overhead. It's a vast, hollow sound that makes her think of a train full of empty boxcars speeding past, much too close. She hears the snow rattling against the house, and envisions the tiny frozen pellets bouncing off the siding. The wind changes pitch, and the house is in the middle of it, surrounded by the rushing river of air, which whistles around the corners, makes the walls creak ominously, as if the structure so much more solid, more massive than their old home, is in fact more fragile, a collection of plywood hastily nailed together into rooms and painted off-white. Somewhere nearby, a tree moans; she thinks it's the big evergreen just outside the back door.

"That's her," Guillaume says, "Elizabeth, Erzsébet, and she's come from very far away, from so far none of us can name it. She's come to blow everything away."

"What are you talking about?" Cynthia says as the wind continues to push against the house, and she wishes her question had less of a quaver in it.

"She's a ship with black sails," her dad says, his eyes alight. "She's come from a place you can't guess to take us somewhere new. She's the end, Cyn, the end of"—he waves his hands, and she would swear the ring is larger, as if engorged on his blood—"of all of it. After her, the world is going to be different. Except for us, it's going to be empty. Tonight, life as we know it finishes. What comes next—"

In the second before the lights wink out, Cynthia is positive her father is wearing the black scarf she thought she glimpsed before. When darkness overtakes the house, he shouts, "Perfect!"

> > >

from: Michael Harket
to: Gaetan Cornichon
date: December 1, 2018 11:00 AM
subject: Somewhere Beyond the Sea

My apologies for not having gotten back to you sooner. (God, it sometimes seems to me I could start just about every email I send with those words. If anyone ever writes my biography, there's the title.) As usual, I'm running late on a story and before I knew it, Thanksgiving was upon us in all its cranberried glory. Then one of the dogs ate something horrible, and we had to rush her to the vet . . . On top of which, at first I couldn't open the file. I know: again? My desktop started acting really weird, to the extent I was afraid it was on the verge of giving up the ghost, a catastrophe I could not afford. Took almost an hour of de-fragging and some additional tweaks, but I was (finally) able to access the story.

Anyway, thanks for letting me have a look at it. It's very cool. (I hope you appreciate how much I'm resisting the impulse to say, "I *told* you you should write about vampires.") I liked the daughter's perspective on her father (which I'm sure has absolutely nothing in common with Rosemary's view of you, right?). (But didn't you say you were going to stop using your family in your work? Or did you mean only Porter?) If I'm not mistaken, there's a bit of *The Sundial* going on here, with the whole world-ending-storm thing. (I'm a big fan of *The Sundial*—I think it's one of Jackson's best books.) The difference is, the storm ends Jackson's novel, whereas here it's the beginning of . . . something. I love the idea of linking the storm from *The Sundial* with the arrival of the *Demeter* in *Dracula*, as if the storm is a vessel. (You even managed to work in references to both Vlad and Elizabeth Bathory—not bad!) The scarf was a nice creepy touch, too—like a miniature cape (or a parasite).

Oh, and the reference to the monastery of Saint-Matthieu: I assume you're nodding to Kostova's *The Historian*. Have we ever talked about the novel? It's about my favorite post-*Dracula* Dracula narrative.

I'm curious to see where you take this next.

from: Gaetan Cornichon
to: Michael Harket
date: December 10, 2018 12:30 AM
subject: Re: Somewhere Beyond the Sea

Glad the story worked for you. I kind of stalled on it after I sent it; I'm not sure when/if I'll get back to it. I mean, I probably will. I don't know. Sorry—I'm kind of under the weather. Honestly, I've been feeling pretty bad for a few weeks—longer, really. Almost like a low-level flu. I'm freezing, then I'm burning up, then I'm freezing again, but the thermometer doesn't show any change in my temperature. My muscles ache like I've been beaten by a bunch of pissed-off critics with baseball bats. I thought I could ride out whatever it is, but haven't, so I finally gave in and scheduled a doctor's appointment for tomorrow (later today, now that I look at the clock). Hopefully, she'll be able to tell me what's wrong.

Oh, and as far as the Kostova goes, yes, like the book a lot. I enjoyed the idea of Dracula having this private archive related to himself.

from: Michael Harket
to: Gaetan Cornichon
date: December 10, 2018 7:01 AM
subject: Sick

Sorry to hear you've been under the weather; hope the doc fixes you up quickly.

Yeah, the archive idea was pretty cool. Seems like there could be a story in that. Wonder if Dracula would have his own copy of the Dracula Ring there?

from: Gaetan Cornichon
to: Michael Harket
date: December 10, 2018 12:10 PM
subject: Re: Sick

No luck with the doctor. She says I've most likely got one of the many viruses currently making the rounds. She took a blood sample, but more as a precaution than anything else. Told me to go home and rest for a couple of days, which is what it seems like I've been doing forever, at this point. You ever feel so awful, even the light hurts your skin?

It's funny: for a short time, right around Halloween, I was feeling pretty good, as in, better than I have in a while, since all the stuff with my heart last year. Don't know what happened.

from: Michael Harket
to: Gaetan Cornichon
date: December 11, 2018 6:49 AM
subject: Re: Sick

Well, the obvious answer would be the Dracula Ring, wouldn't it?

from: Gaetan Cornichon
to: Michael Harket
date: December 11, 2018 8:30 PM
subject: Re: Sick

Yeah, but the ring as what made me feel better, or worse? Or both?

from: Michael Harket
to: Gaetan Cornichon
date: December 22, 2018 9:12 AM
subject: Siodmak Book

Haven't heard from you in a little while. Hope this means you're over whatever's been plaguing you and busy with pre-Christmas insanity. I thought I'd send along something you might find interesting. Instead of finishing my story for you-know-who, I spent the past week reading Siodmak's memoirs. (Did I tell you I'd bought a copy of them for myself? I found a great deal on eBay, and my curiosity won out.) Turns out, they had much less to say about the Dracula Ring than I'd hoped; still a fascinating read (quitter). Siodmak was part of the wave of German Jews who fled the rise of Nazism first for the UK and then the US. Before he left Germany, he was already a novelist, already working in film. When he came to America, he ended up in Hollywood, where he wrote all kinds of scripts, including, most famously, *The Wolf Man*, which invented the modern take on the werewolf. His book ranges back and forth in time, not so much in a stream-of-consciousness way as in an old-man-reminiscing-beside-the-fireplace fashion.

Anyway, he says he's surprised by how many people have asked him about the ring, says he's been pestered by a small but persistent group of fans to divulge its origins. (I wonder if this includes old Forrest Ackerman? He was Siodmak's literary agent at one point and owner of *a* Dracula ring, though whether one of the originals I'm not sure.) Believe it or not, Siodmak was told about a ring associated with Vlad by none other than Bela Lugosi. (Lugosi, you may recall, was Hungarian. Well, he was born in what's now Romania, in a city called Lugoj [the source of his stage name]. This is on the western side of the Western Carpathian mountains. These form one border of the Transylvanian plateau. That's right: Ground Zero for Vlad Țepeș, Dracula, himself. [Although the exact location of his HQ remains in dispute; central-south Romania being a reasonable guess.] If you stretch things a little, you could say that Lugosi's hometown is in the same general vicinity as Čachtice Castle, the home of Elizabeth Bathory [which is in modern day Slovakia]. You can appreciate how much I'd like to find a connection between Lugoj and either someplace associated with Vlad or Bathory's castle, an old trade route, say, but nothing so far has popped up.)

(And no, none of this is information I have at my fingertips. As usual, I fell down the rabbit hole of research, and have decided to share the fruits of my labors with you.)

Apparently, Lugosi had been told about a ring associated with Vlad by his local priest, a man learned in all manner of subjects.

According to this fellow, in his later life, Vlad undertook something called the Blood Pilgrimage, to a monastery somewhere in western Europe, maybe France, maybe Spain. (Shades of Kostova, right? I wonder if she had this in mind—seems too big a coincidence not to be the case.) He was looking for power, for the means to maintain his perilous military supremacy over the Ottoman Turks, not to mention, his local rivals. The Pilgrimage was supposed to give him access to a source of undying strength, but reaching that power was a journey fraught with peril. This is where the ring comes in. It was fashioned to function as a guide, to lead whoever was wearing it safely to something called the Four Communions. Incised in the ring's design was the letter D, for the Latin *Dominus*. (Now there's a word with all sorts of resonance, from "master" to [more distantly] "taming/subduing," "building," and "home.") The ring helped Vlad find what he was searching for, but at a monstrous cost (the whole living dead thing). A hundred-plus years later, the ring was supposed to have found its way to the finger of Elizabeth Bathory. Following her conviction as a mass murderer, and her imprisonment in her chambers, she passed it to an unidentified guard. At some point afterward, it made its way to Greece, where there was a rumor Lord Byron held it before he died.

Siodmak thought the ring would give him the chance to create a new origin for the vampire, much as he had for the werewolf. When he sat down to write the story for *House of Frankenstein* (which I believe was the first of the Universal movies to feature the unholy trinity of Dracula, the Wolf Man, and Frankenstein's monster) he included a scene where the Count connects the ring to the process by which he became a member of the undead. Siodmak stuck pretty close to what he'd heard from Lugosi, the ring as a means to gaining the power of the vampire. He was pretty pleased with what he came up with, but the actual screenwriter, Edward T.

Lowe, chose to omit most of it from his script. There's a bit where Dracula is trying to hypnotize a prospective victim, and he shows her the ring, which gives her a weird vision of a place filled with shadowy forms, but nothing more. I guess it was enough, because the ring subsequently became part of Dracula's regalia, both in the remaining Universal movies and in the Hammer films, where it clung to Christopher Lee's finger.

That's about it for the ring, at least, for what Siodmak has to say about it. One more detail of interest: the design for the ring came from Lugosi, who worked with the costume person on it. I'm not sure if this is as significant as I'd like it to be . . .

I have to be careful—I can imagine this turning into one of those projects that swallows you whole. But hey! nothing's wasted on a writer, right?

Oh, and one more thing: I wanted to have another look at the story you sent me, but when I went to open the file, I got an error message saying it couldn't be accessed due to file corruption. It's likely something on my end, but you may want to check your machine, just in case. And I know you said you were done with it, but if you want to send me another copy . . .

from: Gaetan Cornichon
to: Michael Harket
date: December 26, 2018 10:29 PM
subject: Second Attempt

Wow—it's like having my own research assistant. (What were we saying about Dracula's archive?) Not sure what I'll do with the info, though it gives a bit more weight—more *substance* to this piece of jewelry sitting on my finger. Thanks for passing it on to me.

Weird about the story. Don't worry about it. I can't say I'm feeling any different. The doctor called with the results of the blood test, which were inconclusive, because of course they would be, you know? There was something slightly off in one of the columns, so she wants me to have them redone in another couple of weeks. Can't be anything too serious, right? In the meantime, I've accepted that I'm just going to have to get used to feeling this way and push ahead. It sounds stupid, but you know what helps? The ring. I put it on, and it's as if I'm assuming a role, one where whatever is plaguing me is part of me, something bringing me a kind of twisted satisfaction, even happiness. Once I'm in this head space, writing is easier. It's kind of like the ring is—not dictating to me, but collaborating, helping me to put down what I want to. This is my way of saying, I came up with a (somewhat) different way to tackle what I'm calling the Dracula Ring story, so I decided to sit down at the laptop and see what happened.

Be curious to know what you think.

<Attachment.StopMakingSense.docx>

STOP MAKING SENSE

Ridiculous, to be afraid of her husband, to be lying in bed with her heart galloping, fear potent as moonshine roiling in her stomach.

(Is someone standing in the corner of the room? No. She thinks.)

Afraid for him, sure. In nineteen years of marriage, twenty-three together, there has been no shortage of occasions when Joyce has worried about George: like when he was applying for his first teaching job post college, tenth-grade history at Most Precious Blood, and he didn't have an education degree, just his MA from UConn (because, he said, if you wanted to teach history, shouldn't you have to know history?), and he was working at Enterprise and hating it, and although he confided in her that he wasn't sure he could teach high school, after all, he was so desperately unhappy renting cars anything seemed as if it would be better. And then he was certain he'd blown the interview with the principal, Monsignor Bellew, a man with no sense of humor, and while Joyce reassured him, said it sounded as if his meeting with the priest had gone fine, privately, she had been convinced his nervous attempt at humor ("Don't worry, Father, I'm fine with teaching the Catholic version of history.") had torpedoed the interview before it had left port, and she didn't know what George would do if the job fell through and he was stuck for another six months attempting to talk renters into upgrading their class of vehicle and taking out the additional insurance. She had never witnessed her husband so unhappy, for so long, as if adulthood (if this was what their post-college existence in fact was) had turned out to be a trick, the disappointing toy surprise at the bottom of the box of cereal you'd nagged your mom to buy specifically for its treasure.

Though that was nothing compared to last year, when several incidents of light-headedness sent him to his doctor, who referred him to a cardiologist, who ordered what seemed like every test their insurance would cover—up to and including a portable heart monitor, which George had to wear for two days and which resembled an iPod and hung from his neck in a blue pouch and was attached to his chest by five electrodes whose connecting wires snaked into the top of the monitor, the sight of which, when he pulled off his T-shirt to show her, had made Joyce's head swim, her stomach lurch (not that she had disclosed either of those reactions in front of George: concerned about upsetting him, she pushed down her panic and said, "Oh, they shaved your chest," which the nurse had, in order to ensure the electrodes stayed in place, the observation allowing her to channel her flood of anxiety into humor, into jokes about manscaping, which was the response she maintained for the remaining time George wore the monitor, and then for the additional two days it took the cardiologist to review the results and call to say everything appeared to be fine). It was as if, in a single instant, she had stepped into middle-age, the neighborhood each birthday told her she must be drawing nearer to, possibly residing in already, a message almost comically absurd: she was a mother of young(ish) children, with whom she shared an interest in contemporary music and movies; she was conversant with current technology; she paid attention to fashion trends and adopted the flattering ones. In no part of her life did she display any of the ossification suggested by the words middle-aged, the calcification of taste and knowledge her parents had been overtaken by when she was a teenager and old enough to notice such things. Yet here she was all the same, walking cracked and pitted sidewalks whose surface might collapse at any moment and drop the man she had spent just about half her life with into darkness, into a hole in the ground that would swallow whole him and everything about him, from his passion for basketball (despite knees beginning to protest it) to his love of obscure movies (his current favorite *Ardor*, a bizarre, semi-pornographic French-Canadian take on Dracula) to his absolute loathing for anything pickled—all of it gone, and she and the kids left to cope with the George-size tear in their lives.

No doubt about it, then had been bad, maybe the worst, and there were ways in which she didn't think she'd fully recovered from it, not least of them her new appreciation for the implications of *middle-aged*, namely, that you were halfway across a bridge which only grew more frail and rickety the farther you went on it, and which did not take you anyplace, just broke off in the air and sent you plummeting out of sight, a realization whose short-term impact had been to impart new vigor to her and George's sex life, driving them to bed with a frequency and passion reminiscent of their early years together, before the responsibilities of work and kids had regularized and tempered their physical relationship, and whose long-term impact had been to make Joyce more patient with George, more indulgent when he wanted to drive into Boston on a weeknight to see his favorite band, or when he wanted to go out to dinner even though there was plenty of food in the house, or when he wanted to spend what seemed to her too much on a ring whose claim to fame was its role as a prop in a series of movies right around the time they started to slide downhill. *Better than a sports car*, she told herself after he explained the charge on the Visa, *or a girlfriend*, those traditional remedies to the anxieties of male aging.

This ring, though. Silly to think that her lying here in (*their*) bed began the day George tore the wrapping paper off the box it had been shipped in and eased it onto his finger. Where was the close-up of the ring on his finger, the dramatic music on the soundtrack to foreshadow what was on the way?

It's supposed to be the kind of thing a medieval aristocrat would have worn, proof of status, the raised design on it suitable for pressing into hot wax at the bottom of official documents. Joyce doesn't know if the coat of arms rising in silver lines from the polished wood setting is the crest of an actual royal or noble house, or if it's an invention, designed by a Hollywood costumer; because of its appearance in various horror movies, she's assumed the latter, but the design could have been taken from history, or at least based in it. When George has removed the ring (which he's done less and less, lately), she's studied the silver image on it. At the top, there's a five-pointed crown, with a weird squiggle underneath it, which could be the visor of a helmet or a stylized face. Below, wings outspread, is a bat (the first detail to make her wonder at the image's authenticity: is a bat the kind of animal you'd find on a medieval crest?) hovering over a shield on which two pairs of three-pointed crowns flank a capital letter D (the second feature to cast doubt on the coat of arms: would the first letter of a name whose translation might vary from language to language be appropriate to such a design? [in this regard, the bat actually makes more sense—unless what she's taken as a D is in fact something else, a coffin, maybe]). Despite its size, stretching from the knuckle of George's long middle finger past the first joint, the ring is light, probably because the part of it she took for wood is resin or plastic. (George joked it was bone, stained with blood, which was morbidly amusing at first, now less so.) Whatever the material, it's deeply unpleasant to the touch, prickly in a way belying its apparent smoothness, as if it's covered in tiny bristles, like the abdomen of a tarantula, or needles, like a cactus.

Cost aside (which wasn't too much, not really), as George presented it, buying the former costume accessory made sense as a prop for another role, his as up-and-coming author of smart, self-knowing horror novels that have (astonishingly) drawn praise from several of the writers he and she grew up reading, and whose success has resulted in a steady stream of invitations to appear on podcasts and even network TV on a couple of local morning shows. Before the ring, he was already letting his hair grow out of the short cut he's kept it in for the last decade, allowing his intermittent goatee to take hold and spread up the line of his jaw to join his sideburns, the beard arriving with enough gray to make him appear distinguished, a quality he modified his wardrobe to emphasize. Although still wearing T-shirts printed with the names and logos of his favorite bands, books, and movies, he added unbuttoned shirts and occasionally a dress jacket over them, all in dark colors, navy, charcoal, black, switching his jeans for slacks at the same end of the spectrum, and his Converse for black Doc Martens. For a long time, he looked extremely uncomfortable in the jacket and slacks, self-conscious, the little kid playing the adult, David Byrne in his enormous suit in *Stop Making Sense*. Joyce found this odd. With the exception of the T-shirt and boots, the ensemble was the same one he'd worn to teach history in for nine and a half months of every year for the last sixteen, not to mention, what he dressed in for family functions, holidays, birthdays, graduations, anniversaries, marriages, and funerals. She asked him about it, only to have him insisting she was mistaken, which she was not, but knew better than to argue over. If he wanted to talk about it, he would. This hasn't stopped Joyce reflecting on the matter and (tentatively) concluding that the semi-formal clothes he's worn to his job and family duties are to him a kind of camouflage he dons when he's pretending to be an adult, same as everyone else, nothing to see here, move along—whereas the *Jaws* T-shirt, faded jeans, and Converse are the clothes of the writer, his true identity, not the opposite of an adult, necessarily, but positioned at a weird angle to it. It's its own type of costume, one expressing who he is—or who he wants to think of himself as—as opposed to concealing it. Now, with the continuing success of his fiction requiring personal appearances for which the publicist at his publisher advised him to dress appropriately, he's had to change the clothes in which he was comfortable for ones a little too close to his disguise as just another member of society. Joyce connects his discomfort to an anxiety her husband has confided to her, namely, that each new novel will not be as good as the previous one, resulting in him being found out as a fake, an impostor. It's as if the clothes are an emblem for this complex of emotions.

(Is that a noise in the hallway? A footstep? She listens, listens with her entire being, willing her body to act as a microphone, to pick up the slightest vibration coming from the floor outside the room. *This is ridiculous*, she tells herself, *ridiculous*. The sound is not repeated.)

In this regard, when the ring arrived, it was a good thing, the addition of it to George's wardrobe granting the clothes a theatrical aspect, making them sit easier on him, as if he were the host of one of those Saturday-night horror features from when they were kids, *Creature Feature* or *Chiller Theater*. Though Joyce was repulsed by the feel of it, George claimed not to notice what she was describing, which she found difficult to believe, but for once she could not tell if he was lying, and so allowed her reaction might be caused by some form of an allergy. At first, he kept the ring from his finger until the moment he was sitting down at the computer for a webcast, or on his way out the door to a reading or convention. The rest of the time, he kept it in the square wooden box it came in, on the nightstand on his side of the bed, next to the pile of books he's forever making his way down, and while it's melodramatic, she's come to regard the unfinished blond cube as a coffin for the thing (*the creature*) that over the past two months has spent more and more time on her husband's finger, as he has changed in ways small and large, which gradually made her nervous for him, and now afraid of him.

His turtlenecks, for example. George has never liked turtlenecks, has declared in no uncertain terms his inability to tolerate the feel of the collar around his throat, as if he's being strangled (for much the same reason, he's been reluctant to wear a scarf in all but the coldest weather, and never for long, tugging it from his neck as soon as he's inside a car or building). Joyce doesn't share his phobia, but she respects it, and she's always made sure to remind all of her family members asking what to buy her husband for his birthday or Christmas to steer clear of turtlenecks (scarves, too). And then, maybe a month ago, when George stopped in the living room to kiss her goodbye on his way for a reading down in Providence, he was dressed in a gray turtleneck. So startled was she by the sight, words deserted her; honestly, had he been shirtless, barechested, she would have been only slightly more surprised. Not least among the questions which crowded her brain after his departure was a practical one: how had he had time to shop for new clothing? Between his teaching (and its attendant grading and meetings of one kind or another), driving Lawrence to basketball and SAT prep and writing (and its attendant activities, such as driving to the Brown University Bookstore to be part of a reading with a couple of his friends), George's plate had been beyond full, it was buried under extra helpings of meat and potatoes, vegetables tumbling off the sides, gravy spilling over its rim to stain the tablecloth. Of course he could have ordered it online, which he's done for half the T-shirts folded in his dresser, but she hadn't noticed any packages arriving in the last couple of days, nor had she noticed any clothing-related charges the last time she looked over the credit card accounts. The turtleneck had been joined by four more, in charcoal, navy, black, and maroon, which together became his default choice for writing events, then for teaching, and more recently, for wearing around the house. Upon his return from Providence, Joyce asked about the shirt. But his reply, a shrugged, "I decided it was time for a change," was as unsatisfying as it was banal. There was no way she could see, however, of pursuing the matter that wouldn't sound just the slightest bit unhinged. After all, it was only a shirt. Yet exactly such small changes in someone's behavior signaled greater shifts far beneath the surface of their psyches, the wobbles in the seismograph's needle indicating tectonic shifts miles underground. Joyce would like to say she's grown accustomed to the turtlenecks, except she hasn't. With each passing day, she's had a mounting suspicion that the high collars surrounding George's throat conceal something—a horrible wound or wounds to his neck, long gouges and tears running up the soft skin, muscle raw and red visible and bloody, as if an animal, a dog or wolf, savaged his throat.

A nonsensical idea, yes, though when was the last time she saw her husband's neck uncovered? He's been staying up past her bedtime, rising before her in the morning, a schedule he's attributed to the new book he's started (whose plot, a father and son who may be the last vampires living [undead?] on the run cross-country from the men hunting them, has likely influenced her fantasy about his throat). Even the times they've had sex, it's been in the dark—not a new thing, but one George has gently insisted on, saying it's more romantic. While she can't recall noticing anything different about the contours of his neck with the lights out, the last couple of times she's avoided kissing the skin there, afraid of what her lips might touch, or her tongue taste. At least he's removed the ring before slipping under the covers with her (or so he's assured her—though certainly she would have noticed if he hadn't [wouldn't she?]).

Were it not for the trio of incidents following his switch to turtlenecks, which have left her lying here in (*her*) bed, terror rendering her immobile, Joyce might be able to write off her reactions to the change in George's clothing as silly, a case of her imagination not just running wild, but belting and buckling itself into a race car and roaring around the inside of her skull at two hundred miles an hour. This trinity has reinforced her intuition, her conviction, of the shirts signaling an ongoing (and sinister) transformation in her husband.

The first took place during Elizabeth, the storm the week after Thanksgiving, which knocked out power to the house for a day and a half—inconvenient, but not as bad as it could have been. The night the lights went off, George was restless, full of nervous energy, roaming the house, engaging in brief, fragmentary exchanges with her and Lawrence in the living room, where they were playing Stratego, and with Julia in the kitchen, where she was doing her homework. He skated over the hardwood floors in his socks, broke out in funny little dances to the music blaring from the speaker synced to his phone (the music another weird detail, big-band-style stuff, Bobby Darin, Frank Sinatra, Bing Crosby, pleasant tenor vocals riding melodies comprised of horns and piano, one of the [many] musical styles George has done nothing to conceal his disdain for, condemning it as sentimental, inauthentic—yet here he was, not only shuffling his feet to it, but singing along to most of the lyrics). His behavior was typical of the way he became in the run-up to a major event, his birthday, or Christmas, or a concert he was looking forward to, so full of energy he might as well have been throwing off sparks; albeit, there was a certain degree of tension mixed in with his restlessness, as there was the day before an important review of one of his novels was set to drop. He wasn't exactly bad-tempered, but his normal reactions to things were heightened. As far as Joyce knew, there was no review of his books imminent, which made her attribute his mood to the storm whipping the trees outside. This weather made him anxious, and when the power failed, and the house went dark, and he shouted, "Perfect!" she took his exclamation as a further form of (over)compensation. For a moment, she and Lawrence sat in blackness, the game board with its thinning ranks of rectangular blue and red pieces vanished, Frank Sinatra singing, "*I've got you under my skin*," filling the lightless air. "Hang on," Lawrence said, "I'll get my phone," but, "Save it," she told him, "Dad's lighting the candles," which he was, small tongues of yellow and orange flame flaring to life and settling atop the thick candles George had positioned throughout the kitchen. In their gradually spreading glow, Joyce saw her husband continuing his amateur dancing, slipping over the floor from one candle to the next, a lit match before him in his outstretched hand.

Afterward, she would think she had registered something off about George from the moment the first candle returned him to view, but it would take the addition of another few candles for her to identify what it was: the feet gliding across the kitchen's hardwood surface were hovering six inches above it. Her double take prompted a laugh from Lawrence, who did not see what was happening at the other end of the hallway separating living room from kitchen. Their son's laughter brought a glance from George, who saw Joyce seeing him, seeing him performing this impossible—the word that occurred was *unreasonable*—act, and skated out of view, into the dining room, still half a foot from the floor. It was such a bizarre (*unreasonable*) experience, she did not know how to respond, to process it. Neither of the kids witnessed anything, which of course they wouldn't have, couldn't have, because there was no way it could have happened, what she had seen was a variety of hallucination, there was no other tolerable explanation, even if had lasted for what felt like several seconds, far in excess of the usual tricks of perception that transformed the coat rack at the front door into a tall man standing in the corner. Maybe she would not have felt quite as unsettled by what she had(n't) watched if she could have spoken to George about it, but when she had broached the topic (once the power was safely returned [why did she wait till then, why had she put off approaching him until every light in the house was shining and the TV on besides?]) he had met her incipient remark with a smile whose joy had unnerved her almost as much as the sight of his feet resting in the air. He knew, George's expression said, he knew what she was going to ask him, had been waiting for her to do so, because she had to, it was part of the game, and the answer was yes, she had seen exactly what she thought she had, and it was the start of something . . . (*unreasonable*) . . . for which she was not sure of the word, something connected to the turtlenecks and the ring, yes, the prop once clinging to the fingers of actors whose greatest fame had come from playing versions of the same character. Confronted by his smile, Joyce decided on the spot she did not want to be made privy to whatever secret was powering it, and had switched her question to who was picking up Lawrence from basketball tomorrow. Absent her invitation, George had not offered any information of his own. (Marriage, she has come to realize, is as much about what you don't need to know about your spouse as it is the opposite; though this case has steered the principle into dangerously uncharted waters.)

The second incident took place a couple of weeks later, on

a Tuesday night in the midst of Christmas season, when Lawrence was struck by a nasty stomach bug which confined him
to one of the living room's couches, where he had access to
the PlayStation and the large-screen TV and was five running
steps from the downstairs toilet. In what her father would have
called the wee small hours of the night, Joyce had awakened,
pushed from sleep by the urging of a bladder whose resilience
had not been the same since the birth of her second child,
and after relieving herself in the master bathroom, decided
to check on Lawrence, whom sickness reduced from aspiring
adult to helpless child (a younger version of her son whom
she appreciated the opportunity to visit, however much she
hated to see his cheeks flushed, his eyes glassy with fever).
She padded down the cold stairs and through the dining room
to the kitchen, from which she could see the bright rectangle
of the TV at the far end of the darkened living room, hear the
soundtrack of whatever game he was playing, an electronic
melody whose notes ran through the same progression over
and over again. As she walked toward the couch on which her
son lay, she grew aware of another sound beneath the game's
music, a liquid, messy noise, as of someone slurping soup
from a bowl. She hadn't noticed an open can of Campbell's
on the counter beside the microwave, but neither had she
been looking for one, and it was a good sign if Lawrence had
regained enough appetite to seek out sustenance more substantial than the Gatorade he had subsisted on the past twenty-
four hours. There were grunts mixed in with the slurping,
animal noises of hunger. Since she couldn't see Lawrence's
head above the back of the couch, she assumed he was lying
almost completely on his back, his shoulder wedged into the
leftmost corner of the couch while he spooned soup into his
mouth from the bowl balanced on his chest, his game control-

ler on the carpet next to him. It was his preferred position for using the TV for gaming or watching movies (or to consume food while engaged in those activities) and though she was positive it couldn't be as comfortable as he swore it was, she had learned which battles to pick, and this was not among them.

When she peered over the back of the couch, however, the sight to greet her was not what she had expected. For one thing, Lawrence was lying with his enormous (size 13) feet where she had thought his head would be, on his side, wrapped in the Patriots blanket whose home was the bathroom closet until someone in the family was sick and shivering and needed its well-washed comfort. For another, he was asleep—or she thought he was, because George was bent over him, his arms propped on the cushion to either side, his head inclined to his son's neck. The instant she saw the two of them, George looked up, lifting his right hand from the cushions, fingers down. Backlit by the TV, his face was obscure, unreadable, the length of Lawrence's exposed neck draped in the shadow cast by George's left arm. "Just checking on him," George said, the words seeming to originate to either side of Joyce, in the shadows clustered in the room's corners. George maintained his position—his *pose*, she would later think it—for sufficient time for it to engrave itself on her brain's folds, ensuring her memory of it would remain vivid and the memory stir another, one she could not retrieve on her own and so had employed the assistance of a Google image search to locate. After eight minutes of refining her terms, the search engine turned up the picture George's pose had suggested, a still from one of the classics of silent film, Murnau's 1922 *Nosferatu*, the vampire, Count Orlok, tilting his long white face from the neck of his final victim, his pale right hand held talons-down. Much was different about the scene: unlike the actor, her husband had a full head of curling hair, his ears did not rise to points, and there were no fangs taking the place of his incisors, not to mention, the figure over whom George was leaning was his son, whereas Count Orlok loomed above the young woman who had sacrificed herself to assure his destruction. More fundamentally, where the image of George was dark, the vampire's was light; where the TV shone behind her husband, the rising sun cast its light behind the Count. It was as if the memory of George were the negative of the one from the movie, or maybe vice versa, she couldn't decide. Of course it wasn't necessary, but Joyce checked Lawrence's neck after George rose to go upstairs to bed, only to find (of course) it marked by nothing more serious than a couple of days' stubble.

Despite the evidence of her eyes, her fingertips, she has been plagued by the suspicion, the dread, of having missed something directly in front of her. When she's asked herself what this could have been, she's experienced a brief, startling vision of George's mouth smeared with blood, his nose and cheeks wet with blood, bits and pieces of flesh clinging to his bloody mustache and beard, Lawrence's throat chewed open below him, blood soaking the cushion under her son. It's an image contradicted by Lawrence pushing past her in the morning to retrieve the orange juice from the fridge, by him leaving his sneakers at the foot of the stairs, instead of neatly on the mat with the other shoes, by him lying on the living room couch playing *Outlast* and talking to one of his friends on his phone. Still Joyce has not been able to shake the feeling, the conviction that there's something she's missing. She's reminded of a series of books popular when she was a teenager, the ones whose pages appeared to be full of random geometric shapes until you held the book a certain distance from your face and allowed your eyes' focus to relax, which brought a picture—usually a face—forward from what had been chaos. The problem is, the face promising to reveal itself is her husband's, grown (*monstrous*) different and she is afraid to discover it.

(Is someone standing in the corner of her room? She isn't sure.)

In fact, were it not for what has just happened on the stairs, the third incident, the worst yet, Joyce might very well let the sleeping bear lie (a favorite misquote of her father's, one which has never seemed so appropriate—except "bear" could be swapped out for another animal even more outlandish, an ogre, maybe, or a dragon). Funny, it used to be, whenever she would read about a woman remaining in a bad situation, a relationship or marriage grown toxic, she would think, *Why didn't you leave? You didn't have to do anything dramatic, just get in the car and go somewhere, anywhere.* In all fairness, the solution had been so simplistic, so self-evident that she had immediately recognized she was missing something important, a factor she has become familiar with these last several months, since the ring migrated from the movie screens of decades past to her husband's finger. It's a kind of inertia generated by her combined attachment to her family and her doubt of herself, her daylit skepticism about (over)reacting to turtlenecks, for God's sake, of freaking out over what was likely a trick of the light, a self-generated special effect, of assuming George was imitating a scene from a silent movie when it was probably a case of his knees being stiff. No matter a part of her brain so ancient it warned her ancestors of the approach of saber-toothed tigers and cave bears has been murmuring, then saying, now screaming that she is under the same roof as something similar, a predator wearing her husband's face and playing a sinister game with her, the kind of sport cats have with the mice they're planning to kill and devour, it hasn't been enough to prompt her to any action beyond what just took place on the stairs.

The same cluster of cells tucked deep within the folds of her brain had propelled her from a deep sleep, the kind of descent into unconsciousness she rarely experiences anymore, a consequence of who can count how many nights listening for sounds of distress from one child or the other. In a moment, her feet were on the floor and she was throwing open the bedroom door, traces of the dream she had been immersed in clinging to her, leaving her half thinking she was rushing through the labyrinthine house (in New Orleans?) her subconscious had plunged her into, the photos on the wall to her left windows to another place, a dream beyond her dream. The handful of footsteps it took her to reach the top of the stairs pulled her loose from the last of the fantasy, which meant the tall figure standing on the landing with its back against the wall was no further figment of her imagination, but an actual person, an intruder on his (its) way to the bedrooms, and even as she was thinking that this must have been what dragged her from sleep, her perception of this stranger in the house, she recognized him (it) as George, pressed against the wall he had convinced her to paint black, which in the darkness appeared one end of a great emptiness, an opening to a space of endless night. If asked, she would have described the rictus stretching his lips as a smile, but it could as easily have been the expression of someone in fantastic agony as of someone transported by joy. His hands were crossed over his heart in the position of a corpse laid out in its coffin, the ring on the middle finger of his right hand swollen, as if it were an oversize tick engorged with his blood. She wanted to flip the switch for the chandelier hanging to her left, bathe the scene in brilliant white light, but doing so would have required abandoning her post at the head of the stairs, which would have left access to the second floor open to the half-dozen steps it would have taken George to reach it, and Joyce was certain, she had never been as sure of anything, ever, she did not want this happen, the prospect filled her with dread so pronounced it was nauseating. The atmosphere of the stairwell was curiously thin, as if they were standing at the peak of a high mountain. She had no time to analyze her reaction: George was moving forward from the black wall, almost gliding over the carpet (she couldn't say, exactly, the darkness was especially thick around him, draping his shoulders and wrapping his legs like a cape). Mouth dry, she said, "George." The grin distorting his face did not shift, his eyes did not register her, but his advance halted. "No," she said. "No. You can't come up here. You have to—you have to go. Now."

Time split.

In one branch, George's hands dropped to his sides and he leapt halfway up the stairs before she saw his mouth open, the teeth piercing his gums horrifying, every last one sharp, the canines elongated, a wolf's, his eyes bleeding darkness down his cheeks, a low moan trailing from his throat. Her hands were on their way up to defend herself but it was too late, his teeth were a shock of agony in her throat, her blood spraying hot into his mouth, the noise he was making thrumming against her skin, while she was still trying to understand what was happening.

In the other branch, George retreated (*slid*) back across the landing, becoming harder to see, less distinct, the blackness engulfing him, as if he was sinking into the black wall. The sound of feet descending the stairs filled the air.

Then time rejoined itself and Joyce was standing with her hand at her (*unharmed*) neck, head reeling from the shock of George savaging her with his monstrous teeth (*fangs*). With her other hand, she grasped the railing to keep from collapsing. Her heart, whose beats had paused as the two scenarios played out, started hammering against her chest with such force she feared she was having a heart attack and, using the railing to ensure she didn't topple down the stairs, lowered herself to sitting, allowing her forehead to lean forward until it was resting against her knees. A vulnerable position, should George return, but she could neither hear him moving around downstairs, nor feel the diminished pressure thinning the air on the far side of whatever had just happened to her, which (*maybe*) meant that he had settled himself on one of the living room couches or (*better*) had left the house. What a thing to hope for: were her heart not continuing its mad pounding, her head its wobbling spin, she might have sobbed. As it was, she concentrated on not throwing up in her lap. She remained where she was while the house settled into quiet, until the place nestled within her brain told her she could leave her position and she rose to seek her bed and whatever comfort its mattress could offer a body whose every muscle felt bruised.

She wasn't expecting to sleep, nor has she. She's lain awake with her eyes on the ceiling, repeating to herself how absurd it is to be afraid of her husband, which she is, she most definitely is, the memory of his (*unreasonable*) teeth, of the thunderclap of pain when they plunged into her flesh, echoing in her mind, forming the final link in a chain of events that began with George bidding for that ring online and wound through the turtlenecks to her hallucination of him floating (which wasn't a hallucination, was it?) to the discovery of him crouched over Lawrence's throat (doing what, for Christ's sake, what?). She lies there in the dark attempting to plan her next move, the escape she knows she has to make, grabbing the kids and leaving the house, and how hard can it be? She doesn't have to bring anything else, they could go in their pajamas, the three of them, right now.

The problem is, there might be something standing in the corner of the bedroom where the shadows congregate to the left of the closet. If there is, then it's as tall as her husband but thin, dreadfully thin, its neck wound with what appears to be a scarf, but a scarf fluttering as if caught by a strong wind. Despite everything, Joyce's default reaction is to tell herself it's a trick of her perception; although she does her best not to move, not to let the (*maybe*) figure see that she's seen it. She wonders how long she can keep lying here. She wonders whether the footsteps she heard earlier, when George appeared to merge with the black wall, were walking down the stairs, or climbing up them.

> \> \> \>

from: Michael Harket
to: Gaetan Cornichon
date: January 1, 2019 2:00 PM
subject: Stop Making Sense

Happy New Year! Here's hoping it's a good one for you and the fam and that you (finally) see some improvement on the health front.

Had a quiet time here. Patty was feeling a bit run down, so made an early night of it. Eric and I sat up to suffer through the musical numbers and watch the ball drop. After he went off to Snapchat with his girlfriend, I stayed awake a while longer to read your latest. Jesus, you really went all in on this one, didn't you? Seemed to me you were channeling a bit of Joyce Carol Oates this time, the semi-breathless style she adopts when she wants to take you inside the consciousness of a character in distress. (I mean, you did name the protagonist Joyce.) Although, and I imagine you'll say I'm reaching here, the scene on the stairs reminded me of the part in *The Turn of the Screw* where the Governess confronts the ghost of Peter Quint on one of Bly House's staircases. Needless to say, your version ended a bit more . . . messily. (Or did it? you ambiguous son of a bitch.) (It also occurs to me that Oates wrote a riff on the James—"Accursed Inhabitants of the House of Bly," I'm pretty sure—can't recall if there's a similar moment on the stairs in it, but I don't suppose it really matters.)

Gotta say, you've pushed the autobiographical aspect about as far as I've seen you go with it. Don't take this the wrong way, but there were a couple of moments when I wondered if maybe you'd gone a little too far. I mean, I had a hard time imagining Leslie reading it, you know? On the other hand, it also put me in mind of a Byron passage about the vampire (I'm pretty sure I've quoted it in one story or another) where he describes the condition in this way:

> Then ghastly haunt thy native place,
> And suck the blood of all thy race;
> There from thy daughter, sister, wife,
> At midnight drain the stream of life;
> (. . .) Thy victims ere they yet expire
> Shall know the demon for their sire,
> As cursing thee, thou cursing them,
> Thy flowers are withered on the stem.

It's from a poem called "The Giaour," from a scene where the protagonist is being cursed to live out the rest of his days as a vampire. As far as I know, it's the debut of the vampire in English literature. It also introduces the idea of the vampire preying first on those he's known and loved during his lifetime. (Which derives from one of the central European traditions, I'm pretty sure.) This hasn't been terribly important to most of the vampire narratives we know, but it's there in the monster's background.

All of which is to say, I suppose it would be possible to read your story as an updating of an older trope, if one that in this case I find particularly unsettling. Although as you present it here, the family member seems more distressed at what's happening than the vampire does . . . I guess a vampire sliding from life to (un) life might choose to stay with those familiar to it in order to have a safe and ready source of nutrition while it's navigating its new condition. I remember one writer or another (Lucius Shepard?) speculating about the period of becoming a vampire as one of great intoxication with all this newfound power—whose parameters would be mapped out on those same loved ones.

It appears the ring's a pretty decent collaborator. Just be sure you hang on to the royalties.

But: the black wall makes its fiction debut!

Oh—and I've turned up some more info on the connection between Lugosi and the Dracula ring. It's wild stuff. I have to go now—we're having dinner at Josh and Carmen's—but I'll tell you about it in a day or two.

from: Gaetan Cornichon
to: Michael Harket
date: January 1, 2019 10:01 PM
subject: Re: Stop Making Sense

Happy New Year, and thanks for the good wishes. Health wise, nothing's changed, but I'm continuing my attempt to embrace my condition, whatever it is. Yes to the Oates, at least partially. This piece feels like it might keep going; I suppose time will tell. And yes, the black wall has arrived in print. Can't wait for you to see it when you visit for Boskone.

(Oh, and don't worry about Leslie. Seriously. She's . . . *fine*. *Insert sinister laugh here*)

Hope you enjoyed your dinner. Have to admit, you've piqued my interest. I'm actually curious to hear the next installment of the Dracula Ring saga.

from: Michael Harket
to: Gaetan Cornichon
date: January 3, 2019 8:30 AM
subject: Re: Stop Making Sense

Been a bit under the weather myself, since New Year's—probably picked up something from one of the kids at Josh and Carmen's. Trying to shake it off, but without much luck.

You know, I've been thinking about "Stop Making Sense"—well, as much about the question of what use we make of the experiences of our loved ones. I wouldn't say writers are vampires—

that's a bit too glib, too pat—but there is something vampiric, and specifically in the sense of the Byron poem I quoted, about the way our art draws sustenance from the lives of those closest to us, isn't there? It's funny, years ago, I roomed with this guy in Albany. He knew I was a writer and always acted kind of cautious around me, guarded. I never connected his demeanor with my writing until one night he told me and my girlfriend at the time about this crazy thing that had happened to him. When he was finished, I said something to the effect of, "Oh man, I'm going to have to use that in a story," at which point he practically leapt out of his chair and shouted, "I KNEW it!" as if I had just confessed to the crime he'd suspected me of all along. Freaked me out, enough so that I still remember it.

(And yes, I did incorporate the events he related into something I wrote years later. The guy turned out to be an asshole, which was how I justified it to myself. Even if he hadn't been, though, it wouldn't have stopped me.)

from: Gaetan Cornichon
to: Michael Harket
date: January 3, 2019 6:03 PM
subject: Re: Stop Making Sense

So we're parasites? Leeches? What about everything we give our families, everything we do for them? Isn't this part of the equation? Isn't there some kind of, I don't know, exchange?

from: Michael Harket
to: Gaetan Cornichon
date: January 4, 2019 8:01 AM
subject: Re: Stop Making Sense

Sorry, we're leeches. *Human* leeches, if this makes it any better. (Which sounds like a great idea for an EC Comics–style story.)

from: Gaetan Cornichon
to: Michael Harket
date: January 4, 2019 7:15 PM
subject: Re: Stop Making Sense

Great. Maybe you could use it for one of those anthologies you're supposed to be writing for.

from: Michael Harket
to: Gaetan Cornichon
date: January 5, 2019 7:08 AM
subject: Human Leeches and Ever-Looming Deadlines

To be perfectly frank, I'm so far behind, I'll probably miss the next two deadlines, which is a shame, because one of them is for an EC-themed project the Human Leech thing would be a perfect fit for. The only silver lining is, by the time I finally finish the damned thing, another, similar (or similar-enough) anthology will have rolled around.

Continuing to complicate matters, I still feel like shit. Like you, I went to my doctor, and all he could come up with was an unspecified viral infection. Rest and fluids. How about you? Any change?

from: Gaetan Cornichon
to: Michael Harket
date: January 5, 2019 9:45 PM
subject: Human Leeches

Not really. Funny: I'm sick, then you are. A new kind of computer virus, right? I'd say it's a story idea, except someone must have done it before. Hope you're on the mend soon. Remember fluids. Fluids! I say. You might try some human blood.

Kidding!

(Or am I?)

(Heh.)

from: Michael Harket
to: Gaetan Cornichon
date: January 6, 2019 1:30 PM
subject: The Dracula Ring Part 2

Yeah, the virus-through-the-computer device was a cyberpunk thing, as I recall. I'll pass on the blood, thanks.

Anyway, you wanted it, you got it, the latest fruits of what's becoming a bit of an obsession with me. (Yes, I know, this is the reason I'm always late with everything. But what I found was interesting enough to be worth the delay, even if you stand to be the primary beneficiary of it.) The Lugosi connection turned out to be worth investigating, although initially the idea of the first actor to play the Count on film being the one to pass on (or invent?) the knowledge of the ring struck me as a little too much, a bit of narrative overkill, you know? Someone in a minor part would have been better, aesthetically speaking, but what can you do? I looked online, found a couple of promising biographies of Lugosi. One I was able to buy for my Kindle, the other I had to order through ILL at the college. It came pretty quickly. The Kindle one, *The Immortal Count: the Life and Films of Bela Lugosi*, was solid, but didn't have anything to offer on the subject of the ring. *Lugosi: His Life in Films, on Stage, and in the Hearts of Horror Lovers* had more to say, although the bulk of it was contained in a couple of *loooong* footnotes (and this is coming from a guy who never met a footnote he didn't like).

Gary Rhodes, the author of this second biography, discusses how, as a young man, Lugosi was a member of a traveling theater company performing all over the Austro-Hungarian empire. It was how he truly learned and refined his craft as an actor—I gather his early efforts did not exactly set the stage on fire. Anyway, there's a five-year period in the theater company's history, from 1904 to 1909, Rhodes can't account for. Rhodes says it's likely the players continued to perform along their established route, no big deal. This is where the footnotes come in, which turn the nothing-to-see-here into not-so-fast, maybe-there-is-something-worth-having-a-look-at.

Footnote number one makes reference to a narrative connected to Ed Wood. After Lugosi's death, Wood related a story he claimed came straight from the old man. One of the nights Lugosi was over at the director's for dinner, he talked about something from the beginning of his acting career. In the early years of the century, Lugosi said, the troupe of actors of which he was a part was contacted by a Spanish *conde*, a count, to journey to a remote location in the Pyrénées to perform a special play for the noble and his fellows. When he heard the word "count," Wood assumed Lugosi was on the verge of offering a revelation connected to Dracula; I imagine he was already planning the film he would make from whatever Lugosi told him.

As it turned out, though, Lugosi's story was too fragmentary, too strange, for Wood to figure out what to do with. (I know, which sounds too bizarre itself to be true.) Much of the actors' time was spent journeying, mostly by rail, occasionally by wagon, to their destination, an old monastery of a particularly vile stamp. Much of it was in ruins, and there was in its design something that suggested a faith other than Christianity, a creed older and more sinister. With the exception of a single youth who met them at the gate, the place appeared deserted. Some of the troupe were afraid they had been tricked and urged the others to depart. But if this was a jest, it was an expensive one: their travel costs had been paid in advance, as had half of their considerable fee, by the *Conde de Villanueva*. They continued after their young guide to a spot in the midst of the monastery's buildings, where a natural amphitheater sloped down to a wooden stage. The ground here was bare rock, discolored by generations of stains Lugosi said reminded him of the floor of a slaughterhouse. The edges of the stage had been set with a meal—a feast, serving dishes heaped with meat and vegetables, bottles of wine, trays of bread and cakes. The young man led the actors down into the declivity to the stage, where they found the food was still hot; although there was no trace of whoever had carried all of it into the amphitheater. This didn't stop the actors from devouring the meal (not too different from writers, I suppose—or any artists). Despite the decades separating *now* from *then*, Lugosi said, he could still taste the delicate slices of roast beef, their centers tender and bloody.

After the meal, the youth hauled out from under the stage a pair of large chests filled with all manner of costumes. There were heavily embroidered robes suitable for playing a Medieval king or queen mixed in beside tuxedos and evening gowns, Roman togas next to priestly vestments, uniforms of the officers of centuries of armies tangled with the rags of the peasants their forces had terrorized. The young man invited each of the actors to choose clothing expressing who they truly were, revealing their identity, instead of concealing it. This was the opposite of a theatrical troupe's typical practice, but they had drunk enough of the strong wine to go along with the request. Lugosi chose a tuxedo surprisingly near his size and joined his fellows in changing into the new clothes right there, the wine's potency having lowered the inhibitions of women and men alike.

(And it occurs to me, this detail echoes the discussion of the husband's clothing in "Stop Making Sense." Which is odd, right?)

Perhaps because of the alcohol's effects, the day lurched ahead in fits and starts. One moment, Lugosi was adjusting his jacket, the next he and the other actors were standing around the stage at the points of a strange geometric design whose outline, he saw, was drawn by the stains on the rock. Each member of the troupe was reciting a short phrase in Latin, no two of them the same. Lugosi's was, "*Lucio non uro*," I shine but do not burn—which of course the lone youth had taught him—just as he had positioned Lugosi at this spot—though he less remembered these details than inferred them. The sun dipped behind the mountains, splashing scarlet light across the clouds overhead.

Time stuttered and the darkness of night was split by the flashing lights coming from a quartet of magic lanterns mounted on
slender poles at the corners of the stage. Lugosi couldn't deci-
pher the figures perforating the cover of the lantern closest to
him. Sometimes they appeared to be strange sea monsters, other
times they resembled characters in a language he didn't know.
Where the lights overlapped in the center of the stage, they played
over an enormous, naked man seated on a great throne. The lanterns' projections raced across his muscles, seeming to enact a
weird dance with one another on his flesh. His long hair was thick
and black, as was his beard. He was wearing a crude metal crown
whose irregular points shone in the lights.

Despite the man's inescapable presence, Lugosi had the oddest
impression. The man, he said, was not in fact there: he and his
throne were in some way creations of the very lights and images
flickering over them. Now Lugosi noticed amidst the members
of the troupe other forms, which he took for statues, gray shapes
whose elegant clothing was pitted and pocked, as if from long
successions of rain and snow, of sun and ice. He couldn't recall
where they had come from, or for that matter, the giant of a man
he called the Patriarch. His mouth was dry, his tongue rancid with
the foul aftertaste of the wine, his lips chapped, but he was still
reciting his bit of Latin, "*Lucio non uro.*" He was terribly thirsty.
He thought that the statue to his right, of a middle-aged woman
clothed in the regal dress of centuries passed, moved, but he
was uncertain. It might have been an effect of the dancing lights,
which played tricks on his eyes, giving him the sensation he and
everything around him, the other actors, the statues, the stage
and its naked monarch, had entered another place, a great black
emptiness populated by creatures of fluttering light, projections
from across an incredible distance.

Momentarily, the night lurched to a scene Lugosi hinted at, but either would not or could not describe to Wood. The most he would say was that the Patriarch descended from his throne and the statues learned to move.

Then the sky was showing the first hints of dawn. The stage was empty of the giant, his chair, and the magic lanterns. A third of the troupe were gone, along with the gray statues. Lugosi was mumbling "*Lucio non uro*" through blistered lips. Something weighted his right hand. He opened it, and saw the ring a woman he had thought a statue—or the statue pretending to be a woman— had pressed into his palm seconds before the magic lanterns ceased spinning. Lugosi held on to the ring as he and the remaining actors departed the amphitheater whose stone floor had accumulated a fresh layer of stains. This was pretty much the end for the acting troupe. None of them could talk about what they had been through in the mountains. Lugosi kept the ring with him through the years to come, as he served in the First World War, returned to acting, moved to Hollywood, started acting in the movies that would bring him fame. In time, he told Curt Siodmak about the ring, though he didn't mention his experience at the monastery. Siodmak asked Lugosi to share the design with Vera West, the costume designer for *House of Frankenstein*, and this Lugosi did, though he kept the original safely locked away. Wearing it too often or too long, he said, produced unpleasant results. He wouldn't specify what these were, despite Wood's pleading, but he said the injections he administered to himself were necessary to deal with his prolonged exposure to the ring, to its temptations.

Hell of a footnote, right? Difficult to believe that Kostova didn't run across some version of this story while she was writing *The*

Historian. Also difficult to believe Lugosi wasn't out of his mind on heroin when he told it to Wood.

The second footnote is an equally lengthy and detailed discussion of the connections between the story Lugosi related to Wood and your favorite movie, *Ardor*. Anders Limoge, who wrote the script, hung around with Ed Wood in the mid-sixties and stayed in touch with him into the seventies, when Wood moved into porn, so it's conceivable Wood could have passed on Lugosi's story to him. Rhodes makes a pretty compelling case for its influence on the blood orgy sequence in particular, as well as on the film's portrayal of Dracula as this naked giant who hangs out on his throne. I'd forgotten there's a Dracula Ring in *Ardor*, too, albeit a cock ring. Still . . .

Don't know how much if any of this will be of use to you, but I find it fascinating. I really need to get back to my own writing, but it seems the more I learn, the more I want to learn, the more information I want to collect to feed to you. (Now there's a disturbing image.) Or, what was it you said before, about the research giving the ring more weight? Maybe this is what's going on. It's like I'm some kind of knock-off Renfield to your off-brand Dracula. Heh, as you would say.

from: Gaetan Cornichon
to: Michael Harket
date: January 7, 2019 10:14 PM
subject: The Dracula Ring Part 2

You as Renfield to my Dracula. Sure, why not? You'd make a fine assistant. (Assistant? Henchman? Slave? Do we have to put names on these things, as long as you do what I tell you to?)

from: Michael Harket
to: Gaetan Cornichon
date: January 12, 2019 5:30 AM
subject: From the Department of Strange Occurrences

I wanted to have another look at "Stop Making Sense," but when I went to pull it up on my computer, I could not find it. No trace of it, *nada*. I thought I might have deleted it by mistake, but it wasn't in my trash bin, either. I checked my school e-mail in case you'd sent it there, but nope, nothing. I've been in that kind of feverish state where everything seems just the slightest bit off, and I had the strangest sensation of not having read the story at all, of having invented the whole thing, or that I'd somehow watched it play out, as if you'd beamed it directly into my brain.

from: Gaetan Cornichon
to: Michael Harket
date: January 12, 2019 11:50 PM
subject: Newer Story (But Maybe It's All the Same One)

Huh. Weird. Don't worry about that thing. Try this. It's the latest the ring and I have come up with.

THE SHARK APPROACHES

"Little shark," his father used to call him, when Dean was a kid and they'd go to the beach, usually one somewhere along the Bay's great sweep, Sagamore down beside the Cape Cod canal, or Duck Harbor way out in Wellfleet, and he and Dad would hotfoot it over the burning sand to where the waves broke in frothing sheets of water which spread up the beach to meet the

two of them, their welcome coolness climbing Dean's shins as
he splashed into them, the next line dashing against his knees,
his father already a handful of steps behind, slower despite his
ridiculously long legs, calling for Dean to wait up, but the wave
after rose unexpectedly high, crashing against his belly and
holy-shit-was-that-cold his balls, and since the worst was over
he might as well dive in, so he put his hands palms together as
if he were praying and leapt at the following wave, the ocean
taking him into its salt embrace as he kicked his feet and swept
his arms, pushing against the motion trying to return him to
shore, the steady roar muffled on this side of it, sunlight filtering brightly through the heaving water, schools of tiny fish flitting across the scalloped sand below him, his shadow rippling
over them. He would emerge into the air fifty feet from where
he'd plunged under the waves, his dad standing scanning the
water, trying to locate him, and the minute Dad's eyes locked
on him, the anxiety threatening to overtake his face would dissolve, swept away by his relieved grin, and he'd call out, "Little
shark! Wait for me!" And Dean would shout back, "Come on,
big shark!"

He knew at the time his father's nickname for him connected to the movie *Jaws*, which Grandpa and Grandma had
taken Dad and Aunt Kristin to see at the drive-in when he was
very young, and which Dad said was one of the scariest things
he'd ever seen, maybe the scariest, so frightening it kept him
away from the water, even his friends' pools, for the rest of the
summer. (At Dean's insistence, his father had recited a bare-
bones summary of the plot, most of which hadn't sounded
particularly frightening, except the bit about the shark fling-
ing itself half out of the ocean onto the old fisherman's boat
and him sliding down into its waiting mouth: something
about the way Dad described the scene—maybe it was the

blank expression on the shark's face, its empty black eyes—
made it the source of a few nightmares, much to Mom's irritation.) The thing was, even as the film was scaring him and
all his classmates off the beach, it was awakening a fascina-
tion with sharks, fostered by a flood of coloring, activity, and
informational books rushed into print by publishers eager to
take advantage of the interest of those housebound kids. As
a result, Dad was a font of useless information about sharks,
much of which he passed on to Dean, who remembered more
of it than he thought necessary to enjoy a happy and produc-
tive life. Sharks were closer to rays and skates than they were
to actual fish with their bony skeletons. A shark's interior
structure was provided by cartilage, the same stuff the tip of
your nose was built from; the lightness of the cartilage helped
them to float, as did their livers, which were full of buoyant
oil. Some sharks couldn't draw water into their gills on their
own; instead, they had to maintain constant motion, forcing
water through the gills. If these stopped moving for any length
of time, they died, suffocated. Depending on their diet, their
teeth varied, but those of the Great White, the shark in *Jaws*,
were triangles, serrated like the carving knife Dad brought
out for Sunday roast beef. The same shark could smell a single drop of blood in a million drops of water, and the slim,
mucous-filled channels lining its body helped it detect motion
across great distances. Mature Great Whites grew to eleven
feet if they were male, fifteen if female, but twenty-plus feet
was not out of the question. Should a Great White attack you,
you were almost certainly dead, unless you could find a way to
strike it in the gills, which might drive it off.

And so on. For a few years in his early teens, when it was
Shark Week on the Discovery Channel he, Dad, and Judy would
gather in front of the living room TV each night to watch two-

hour blocks of divers in cages being eyed by enormous sharks sliding alongside the bars, divers floating unprotected amidst schools of smaller (but no less dangerous) sharks circling them, and recitations of shark attacks combining video recreations of the events leading up to the bites with black-and-white photos of the actual wounds.

Eventually, Shark Week's allure faded, and while Dean remained a fan of *Jaws*, which he finally watched when he was twelve, the movie and two sequels he sat through had little lasting impact on him. At the beach, Dad continued to call him "little shark," but since Dean was approaching the same height and weight as his father, the name had the quality of a dad joke. Long before he took his Introduction to Psychology class second term of his junior year, Dean recognized a degree of ambiguity in his father nicknaming him for the creature so terrifying to his childhood self, but couldn't figure out its significance. Was it Dad's way of expressing some kind of fear about Dean? But why should he be afraid of his son? Unless it was the anxiety of beholding someone who was going to outlive him: that made sense. Or was the name mocking, comparing him to an animal next to which he was harmless, ineffectual?

It's funny: he hasn't devoted this much attention to sharks for years. "Little shark" hasn't registered as much more than a kind of verbal beach furniture, a way Dad refers to him when they're at the shore. If he can't stop thinking about the name and the creature now, it's because of what he saw when Dad took him into the black wall, into those endless black depths, a huge, pale shark swimming through the inky air toward the two of them.

At least, he thinks it's what he saw. He's been confused about a lot of things since—

(*the blood*)

—actually, since before the black wall, since the night on the living room couch the time he was sick. He had been running a pretty high fever, and everything had the weird, wavery feel it did when the numbers on the digital thermometer showed over 101. His mind was restless, unfocused, slipping from menacing dreams to strange waking and back again, or maybe it was vice versa, he couldn't say. He was supposed to be playing *Outlast*, using the game's graphics and narrative to distract him from his sickness, but the fever made the forms moving on the TV disturbingly real, liable to step out of the large screen and onto the throw rug in front of it at any minute, while the game's story was hopelessly snarled. Eventually, after yet another stumble to the bathroom, which confirmed nothing left in his system, he fell into a light sleep.

Somewhere behind his eyelids, he was aware of someone entering the living room, a presence as much an absence (whatever the fuck *that* meant), which registered in his unconscious as a tall, slender shape from whose neck a ragged length of shadow fluttered. The figure bent toward him, allowing Dean to see its face was a great hole, a cavern of blackened flesh studded with stained fangs. The thing pressed its empty face to his neck, the sensation of its rotted flesh against his skin awful. His fever flared, his pulse pounded in his throat. His arms, his legs, his chest were hollow, balloons he couldn't move. In a dozen places, the fangs dug into his neck. Blood sprayed into its hollow face, streamed down Dean's flesh to the couch. Pain which should have ejected him from this dream only bound it to him. He was rushing out of his body along with his blood, carried from himself through the tears in his throat, his (un)conscious dissolving into darkness—

—and he was awake, or in a state approaching it, his father rising from where he'd been leaning over him, his mother surveying the two of them from the other side of the couch, her face contorted in an expression Dean didn't recognize (but later realized was horror). He heard Dad say, "Just checking on him," an explanation which had to be true, since Dean could feel the skin of his neck whole and uninjured (though the memory of the dream remained vivid, as if he were recalling an actual event, not the by-product of a virus). Mom was less than convinced, her features shifting to wary disbelief. When she pressed her fingers to Dean's throat, it was as if she'd shared in his dream, which so surprised him, he almost jumped from the couch. He couldn't escape from his half-waking state, however, and he remained where he was until she departed the room. Finally able to move again, he pushed himself off the couch and staggered into the bathroom on legs stubbornly numb. He flipped up the light switch, and for an instant saw something wrapped around his neck, a tattered length of blackness shining with blood. In the time it took his heart to leap in his chest, the scarf was gone, a scrap of dream escaped back to his unconscious. He inspected his throat, but found no evidence of even the slightest injury.

Since that night, his life has continued: he's gone to school, spent time with his girlfriend, played basketball, binged a couple of Netflix series. But on some level he's aware of but cannot name, it's as if nothing has occurred in the intervening weeks. It's as if he's remained in front of the mirror, looking at the black scarf wound around his neck. Under normal circumstances, he would have confided in Kara, his girlfriend, but some impulse, some internal censor, has prevented him from telling her anything beyond he's been really sick and had these insane nightmares, whose details she thankfully hasn't pressed him for. Nor has he been able to speak to his other friends, with whom he's shared all manner of things his parents will never know about. Maybe it's because this involves his dad and mom? He's wanted to talk to his mother about it, but the words to start such a conversation have proven elusive. For the first time in a while, Dean has wished she would just talk to him, corner him the way she used to when he was a kid and she decided they needed to have a conversation about sex, or drugs, or whatever. Mom, however, has been increasingly preoccupied, with what exactly Dean isn't sure, although the looks she gives Dad when she thinks no one's watching her are full of worry. Dean's made a couple of halting attempts to speak to his younger sister, to ask Judy if she's noticed anything different about him, but she's shrugged off his question in favor of what's on her headphones. As for talking to Dad, well, wouldn't that be an awkward conversation? "How come I dreamed your face turned into a mouth and you tore out my throat?" Not to mention, his dad has been acting weirder and weirder—another reason for Mom's secret glances—everything he does, from walking the dog to eating dinner to washing the dishes, accented by a manic humor always on the verge of tipping into out-and-out hysteria.

At some point—possibly last night, possibly weeks ago—his father took him *into* the black wall. From staring at himself in the bathroom mirror, he was standing on the landing facing the wall Dad had argued would look cool if it were black, until Mom gave in and agreed to painting it a glossy color the hardware store labeled Midnight but Dean and Judy together named Shiny Emo, which their father had not found nearly as amusing as the two of them had. It must have been late, hours after Mom and Judy had gone to bed, the lights out, the house quiet in the way peculiar to the deep hours of the night, when the sun was hours gone and hours to return. Dean couldn't remember descending the stairs from the second floor, nor could he recall how his dad had come to be standing behind him, his hand—the one with the ring—resting on Dean's shoulder. Despite the lack of light, the wall dimly reflected the two of them, a parody of a father-son portrait. The air in the hall was thin, difficult to breathe. Dad pushed him forward, toward his mirror self, and while the pressure he exerted was minimal, Dean couldn't resist it. He was certain his father intended to crush his face against the wall, but when the tip of his nose touched its surface, the wall yielded, admitting him into something like a sheet of liquid—not water, a more viscous substance. His pulse surged with panic at not being able to breathe, but he was unable to fight his father's steady press. The substance enveloped him—them, as Dad followed Dean into it. He couldn't breathe, but this was suddenly less important than it had been the moment prior, rendered so by the immense sensation of stillness surrounding him. His father had brought him inside a vast space, an area whose parameters were boundless—impossible, yes, except here they were walking through syrupy blackness he couldn't draw into his lungs but was able to survive within, anyway. Dad's hand did not move from his shoulder, the ring on it giving off a cold, flickering light that did little beyond hurting Dean's eyes. In the distance to either side of them, Dean had the impression of enormous shapes, what might have been the ruins of great buildings (although there was a curvature to what he could make out of their designs suggesting gigantic beasts, behemoths and leviathans, dragons, crouched in either watchfulness or death). Gradually, he and his father came to a place more open. The light from the ring leapt over a block of unfinished stone directly in front of them, its rough top a table for a quartet of plain metal goblets arranged at the four points of the compass (or of a diamond, Dean supposed). Dad spoke, his words warped by their dark surroundings; Dean picked out something that was either "you" or "use" or maybe "choose"; another that might have been "goblet" or "gullet" or even "swallow." The indication was clear. Dean reached out and lifted the vessel on the right. Its surface was warm, as if someone had been holding it moments before. When he grasped it, the cup was dully empty, but as he raised it to his lips, it filled with black liquid, the air condensing inside it. Dad murmured encouragement. *Why am I doing this?* Dean thought, but tasted the cup's contents anyway. It had the flavor of nothing, not even the mineral tinge of their tap water.

Overhead, a huge shape swam through the darkness. Dean jumped, almost dropped the goblet (which, he understood, would not have been a good thing). "Steady," his father said, or, "Ready." Dean returned the cup to its place as the shape continued past them and turned in their direction with a lazy slowness. What Dean could distinguish of it in the flashes of his father's ring reminded him of a shark, one the size of a city bus, a gaping mouth full of teeth like butcher knives at one end of a dim body streamlined as a torpedo. Dad said, "Erzsébet," or, "There's a bed," or "There's the bet," the syllables full of reverence. The shark (except it wasn't a shark, it was something a shark would flee as fast as its fins would allow it, it was something that would devour any predator foolish enough to confront it) moved from side to side, allowing each of its huge black eyes to sweep over Dean, then, with a flick of its tail, was on him.

He isn't sure what happened next. The (not) shark slammed into and *through* him, the force of the blow stunning him. He had the impression of being hurled out of his body, which he saw at the other end of a long tunnel, staggering backward at the impact tearing the blood from it all at once, the blood hanging wetly in the air in a dark column before splattering to the ground. Agony so extreme he had nothing to compare it with yanked him back into himself, together with the surrounding darkness, which rushed through his skin, seeking and flooding his arteries and veins, the chambers of the heart yet to stop beating. Emptied, insubstantial, he was lifted and carried along behind the shape that had stripped him of his blood, an empty paper cup swept up by the slipstream of a tractor trailer. In almost no time, he traversed a great distance, a roaring in his ears, his father flying beside him, arms against his sides, a mad grin on his face. Dad shouted, but Dean couldn't hear what he was saying. They were moving faster and faster—

—and he was floating in front of the black wall, hovering in the stairwell, rotating slowly in the darkness, almost close enough to the chandelier to reach out and brush his fingers against its candle-shaped bulbs. While still aware of pain, tremendous pain, astonishing pain, the highways and byways of his nervous system burning white phosphorous hot, he knew this conflagration was holding him aloft, the fire lifting the hot air balloon. On the stairs beneath him, his father was standing, gazing up at him with an expression of lunatic joy. "Little shark," he said, rising into the air like Peter Pan, like Superman, "let's go for a swim."

It was as if the pair of them were sharks, the rooms in the house a series of pools he might swim between with no difficulty. From the stairwell, he and Dad dove into and through the wall separating them from the kitchen, skimming the surface of the counter, the sink, shooting down the hallway to the living room, circling it, soaring to the vaulted ceiling and dipping to the floor, racing back along the hall and through the kitchen to the dining room, where they slid over the dining room table and up, through the ceiling to Judy's room, where she lay sleeping against Auggie the dog, who snarled in his dreams as Dean and his dad passed out to the upstairs hall and into his parents' room, where his mom was lying flat on her back in the queen-size bed, her open eyes darting from corner to corner of the ceiling, as if she was aware of but unable to see Dean and his father darting around above her. Although his agony was unchanged, Dean was exhilarated, a child playing the best game ever, the corners of his mouth pulled into the widest smile ever. Dad turned his face to him and it dilated, his features opening into a cavern fringed with fangs, while the rest of his body lost definition, blurred into black smoke. The transformation did nothing to blunt the inky joy suffusing Dean; it seemed only another part of their marvelous game, a scene from *Beetlejuice*. From the depths of the maw, his father's voice said, "Now you."

Now him, and how to think about what followed? The dark delight circulating through him spilled out of his smile, raising his teeth to sharp points as it flowed over them, streaming along the length of his body, smoothing its contours to a shape sleek and dynamic. "Little shark," indeed, except he was no longer little, and he was not a shark, he was kin to the thing (*Erzsébet*) which had separated him from his blood. In his new form, he was aware of the blood pounding through his mother's terrified body in a way he never had been before—in a way he'd never been aware of his own blood. He could hear the ka-THUD ka-THUD ka-THUD of her heart, the whooooosh of the blood streaming in her arteries; he could smell the fluting copper odor of it under the skin it lit with faint radiance; he was aware of Judy's pulse counting its slower beat across the hall; the wealth of sensations causing the pain he had been

able to accommodate while flitting around the house to crescendo, to overwhelm him, to rage through him in incandes-
cent madness. His mind was a white inferno. If only he could
get to the blood, to all the blood, it would dim the pain, if only
he could taste it—

(*No*)

Dean

(*blood soaking the pillows*)

is

(*blood drenching the blankets*)

in

(*blood spattering the walls*)

the car with his dad,

(*who is that screaming?*)

huddled in the back seat, dressed in his sweats, a fine layer of soil

(*soil?*)

sprinkled over him. He's listening to the turn signal making its
tic-tic-tic sound as Dad steers onto 27 toward Sharon. His hair
is clotted with dirt and something else, something wet-going-to-

tacky. His jaw aches, and a flat, metal taste clings to his teeth, his tongue. Nausea threatens the top of his throat. He swallows, succeeds in croaking, "Where are we going?" without vomiting.

"Visiting," his father says. He drives with one hand on the wheel, the ring perched atop his finger shining with dull light.

(a pool of blood at the base of the black wall)

(who was screaming?)

(Mom? Judy?)

from: Michael Harket
to: Gaetan Cornichon
date: January 18, 2019 5:05 AM
subject: The Shark Approaches

Wow. That was some fucked-up shit. Probably not the best thing to read in my current mental state, but all the same, I'm glad I did. I think. So much for concerns about using your family in your writing, I suppose. If I didn't know you and them, I would be worried. Hell, I'd be panicking. I did think the piece was unusually direct for you, as far as the supernatural elements go. It's cool to see you trying new things, though, like the megalodon-kaiju-whatever the fuck. Makes me wonder what role Elizabeth Bathory is supposed to be playing in all this. I mean, the story's about the *Dracula* Ring, right?

Have to say, if Porter wasn't thrilled with his inclusion in *Split Rock*, I can't imagine he's going to be any happier with this.

from: Gaetan Cornichon
to: Michael Harket
date: January 18, 2019 11:36 PM
subject: Re: The Shark Approaches

Porter's a good boy. No need to worry about him. As for *Erszé-bet*, she's the harbinger. The ring draws her. Dracula is—he's a disposition, you could say. I think. It's complicated. Or I don't understand it.

What about the research, Renfield? Anything new and juicy?

from: Gaetan Cornichon
to: Michael Harket
date: February 2, 2019 10:01 PM
subject: Yoo Hoo

Haven't heard from you in a couple of weeks. Everything okay? Renfield? Hello?

from: Michael Harket
to: Gaetan Cornichon
date: February 3, 2019 5:50 AM
subject: Blood in the Corn

I'm sorry not to have been in touch (almost added "Master," but I'm resisting taking the joke so far, because I'm afraid it isn't a joke, or not one I should be laughing at). The rabbit hole has become a warren I cannot escape. This particular chamber (to extend the metaphor) has—there are strange things about it, especially in light of the stories you've sent me. Or maybe not, and it's a case of I've been staring at the monitor screen too long. I don't know. My head is awfully fuzzy, lately. I'm not well.

It turns out, Lugosi himself drafted a script related to the Dracula Ring. I'm not clear exactly when, but it was during the long slump at the end of his career, around the time he was working with Ed Wood. He wrote to John Carradine, tried to convince him to star in it with him. Carradine expressed mild interest, but he was already committed to working on *The Ten Commandments*. After Lugosi's death, the screenplay passed out of Carradine's hands and eventually wound up in Dino De Laurentiis's possession. This was around 1961. De Laurentiis contacted Lucio Fulci, who was better known at this point for his comedies, if you can believe it. Fulci was intrigued, and worked with De Laurentiis to tweak the script. He hired a pair of comedic actors, Franco Franchi and Ciccio Ingrassia, to play the leads, which was a gamble. These guys were the Italian equivalent of Laurel and Hardy. But Fulci saw something in the pair he thought would help the film to succeed, a certain gravitas in Franchi, and a melancholy to Ingrassia. As for the actors, they were willing to give the material a try. If nothing else, it was a paycheck.

Fulci completed principal photography on what would be released as *Sangue nel Grano (Blood in the Corn)* in a few weeks. He filmed in black and white, with a minimal musical soundtrack. It's a short movie, about seventy minutes, which you can find a not terrible copy of on YouTube. The story is set in the US, Oklahoma during the dust bowl. (Lugosi's original setting.) There wasn't money to shoot in America, so most of it was filmed on a sound stage, although there are a couple of exterior scenes where the Italian countryside is meant to stand in for Oklahoma (which, as you can guess, it doesn't). There's a farmer, played by Ingrassia, whose farm is on the brink of failure, its cornfields shriveling and dying. His wife, son, and daughter know the end is in sight. Every day, they watch vehicles passing by on the road on one edge of their property, cars full of families like them, trucks whose flatbeds are jammed with whatever could be taken from the houses they've left, mattresses, headboards, dressers, tables, chairs, trunks, suitcases, and other more exotic objects, an upright piano, a chandelier, a framed painting. Some nights, a car or truck or two will stop at the farm, ask if they can rest the night there. Mom welcomes everyone. The sister looks worried as her mother takes more from the dwindling supplies on the pantry shelves. The brother makes resentful remarks, which earn him a rebuke from his mother, and then a slap when he won't stop complaining. Dad doesn't say much, just stares at the horizon and broods.

(From the moment the camera settled on him, something about Ingrassia bothered me. I'm not sure how long it took me to realize his striking resemblance to you, at least in this role. The instant I noticed this, I saw his wife as Leslie, his kids as Porter and Rosemary. I'm not sure exactly how to put this, but I have the sense none of these similarities is as intense as I perceive it to be, though I don't know what this means.)

Anyway, one night, a car turns up the driveway. It's long, black, with tinted windows, not the type of thing the family's been used to seeing. Its hood ornament is the figure a woman wrapped in robes streaming out behind her. I'm not much on cars, but I did some digging (research about the research) and identified the vehicle as a 1931 Duesenberg Model J. Very pricey; I'm not sure how Fulci afforded it for the movie. The man driving the car, Franchi, is in a bad way. He's dressed in typical vampire finery, but his tuxedo is dirty, his shirt collar open, the button missing. No cape. His hair is a mess, his cheeks sunken, his eyes hollow. He's wearing the Dracula Ring, though, and he moves with regal elegance. Franchi was a gifted physical actor, and it's something to watch him: he invests his performance with a mix of grace, frailty, and occasionally anger. While his character is never named (even in the credits, he's listed as "The Visitor"), it's pretty clear he's Dracula, on the run from an unspecified catastrophe in the Ozarks, an appealingly odd detail. He asks for shelter for the night, and while Dad is clearly suspicious, Mom agrees.

There's a dinner scene during which The Visitor joins the family at the table but refuses to partake of the soup and bread set before him, his explanation a rare condition making his dietary needs rather . . . unique ("*unica*"), a word Franchi pronounces with all the emphasis Lugosi gave to *wine* in the Browning film. The Visitor asks the father about the farm. "Isn't it obvious?" Dad says. The farm is already dead. All of them are dead, too. Here the son breaks in. Things wouldn't be so bad, he declares, if they didn't have to share what they earned with the sweat of their brows with every tramp who knocks on their door. Mom reproaches him, but The Visitor raises his hand (the one with the ring on it), tells her not to criticize the boy. It is right, he says, for a man to take pride in his work, in what his hands have wrought from the earth. What claim should any of these travelers, these *Gypsies*, have on the farm's yield? Junior's eating this up, but Dad brings everything to a crashing halt when he says the only yield of these acres is dust, and he does not begrudge any man his share of it.

As the brother and sister clear the plates from the table, The Visitor says he has a favor to ask of Dad. He needs a place to house his car for a few days, possibly a week. The vehicle requires repairs, which he can make, but he must obtain the part from a mechanic in Oklahoma City. Is he asking for a ride? Dad says. No, The Visitor says, only for a berth in the barn behind the house. If the father can accommodate him, he is prepared to recompense him handily. Perhaps they could take a walk outside, examine the barn together?

Dad agrees, and the two of them exit, The Visitor kissing Mom's hand on the way out. Some time later, Dad returns. There's a distracted expression on his face, the collar of his shirt is a mess, and he's wearing the Dracula Ring on his right middle finger. Mom notices. Dad says it was a down payment for agreeing to keep the car. What happened to the man? Mom says. He left, Dad says. Walked off into the corn. Said he was going to meet someone.

The next day, Dad is in a much better mood, so much so Mom and the kids exchange suspicious glances. When a family turns its truck up the driveway later on, searching for a place to rest for the night, Dad welcomes them warmly, invites the six of them to join him and his wife and children for supper. The newcomers are grateful, and spend the meal bemoaning the loss of their farm, the generally terrible state of the economy, of everything. Dad nods in agreement, all the while rubbing the ring with the thumb of his left hand.

After dinner, Dad invites the father to accompany him on a walk around the property, which the man is happy to do. Mom and the man's wife clean the table, wash and dry the dishes, prepare the children for bed. All the while, they continue to talk about how desperate everything has become, a conversation that goes on at the table over a couple of cigarettes. The toll all of this is taking on their husbands, they agree, is worrying, but the way Mom discusses Dad, you know she's thinking about more than the state of the farm. The door swings open, and the women jump. The visiting father is standing there, backlit by the full moon, which has risen and is impossibly large. He stumbles into the house, tells his wife to fetch the kids, he has something he wants all of them to see. He isn't really coherent. What, Mom says, what's so important the children have to be wakened? Over Mom's protests, the wife wakes their children and then herds them toward the door in their nightgowns and pajamas. All the hubbub has roused Mom's kids, who want to go outside with the others, but she orders them back to bed. By the time she's managed this, the visitors have all left the house. Mom follows them a couple of steps into the yard, only to stop at the sight of Dad, waiting between two rows of withered corn. As she watches, he turns and starts off into the field, the visiting family proceeding single-file behind him.

For a moment, it looks as if Mom might race after them. She doesn't. She flees back inside and slams and locks the door. She considers looking out a window, but opts not to. Sometime later in the night, while she's lying in her bed, the lock opens, the door swings in, and Dad enters the house, cleaning his hands with a cloth.

At daybreak, there's no sign of either the visitors or their truck. Dad's bustling around the kitchen, cooking flapjacks and bacon. This does nothing to quell his family's suspicions. (I almost wrote "your family's suspicions.") Mom asks him what became of their guests. Dad hesitates, and it's obvious he's inventing an answer. He settles for telling her they departed early, had intentions of reaching Albuquerque by nightfall. In that truck? Mom says. I know, Dad says, but they were determined to try. Mom isn't happy—she lets Dad and the kids see her displeasure—but doesn't say anything else. Dad says he's going outside to work and requests both kids accompany him. By the looks of things, there's bad weather on the way, and he needs their assistance in preparing for it.

(Lugosi and Fulci obviously had little interest in portraying a real, working farm. Given its size, there should be at least a few farmhands to help with the running of the place, even in the family's straitened circumstances.)

Later in the afternoon, a dust storm rolls over everything. The sunlight dims, a strong wind kicks up, and soon the air is full of dust. Mom shutters the windows, pushes a throw rug against the bottom of the front door. The whistle of the wind and the hiss of the dust against the house are deafening. She paces anxiously, glancing at the door every few seconds. Finally, someone pounds to be let in, and she rushes to admit them.

It isn't Dad, or either of the kids. Instead, a man wearing a duster and a cowboy hat, holding a handkerchief over his nose and mouth, asks if he can speak with Mom. She steps back to allow him in from the storm, then pushes the door shut behind him. He lowers the handkerchief and removes his hat, apologizing for the mess he's making all over her nice clean house. He's not a young man, but his hair and mustache are still dark. He tells Mom he's a Texas Ranger, in pursuit of a very bad character. He's a long way from Texas, Mom says. Yes he is, the man says. It's just one of the many peculiarities associated with this case, which is of sufficient desperation to necessitate his bypassing the usual pleasantries of conversation with such a fine woman as herself to speak more directly and ask her if she's seen a particular automobile pass by her property, a big black car of the type he for one could work his entire life and not be able to afford. Mom's reaction gives the Ranger the answer to his question, but before she can speak, he goes on, telling her the fellow behind this car's wheel is about as dastardly a villain as he's encountered in twelve years dealing with such types. The last time he and the Ranger crossed paths, a few days ago, they exchanged gunfire, and the Ranger is reasonably sure he winged the man, using a kind of ammunition the man would find of especial hurt. Mom doesn't understand what the Ranger means. It doesn't matter, he says, what does is, with this bullet stuck in him, the man will be more desperate than usual, the way a wounded animal is extra dangerous. Though the Ranger hasn't seen the rest of her family, if the man he's pursuing is about, every last one of them is in mortal peril.

Mom leads the guy outside, into the chaos of the dust storm. Together they struggle across the yard to the barn, her holding a shawl over her head, him with one hand on his hat, the other holding a long-barreled revolver. At the barn, they shoulder open the door just enough to allow them to squeeze inside. Once on the other side of it, they push the door closed. Both cough, but the Ranger's gun is already up, sweeping the barn's darkened interior. Sure enough, there's the car, parked at the other end of the space, where the shadows are thickest. Mom calls out for Dad and the kids. The Ranger hushes her and proceeds across the barn. This part happens very quickly. When he reaches the car, he stalks past the blank windshield (which the camera lingers on), past the driver's door to the rear passenger door. He grabs the handle and hauls the door open, leaping back as a wave of earth pours out of the car. He keeps his gun aimed at the interior of the vehicle as dirt continues to stream onto the barn floor, revealing first a hand, then the sleeve of a black tuxedo jacket, then the breast of a dress shirt into which has been plunged a short length of wood, the broken handle of an axe or scythe, by the look of it. The final thing the dirt slides away from is the face of The Visitor, himself, his eyes open and flecked with soil, his lips drawn back in a snarl, his fangs visible, his mouth stopped up with dirt.

Confused, the Ranger steps away, into the waiting embrace of Dad, who catches him around the throat with his left arm, and seizes the wrist of his gun hand with his right hand. The Ranger struggles, emptying his pistol into the air as Dad brings his mouth to the man's neck. The Ranger shakes, goes limp, and drops the revolver. Dad lowers him to the ground almost tenderly. He stands, wiping his mouth with the back of his hand, and he looks more like you than ever. Mom—who is Leslie, I don't know how this is possible, but she is—asks him what's happening. A sound above her startles her, makes her look up to the loft, where she sees her son (who is Porter) crouched over her daughter (Rosemary, and this is horrible, it's too much), his mouth dark with her blood. Mom screams as Dad advances toward her. The camera zeroes in on her terrified eyes, then on Dad's blood-smeared teeth, then alternates between eyes and teeth, eyes and teeth, until you grab Leslie by the shoulders and hiss and bring her to you, her neck to your waiting mouth. As she screams again, the screen goes dark.

The movie's final scene begins with the growl of the Duesenberg's engine and a close-up of its hood ornament (who is Erzsébet?). From the way the figure is vibrating, it's obvious the car is on the road. The camera slides along the hood to the darkened windshield, passing through the glass to show us you in the driver's seat, your right hand resting at twelve o'clock on the steering wheel, the Dracula Ring visible on your middle finger. Over your shoulder, we see the back seat heaped with stalks of corn and dirt. If we freeze the movie so we can study the image, we see part of

Porter's face, his eye closed, where the earth has shifted from it. It's difficult to say for sure, but you might be smiling.

There's something else, but I don't want to write about it right now.

From the outset, the movie was a flop. De Laurentiis wanted Fulci to shoot additional footage, re-edit the thing into a comedy, but the director refused. So old Dino brought in a TV guy to film a dozen new scenes, including a new climax and ending. What resulted went by the new title *Qualcosa di Clandestino sta Accadendo nel Grano!* Which translates literally as *Something Clandestine Is Happening in the Corn!* You could describe it as a sex-farce with vampires, albeit, one whose tone veers wildly. If I'm not mistaken, Karen Russell mentions it in "Vampires in the Lemon Grove." Poor Lugosi. At least before all of this happened, he was safely dead.

from: Gaetan Cornichon
to: Michael Harket
date: February 3, 2019 11:13 PM
subject: Re: Blood in the Corn

Is this the part where I say, Perhaps it was me?

from: Michael Harket
to: Gaetan Cornichon
date: February 4, 2019 5:18 AM
subject: Re: Blood in the Corn

No, it's the part where I say it was me. I was sitting in my office chair, hunched over in front of my computer screen, and then I was beside you in the front seat of that car, its interior full of the smells of earth and blood, of leather seats and green ears of corn. The tires hummed on the blacktop as you drove roads winding between dark stands of trees and beside low stone walls. Something tickled my skin, and I saw white letters, words, names and titles and locations rolling over me, you, the car, the closing credits playing on us while you sped along. You didn't look at me, but I knew you were aware of me there. "Soon," you said. "Very soon."

from: Mail Delivery Subsystem
to: Michael Harket
date: February 4, 2019 5:19 AM
subject: Message Not Delivered

There was a problem delivering your message to Gaetan Cornichon (otherson72@gmail.com). Error Message 417: Invalid Address. Please check the address and try again later.

From BostonGlobe.com | Metro Section

Police Investigating Disappearance of Stoughton Author and Family

By Natsuo O'Brien, Globe Correspondent | February 4, 2019, 4:58 p.m.

STOUGHTON—Police are investigating the disappearance of a writer and his family under what law enforcement officials are calling troubling circumstances. At approximately 8:00 a.m. this morning, one of Gaetan and Leslie Cornichon's neighbors approached their house in response to what she described as an hour's worth of unceasing howling by the Cornichons' dog, Tulip. Finding the front door open, the neighbor (who does not wish to be identified), discovered the dog tied to one of the dining room table's legs. She also found what she described as a "horrifying" amount of a liquid she suspected was blood at the base of one of the house's walls. She fled the house, taking the dog with her, and called 911. The police confirmed that the substance at the foot of the wall (which was apparently painted black) was blood; though whether it is human blood, much less, that of the Cornichons and their two children, Porter and Rosemary (ages eighteen and fourteen respectively), has not been disclosed. As of this writing, police have not been able to locate any of the Cornichon family. Since all of their vehicles have been accounted for in their garage and driveway, police are concerned for the family's safety. Anyone with knowledge of their whereabouts is urged to contact the Town of Stoughton police.

A local celebrity, Gaetan Cornichon is the author of several popular suspense-thriller novels, including *Pitchfork Days*, *Split Rock*, and *The Book of Bad Decisions*. Recently, *Pitchfork Days*, which *Time* magazine called the decade's most frightening novel, was optioned for a movie to which actor Chris Evans is rumored to be attached.

from: Michael Harket
to: Gaetan Cornichon
date: February 5, 2019 7:01 PM
subject: What the Fuck is Going On?

I don't know what's happened to your email—to you. It isn't anything good, is it? I've misunderstood what's been happening, haven't I? Taken for tropes and narrative conventions what's been screaming and blood, evaded what's been staring me in the face from the blank and pitiless screen of my computer. I guess the final question for me is, what is the ring? What exactly is its role in all of this (whatever all of this is)? I don't think I can stop my research (which I envision as me wandering lost through endless rows of bookcases, navigating a maze of information that refuses to cohere into significance, into an exit), but I suspect it's not going to bring me the answer to this particular question. So if you have any insight, I would consider it a kindness to a friend. If such a thing means anything to you, anymore.

from: Mail Delivery Subsystem
to: Michael Harket
date: February 5, 2019 7:02 PM
subject: Message Not Delivered

There was a problem delivering your message to Gaetan Cornichon (otherson72@gmail.com). Error Message 417: Invalid Address. Please check the address and try again later.

from: D <theblackcar@themidnighthighway.com>
to: R <archivist@thearchive.com>
date: The Advancing Night
subject: The Kindness of Blood

The ring? The ring is the closed circle. It's Erzsébet. It's blood and blood and blood. It's the moon full and the moon dark. It's the Patriarch with his iron crown. It's rising and feeding and rising and feeding. It's the reel of film unwinding. It's death and death and death, death rolling out ahead in an endless highway. It's me and you, me on my way to you.

> > >

For Fiona, and for Paul Tremblay

ABOUT THE AUTHORS

KELLEY ARMSTRONG is the author of the Rockton thriller series and stand-alone thrillers. Past works include the Otherworld urban fantasy series, the Cainsville gothic mystery series, the Nadia Stafford thriller trilogy, the Darkest Powers & Darkness Rising teen paranormal series and the Age of Legends teen fantasy series. Armstrong lives in Ontario, Canada, with her family.

DALE BAILEY is the author of eight books, including *In the Night Wood*, *The End of the End of Everything*, and *The Subterranean Season*. His short fiction has won the Shirley Jackson Award and the International Horror Guild Award and has been nominated for the Nebula and Bram Stoker Awards. He lives in North Carolina with his family.

NATHAN BALLINGRUD is the author of *North American Lake Monsters*, *The Visible Filth*, and the forthcoming *The Atlas of Hell*. Several of his stories are in development for film and TV. He has twice won the Shirley Jackson Award. He lives somewhere in the mountains of North Carolina.

LAIRD BARRON spent his early years in Alaska. He is the author of several books, including *The Beautiful Thing That Awaits Us All*, *Swift to Chase*, and *Black Mountain*. His work has also appeared in many magazines and anthologies. Barron currently resides in the Rondout Valley, writing stories about the evil that men do.

PAUL CORNELL is the writer of the Lychford novellas from Tor.com Publishing, and the creator-owned comics *Saucer Country* and *This Damned Band*. He's also written widely for television and is the cohost of *Hammer House of Podcast*.

GEMMA FILES was born in England and raised in Toronto, Canada, and has been a journalist, a teacher, a film critic, and an award-winning horror author for almost thirty years. She has published four novels, a story cycle, three collections of short fiction, and three collections of speculative poetry; her most recent novel, *Experimental Film*, won both the 2015 Shirley Jackson Award for Best Novel and the 2016 Sunburst Award for Best Novel (Adult Category). She has two new story collections from Trepidatio (*Spectral Evidence* and *Drawn Up From Deep Places*), one upcoming from Cemetery Dance (*Dark Is Better*), and a new poetry collection from Aqueduct Press (*Invocabulary*).

JEFFREY FORD is the author of the novels *The Physiognomy*, *Memoranda*, *The Beyond*, *The Portrait of Mrs. Charbuque*, *The Girl in the Glass*, *The Cosmology of the Wider World*, *The Shadow Year*, and *Ahab's Return*. His short story collections are *The Fantasy Writer's Assistant*, *The Empire of Ice Cream*, *The Drowned Life*, *Crackpot Palace*, and *A Natural History of Hell*.

CHRISTOPHER GOLDEN is the *New York Times* bestselling, Bram Stoker Award–winning author of such novels as *Ararat*, *The Pan-*

dora Room, and *Snowblind*. With Mike Mignola, he is the cocre-ator of two cult favorite comic book series, Baltimore and Joe Golem: Occult Detective. As an editor, he has worked on the short story anthologies *Seize the Night*, *Dark Cities*, and *The New Dead*, among others, and he has also written and co-written comic books, video games, and screenplays. Golden cohosts the podcasts *Three Guys with Beards* and *Defenders Dialogue*. In 2015 he founded the popular Merrimack Valley Halloween Book Festival. He was born and raised in Massachusetts, where he still lives with his family.

BRIAN HODGE is one of those people who always has to be making something. So far, he's made thirteen novels, more than 130 shorter works, five full-length collections, and one soundtrack album. His most recent books are the novel *The Immaculate Void* and the collection *Skidding Into Oblivion*, companion volumes of cosmic horror. His Lovecraftian novella *The Same Deep Waters as You* is in the early stages of development as a TV series. He lives in Colorado, where more of everything is in the works. Connect through his website (www.brianhodge.net) or Facebook (www.facebook.com/brianhodgewriter).

STEPHEN GRAHAM JONES is the author of seventeen novels and six story collections. His novella *Mapping the Interior* published by Tor.com won the Bram Stoker Award for Long Fiction. Coming next is the novel *The Only Good Indians* from Saga Press and *Night of the Mannequins* from Tor.com. Stephen lives and teaches in Boulder, Colorado.

RICHARD KADREY is the *New York Times* bestselling author of the Sandman Slim supernatural noir series. *Sandman Slim* was included in Amazon's "100 Science Fiction & Fantasy Books to

Read in a Lifetime," and is in production as a feature film. Some of Kadrey's other books include *The Grand Dark*, *The Everything Box*, *Hollywood Dead*, and *Butcher Bird*. He's also written for *Heavy Metal* magazine, and the comics *Lucifer* and *Hellblazer*.

CASSANDRA KHAW is a scriptwriter at Ubisoft Montreal. Her work can be found in places like the *Magazine of Fantasy and Science Fiction*, *Lightspeed*, and Tor.com. She has also contributed writing to games like *Sunless Skies*, *Falcon Age*, and *Wasteland 3*.

JOHN LANGAN is the author of two novels and three collections of stories. His novel *The Fisherman* was recognized with several awards, including the Bram Stoker Award. He is one of the founders of the Shirley Jackson Awards, and occasionally reviews horror and dark fantasy for *Locus* magazine. He lives in New York's Mid-Hudson Valley with his wife, younger son, and the sound of electric guitars.

JOSH MALERMAN is the author of *Inspection*, *Unbury Carol*, and *Bird Box*, which was turned into the hit Netflix movie starring Sandra Bullock. He's also one of two lead singers for the Detroit rock band the High Strung, whose song "The Luck You Got" can be heard as the theme song to the Showtime series *Shameless*. He lives in Michigan with his wife, the artist and musician Allison Laakko.

USMAN T. MALIK is a Pakistani writer who divides his life between Florida and Lahore. He has won the Bram Stoker and British Fantasy Awards and been nominated for the Nebula, World Fantasy, and storySouth Million Writers Awards. His stories have been reprinted in several Best of the Year anthologies.

In his spare time, Usman likes to run distance. You can find him on Twitter @usmantm.

LISA MORTON is a novelist, screenwriter, author of nonfiction books, and six-time winner of the Bram Stoker Award whose work was described by the American Library Association's *Readers' Advisory Guide to Horror* as "consistently dark, unsettling, and frightening." Her most recent release, *Ghost Stories: Classic Tales of Horror and Suspense* (coedited with Leslie S. Klinger), was called "a work of art" by *Publishers Weekly* (starred review). Lisa lives in the San Fernando Valley and online at www.lisamorton.com.

New York Times bestselling author GARTH NIX has been a full-time writer since 2001, but has also worked in various roles in publishing and marketing, and as a part-time soldier in the Australian Army Reserve. Garth's books include the Old Kingdom series beginning with *Sabriel*; the Seventh Tower sequence; the Keys to the Kingdom series beginning with *Mister Monday*; and many more. His work has been translated into forty-two languages.

A. C. WISE's fiction has appeared in publications such as Tor.com, *Shimmer*, and *The Best Horror of the Year*, Volume 10, among other places. She has been a finalist for the Lambda Literary Award and winner of the Sunburst Award. Both of her collections are published with Lethe Press, and her novella, *Catfish Lullaby*, is published with Broken Eye Books. In addition to her fiction, she contributes a regular review column to *Apex Magazine* and the Women To Read and Non-Binary Authors To Read series to *The Book Smugglers*. Find her online at www.acwise.net.

ABOUT THE EDITOR

ELLEN DATLOW has been editing science fiction, fantasy, and horror short fiction for forty years as fiction editor of *Omni* magazine and editor of *Event Horizon* and *Sci Fiction*. She currently acquires short stories and novellas for Tor.com. In addition, she has edited about one hundred science fiction, fantasy, and horror anthologies, including the annual *The Best Horror of the Year* series, *The Doll Collection, Children of Lovecraft, Nightmares: A New Decade of Modern Horror, Black Feathers, Mad Hatters and March Hares, The Devil and the Deep: Horror Stories of the Sea, Echoes: The Saga Anthology of Ghost Stories*, and *The Best of the Best Horror of the Year*.

She's won multiple World Fantasy Awards, Locus Awards, Hugo Awards, Bram Stoker Awards, International Horror Guild Awards, Shirley Jackson Awards, and the 2012 Il Posto Nero Black Spot Award for Excellence as Best Foreign Editor. Datlow was named recipient of the 2007 Karl Edward Wagner Award, given at the British Fantasy Convention for "outstanding contribution to the genre," was honored with the Life Achievement Award by the Horror Writers Association, in acknowledgment of superior achievement over an entire career, and honored with the World

Fantasy Life Achievement Award at the 2014 World Fantasy Convention.

She lives in New York and cohosts the monthly Fantastic Fiction Reading Series at KGB Bar. More information can be found at www.datlow.com, on Facebook, and on Twitter at @EllenDatlow. She's owned by two cats.

PERMISSIONS

"Das Gesicht" by Dale Bailey, copyright © 2020 by Dale Bailey. Used by permission of the author.

"Drunk Physics" by Kelley Armstrong, copyright © 2020 by Kelley Armstrong. Used by permission of the author.

"Exhalation #10" by A. C. Wise, copyright © 2020 by A. C. Wise. Used by permission of the author.

"Scream Queen" by Nathan Ballingrud, copyright © 2020 by Nathan Ballingrud. Used by permission of the author.

"Family" by Lisa Morton, copyright © 2020 by Lisa Morton. Used by permission of the author.

"Night of the Living" by Paul Cornell, copyright © 2020 by Paul Cornell. Used by permission of the author.

"The One We Tell Bad Children" by Laird Barron, copyright © 2020 by Laird Barron. Used by permission of the author.

"Snuff in Six Scenes" by Richard Kadrey, copyright © 2020 by Richard Kadrey. Used by permission of the author.

HAPPY DEATH DAY & HAPPY DEATH DAY 2U
by Aaron Hartzler

In *Happy Death Day*, Teresa "Tree" Gelbman's birthday is the worst day of her life, starting when she wakes up in a stranger's bed. It's also the last day of her life, ending when she's killed by a psychotic killer with a knife. She's dead. Then she wakes up in a stranger's bed, it's September 18, and she has to live it all over again. It's a Groundhog Day situation, only with murder, guns, and mean girls. Tree's only shot at living to see the next day is to relive the day of her murder, over and over, until she discovers her killer's identity. *Happy Death Day 2U* picks up the story without missing a beat. Tree Gelbman thought she'd finally lived to see a brand-new day. But when she wakes up on her same birthday and a new psychopath in a mask is out to kill her and her friends, she's going to find out that all the rules have changed. Death makes a killer comeback.

Horror

THE BLUMHOUSE BOOK OF NIGHTMARES
The Haunted City
Edited by Jason Blum

Jason Blum invited sixteen cutting-edge writers, collaborators, and filmmakers to envision a city of their choosing and let their demons run wild. *The Blumhouse Book of Nightmares: The Haunted City* brings together all-new, boundary-breaking stories from such artists as Ethan Hawke (*Boyhood*), Eli Roth (*Hostel*), Scott Derrickson (*Sinister*), C. Robert Cargill (*Sinister*), James DeMonaco (*The Purge*), and many others.

Horror

BLUM HOUSE
BOOKS
VINTAGE BOOKS & ANCHOR BOOKS
Available wherever books are sold.
www.blumhousebooks.com
www.vintagebooks.com
www.anchorbooks.com